BACHE[...]
THE BABY WARD

BY
MEREDITH WEBBER

First published in Great Britain 2010
Harlequin Mills & Boon Limited,
Eton House, 18-24 Paradise Road, Richmond, Surrey TW9 1SR

© Meredith Webber 2010

ISBN: 978 0 263 87920 9

Harlequin Mills & Boon policy is to use papers that are natural,
renewable and recyclable products and made from wood grown in
sustainable forests. The logging and manufacturing process conform
to the legal environmental regulations of the country of origin.

Printed and bound in Spain
by Litografía Rosés, S.A., Barcelona

The thing about Kate, he'd discovered, was that she refused to be beaten by what life threw at her. She kept going, kept smiling, always positive, always upbeat, seeing the best in situations, the best in people.

Angus was not sure where all this rational thinking was getting him, although he now had a much fuller picture of the woman he loved.

Loved?

He set the cup back carefully in its saucer, certain it had been about to slip from his grasp.

Loved?

How could he love her? He barely knew her. But even as this excuse sprang from his brain, another part of his mind was denying it. Of course he knew her.

He pictured her on the yellow sofa, an arm around his son, and remembered the stab of jealousy he'd felt. But what he should have felt was pleasure—that finally he'd found a woman who would make the ideal mother for his son…

Meredith Webber says of herself, 'Some ten years ago, I read an article which suggested that Mills and Boon were looking for new Medical™ Romance authors. I had one of those "I can do that" moments, and gave it a try. What began as a challenge has become an obsession—though I do temper the "butt on seat" career of writing with dirty but healthy outdoor pursuits, fossicking through the Australian Outback in search of gold or opals. Having had some success in all of these endeavours, I now consider I've found the perfect lifestyle.'

Recent titles by the same author:

DESERT KING, DOCTOR DADDY
GREEK DOCTOR: ONE MAGICAL CHRISTMAS
CHILDREN'S DOCTOR, MEANT-TO-BE WIFE*
THE HEART SURGEON'S SECRET CHILD†

*Crocodile Creek
†Jimmie's Children's Unit

CHAPTER ONE

'But I'd assumed—'

A quick frown from her boss, Alex Attwood, failed to halt Kate Armstrong's angry protest.

'—that when Phil and Maggie left to go back to England, I'd take Maggie's place as anaesthetist on *your* team, not be working with some total stranger.'

Alex's frown turned to a sigh.

'Have you any idea how hard it is to juggle so many new people on the two teams?' he asked, only slight exasperation showing in his voice. 'I've left you in the second team—and you know darned well that doesn't mean second in importance—because you know the ropes and you'll be a help to Angus, whom, by the way, you should meet!'

Alex paused to grin at her.

'That way he won't be a *total* stranger!' He turned towards the door behind Kate and added, 'Come on in, Angus. We were just discussing you.'

Kate was torn between wishing the floor would open up and swallow her, and wondering why a quick, embarrassed glance at a tall, dark-haired stranger should make her stomach feel uneasy.

Angus McDowell had more on his mind than some redheaded termagant—one of his mother's favourite words—who obviously didn't want to work with him. Hamish had thrown out a rash, the quarantine kennels had phoned to say McTavish was sick and, as he'd left the house, Juanita had given him a shopping list a mile long, telling him that as she didn't know where the supermarket was—he'd have to find one.

But apparently the termagant was going to be working with him whether she liked it or not, so he offered her a practiced smile, and held out his hand, politely ignored the fiery blush that had swept into her cheeks.

'Angus McDowell,' he said as she slipped fine-boned fingers into his clasp, then quickly withdrew them, tucking her hand into the pocket of her jacket as if to save it further contamination.

'Kate Armstrong,' she said, her voice deeper than he would have expected in a small, slim woman. Slightly husky, too, the voice, although maybe that was a hangover from the argument she'd been having with Alex. 'I'm to be your anaesthetist.'

It had to be jet lag that made Angus feel a splinter of ice run through his veins—she wasn't talking about anaesthetising *him*! He pulled himself together and managed another smile.

'Great,' he said. 'Most important part of the team, the anaesthetist—well, alongside the perfusionist—'

'And the second surgeon, and the surgical assistant, and the scrub nurse, and the circulating—'

He held up his hands in surrender.

'You're right, we're a team, and every member of it is equally important, although your job carries a lot of pressure, because you have more pre- and post-op contact with the patient and his or her parents.'

She looked at him then—really looked—pale green eyes meeting his, offering a challenge.

'Soft-soaping me?' she said, softening the challenge with a slight smile. 'You obviously heard the argument I was having with Alex.'

She shrugged, shoulders in a crisp white shirt lifting slightly.

'It was nothing personal—not against you. I'd just been looking forward to working with Alex. Not that I haven't done ops with him—we all switch around from time to time—but I find I learn different things from different surgeons.'

It sounded weak and Angus wondered if there was some other reason this woman wanted to be on Alex's team—a personal reason. But he couldn't be worrying about such things when he had enough personal problems of his own to sort out.

Hamish for one, even apart from the rash…

He shut off the dark cloud of the past, concentrating on the present. He said, 'Then I hope you will find working with me as instructive.'

He moved away from her as other members of the team filtered into the room.

Kate looked around at the newcomers. She'd met Oliver Rankin, the new paediatric surgical fellow who would be working with both teams, a few months ago when he'd spent several weeks with the paediatric cardiac surgical unit at Jimmie's—as the St James Hospital for Children was affectionately known. But this was the first time she'd seen Clare Jackson, the new perfusionist, and from the way every male eye in the room turned to Clare as she walked in, the perfusionist was going to cause a stir in the tight-knit unit.

Admittedly it wasn't Clare's fault that she was tall, dark-haired and strikingly beautiful. Kate tugged at her scraggly red locks which, no matter how she tried to tame them, were always breaking out of their confinement, and wondered what it would be like to be beautiful, to be so much the centre of attention....

Not that she'd like the attention part.

The talk had turned to patients, those who had been operated on and their progress, before moving to a rough plan for the operations for the week. Rough because no-one ever knew when some baby would be born with a congenital heart defect that would need immediate attention.

'Angus, we've been advised of a baby with a TGA coming down from a regional hospital on the north coast hopefully tomorrow,' Alex said. 'They want to stabilise him before the airlift. I know you've made something of a speciality of transposition of the great arteries so I'd like your team to take him when he comes.'

The new surgeon nodded, though Kate noticed he looked worried at the same time. Surely he couldn't be concerned about the operation, not if he specialised in it and when it was one that was performed successfully so often these days.

The little frown between his eyes made him more human somehow, Kate decided, studying the face that had at first appeared stern and unyielding to her. Was it the darkness of his hair and eyes that made him seem that way, or the strong bones beneath olive skin that stretched tightly over them so the long nose between broad cheekbones and the firm jawbone were accentuated?

'Kate, you with us?'

She looked across at Alex and nodded, though she'd have liked to bite him for drawing attention to her momentary lapse in concentration.

'Of course!' she snapped.

'Then off you go. Take Angus down to the childcare centre, and when you've finished there, give him a general tour of the area. Apparently he's got some shopping to do.'

She looked from Alex to the stranger with whom she was going to be working, really regretting now that she'd missed the bit of the conversation where she'd been stuck with being his tour guide. Angus was on his feet and coming towards her, smiling again....

The smile, though it seemed practiced and didn't quite reach his eyes, caused another weird sensation in the pit of her stomach. Although maybe that was the slightly mouldy bread she'd used for toast that morning. But just in case, she turned away from the smile and hurried out of the room, assuming he would follow.

'You've children yourself that Alex appointed you to show me the childcare centre?'

If she'd been a sucker for accents this one would have won her over, a soft Scottish burr overlaid with a little bit of North American. The effect in the deep voice was totally enthralling.

'Children?' he repeated, and she knew she had to pull herself together.

'Not yet,' she said, 'but I'd like to have a family and I'd also like to keep working, at least part-time, so somehow I became involved—'

She was used enough to this conversational subject to be able to keep her voice casually light, but they'd reached the elevator foyer and she could no longer pretend she had to look where she was going, so had to turn to face him.

'—with a move to expand the hours of the centre. It made sense to me to have it open twenty-four hours a day, so people on night shifts, or staff called in unexpectedly at night as our team often is, have somewhere to leave their children.'

Definitely too much information but the uneasiness in her stomach—not to mention the disturbing shadows she now saw in his dark eyes—had her prattling on.

The elevator arrived and they crammed inside, the conversation, fortunately, ceasing as they rode down to the ground floor where most of the passengers exited.

'It's in the basement?' Angus queried, wondering about the reasoning behind keeping children in a dingy, dark environment.

His reluctant guide—he'd seen her sigh when Alex suggested she take him around—smiled, small, even white teeth gleaming in her pale face.

'Ah, but there are basements and basements?'

'Mostly, in hospitals, used for the morgue,' he reminded her, while he wondered why small, even teeth should have made such an impression on him.

Teeth?

Surely he wasn't developing a tooth fetish.

'Not here,' she said cheerfully, leading him out of the elevator and along a wide corridor decorated with a bright mural depicting zoo animals.

She pushed open a door and they entered a small, fenced-off foyer, beyond which Angus could see a big, bright room, bright because the whole of one wall was glass, and beyond the glass was a playground—a sunlit playground!

'We're in a basement?' he queried as he took in the children in groups around tables in the big room, and beyond it another room with a wide window so he could see cots set up within it.

'The hospital is built on a hill. It wasn't hard to excavate a little more on this side so the children had an outdoor area.'

A woman came towards them, greeting Kate with genuine delight.

'You've been a stranger,' she said. 'After you did so much to help get the after-hours arrangement set up, we all felt you were part of our team.'

To Angus's surprise, Kate Armstrong looked embarrassed by the praise, but she rallied and introduced him.

'Mary is the director of the centre,' Kate explained, 'so if you want to get your children in, she's the one you need to talk to.'

'Of course, the children of hospital staff get priority but we do take in children from the local area, as well,' Mary explained. 'You'll be looking for something—for how many children and what ages?'

'Just the one,' Angus replied. 'Hamish is four and moving to Australia is a big change in his life. I feel if he can make some friends here, he'll settle in more easily.'

'Of course he will,' Mary assured him. 'And we can take another child in our four-year-old group. In fact, we'll be particularly happy to have a boy, as we're a bit top-heavy with girls in that group. Would you like to come in and look around now, or would some other time suit you? Perhaps a time when you can bring your wife?'

Angus closed his eyes briefly. There always came a moment! He shored up the defences he'd built around his heart and answered calmly.

'I'm a single parent,' he said, happy the phrase was so familiar these days that no questions followed it. 'But as Kate's been seconded to show me where the supermarket is, and I don't want to take up too much of her time,' he added to Mary, 'perhaps I could come back this afternoon?'

'Any time,' she said. 'And you're in good hands with Kate. If anyone knows her way around a supermarket, it's our Dr Armstrong.'

'Why would she say that?' he asked his guide as they walked back to the elevator.

The redhead shrugged, looking thoroughly embarrassed once again. He knew it must be her colouring but it was unusual—refreshing?—to see a woman blush these days. But as they waited for the elevator, she shook off her embarrassment and explained.

'When the childcare centre first asked the hospital powers that be about extending hours, the usual objections were raised—costs, and where would the money come from, et cetera—so a few of us, mostly parents and childcare centre staff, began to fund-raise with the aim of getting enough money to trial the idea. We baked a lot of cakes over a couple of months, selling them within the hospital to patients, visitors and staff. We used the kindergarten kitchen after hours and as my hours were fairly erratic—and to be perfectly honest I'm not much of a biscuit or cake cook—I was the chief shopper.'

'And you don't have children?'

The elevator had arrived but she didn't move, looking at him again, the defiance in her eyes echoed in the slight tilt of her chin.

'No, but that's not to say I won't ever have them.'

Did she feel she'd been too adamant that she added quickly, 'And a lot of the people involved in the fundraising were my friends.'

They rode back up to the ground floor, the questions he'd have liked to ask—was she married, did her husband work at the hospital—were too personal when they'd just met. There was something about her—pale skin, delicate features and a slim dancer's body, straight-backed, head held high—that reminded him of the delicate porcelain figurines his mother collected, so he kept sneaking looks at her.

At least, he thought that's why he kept looking at her. It had to be; he didn't look at women any other way these days—well, not often, and definitely not at women who were colleagues.

Yet he was intrigued enough to ask the questions anyway.

'You seem positive about the children in your future. Are you already married to their father? Engaged?'

They were walking through a fairly crowded foyer so someone bumped into her when she stopped abruptly and he had to put out his hand to grab her shoulder and steady her. But the people around them didn't seem to bother her as she studied him for a moment, then gave a rueful smile, cheeks pink again.

'Not married, not even engaged, but all I've wanted to be since I was eleven is a grandmother, and, being a doctor, I do understand I'll have to be a mother first.'

She'd made a joke of it, but underneath her light-hearted confession, Angus sensed a deeper emotion and wondered if this was a stock answer she gave to fend off further questions. It must have some basis in truth, so what had happened when she was eleven?

And why was he wondering?

Then she added, 'Maybe,' and the word had such sad undertones he wanted to hug her—a comforting hug, nothing more, but not something he made a habit of doing with colleagues.

It was strange that the man's questions had Kate coming out with something she'd never told a soul, not even her best friend. And while it was true it *had* been an ambition since childhood, she'd blurted it out it because the pang she always felt when the question of children arose had surprised her today with its intensity.

Had he fallen for the grandmother excuse? Who would? A diversion—that's what she needed.

'There's a coffee shop here that does good coffee and great friands, a sort of pastry. Let's fortify ourselves for the shopping trip.'

She waved her hand in the direction of the coffee shop, then realised half the hospital could be taking a break there. Walking in with a man who'd immediately be established in the hospital's top-ten most handsome could give rise to the kind of gossip she hated.

'No, a better idea would be to show you the best little eating place around here. The breakfast crowd will have gone and the morning coffee crowd not arrived. It's a bit of a walk but through a nice park. Come on.'

What was she doing? It had to be more than strangeness in her stomach from mouldy bread that had her confessing her grandmother obsession to the man one minute, then asking him to Scoozi for coffee the next.

Someone in the hospital coffee shop she didn't want to see? Angus wondered, but he followed her out of the hospital, across a road and into the big park that stretched away for what seemed like miles.

'I've a hospital house down that road,' he said, pointing across the intersection where solid, old, two- and three-storeyed houses lined a tree-shaded street. 'My house is opposite a park. Is this the same park?'

His guide turned towards him, a frown on her face—a face which, unlike his mother's porcelain figurines, showed every emotion.

Right now it was a picture of dismayed disbelief.

'You're living in one of the hospital houses?'

Unable to see why it should worry her, he nodded.

'I gather it's the one Maggie and Phil left,' he explained. 'It's actually two flats which is perfect for me as Juanita, my housekeeper-nanny, likes her own accommodation. She says she's not my wife or mother and is entitled to her own space.'

He can't be living in Maggie and Phil's place! The wailing words raced through Kate's brain, but she knew someone was—she'd seen a removal van there yesterday and wondered who could afford to pay for one on a Sunday.

She could move! It didn't matter that she'd decided she had to face her ghosts. She could do that next year, or the year after. She'd had good tenants in the house before, and the renovations she wanted to do could wait.

Except that she'd already stripped the wallpaper off most of the living room walls—

'Are you all right?'

The last word, with its rolled *r* only made her mad, panicky reaction worse, but she steeled herself to calm down. It was the man's accent, that was all, the deep Scottish voice would make anyone shiver.

That and the shadows in his dark eyes.

'I was thinking of coincidences,' she said, aware of the lameness of this excuse. 'I live next door.'

'Next door towards the hospital?' His eyebrows rose as he asked the question, and there was a puzzled look on his face, much like the one he'd worn when he'd asked her about her marital status—puzzled and a bit amused at the same time, though once again his eyes weren't smiling.

'Next door the other way,' she corrected, then before he could make some polite remark about the state of her overgrown garden or the junk from the living room she'd been depositing in the front yard, she added, 'It was my family home but it's been rented out for the past few years. I'm doing a bit of renovating now that I've moved back in.'

She didn't add, *With the ghosts*, although that was how it felt—just herself and the lonely ghosts in a house made for families, a house that should ring with children's laughter. Her mind flashed back to that day when she was eleven, staying with her friend Beth and visiting Beth's grandmother's house for the seemingly old lady's sixtieth birthday. *That* house had been filled with laughter while the children, all related in some way—connected and secure in the connections—had dashed around like restless puppies. This is a family, Kate had realised. *This* is what I want!

She shut the door on that memory, and fast-forwarded to years later and her adamant refusal to have a termination when Brian had suggested it. The baby would have been her family—*would have been*. She continued on her way. By now they were halfway across the corner of the park, and a short detour to the right took them to the road opposite Scoozi.

'That's the café,' she said, pointing to a place that had seen so much drama played out among hospital personnel, the walls were probably impregnated with emotion.

In order to avoid any further asinine confessions, once they had coffee and carrot cake, which happened to be the cake of the day, in front of them, Kate introduced work topics, asking him why TGAs had become something of a specialty with him.

Serious, dark brown eyes studied her across the table and for a moment she thought he might not answer her question, but apparently he was only mustering his thoughts—not coming out with the first thing that came into his head, as she was wont to do!

'My first operation—the first I did as lead surgeon in a team—was a TGA and things went wrong. The coronary arteries were twisted around the heart, one of them going through the heart walls, and although we got there in the end, it was enough to make me realise that TGAs weren't the piece of cake I'd been considering them.'

Kate nodded, picturing the subdued panic in the theatre as the team fought to sort out the problems that tiny heart would have presented.

'So you made a speciality of them?'

He smiled at her, a slow, lazy smile that made her stomach flip. Mouldy bread or something far more serious?

'Well, I did a lot more study into previous TGA cases and the complications the team could encounter during the operation, and tried to work out the best way of handling them.'

'Including coping with coronary arteries that wound through the heart wall?' Kate teased, unable to stop herself smiling at this stranger.

Not that he'd be a stranger for long, because they were neighbours, as well as colleagues. The thought caused another quiver in her abdomen, although she knew they'd only be friends. A man as good-looking as Angus McDowell could have his pick of women— should he want a woman—and scraggly redheads were unlikely to be on the top of his list.

'Including—in fact, especially—that,' he was saying. 'Now, you're doing me a favour, showing me around, so I'll pay for our coffee.'

He stood and walked towards the till, leaving Kate wondering what she'd said that had caused such an abrupt departure.

And such a shift in mood, which had been becoming, well, neighbourly!

Angus knew he'd spoken curtly, not to mention practically knocking over his chair in his haste to get away from the table, but the redhead's smile—talking about coronary arteries of all things—had caused a physical reaction in his body, one he hadn't felt in a long time, and didn't want to dwell on now.

Jet lag might explain it.

Or concern about Hamish's rash.

Hamish…

Better to think about Kate's smile than the little boy he loved but knew he wasn't bonding with the way he should—the little boy who was the image of his mother.…

He paid for the coffees, but thinking of Kate's smile had him wondering if he could politely ask directions to the supermarket so they could part company and he could sort out what was happening to him.

Hardly!

Nor was he going to be able to avoid her in the future, given they'd be working on the same team—working closely.

Kate took him to the local shopping mall, within walking distance, and pointed out the best places to shop for meat and fruit.

'Stupid of me not to have thought of getting the car before we came here. Do you have a car?' Although she needed to shop herself—fresh bread for one thing—she was too eager to get out of his company to do it now, so added quickly, 'All the shops deliver, or you could get a cab. Will you be all right?'

Angus was forced to look at her now, although since the smile he'd been avoiding eye contact. The neat-fetured face was turned towards him and it seemed to him there was a shadow of anxiety in her pale green eyes.

For him?

Surely not! He was a grown man and quite capable of shopping and getting a cab home.

But it could hardly be for herself.

'Thank you, yes, of course I'll manage,' he responded, but at the same time, contrary now, he wished she'd stay—shop with him, share the cab, maybe come in and meet Hamish and Juanita—neighbourly…

'Stop kidding yourself,' he muttered under his breath when, goodbyes said, he was striding down the refrigerator aisle in the supermarket. 'One silly little smile across a coffee table and suddenly you're attracted to the woman!'

Not that anything could happen! It was Sod's Law once again. The one woman in the world he'd felt a physical response to in four years and she wanted children.

Well, she wanted to be a grandmother.…

Why?

He recalled a depth of emotion in her voice and guessed the grandmother thing might be a cover for something else.

He shoved yoghurt and butter into his trolley, then had to go back for cheese, knowing it wasn't quite true about the physical attraction. There'd been a couple of women but nothing serious, nothing he'd wanted to pursue.

So maybe an affair with this woman…

What *was* he thinking! He'd barely met her, didn't know her at all, and just because she looked like one of his mother's figurines, it didn't mean he had to go loopy over her. Besides, there were a whole raft of reasons why he shouldn't get involved. The effect it would have on his relationship—what there was of it—with Hamish for one. Two, she was a colleague. And three, well, he wasn't certain about three, although he knew there must be a three—didn't things always come in threes...?

Having worked the previous weekend, Kate had what was left of Monday off, but given the proximity of their houses and not wanting to run into Angus McDowell again, she chose instead to go back to work. There was always book work to be done, and reports to write up— work she was usually happy to ignore until the last possible moment.

It was almost dusk when she finally walked down the road to her house, dawdling until she reached the place where Angus McDowell now lived, then hurrying, looking busy, in case he happened to see her. But once past the boundary fence, she paused and surveyed the mess in her front yard. She should have hired a skip before she began moving the old furniture. She could have thrown things straight into it.

'It's a terrible mess.' The young, accusatory voice came from somewhere behind an old yellow sofa and the rolled *r*'s told her it must be the four-year-old from next door.

'It is indeed,' she agreed, walking towards the sofa and peering over the back to see the little boy with wide blue eyes beneath a tousled thatch of white-blond hair, crouched there, a tunnel through the hedge behind him revealing his access from the neighbouring yard. 'Does your dad know you're here?'

'He's out…' It sounded like 'oot' to Kate, who had to smile, though if the child had been living in the U.S., surely his accent should be American rather than Scottish.

'And Juanita told me to get out from under her feet,' the small explorer finished. 'I was looking for an adventure. Me and McTavish—he's my dog but right now he's quantined—we like adventures.'

Kate nodded. She'd liked adventures herself when she'd been four. Unexpected pain hit her as memories of Susie's death flashed before her eyes. They'd shifted to this house soon after and here the family had fallen apart.…

'Adventures can be fun but you need to be careful where you have them,' she told him. 'Perhaps you and McTavish, when he's back with you, should have your adventures in my backyard. Come on, I'll show you.'

She opened the side gate and led the way around her house, pushing through the branching arms of the untrimmed camellia hedge, to where the bushes grew even more thickly in the backyard, although there were patches of rather dry lawn here and there.

'See, you can come through the hedge here—' she pointed out another little tunnel '—and play safely. With the gate shut, McTavish won't be able to run on the road.'

'Hamish!'

The thunderous roar startled both of them, but Kate was first to respond.

'He's here, in my backyard. You won't fit through the tunnel so you'll have to come around the side.'

There was some muttering from the other side of the hedge, then the sound of next door's side gate opening.

Hamish, meanwhile, had read the situation well and disappeared through the hole in the hedge, back into his own yard and was even now calling out to Juanita, so when a scowling Angus McDowell appeared, Kate was the only one in his sights.

'Didn't you think to check that someone knew where he was?' he demanded. 'Surely if you've been involved with the childcare centre you've some notion of children's behaviour! We're going demented in there, looking for him and you're here chatting to him in your own backyard.'

There was more than anger in his eyes, there was fear, as well, but his tone had tightened Kate's nerves and she was in no mood to be conciliatory.

'Well, I'd hardly be chatting to him in your backyard, now would I?' she demanded. 'You were "oot," he told me, and Juanita sent him to play. As it happens, I found him in my front yard, and because there's only a low brick fence that a crawling infant could get over, and a front gate that doesn't shut properly, I brought him around the back to suggest if he goes adventuring he should use the backyard.'

She considered setting her hands on her hips and giving him a good glare but the shadows she saw again in his eyes had killed her anger. This man had suffered pain. Was still suffering it? Was his move to Australia part of a healing process?

It's none of your business, her head warned, but having known pain—strong emotional pain—she couldn't help but wonder.

'Adventures! It's all he thinks about,' Angus muttered, still angry in the aftermath of anxiety but not seething any more. 'Some fool gave him a book that has a story about a boy and his dog that go on adventures and he's been mad for them ever since.'

He looked at the woman he'd been yelling at only minutes earlier and caught a hint of a smile she'd tried to hide.

'It isn't funny,' he snapped, not sure it was the smile or his reaction to it that had riled him.

She looked up at him, really smiling this time.

'It's a little bit funny,' she pointed out. 'Four years old and he's trespassing on my property and telling me it's a terrible mess. I'm sorry I didn't call out to Juanita to tell her he was with me, but it was a matter of a minute or two to show him the backyard where I knew he'd be safe. Take a look—could you get a better place for an adventure? And wouldn't you be more worried about him if he wasn't off having adventures? If he did nothing but sit around in front of the television all day?'

Angus sighed. Of course he'd be worried if Hamish wasn't always pushing himself to see more, do more, learn more. But did he want to admit it to this woman?

'I guess so,' he said, although reluctantly, 'and I know he misses the dog. Apparently we can visit him in quarantine but I haven't sorted out a vehicle yet so can't get to the quarantine station.'

'Well, that's easily fixed,' his neighbour replied. 'I'm on call at the weekend, so feel free to take my car. I've got a sat nav you can use so you won't get lost.'

Angus stared at her. Every cell in his body told him not to get more involved with this woman, but she wasn't inviting him to dinner, nor showing any signs she felt the slightest interest in him as a man; she was simply being neighbourly.

So why was he so hesitant to accept her offer?

'Or not,' she added with a shrug that showed little concern over his rudeness in not replying. 'Now, I've got to get inside, I've some stripping to do.'

Stripping?

It *had* to be jet lag that had his imagination working overtime, seeing that slight body slowly revealed as she eased off her clothes!

She started towards the back of the house, pausing to remove a key from under a lichen-covered Buddha, then as she straightened she turned back towards where he still stood, puzzled and disturbed, in her backyard.

'I've just remembered,' she said, 'there's a gate down the back between the two properties. Dad let the hedge grow over it when the house you're in was sold for rentals years ago, but if you hack away at the hedge and free the gate, Juanita will be able to get in here more easily if she needs to find the adventurers.'

'That's the first place burglars would look for a spare key,' he muttered, ignoring her advice about gates and hedges but finally getting his legs to work and moving towards her rather than the side gate.

Now she laughed.

'No way. They look under the doormat first, then under the flowerpots—look at all of them.' She waved her hands towards the mass of flowerpots clustered on mossy paving stones around the back door.

Angus *did* look. Looking at pot plants was infinitely preferable to the mental image lingering unwanted in his head.

Although she couldn't have meant that kind of stripping…

He turned more of his attention to the pot plants—a lot more.

'Herbs? I thought you said you couldn't cook. Why all the herbs?'

'I can cook, I just can't bake. When it comes to things like cakes and biscuits—I'm hopeless at those.'

It was one of the most inane conversations Kate had ever been involved in, but somehow she couldn't move away from the man who was now examining her herbs with an almost professional interest.

Or what seemed like one!

Why hadn't he left?

Why walk towards her rather than the side gate?

Surely the strangeness she was feeling in his presence wasn't reciprocated? Not just attraction as in physical awareness but attraction like iron filings to a magnet—a kind of inexorable pull.…

'I've got a wall to strip and someone's calling you,' she said as a shrill, 'Daddy' wafted across the hedge.

'Yes,' he said, but still he didn't move, except to straighten up from his examination of the herbs and look directly at her, the shadows in his eyes not visible in the gathering dusk, so he was just a tall, dark and very handsome man!

'Yes,' he said again, then finally he turned away, calling back to Hamish, telling him he was coming, and disappearing around the side of the house.

Weird!

CHAPTER TWO

KATE left early for the hospital, telling herself it had nothing to do with not wanting to accidentally run into her neighbour and so having to walk with him. But maybe he'd had the same idea of avoiding her, or he always arrived at work an hour early, for he was the first person she saw as she entered the unit.

'The baby being transferred has arrived,' he said, a slight frown furrowing his brow.

'Bigger problem than you thought?' she asked, sticking to professionalism mainly because the toast she'd had that morning hadn't been made from mouldy bread but her stomach was still unsettled.

'No, the scans show really good coronaries, as far as you can ever tell from scans, but he hasn't got a name.'

Now Kate found herself frowning also.

'Hasn't got a name?' she repeated. 'But that's ridiculous. Of course he must have a name.'

'Baby Stamford,' Angus replied, his frown deepening.

'Oh, dear,' Kate muttered, hoping the first thing that had entered her head was the wrong one. 'But sometimes parents wait until their baby's born to name him or her, thinking they'll know a name that suits once they've seen the baby.'

Now Angus smiled, but it was a poor effort, telling Kate he knew as well as she did that sometimes the shock of having a baby with a problem affected the parents so badly they didn't want to give the child a name—didn't want to personalise the infant—in case he or she didn't survive.

Her heart ached for them, but aching hearts didn't fix babies.

'You're operating this morning?' she asked Angus.

He nodded.

'Good! That gives me an excuse to speak to the parents, to explain what my part will be, before, during and after.'

She looked up at him.

'Shall we go together? A double act?'

Angus studied her for a moment, almost as if he was trying to place her in his life, then he nodded.

'The mother came by air ambulance with the baby, and the husband is driving down. Somewhere called Port something, I think they come from.'

'Port Macquarie,' Kate told him, 'and as far as I'm concerned, that's in our favour, the mother being here on her own. We might find out more from her than we would from the two together.'

'I prefer to speak to both parents,' Angus said in the kind of voice that suggested he was coolly professional in his approach to his job, not someone who got involved with the parents of the infants on whom he operated.

Which was fine, Kate admitted to herself as they walked down the corridor towards the parents' waiting room. A lot of paediatric surgeons were that way, finding a certain detachment necessary in a job that carried huge emotional burdens.

Although he was a single father himself—wouldn't that make him more empathetic?

And why, pray tell, was she even thinking about his approach to his job when it was none of her business? All she needed to know was that he was a top surgeon!

The waiting room was empty.

'The baby was born by Caesarean, so the mother is still a patient,' Becky, the unit secretary, told them. 'She's one floor up, C Ward, room fifteen.'

'Let's take the stairs,' Kate suggested, and when Angus grimaced she added, 'Not keen on incidental exercise? Don't you know that even the smallest amount of exercise every day can help keep you healthy?'

Far better to be talking exercise than thinking about empathy....

'I lived in America for five years, where everyone drives, and already today I've walked to work—incidental exercise, but mainly because I don't have a car.'

'You lived there for five years?' Kate queried, taking the second flight two steps at a time, only partly for the exercise. 'Yet Hamish has a broad Scots accent?'

Angus caught up with her as she opened the door.

'When my wife died, my mother came out to mind the baby, then my father took early retirement, so he and my mother were Hamish's prime carers when he learned to talk. They stayed until Hamish was three, then found Juanita for me before they returned to Scotland, where my father's old firm was only too happy to have him return to work.'

When his wife *died*?

There were plenty of single parents around, but most of them didn't have partners who had *died*!

No wonder he had shadows in his eyes....

Kate tried to make sense of this—*and* make sense of why a casual answer to her question was having such an impact on her—as she led the way to C Ward, but once inside room fifteen, Angus's marital state was the last thing on her mind.

'I really don't care what you do,' the woman in the bed in room fifteen announced when they'd introduced themselves and explained the reason for their visit. 'This is just not the kind of thing that happens to people like us. I mean, my husband has his own business and I'm a barrister—we're both healthy, and we run in marathons. I keep telling people that the babies must have been mixed up. I held my baby when he was born and there was nothing wrong with him, and then suddenly people are saying his heart's not right and flying me off to Sydney, even refusing to take my husband in the plane.'

The tirade left Kate so saddened she was speechless, but thankfully Angus was there. He sat down carefully by the side of the bed, and spoke quietly but firmly.

'Mrs Stamford, I realise this is a terrible shock to you, but with this defect babies always seem perfectly healthy at first. It's only when a little duct between the two arteries starts to close and oxygenated blood keeps circulating through the lungs rather than around the body that a blueness is noticed, usually in the nail beds and lips of the infant.'

Kate saw the woman's fury mount, and expected further claims of baby-swapping, but to Kate's surprise, Mrs Stamford's anger was directed at Angus's choice of words.

'Defect? You're saying my baby has a defect?'

Time to step in before she became hysterical, Kate decided.

'It's fixable, the problem he has,' she said gently. 'That's why we're here. We need to explain the operation to you and get your permission to perform it.'

'And if I refuse?'

Oh, hell! Kate tried to think, but once again Angus took over.

'There could well be legal precedents that would allow us to operate anyway,' he said. 'I'm new to Australia but in many of the states in the U.S.—'

'Well, I very much doubt that,' Mrs Stamford interrupted him, although she seemed to have calmed down somewhat. Kate sought to reassure the woman.

'It's an operation that's frequently performed, and with excellent results,' she told her, 'and we're lucky to have Dr McDowell here as he specialises in it.'

She looked at Angus, expecting him to begin his explanation, but he hesitated for a moment before taking a small notebook and pen out of his shirt pocket.

'This might explain it best,' he said to Mrs Stamford.

Kate wondered about the hesitation—was it to do with the detachment she'd sensed earlier?—although now he was drawing a small heart on a clean page of the notebook, carefully inking in the coronary arteries which clasped the heart like protective fingers, then showing the two major arteries coming out the top of the organ.

'These coronary arteries which feed oxygenated blood to the heart muscle to keep it beating come off the aorta, the bigger of the two arteries coming out of the heart. The aorta is supposed to come out of the left ventricle while the pulmonary artery that divides in two and goes into the lungs comes out of the right. On rare occasions these two arteries are transposed and the aorta comes out of the right ventricle, with the pulmonary artery coming out of the left.'

Mrs Stamford was at least interested enough to look at Angus's drawing, and as she was quiet, he continued.

'What we have to do is first move the two coronary arteries, then we swap the major arteries, cutting the aorta and fixing it to the pulmonary artery where it comes out of the heart, and stitching the pulmonary artery to the aorta so the two arteries are now doing the jobs they're supposed to be doing.'

'For ever?' Mrs Stamford demanded.

Angus hid a sigh. She was right to ask, and had every right to know the truth, but this was one of the reasons he hated getting too involved with parents, having to tell them that the future could hold more operations, having to tell them that, although their child could lead a normal life, there was no guarantee of a permanent fix. Every conversation led to more emotional involvement—and often more pain for the parents.

'There's a chance the baby will need another operation when he's older.' He spoke calmly and dispassionately—straight medical information. 'The valves on the pulmonary artery are smaller than the aorta's valves and as these valves are left in place they might sometimes need to be expanded.'

'Leave the diagram,' Mrs Stamford said. Ordered? 'I'll speak to my husband and then talk to you again.'

She was dismissing them, and Kate waited while Angus pulled the page from his notebook, then they both left the room.

'*Is* there a legal precedent in some places to go ahead without permission?' Kate asked him.

'I've no idea,' he replied, 'but the woman was getting hysterical and I thought, as she's a barrister, legal talk might calm her down.'

'I think she's entitled to a *little* hysteria,' Kate muttered, wondering if Angus could really be as detached as he appeared.

She shrugged her shoulders, trying to ease the tension that had coiled in her body.

'It must be terrible for the parents,' she reminded him, 'to learn that there's something wrong with their child.'

Worse than losing an unborn child?

She thrust the thought away and turned her attention to what Angus was saying.

'Particularly parents who are barristers and run marathons?' he queried, the dryness in his voice suggesting he hadn't taken to Mrs Stamford, not one little bit. 'I wonder who she thinks *do* have children with heart defects? Common people like doctors and teachers? People who don't run marathons? I'm glad the baby is our patient, not the mother.'

'That's if the baby *is* our patient,' Kate reminded him, although she was wondering why Angus had chosen this specialty if he didn't like dealing with parents. Surely that was as important as successfully completing a delicate operation? Or nearly as important…

'He will be,' Angus assured her, moving to avoid a passer-by and accidentally bumping against her shoulder. 'I doubt any mother would deny her child a chance at life.'

'I hope you're right!' Kate murmured, though fear for the tiny scrap of humanity fighting for his life right now made her feel cold and shivery.

Except for a patch of skin on her shoulder which was very, very hot!

'Do you want to read his file? A paediatrician in the hospital where he was born gave him prostaglandin to keep the ductus arteriosus open and opened a hole between the atria to mix the oxygenated blood as much as possible but it won't hold him for long.'

Kate sighed.

'No, I'll read the file later. Right now I should go back in and talk to her.'

'Better you than me,' Angus said, although even as he spoke he felt saddened by his reaction and wondered just when he'd lost the empathy he used to feel with parents.

Fool! No need to wonder when he knew the answer. It was back when Jenna died—

'You make it sound as if I'm walking into an execution chamber,' Kate teased, jerking him out of the past. He found himself wishing she wouldn't do it—wouldn't talk to him so casually, as if they were old friends, and smile at the same time. It was affecting him in a way he didn't understand and certainly didn't want to consider. He didn't *do* emotion! Not any more.…

'I didn't mean it that way,' he told her.

'No?'

Again the teasing smile, and again he felt a physical reaction to it, but before he could analyse it, Kate was speaking again.

'I can understand her anguish. Not only fear for her little son, but that terrible "why me" feeling she must be experiencing.'

'"Why me"?' Angus repeated, then he shook his head as he admitted, 'You're right. There's always a lot of "why me" isn't there?'

He looked unhappy and Kate realised that's exactly what he must have thought when his wife had died, as he tried to cope with his own grief and anguish, not to mention his son's loss of a mother.

And she, Kate, foolish woman that she was, had caused him pain by bringing it up!

But the 'why me' feeling was familiar to her, and although she wouldn't—couldn't—think about the really bad times she'd felt that way, maybe a couple of her less traumatic 'why me's' would cheer him up, chase the shadows from his eyes if only for a few minutes.

And lighten the atmosphere before she went back in to see Mrs Stamford!

'For my part they've been totally minor.' That was a lie but he'd never know. 'Things like a date passing out in his soup in the most expensive restaurant in town—a diabetic coma not drunkenness—and as it was a first date, it wasn't entirely surprising the relationship came to nothing. Then there was the one and only time I was persuaded to try skydiving. I got caught up in a tree and it took five hours to get me down, with full television coverage of a local drama. I know these are very trivial things compared to what Mrs Stamford is going through, but they do give me just some inkling of her "this can't be happening to me" feelings.'

Angus smiled and Kate felt a little spurt of happiness that she'd been able to make him smile, but the happiness faded as she remembered the task she'd set herself. She returned to Mrs Stamford's room.

'I thought you might like someone to talk to,' she said, giving the woman a quick professional once-over and not liking the pale, haggard face and red-rimmed eyes. 'There are counsellors, of course, that we could bring to you, but they wouldn't know the ins and outs of the op the baby needs. If you want to talk it out I'm willing to sit here and listen.'

'You said you were a doctor,' Mrs Stamford muttered in accusing tones. 'Don't you have other duties, people waiting for your services? We keep reading about the waiting lists for operations in hospitals, yet you've got time to sit and chat.'

Kate bit back a defensive retort. The woman was in terrible emotional pain; she was entitled to lash out.

'My job this morning was to prepare your baby for surgery,' Kate responded, speaking gently but firmly. 'As the anaesthetist I'm in charge of everything that goes into his blood and lungs until he goes onto the bypass machine, then afterwards until he's out of the post-op room. But I'm also a woman, and although I can't imagine the depth of the pain you're going through, I thought you might like a sounding board. Or to ask questions. Or just to have someone sitting with you for a while.'

Mrs Stamford's stiff upper lip did a little wobble, as did her lower lip, then she sniffed deeply as if to control tears that longed to flow.

'Will he die if he doesn't have the operation?' she asked, even paler now, if that was possible.

Kate hesitated.

'We can keep him alive for a while, but because most of the oxygenated blood is circulating back through his lungs and not getting to his heart and brain, the answer's yes. But we have kids that have had this op coming back to visit us years later, fine healthy young girls and boys.'

The only response was another sniff, although the way the woman was twisting her hands told of her terrible agitation.

Kate longed to help her but wasn't sure how.

Maybe…

'Have you thought what you'd have done if you'd known the baby had a problem early on in your pregnancy. Would you have had a termination?'

Now colour rose in Mrs Stamford's cheeks.

'You mean, an abortion? No, I'd never have done that. A life's a life—my husband and I both agree on that.'

But now the baby's here you'd let him die? Kate thought, but she couldn't say it. Nor could she understand Mrs Stamford's thinking now, until the woman sighed and said, 'You're right. Of course I can't let him die. It was the shock! Give me whatever I have to sign, then go ahead and operate.'

Kate had won, so why did she feel as if she'd lost?

Because things were never that easy!

'He could still die,' she said, even more gently than she'd spoken earlier. 'These operations are performed quite often and with great success, but with any operation at any age there's a risk. You understand that.'

'Scared you'll be sued if you don't dot all the *i*'s and cross all the *t*'s?' Mrs Stamford snapped, but Kate heard the pain in her voice and knew the woman was close to breaking.

'I'm more afraid that having given permission if something does happen you'll blame yourself,' she said. 'You're already doing that, aren't you? Somehow you've convinced yourself this is all your fault, but congenital abnormalities can happen anywhere, any time.'

She stood up and moved closer to Mrs Stamford, putting her arms around her and holding her as the woman wept and wept.

'This is the damn problem with only having units like this in the capital cities,' Kate ranted to Angus a little later, the signed permission form in her hand. 'The patient, and usually the mother, are whisked away and end up miles from family support. She's got no-one, that woman, until her husband gets here. I know we can't have units like this in every hospital in Australia, but there should be a better way of doing things.'

Angus gave her shoulder a comforting pat, the physical effect of which jolted her out of her worry over Mrs Stamford's isolation, especially as she'd written her colleague down as a man who remained detached—too detached, she'd thought, for comforting pats!

'She's got the baby,' he reminded her, and Kate looked up at him.

'You mean…?'

'You've already achieved one miracle this morning,' Angus told her, 'so why not go for two. Go back in there and ask her if she'd like to go with him as he's wheeled to Theatre. We can get a wheelchair and she could touch him, hold his hand. Although if she doesn't want to bond with him in case he doesn't live—'

'She *thinks* she doesn't want to bond with him.' Kate interrupted his objection, excited now by the idea. 'But maybe she's changed her mind about that, as well.'

She'd sounded positive about it, but deep inside she had her doubts, even wondered if it was wise to push Mrs Stamford this little bit more. But Angus seemed to think it was a good idea and he was looking far happier now than he had been earlier, so the least Kate could do was try.

She returned to the room where Mrs Stamford was lying back against the pillows, her eyes closed and only a little more colour in her face than when Kate had first seen her.

'We'll be taking him to Theatre very soon, and I wondered if we arranged a wheelchair for you and a wardsman to push it, you'd like to come up to the PICU and go as far as the theatre with him.'

Mrs Stamford's eyelids lifted and dark brown eyes stared fiercely at Kate.

'What are you? Some kind of avenging angel, determined to push me further and further?'

'I just wondered,' Kate said lamely, 'seeing as you're here on your own until your husband arrives and he, the baby, is on his own, as well. Maybe you could support each other.'

Oh, boy! Wrong thing to say! Mrs Stamford was in tears again, flooding tears and great gulping sobs.

Kate held her again, and it was only because she was holding her, she heard the whispered instructions.

'Get the bloody wheelchair, but I want a nurse not a wardsman wheeling me. Men don't understand.'

Uh-oh! Was it Mr Stamford, not Mrs Stamford, who'd found it hard to accept a less-than-perfect child? Had she consulted him—phoned him—before she signed the permission-to-operate paper?

And while Kate could have argued that some men were far more understanding and supportive than some women, she held her tongue. She gave Mrs Stamford a final hug and darted off, not wanting to give the woman time to change her mind. She arranged the transportation, then raced back up to the floor above, knowing she had to be there to intubate Baby Stamford and prepare him for his lifesaving op.

'So tiny, the veins.'

She didn't have to glance up to know it was Angus hovering beside her in the treatment room as she put a peripheral line into the baby's foot, already having secured one in his jugular and administered the first mild sedative.

'So tiny we need to work out better ways of doing this—smaller, more flexible catheters. You'd think it would be easy but I've been working with technicians from one of the manufacturing companies for over a year now, and we're no further advanced. Too fine and they block, or twist or kink—it's so frustrating!'

Angus studied the back of her head—a coloured scarf now hiding the bright hair—as she concentrated fully on her task.

She'd been working with techies to improve catheters? Kate Armstrong was full of surprises, not least of which had been the way she'd talked Mrs Stamford out of her indignation and allowed the woman's natural maternal instincts to come out.

The redhead's body brushed against his as she straightened up and *his* body went into immediate response mode. Not good where Kate Armstrong was concerned. She wanted kids—well, grandkids, which meant, as she'd pointed out, having kids first.

She was not for him!

Even though the 'grandmother' thing intrigued him! Not to mention whatever lay behind it….

Was it because of the familiar noises in the operating theatre, the sizzle of the bovie as it cut and cauterised tiny vessels, the bleeps of the monitors as they kept Kate up-to-date on Baby Stamford's condition, the subdued chatter of the staff, the music playing in the background, that Angus felt so at home? Although this was not only his first operation at Jimmie's but the first time he'd worked with any of the team.

Oliver Rankin was assisting. He was quiet, neat and efficient, although Angus rather thought he was casting glances in Kate's direction a little too often. Clare Jackson was operating the bypass machine, waiting for the order to use it to take over the work of Baby Stamford's tiny heart. Clare Jackson might not want children, Angus thought, standing back so Oliver could lift the pericardium away from Baby Stamford's heart.

The thought startled him, and he shut it down immediately, dismayed to find himself, for the first time in years, thinking of something other than the operation while in Theatre. He prided himself on his total concentration on the job, and although he often joined in the general chat and jokes, his mind never strayed far from the tiny patient on the table.

She was far better looking, beautiful, in fact—Clare Jackson—so why was he, too, glancing up at Kate from time to time.

Because she's the anaesthetist, of course, and she's the one who knows how the baby's doing, down there, all but hidden with the cage to protect his head and wrappings covering all his little body except his chest.

'Blood gases fine,' the woman he was trying to block from his mind said. 'Heartbeats 130 a minute.'

With the little heart fully exposed, Angus inserted cannulas into the aorta and an atrial vein; Oliver attached the tubes that would put Baby Stamford on bypass—the tubes connecting to the machine which would oxygenate his blood and pump it through his body.

'Pressure's up,' Kate said, reassuring everyone, although Clare was now controlling what happened to the baby's blood pressure.

'Check blood gases and start cooling him.' Angus gave the order, one hundred percent of his attention back on his patient, the information coming in from Kate and Clare clicking computerlike into his brain, his mind whirling as he worked, total concentration on what he was doing but thinking ahead, always anticipating any problem, at the same time.

'Why do we cool them?' the circulating nurse asked, her voice suggesting she'd often wondered but for some reason had never wanted to ask.

'It cuts down the risk of organ damage when the flow of blood to the brain and other major organs stops—when we stop the heart to do the repair.'

Oliver explained, while Angus inserted a tiny tube into the aorta, where it was rising out of the heart. Through this he'd put the poison that would stop the heart beating and, once that went in, it was a matter of timing every second of the operation.

Kate watched him at work, waiting patiently until all the blood drained from Baby Stamford's heart, then switching the coronary arteries so neatly and quickly she didn't realise they were done until he stood and stretched.

Once straightened, he looked across at her, and she nodded and held up a thumb, but there'd been something in his dark eyes that had suggested he was looking at *her*, not at the anaesthetist. Ridiculous, of course, but she shivered in spite of herself, then turned all of her attention back to the patient on the table and the machines that told her what was happening.

Less than an hour later the baby's heart was beating on its own, the little hole in his heart repaired, the arteries switched so they would now do the jobs they were intended to do. And though Angus had left a pacemaker in Baby Stamford's chest to keep his heart rate stable, and various drainage tubes and measuring devices were still attached to him, he was doing well.

Kate had to smile as she accompanied her tiny comatose patient to the intensive-care room. He would be her responsibility until he regained consciousness, although Clare was in charge of the machine that was keeping him breathing.

'Getting him off the ventilator is the next hurdle,' Clare, who was walking beside Kate, said.

'Only if he needs it for a long time, but he's come through very well—all his blood values were good,' Kate replied, and Clare smiled.

'You're a glass-half-full person, right?' she said.

Was she?

'I've never thought about it,' Kate admitted honestly.

'Never thought about what?' a deep voice asked, and she turned to see Angus had joined them in the small room.

'Whether I'm a pessimist or an optimist,' she said, thinking of the times when sadness and loss had threatened to overwhelm her and whether that was pessimism.

'Oh, definitely an optimist, I'd say,' Angus told her, almost smiling, almost teasing. 'What else would you call a woman who organised childcare for children she doesn't yet have?'

'You what?' Clare demanded, but Kate silenced Angus with a 'don't you dare' look.

Bad enough she'd admitted her grandmother obsession to one person without the entire hospital knowing it.

'What about you, Angus,' she asked to divert the conversation. 'Are you a glass-half-full or a glass-half-empty person?'

He studied her for a moment.

'You know, I've never thought about it. Definitely half full as far as patients are concerned. I could never do an operation if I doubted I'd be improving a child's quality of life.'

'You've children yourself?' Clare asked, and Kate felt a surge of something that couldn't possibly be jealousy flood through her veins at the other woman's interest.

'One, Hamish—he's four,' Angus answered, while Kate wondered why Alex couldn't have found a less beautiful perfusionist.

'Probably ready for a little sister or brother,' Clare suggested, and though Kate knew this was just idle talk as they all watched the monitors that told them Baby Stamford was doing well, she resented the other woman's interest. Although Clare probably didn't know Angus was a widower.

'Not for Hamish, I'm afraid,' Angus replied. 'He's going to be an only child for life.'

Poor kid, Kate thought, but before she could point out the disadvantages—the haunting loneliness she'd felt as an only child—Clare was talking again, talking and smiling.

Flirting?

'Good for you!' she said. 'I'm one of four and the number of times I've wished I was an only child! You've no idea. Having to share toys, wearing hand-me-downs—not that we lived on bread and jam or the hand-me-downs were rags, but I think I was born to be an only child.'

Selfish! Kate muttered to herself, but there was something so open and honest about Clare that she found herself looking past the beauty to the woman within.

And liking her!

Damn!

Double damn if Angus were to fall for her, and why wouldn't he?

Not that it was any of Kate's business who he fell for, so why was she still thinking about Clare, thinking perhaps she was attached—*surely* she was attached; how could someone so beautiful be unattached?

'Look, there's no point in all three of us being here. Why don't you two grab a coffee break—in fact, it's past lunchtime. The canteen is good, and cheaper than the coffee shop on the ground floor. You know where to go?'

Was she pushing them together? Angus wondered. Then knew it was only because, for some indefinable reason, he was attracted to Kate Armstrong that he'd even consider she might be doing such a thing. This was work—two colleagues sharing lunch. He had to get his mind off Kate Armstrong and, having decided that, lunch with the beautiful Clare might be just what he needed.

Kate watched them depart, telling herself it was for the best, particularly now she'd heard Angus being so adamant about not producing siblings for Hamish. Given that fact, Angus McDowell was definitely not the man for her.

Not that he'd shown the slightest sign of wanting to be, so why she'd been idly fantasising about him she had no idea!

No idea apart from the attraction that had startled her body into life when she'd first met him. *Her* body, that was usually biddable and dependable and had rarely felt anything more than a lukewarm interest in any man since Brian and even he hadn't provoked much physical reaction.

Enough of attraction; she'd think about something else. Like why was Angus so definite about not wanting more children? Perhaps it was another way of saying he'd never marry again?

Get your mind back on work!

She checked Baby Stamford, wishing he had a name, then was surprised to hear the whirr of a wheelchair coming towards her. Mrs Stamford, pushed by a man who definitely wasn't a wardsman.

'They said he'd come through very well.' Mrs Stamford's voice was back in accusatory mode, daring Kate to argue this piece of good news.

'He's a little champion,' she assured the still-pale woman, then she held out her hand to the man. 'I'm Kate Armstrong, the anaesthetist. I'll be keeping an eye on him for the next few hours.'

'Pete Stamford,' the man responded, shaking Kate's hand, although all his attention was on his baby son who was so dwarfed by wires and tubes it was hard to see much of him. 'You keep a personal eye on him? Not just watch monitors?'

'I like to be here most of the time,' Kate told him, and was surprised when the man's face darkened.

'Then it's obvious to me he's not out of the woods yet,' he said, his muted voice still managing to convey anger.

'He's been through a huge ordeal for such a tiny baby,' Kate said gently. 'Being on bypass takes a lot out of them, and we stop his heart while the switch happens, poor wee mite, but there's no cause for anxiety. I stay because I like to watch until I'm certain he's over the effect of the anaesthetic and sleeping naturally. I can't always do it, because I've usually other ops scheduled, so today it's a bit of a treat for me.'

Pete Stamford eyed her with great suspicion and Kate was glad he hadn't come when all three of the specialists had been in the room. Then he would have been truly alarmed.

And she was even gladder—or should that be more glad, she wondered—when she realised that Mrs Stamford had wheeled herself closer to the cot, put her hand through the vent and was softly stroking her baby's arm, talking quietly to him at the same time.

Kate felt her heart turn over at the sight, then realised Baby Stamford's father was also looking at his wife, while tears streamed down his cheeks.

Unable to resist offering comfort, Kate put her arm around his shoulders and he turned to her and sobbed, his chin resting on her head.

'It's okay,' she said, more or less to both of them. 'You've been through such an ordeal and it isn't over yet, but the worst part is behind him, so maybe, little champ that he is, he deserves a name.'

To Kate's surprise, Pete straightened. He stepped towards his wife, taking her hand as they both chorused, 'Bob.'

Bob?

They were going to call the baby Bob?

What about Jack and Tom and Sam, simple syllable names that were in vogue right now? What kind of a name for a baby was Bob?

It was Mrs Stamford who eventually explained.

'We had a dog once, a border collie, who was the most faithful animal God ever put on earth. Even when he was dying of some terrible liver disease, he would drag himself to the doorway to greet Pete every night, and every morning he'd bring in the paper and drop it at my feet, right up to the day he died. He had more strength and courage than any human we've ever known, so it seems right to name this little fellow after him.'

Now Mrs Stamford was crying, too, and Kate quietly backed out of the room, wanting to leave the pair of them to comfort each other—and to get to know their little son.

Bob!

Angus returned as she was standing by the main monitors in the PICU. He peered into the room where the couple were, then turned to Kate, his eyebrows raised.

'They're okay,' she told him. 'They've called him Bob.'

'Bob?' Angus repeated. 'Ah, after a grandfather no doubt.'

'After their old dog,' Kate corrected, then she laughed at the expression on Angus's face. 'Thinking how it would be to have a child called McTavish?' she teased, and although he smiled, once again the smile didn't reach his eyes.

'I meant it when I said earlier there'd be no more children in my family,' he said, and Kate sensed he was telling her something else.

Telling her he, too, felt an attraction between them but it couldn't be?

She was not sure, but her body seemed to take it that way, disappointment forming a heavy lump in her chest.

CHAPTER THREE

'His name's Pete—Mr Stamford, that is,' she said to Angus, anxious to get him out of her company. 'I'm sure he'd appreciate meeting you and talking to you about the op and Bob's expected progress.'

Her tongue stumbled over 'Bob,' and Angus smiled at her, restarting all the sensations she didn't want to feel. Surely if she ignored them they'd go away, and for all the fancy she'd had earlier, she doubted Angus would be attracted to her. Especially not with a beauty like Clare around.

Or perhaps he no longer felt attraction for anyone. Perhaps his adamant declaration that Hamish would be an only child was because he was still in love with his dead wife—that was a possibility.

In which case he should do something to dampen down *his* attractiveness, Kate thought gloomily.

He walked away and she looked through the window to where he stood, talking to Pete and Mrs Stamford, and though she couldn't hear what they were saying, in her imagination she heard his seductive accent and knew ignoring the manifestations of attraction would be difficult to do.

Perhaps an affair—

He's not interested in you!

One part of her head was yelling at the other part. She tried to remember back to lectures on the brain and which bits controlled what. She'd never been particularly interested in neurology and worked quite happily on the theory that half her brain did emotion while the other half did common sense. And while the common-sense half—maybe that part was more than half in her case—usually held sway, she knew once the emotion part was awoken, it could be difficult to ignore.

Double damn again.

'You talking to yourself?'

The nurse sitting at the monitor looked up and Kate realised she'd sworn aloud.

'Probably,' she told the nurse. 'Early dementia setting in.'

'Not surprising, the work you do, anaesthetising tiny babies. I couldn't do it. I find it hard enough to watch them on the monitor. I'm getting married next week and we want to have kids, but I'll have to transfer out of the PICU before I can even think about it. Pregnancy's scary enough without knowing all the things that could be going wrong with the baby!'

Kate watched the monitor and considered this. It was what she did, caring for babies during lifesaving operations, so she'd always seen the work as positive, but as Angus and the Stamfords left Bob's room and she returned to it, she wondered if knowing the things that could happen would make pregnancy better or worse.

Better, surely, for there would be no unknowns.

But had she chosen it, subconsciously steered her career this way, because of the baby she'd lost?

No, that had been back in second year at university, before she'd begun her medical training, when medicine had still been only one of the options she'd been considering.

But her affinity for babies came from somewhere....

She shook her head, shaking away thoughts that had been safely locked in some dusty closet in her mind for many years.

'You handled Mrs Stamford very well. Are you able to feel that empathy for all your patients' parents?'

Angus appeared when Kate, some hours later, was in the surgeons' lounge checking the operating list for the following day, baby Bob now in Clare's care.

Kate turned towards him, but though looking at him usually produced a smile, this time it was forced.

'That's a strange question,' she told him, still puzzling over the man who'd asked it. 'I would think anyone would feel empathy for someone with a sick child.'

'Perhaps!' He shrugged off her assertion with that single word, as if to say *he* didn't, but she'd seen glimpses of an empathetic man behind the cool detachment he wore like a suit.

Or maybe armour?

'Not "perhaps" at all,' she argued. 'I bet you feel it or have felt it. In fact, I'd like to hazard a guess it's because of the children you see with problems that you've decided not to have more children.'

'You couldn't be more wrong.'

The blunt statement struck her like a slap and she felt the colour she hated rising in her cheeks. He must have seen it, for his next question was conciliatory, to say the least.

'But on that subject, you see these infants yourself, yet you still want to have children. Why's that?'

He'd asked the question to turn the conversation back on her, Kate knew that, but it was something she'd been thinking about since talking to the nurse earlier at the monitors. She'd locked the memory of her unborn child back into that dusty closet where it belonged, but the other issue was, and always had been, family.

How could she explain the loneliness she'd experienced as a child, and the ache for family, accentuated this time of year as Christmas drew near? Oh, she had friends who always welcomed her, but Christmas was for families, and since she was a child, she'd dreamed that one day she'd be the one cooking the turkey—she'd be the one with the children....

Pathetic, she knew, so she answered truthfully—well, partly truthfully.

'It's more a family thing,' she admitted. 'I was—I was an only child of parents who had no siblings living in Australia so I had no cousins or aunts or grandparents. Then one day—'

'When you were eleven,' he interrupted, and she nodded.

'—I was staying with a friend and we went to her grandmother's sixtieth birthday party and I saw a family in action and knew it was what I wanted.'

She kept her eyes on him as she spoke, daring him to laugh at her, wondering why the hell she was pouring out these things to a virtual stranger when she'd held them close inside her lonely heart for all these years!

He didn't laugh, but nor did he respond, the silence tautening between them.

'Besides,' she said, determined to get back to easy ground, 'why wouldn't I want to pass on the genetic inheritance of pale skin and red hair—so suitable to a hot Australian climate.'

Now he did respond, even smiling at the fun she was poking at herself.

'Ah, selective breeding. I do agree with that, but you could do that with one child—even be a grandmother with one child—so why children plural.'

Now Kate's smile was the real deal, and she shook her head as she replied.

'You're a persistent cuss, aren't you? We barely know each other and you're asking questions even my best friends don't ask. They just accept—Kate, yes, the one who wants kids. They usually emphasise the *want* and sigh and roll their eyes because they already have children and are often wondering why on earth they thought it was such a good idea.'

'Which gets you very neatly out of answering my question,' Angus said, but he didn't persist and Kate was happy to let the subject drop, as memories of her father's long illness and eventual death when her aloneness really struck home—no-one to share the caring, or share the pain and loss—came vividly to mind, bringing back the surging tide of grief she thought she'd conquered years ago.

Had her colleague seen something in her expression—a change of colour in her cheeks—that he held out his hand?

'Come on, baby Bob is fine, and we've a full day tomorrow. I'll walk you home.'

Kate considered arguing, making the excuse that she wanted to check the children on the next day's operating list, but weariness was seeping through her bones and, dodging the hand he'd offered to guide her through the door, she led the way into the corridor.

Why did she intrigue him? And why so suddenly was he attracted, he who didn't believe in instant attraction? Angus pondered this as they walked down the leafy street towards their houses. The summer sun was still hot, although it was late afternoon, and sweat prickled beneath his shirt, but that was nothing to the prickling in his skin when he saw this woman unexpectedly, or an image of her flicked across his inner eye.

'Does it get much hotter?' he asked, thinking an innocuous conversation about the weather would distract him from considering his reactions to his companion.

'Much,' she said cheerfully. 'It's only late November. Summer doesn't officially begin until December, and February can be a real killer, but at least you've got a nice olive skin. You can go to the beach to cool off and not risk turning as red as a lobster and coming out in freckles the size of dinner plates.'

'Dinner plates?' he queried, smiling, but more, he feared, because she'd said he had nice skin than at her gross exaggeration.

'Well, very freckly,' she countered.

'Ah, the great genetic inheritance you want to pass on to your children!'

She sighed and ran a hand through her tangled red curls.

'I'm very healthy—surely that's important,' she pointed out.

It was a silly conversation but the children thing nagged at Angus. He could accept that it was natural for a woman to want children, but Kate's desire seemed slightly out of kilter—more like determination than desire.

And he was obsessing about this, why?

Because he was attracted to her, of course!

Stuff and nonsense, as his mother would say. It was jet lag, not attraction—attraction didn't happen this fast.

'Can Hamish swim? He'll need to learn if he can't. There are learn-to-swim classes for children in every suburb.'

Had Kate been talking the whole time he muddled over attraction or had she just come out with this totally unrelated question?

Either way, he'd better answer her.

'*Need* to learn?' he repeated.

Her easy strides hesitated and she looked towards him.

'*I* think so! There are far too many drowning fatalities of small children in Australia each year. No matter what safety measures are put in place, and what warnings are issued, the statistics are appalling.'

Something in her voice sent a shiver down his spine and he hurried to reassure her.

'He *can* swim. Loves the water but has no fear, which is always a bit of a worry.'

She was standing looking at him, and he almost felt her shrugging off whatever it was that had bothered her earlier, although when he really looked at her, he saw the pain in her eyes.

'Someone you knew drowned?' he guessed, then regretted the casual question when all the colour left her face.

But she didn't flinch, tilting her chin so she could look him in the eyes.

'My sister—she was only two. It was a long time ago, but you don't forget.'

He reached out and touched her arm.

'I'm so sorry, I really am. I shouldn't have persisted.'

She rallied now, shrugging off the memories.

'That's okay, you weren't to know. Things happen. But you can understand why I'm a wee bit obsessive about children learning to swim.'

'Of course you are.' He squeezed her arm where he was holding it, feeling her bones beneath the flesh. 'Well, be assured Hamish will be fine in the water. We're quite near the beach, I believe.'

Her smile caught him by surprise, as did his gut's reaction to it.

'Quite near the beach? You really were thrown straight in the deep end,' she said. 'You haven't had time to work out your surroundings at all.'

Then, as if their previous conversation had never happened, she looked up at the sky, where the sun was heading slowly towards the west.

'With daylight saving, it'll still be light for a while. What if I pile you and Hamish and Juanita into my car and we do a quick tour of the neighbourhood. We can have a swim and finish with fish and chips at the beach—if Hamish is allowed to eat fish and chips.'

She was being neighbourly, possibly to banish memories his careless question had provoked, but the offer told him more about Kate Armstrong than she'd probably intended it to. She was the kind of person who would always put herself out for others. She'd had no need to go back into Mrs Stamford's room that morning, but had known the other woman was in deep emotional pain and had decided to make one more attempt to help her.

Now she was offering to drive his little family to the beach.

She *should* have children! A giving person like Kate would be a wonderful mother. Angus remembered a book he'd read on parenting that explained no matter how hard a father tried he could never fully replace a mother. Something to do with wiring…

If Hamish had a mother, would that let Angus off the hook? Allow him to feel less, not exactly guilty, but disquieted about his interaction with his son?

He shook his head as if to shake away the notion. He was fine as a father, spent time with Hamish, did whatever he could for him.…

'Well?' Kate demanded, and Angus pulled himself together.

'We'd be delighted, and thanks to his early upbringing Hamish loves fish and chips. It's practically a staple diet back home in Scotland.'

What was she doing? Was she mad, getting more involved with her neighbours instead of less? Kate left him at his gate and strode ahead, then found Hamish and a woman who must be Juanita sitting on her yellow sofa.

'I thought I told you the backyard was for adventures,' she scolded Hamish, although she softened the words with a smile.

'This isna an adventure,' he told her, four-year-old scorn scorching the words. 'I'm with Juanita. We're waiting for you to come home so I can—'

'Introduce me,' the woman said, standing and holding out her hand to Kate. 'I am Juanita Cortez.'

She was a solid, olive-skinned woman of about fifty, Kate guessed as she introduced herself, and asked Juanita how she was settling in.

'We are nearly there,' Juanita replied. 'Angus has sorted a kindergarten for Hamish and I've found an organisation for ex-pat Americans that meets once a month, and another place where I can go to play bridge, so I will soon meet plenty of people.'

'Well done you,' Kate responded, admiring the other woman's nous in getting organised, but she was watching Hamish as she spoke, watching Angus swing his son into the air before depositing him on his shoulders, normal father stuff but somehow Angus was never looking at the little boy.

Not directly.

Seeing them together, so unalike, Kate wondered if Hamish looked like his mother, and therefore was too painful a reminder....

Oh, dear!

'Come on,' Angus said, 'let's get changed. Kate's taking us to the beach.'

'Are you, Kate? Are you really?' the little boy perched on Angus's shoulders demanded.

Stupid, this is stupid getting more involved with them, but something in the anxious young eyes made her reply immediately.

'Of course. Get your swimmers, or whatever you Yanks and Scots call swimming costumes and meet me at the shed in my backyard in half an hour.' Kate turned back to Juanita. 'You'll join us.'

Juanita looked far less interested in a trip to the beach than Hamish had been.

'If you don't mind, I'd prefer to stay at home. I need to send some emails to my family to let them know we've arrived and are settling in, then I must make some phone calls about the ex-pat organisation and bridge club.'

As Angus and Hamish had disappeared into their house, Kate assumed this would be okay with him, so she nodded to Juanita and hurried inside herself, worrying again because a swim was just what she needed to wash away the tension of the day. But on the other hand, letting Angus McDowell see her lily-white body in a swimsuit, especially on a beach full of bronzed bathing beauties, was a very embarrassing idea.

As if he cared what she looked like in a swimming costume, the common-sense half of her brain told her, though the sensible admonition wasn't strong enough to stop a rather wistful sigh.

She changed into her swimming costume, pulled shorts and a T-shirt over it, then dug through the kitchen junk drawer in search of the car keys. She used the car so rarely, the keys got buried under spare change, receipts and reminder notices from the library—even an apple core, today, although how that had got in there, Kate had no idea.

Then out the back door, locking it, and casting a quick glance at her pots to check if they needed watering. Later—she'd do that later, because excited voices from the far end of her backyard told her Angus and Hamish had arrived.

'We came down the lane,' Angus explained, 'although I've found the gate between the properties. I just haven't had time to hack through the jungle to release it.'

It's because he's got this outer carapace of an easy-going man that I feel as if I've known him for ever, Kate decided as she unlocked the shed and turned on a light, revealing her father's ancient old car. *But all he lets people see is the outside....*

'That's your car?'

Two voices chorused the question, the younger one excited, the older one full of disbelief.

'It goes,' Kate said defensively.

'I think it's super,' Hamish announced. 'Like something out of a storybook. Has it got a name?'

As a person who thought giving names to inanimate objects was stupid, Kate longed to say no, but if she did, the car would probably hear her and refuse to start.

'My father called it Molly,' she admitted, hoping maybe Angus, who was walking around it, examining it the way one would an antique, hadn't heard, but just in case he hadn't, Hamish made sure he knew.

'Did you hear that, Dad? We're going for a ride in Molly.'

He was patting the car's pale blue paintwork, his little hands leaving prints in the dust, so Kate was squirming with embarrassment before she'd even opened the doors. She did that now, helping Hamish into the back seat, pulling down the booster seat and fastening the seatbelt around him, then getting in the car herself.

'Molly?' Angus queried softly as he slid into the passenger seat beside her.

'My father named her.' Defensive didn't begin to describe how Kate felt, until she remembered—'And if you want to borrow the car to visit your dog at the weekend, then I don't want to hear another comment, thank you.'

Before Angus could reply, Hamish began chattering about McTavish and how much he would like a car called Molly, and the child's innocent delight in the situation eased Kate's tension, so by the time they'd driven around the immediate neighbourhood and arrived at the beach at Coogee, she'd even stopped worrying about Angus seeing her in a swimming costume.

He'd have been better not having seen her in a swimming costume, Angus decided as their chauffeur slipped out of her shorts and shirt, revealing a pale but perfect body. All of his mother's figurines were decorously covered, so it wasn't a similarity to one of them that sent his heartbeat into overdrive.

It must be the prolonged period of celibacy his libido had been suffering. His last female friend had fallen out with him six months ago over the amount of time he spent with Hamish. The argument had been fierce, mainly because Angus knew he spent the time with Hamish in an attempt to make up for what he didn't give the child. Not love, exactly, for he loved him deeply, just… He didn't know what the 'just' was, except that it was there—a missing link.

But the outcome of that argument had been that he'd decided it was easier to stay out of relationships for a while, especially as by that time he'd been offered the job in Sydney and had known he'd be moving on.

So, have a swim and settle down, he told himself, shucking off his own shorts and polo shirt, then following his son and Kate down to where green waves curled, then broke into foaming swirls that slid quietly up the beach.

'These are big waves.' The awe in Hamish's voice made Kate smile. 'In Scotland we have little waves and in America there aren't any beaches.'

'Not where you lived,' Kate reminded him, forbearing to point out America had thousands of miles of coastline on two oceans. He was jumping the waves as they washed towards him, shrieking with glee, and Kate's heart ached with wanting. To have a child, her own child—any child, she was beginning to think.

Although it was a baby her arms ached for....

'Want to go out deeper?'

Angus scooped up his son and strode towards the curling waves.

Presumably Angus could swim.

Kate watched them go, the ache still there—stronger if anything. It was all to do with family. Were Angus and Hamish a family? Was the base of family solid beneath the little boy? Had it not been solid in her case, even before Susie drowned? Had her family been doomed to disintegrate like so many families did these days, even before Susie died?

She could see the pair in the deeper water, ducking under waves, and remembered times, after her mother died, when she and her father had come to the beach.

He would take her out into deep water and throw her over the waves. He'd loved her, Kate had no doubt of that, but it had been a detached, distracted kind of love, the kind one might give to a specially favoured pet, the concept of family perhaps as unfamiliar to him, another only child, as it was to Kate.

Enough! She dived beneath the next wave, surfaced for a breath, then dived again, coming up beyond the breakers, feeling the water wrap around her body, cooling and soothing her, reminding her of all the wonderful things in her life, counterbalancing the aches.

A good wave was coming, rising up above the others, curling early. Swimming hard she caught it and rode it to the beach, aware of passing Angus and Hamish on her way. She lay where the wave had left her on the sand until an excited little boy joined her.

'Will you teach me to do that, will you, Kate, will you?'

Kate rolled over and smiled up at him.

'I surely will, champ,' she said. 'Next time I'm at the shops I'll get you a little boogie board. It's easiest to practise on that in the shallows, then I can take you out in front of me on my bigger board. One day when you're older, if your Dad decides to stay in Sydney, you might learn to surf. See the people at the far end of the beach, standing up on their surfboards?'

'Can you do that? Can you teach me that?'

His excitement had him hopping up and down, splashing her with water.

'There are better teachers than me, for board surfing,' she told him, sitting up and looking around for Angus.

Perhaps she *should* have asked if he could swim! Then his body, sleek as a seal's, slipped onto the beach beside her.

Angus sat up and shook the water from his hair.

'I didn't catch it way out where you did,' he said to the woman he'd been watching since she was deposited on the sand, a slim white mermaid in a green bathing suit. 'I just surfed the broken bit. It's been a long time since I caught a wave—student days at St Ives in England, an annual summer pilgrimage.'

He'd flopped onto the tail end of the wave to stop thinking about her, but now, this close, not thinking of her was impossible. The beautiful skin, so fine and pale he could see the blue veins in her temples, and in the slender lines of her neck, then the fiery red hair, darker now, wet and bedraggled, framing her face like a pre-Raphaelite painting.

'Kate is going to teach me how to ride on the waves,' Hamish announced, and now colour swept into her cheeks.

'I wasn't sure if you knew how. He asked me, but of course, you're a surfer, you can teach him.'

'Maybe we could both teach him.'

Angus heard the words come out and wished there was some way he could unsay them. How could he include someone else in his family before he'd made sure it *was* a family? It had obviously embarrassed her, as well, for the colour in her cheeks had darkened, and she stood and headed back into the water.

'I'll just catch another wave.' The words floated back over her shoulder before she dived beneath the breakers.

'Can I do that? Can I?' Hamish demanded, so Angus put thoughts of pale-skinned mermaids right out of his mind and concentrated on teaching his son to dive beneath the waves.

'Time for a shower and something to eat?'

Angus and Hamish, the diving lessons over, were sitting on the beach, making sandcastles, when the mermaid surfed right to their feet, lifting her head to ask the question.

'We can shower up on the esplanade,' she added, pointing towards the road, then, as if that was all the information he would need to realise the swim was over, she stood and walked back to where they'd left their towels and clothes. Angus hoisted Hamish onto his back and followed, thanking Kate as she picked up their clothes and handed them to him.

'There are changing rooms if you don't want to put your clothes on over your swimmers,' she said, 'but I find it's cooler to stay wet underneath, and as we can eat our fish and chips in the park, it doesn't really matter.'

Very matter-of-fact, yet that was what this outing was, a neighbourly gesture.

So why did he feel disappointed?

Feel as if something had changed between them?

For the worse!

She held their clothes while he showered with Hamish, then dried the little boy with her towel while Angus dried himself.

Being busy with Hamish meant Kate didn't have to look at Angus's sleek, wet body. She'd always considered herself immune to hormonal surges of attraction but the man next door was definitely setting her hormones in a twitch. What to do about it was the problem.

Keeping her distance from him would be one answer, but that was impossible when she not only worked with the man on a daily basis but also lived next door to him.

So she'd have to fake it—pretend to a platonic neighbourliness she was far from feeling.

'The Frisky Fish is the best for fish and chips, or it was last time I bought any.' She finished dressing Hamish and straightened up as Angus, his body now suitably covered, came to join them.

'That one just across the road?'

Such a simple question but his accent really was to die for! She was thinking accents when she should have been answering but now it was too late, for he was speaking again.

'I'll buy our dinner,' he announced. 'I know what Hamish eats, what about you—a serve of fish and chips?'

The dark eyes were fixed on her face and Kate found it hard to pretend when just this casual regard made her feel warm inside.

'I'm more a calamari person—not into fish at all— and could I have a battered sav, as well?'

'Battered sav?' Again man and boy made a chorus of the question, though Hamish added, 'Oh, I want one of those, as well.'

'Just ask for it, you'll see,' Kate told Angus, smiling at his bewildered frown. 'Hamish and I will bag us a table.'

She took the excited little boy by the hand and they walked through the park until they found a vacant table.

'I'm going to kindy tomorrow—Dad's taking me,' Hamish told her, and though he sounded excited there was a hint of anxiety in his blue eyes.

'That will be such fun for you,' Kate said. 'Meeting lots of new friends, finding people to play with at the weekends. Maybe we can bring some of your friends to the beach one day.'

'When I can ride the waves so I can show them,' Hamish told her, and Kate wondered at what age children developed a competitive streak.

She asked about his friends back in America and laughed at the adventures he and McTavish had shared, so she was surprised to see nearly an hour had passed and Angus hadn't returned. The Frisky Fish was popular and you usually had a wait while your meal was cooked, but this long?

'Here's Dad! He's remembered drinks even though we didn't tell him.'

Kate turned to see Angus approaching, holding white-wrapped parcels of food in one hand, a soft drink and a long green bottle in the other. He reached the table and put down the white parcels, gave Hamish his drink, then deposited the bottle on the table.

'I haven't a clue about Australian wines. I drank a fair bit of it in the U.S., but none of the names were familiar so I asked the chap behind the counter what went with battered savs.'

He was pulling two wineglasses from his pocket as he spoke, then he looked apologetically at Kate.

'I do hope you drink wine. I didn't think—should I have got you a soda, as well?'

'I'd love a glass of wine,' Kate assured him. 'Especially a glass of this wine. The bloke at the wine shop saw you coming, and sold you something really special—really expensive, I would think!'

Angus smiled at her, destroying most of her resolution to pretend she felt no attraction.

'Phooey to the price, as long as you enjoy it. We can both have a glass now and you can take the rest home to enjoy another time—it's a screw-top.'

He poured the wine, then busied himself unwrapping Hamish's dinner, showing him the battered sav.

'It's a kind of sausage called a saveloy that's fried in batter,' he explained to Hamish, who was squeezing tomato sauce onto it with the ease of an expert in takeaway food.

'And don't think you'll get one too often,' Angus added. 'Full of nitrates, then the batter and the frying in oil—just about every dietary and digestive no-no.'

'You're just jealous you didn't get one,' Kate told him, biting into hers with relish, then she laughed as Angus delved into his white package and came up with one.

'Well, I had to try it, didn't I?' he said defensively, but as he bit into it, he pulled a face and set it back down, deciding to eat his fish—grilled not fried, Kate noticed—instead.

'They're not to everyone's taste,' she said, 'but my father was the food police like you and I never got to taste one as a child, so I became obsessed later on in life.'

'Obsessed by battered savs?' Angus teased.

'Better than being obsessed by some other things I could think of,' Kate retorted.

Her next-door neighbour for one!

CHAPTER FOUR

KATE stopped the car in the back lane outside their gate and watched the two males walk into their yard, the taller one looking straight ahead, although Hamish was chattering at him.

He was a good father, Angus, Kate told herself as she pulled into the shed that did service as a garage for Molly, but she sensed that something was amiss in his relationship with his son. Back when she was young, she'd felt guilt—blamed herself—for her family's disintegration, thinking that if somehow she had managed to save Susie, everything would have been all right. It was this, she knew, that had led her to accept that, although her father loved her, there would always be a wall between them, so even when he was dying they couldn't talk about the past.

Had his wife's death built the same kind of wall between Angus and Hamish, or had Angus simply shut himself off from *all* emotion to shield himself from further pain?

And just what did she think she was doing, pondering such things? she asked herself as she closed the double doors of the shed. Why was she considering the convoluted emotional state of someone she barely knew?

Because you're interested in him.

The answer was immediate and so obvious she felt a blush rising in her cheeks and was glad that Angus wasn't around to see it. A dead giveaway, her blushes.

She thought of Clare instead, of the dark-haired beauty, and reminded herself that if Angus McDowell decided to be interested in a woman on their team, then Clare would surely be the number-one choice.

Kate grumped her way inside, a depression she rarely felt dogging her footsteps, but as she showered she thought of baby Bob and realised how little she really had to complain about.

Refreshed, she opted not for lounging-at-home clothes—in her case a singlet top and boxer shorts, her pyjamas of choice—but for respectable clothes—long shorts and a T-shirt, reasonable hospital visiting clothes. She'd just pop up and check not only on Bob but on Mr and Mrs Stamford, as well, to see how they were coping.

'There's something wrong? You've been called in?'

The panic she'd felt when she saw Angus by Bob's crib was evident in her voice, but when he turned and smiled at her she realised she'd overreacted.

'Did you think you were the only one who likes to check on patients, even when there's no reason for alarm?' he said.

Damn the blush.

'Of course not,' she managed stoutly. 'It was just that seeing you there with him gave me a shock. Mr and Mrs Stamford?'

'Gone to get a bite to eat. I said I'd stay.'

Was there an edge of strain in his voice that the statement pinged some memory in Kate's head?

'I got the impression you didn't like getting too involved with patients and their parents?'

He frowned at her but she was getting used to that.

'I think a certain degree of emotional detachment is necessary in our job.'

But even as Angus said the words he knew it hadn't always been that way. He also knew that it was seeing Kate Armstrong's empathy with Mrs Stamford that had broken through a little of his own detachment, enough to lead him to suggest he stayed with Bob while the couple ate together.

Was this good or bad, the breakthrough?

He was so caught up in his own thoughts it took him a moment to realise Kate was talking to him, pointing out the oxygen level in Bob's blood, suggesting they might be able to take him off the ventilator sooner, rather than later.

Dragging his mind back to his patient, he nodded his agreement.

'The operation is so much simpler when the coronary arteries are good,' he said. 'I was thinking the same thing about the ventilator when you came in. Maybe tomorrow morning we'll try him off it.'

They stood together beside the crib, Angus so conscious of the woman by his side he knew he had to be very, very wary of any contact with her outside working hours. Admittedly, her taking them to the beach, her offer to lend her car at the weekend, were nothing more than neighbourly gestures, and he wouldn't want to rebuff her or offend her, but every cell in his body was shouting a warning at him—danger, keep clear, problems ahead.

Kate felt him closing off from her and wondered if he'd been offended by her comment earlier—the one about detachment. But if he *was* closing off from her, well, that was good. It would be easier for her to pretend that's all they were, neighbourly colleagues, in spite of how her body felt whenever she was in his company.

She felt hot and excited and trembly somehow, physical manifestations she couldn't remember feeling since she was fifteen and had had a crush on the captain of the school's football team. Not that he'd ever looked at her, nor even stood close to her.

She stepped away from the crib, turning to greet the Stamfords, who'd returned from their dinner.

Pete Stamford eyed her with suspicion, and she wondered if he was worrying again, thinking the presence of two doctors by his son's crib meant there were problems.

'It's a habit,' Kate was quick to assure him. 'I find I sleep better if I do a final check of my patients before I go to bed.'

Pete nodded and Mrs Stamford, who still hadn't offered them the use of her first name, shook her head.

'Maybe all the horror stories we hear about health care are exaggerated,' she said, and Kate knew it was an apology for her anger of the morning.

'I don't think the news channels would attract an audience if they didn't exaggerate a bit,' she said, then she said goodnight to the couple, including Angus in the farewell, and left the PICU.

Angus caught up with her in the elevator foyer, and though he'd told himself he should linger with the

Stamfords until Kate was well away from the hospital, he felt uncomfortable about her walking home on her own this late at night.

'Oh, I do it all the time,' she said when he mentioned the folly of a woman walking the streets on her own. 'There are always people around near the hospital. Cars and ambulances coming and going, police vehicles—we're not quite in the middle of the city, but we're close enough and the streets are well-lit.'

'There's that dark park across the road,' he told her, stepping into the elevator beside her and wondering if it was the enclosed space, or her presence within it, that was making him feel edgy.

'The park's well-lit, as well,' she told him, smiling up at him. 'I'm not totally stupid, you know. I wouldn't take any risks with my personal safety, but around here, well, you'll see.'

And see he did, for there *were* plenty of people around as they walked down the street towards their houses. People, cars, ambulances and, yes, police vehicles.

Too many people really.

Far too many!

The thought jolted him—hadn't he just decided that Kate was nothing more than a neighbourly colleague? But the light steps of the slim woman by his side, the upright carriage and slight tilt of her head when she turned towards him…something about her presence was physically disturbing. So much so he wanted to touch her, to feel her skin and the bones beneath it, to tilt her head just a little bit more, run his fingers into the tangled red hair and drop a kiss on lips so full and pink they drew him like a magnet.

Attraction, that's all it was. He could cope with it, ignore it. And tomorrow he had a full day of appointments, no operations, so he wouldn't see her. All he had to do was walk her home, say goodnight and that was that.

Except that Hamish was sitting in her front yard on the discarded yellow couch!

Admittedly Juanita was beside him, but still Angus felt the anger rise inside him.

'You should be in bed,' he told his son, his voice stern enough to make the child slide closer to his nanny.

'McTavish is sick,' Hamish whispered, and the woman Angus was ignoring reacted far more quickly than he did. She knelt in front of his child and took him in her arms.

'It's probably just the water here in Sydney,' she assured him. 'I get sick when I go to different cities and drink different water. But the sickness doesn't last. It's always over in a day or two.'

Was this why children needed a mother?

Because women reacted more instantly—instinctively perhaps—to a child's misery?

His mind had gone to McTavish's health, to wondering what could be wrong with the dog. And to the other puzzle Hamish's presence presented. He went with that because it was useless to speculate about the dog's illness.

'And just why does that mean you're sitting in Dr Armstrong's yard, not at home in our living room?'

'Because Kate has a car and she *said* I could call her Kate!'

For a very biddable little boy there was a touch of defiance in the words and Angus found himself frowning, though at Juanita this time.

'What exactly is going on?' he demanded.

She shrugged her thick shoulders.

'It's as he says. The quarantine office phoned to say McTavish wasn't eating and there was nothing for it, but Hamish had to visit him, although I told him we couldn't see him tonight. He insisted he come and wait for his friend, sure she'd take him to see the dog.'

Angus could imagine what had happened, and understood that if Juanita had tried to insist on Hamish going to bed, the little boy would only have grown more upset, and with the move, and missing his dog, he was already emotionally out of balance.

But knowing how this had come about didn't help him in deciding what to do, although now Kate Armstrong seemed to have taken things into her own hands. She was sitting on the couch beside Juanita, holding Hamish on her lap.

'Juanita's right,' she was telling Hamish, 'we can't visit McTavish at this time of night because if we did all the other dogs and cats and birds and horses there would be disturbed and upset and they would want their owners to be visiting them, as well. But your father can phone them and ask them how McTavish is now. Perhaps he can tell them what McTavish's favourite food is, and the people who are minding him can try to coax him to eat a little of it. They have vets—animal doctors—at the quarantine centre who will be looking after him, just as your Dad looks after the babies at the hospital.'

'My mother died.'

Angus's heart stopped beating for an instant and a chill ran through his body. He'd never heard Hamish mention his mother, but it was obvious the little boy assumed Jenna had been ill before she died, and now he was thinking McTavish could also die. He knelt in front of his son and lifted him from Kate's knee.

'McTavish won't die,' he promised, knowing the assurance was needed, although he also knew he couldn't guarantee such a thing. 'Kate's right, let's go inside and phone the quarantine centre and tell them that he really likes—'

What did the dog really like?

'Biscuits,' Hamish told him, his fears forgotten in this new excitement.

'Not exactly a dietary imperative,' Angus muttered, but if biscuits could coax McTavish to eat, then he'd certainly suggest them.

He carried his son towards the house, pausing for Juanita to catch up with them and to nod goodnight to Kate. But the image of her sitting on the old yellow couch, his son in her arms, remained with him long after his conversation with the quarantine office and the reassuring return phone call that, yes, McTavish had eaten some biscuits and even eaten some of the dried dog food the carers had mixed in with the broken biscuits.

The image of her accompanied him to bed, aware of her in the house next door, so close, too close.

Any woman would have comforted Hamish in that situation, he told himself, but some instinct deep inside was telling him she wasn't just any woman, this Kate Armstrong. She was special—special in a way no woman had been since Jenna.

Which was another reason he had to avoid her....

It proved, as he'd known it would, impossible, for the teams met regularly. He operated with her, and discussion of patients was inevitable. But he managed to avoid her out of work hours until the day he came home early enough to attack the hedge around the garden gate.

Kate had been sensible in suggesting that if Hamish wanted to adventure he do it in her backyard, so freeing the gate had become a necessity. He'd bought a pair of hedge trimmers at the local hardware store and, some three-quarters of an hour of reasonably hard labour later, had cleared his side enough to push the gate open. Now all he had to do was trim her side.

Should he phone her first to ask if it was okay to come in and do it?

Phone her when she lived next door?

Well, he wasn't going to go over and ask; just seeing her each day at work was enough to tell him the attraction was going to take a long time to die.

He was debating this when Hamish returned from his job of stacking all the cut-off hedge branches in a pile near the back fence.

'Oh, look, we can get into Kate's garden.'

He ran through the gate before Angus could stop him, calling back to his father in even greater excitement, 'And here's Kate, she's right up a ladder!'

Right up a ladder?

A child suddenly calling out?

She could be startled!

Fall!

Angus dashed through the open gate to find his son confidently climbing up a very long ladder, at the top of which stood the team anaesthetist, a measuring tape, a pen and a notebook clamped in her hand.

She was peering down uncertainly, no doubt partly because Hamish's enthusiastic attack on the ladder rungs was making it wobble.

'No, Hamish dear,' she said gently. 'You can't have two people on a ladder at once. It might tip over.'

Once again the first thought, beyond the anger fear had wrought in his chest, was that this woman would make a wonderful mother. She was always fair. She always explained in a common-sense way that a child would understand.

Although, Angus realised a little belatedly, the child in question hadn't taken much notice and was still six rungs up the ladder and teetering there a little uncertainly.

Angus rescued him, set him on the ground, then looked up at the woman above him.

'And just what are you doing up there?'

He'd meant it as a neighbourly question, but it came out as a demand because the ladder seemed old and highly unstable and she was at the roof level of a two-storey house.

'Possums,' she replied, apparently not taking exception to his tone. 'I wouldn't mind the little beggars living in the roof if they'd just stay in one place, but it seems they live on one side and feed on the other so they're galloping across my ceiling in what sound like hobnail boots all night.'

'Possums?'

He realised there'd been a lot of conversation after that, but his mind had stuck on the word.

'Little furry animals, big eyes and long tails, cute as all get out but *not* much fun if they're living in your ceiling.'

'Oh!'

The word was obviously inadequate but Angus wasn't certain where to take the conversation next, and the uncertainty was only partly to do with the fact that Kate appeared to be wearing very short shorts, so from where he stood her pale legs went on forever and he found it hard to focus on anything else.

Fortunately Hamish was less inhibited.

'Possums!' he shrieked. 'Can I see them? Can I, Kate, can I?'

'Later,' she said. 'Just let me finish here and I'll come down and explain.'

Angus found himself wanting to order her down right away—wanting to tell her he'd do whatever it was she was doing—but having no notion of possums' habits, nor of what she could be arranging for them, he knew he'd be making a fool of himself if he said anything at all. So he stood and held the ladder steady, and not, he told himself, so he could watch her as she climbed down it. In fact, he turned resolutely away, determined not to have his resolve weakened by long pale legs in short shorts.

Kate told herself that of course she could climb down a ladder that Angus was holding; after all, hadn't she been successful in avoiding him these past few days, limiting their encounters to purely work contact? But her legs trembled as she came closer to where he stood and it took an effort of supreme will not to climb back up the ladder and perch on the roof until he grew tired of standing there.

'What exactly were you doing?' he asked as she passed him, very close—close enough to see a beard shadow on his cheeks and lines of tiredness around his eyes.

Wasn't he sleeping well?

She wasn't exactly enjoying night-times herself, finding it hard to sleep when images of him kept flitting through her mind.

He was so *close*....

'There's a hole,' she said, reaching the ground and backing away from him, lifting a hand to stop him moving the ladder. 'That's how they're getting in and out. I had to measure it.'

'So you could make a door for them?' Hamish asked, dancing around with excitement at the thought of a possum door.

'Not exactly,' Kate admitted, 'although I suppose you could call it a door, but I intend to keep it locked.'

'You want to lock them in?' Angus asked. It must be something to do with the air in Australia that so many of the conversations he had with Kate had a feeling of unreality about them. Battered savs came to mind....

'So I can keep them out,' she replied, speaking to him but squatting down so her face was level with Hamish's. 'There are plenty of other places the possums can live, think of all the trees here and in the park. That's where possums should live—in holes in the trunks and thick branches of trees. Once I fix my hole, they'll find somewhere else very easily.'

Hamish nodded his understanding, then asked the obvious question.

'But how will you get them out?'

Kate smiled at him, though Angus imagined there was sadness in the smile. Was she hurting for her own lack of children? Were they *so* very important to her?

Maybe one child would do her?

Hamish—

The thought shocked him so much he straightened his spine and clamped down on his wandering mind, thinking he'd go and cut the hedge on this side, departing forthwith, but she was talking again, explaining to Hamish, and Angus couldn't help but listen.

'I've been feeding them every night since I came back here to live,' she told Hamish. 'Are you allowed to stay up until eight o'clock because that's when it starts to get dark and they come out of the roof and down here to the garden to eat the fruit I put out. There's a whole possum family—a mother and a father and two little ones that sometimes ride on their mother's back but who are learning to climb themselves now.'

'Can I come and see, can I, Dad?'

The excitement in his son's voice meant Angus had to look at him, *really* look at him, something he usually avoided as Hamish's resemblance to Jenna was like a knife blade going through his skin.

And the excitement in Hamish's voice was mirrored in his little face. Seeing it, Angus could only nod. He even found himself smiling.

'You'll come and see them, too?' Hamish persisted, and Angus lost his smile, knowing for sure he'd have suggested Juanita take the little boy to see the possums. It wasn't that he didn't love Hamish dearly, but with the move and settling in to a new routine, the bond between himself and Hamish had seemed to weaken rather than strengthen. Besides which, more out-of-work hours' proximity to Kate Armstrong was something he needed to avoid.

'Of course,' he responded, suddenly aware that it was selfish to refuse—a kind of self-protection because Hamish looked so like Jenna.

Angus didn't sound overly excited by the idea, Kate decided, but then she wasn't so chuffed, either. She wanted to see less of Angus McDowell, not more.

'Eight o'clock, then,' she said, and headed for the shed where she hoped she'd find a piece of timber the size she wanted. Unfortunately the gate was in that direction so Angus fell in beside her, while Hamish raced excitedly back to his place to tell Juanita about the possums.

'Just what do you intend doing about the hole?' Angus asked.

Ah, easy question!

'I'll cut a piece of timber to fit over it and nail it in place. From the look of it, someone's tried to fix it before using some kind of magic glue to stick fibro over the hole but the possums were too cunning for that. They just ate the glue, or got rid of it some other way.'

She realised Angus had stopped walking and turned back to check on him. He was standing stock-still, staring at her with an unreadable expression on his face.

'What's up?' she asked, although she knew what was wrong with *her*. Just looking at the man raised her heart rate.

'The way I figure it, you wait until the possums come out, then you go and cover their hole, that right?'

Kate nodded.

'Up that rickety old ladder, *and* in the dark because they won't come out 'til dusk? You were going to do that yourself, telling no-one who'd go looking for you if you fell, asking no-one for help?'

Kate nodded again, although she was starting to feel peeved. It was none of his damn business what she did, yet he was sounding like a father admonishing a wayward teen.

'Didn't it occur to you how dangerous that was?' he demanded, and she forgot peeved and smiled.

'Angus,' she said gently, 'this is the twenty-first century. Women do these things. They take care of themselves, and if that includes minor repairs to their homes, then that's part of it. Actually,' she added after a momentary pause, 'they've been doing it for centuries. I bet it was often the woman who climbed on top of the cave to move dirt and stones over places where the rain got in. The men would have been off chasing bears and wouldn't have considered a bit of water over the fire an inconvenience.'

'I wasn't thinking about sexism or what women can or can't do. There's a safety issue,' he countered, but something in the way he said it didn't ring true.

Kate, however, went along with him.

'The ladder might look rickety but it's perfectly safe,' she assured him, but he didn't look any happier than he had when the whole stupid conversation had begun.

They parted, Kate leaving Angus hacking at the hedge while she continued on to the shed, not thinking about oddments of timber at all, but about a little warm place inside her that seemed to think Angus's concern might have been personal.

Fortunately it turned out to be one of those afternoons when the sensible part of her brain held sway. It seemed to laugh so loudly at the thoughts of the emotional part that she knew she'd got it wrong.

Which was just as well, she told herself, although a heaviness in her chest told her she did not believe that at all!

CHAPTER FIVE

THEY came, the tall man and the child, as dusk was falling, filling Kate's backyard with shadows. Urging Hamish to talk softly, she led them into her kitchen and lifted him onto the bench beneath the window.

'See,' she said quietly, 'just there under the lemon tree, I've a little table with cut-up apple and banana and some cherries on it.'

She had the outside light on, knowing its soft yellow glow didn't disturb the nocturnal animals.

Holding Hamish steady on the bench, she was aware of Angus moving up behind her, aware of the warmth of his body close, and even the scent of him, citrusy yet still male. It was some primordial instinct that had her body responding, she told herself, trying hard to concentrate on Hamish in order to blot out the effect Angus was having on her hormones.

'Listen,' she whispered to Hamish, 'can you hear them scrabbling down the tree?'

Hamish nodded, his little body rigid in her hands, though she could feel excitement thrumming through him. The longing for a child—her child, family— zapped through her like an electric current, shocking her

with its intensity. It had to be because she was holding
Hamish, because normally the longing was no more
than a vaguely felt dull ache.

Well, at least it had shocked her out of focusing on
the man behind her.

'Look, Dad, look!' Hamish said excitedly, and Kate
was happy to yield her place to Angus so he could hold
his son and share the excitement as the small furry animals with their pointed noses and big bright brown eyes
landed on the fruit table, the older pair looking around,
checking their safety, while the two youngsters began
to eat.

'Oh, they've got little hands!' Hamish cried as one
of the possums turned towards them, a piece of apple
in its paws, sharp white teeth nibbling at it.

'They've got wonderfully expressive faces,' Angus
said, a note of genuine delight in his voice as he turned
to smile at Kate.

'I know,' she agreed, 'and I love them to bits, but they
are *not* going to continue living in my ceiling!'

They watched in silence, broken only now and then
by Hamish's exclamations of wonder and delight. Then,
the feast finished, the possums leapt into the branches
of the lemon tree and, from there, scrambled into a jaca-
randa, scurrying up the trunk, then out along one of the
top branches, from which they leapt into a eucalypt.

'There's a hole in the trunk of that tree where they
can live,' Kate told Hamish. 'They could go and live
in the park but they probably won't because they know
they get fresh fruit here every night.'

She'd lifted him off the bench and carried him outside as the possums departed, and though she enjoyed the heaviness of his tired body in her arms she knew she had to hand him over to his father.

'Can I come and see them again?'

She was about to answer when she realised it was probably way past his bedtime. Fortunately Angus answered for her.

'Perhaps in winter when it gets dark earlier,' he said, 'although maybe we should think about putting out some fruit some nights, just as we used to put out bird feed for the birds in winter back home.'

Back home!

The phrase echoed in Kate's head as Angus lifted his son from her arms and, after thanking her, walked towards the gate in the hedge.

It was a reminder that on top of all the other reasons she shouldn't be attracted to this man, he didn't really belong here. Although as far as she knew he wasn't on a time-limited contract. Silly woman! Stop thinking about him. Get on with the job you have to do!

Angus kissed Hamish goodnight and left him with Juanita, determined to get back to Kate's place before she began her precarious task on the ladder. He'd go up and do it himself, and to hell with her 'liberated woman' attitude. After all, what use was an injured anaesthetist to him?

Too late! By the time he returned to his backyard she was already at the top of the ladder, and he could hear the hammering even before he walked through the gate.

Now he was in a dilemma! He didn't want to startle her, but he couldn't *not* approach. The least he could do was hold the ladder steady.

'I've come back,' he said, speaking quietly. 'And if you climb down, I'll do that for you.'

'I'm nearly done,' she answered cheerfully. 'Once I had the size it really wasn't difficult. There were studs under the soffit I could nail to, and though I feel just the teensiest bit guilty about shutting the family out of their home, at least I'll get to sleep more easily.'

'Which is more than I'm doing at the moment,' Angus muttered to himself.

He only realised he'd spoken the thought out loud when Kate said, 'I beg your pardon?'

'Oh, nothing,' he told her. 'I was just wondering why you haven't someone in your life you can get to do these jobs.'

Well, he *had* been wondering that earlier! The 'someone' might be a boyfriend or partner and he was far more curious about her single status than he should be!

'Are we back on the "man's job" thing?' she asked, beginning to come down the ladder so it moved in his hands.

'Not really,' he admitted, 'but it's hard for most men to think a woman is just as capable at odd jobs as they are. In fact, you're probably far more capable than I am. I'm a total fool when it comes to hammers—I seem to hit everything but the nail.'

Blithering, that's what his mother would say he was doing, but as Kate came closer he realised he'd either have to change the way he was holding the ladder, or let her finish her climb to the ground right through his arms.

The silly conversation ceased but he couldn't let go of the ladder, and although he pushed himself as far back as he could he still feel her body slither against his as she reached the lower rungs. A slight sway of the ladder and she was in his arms, all reason forgotten as he lifted her off the second bottom rung, setting her on the ground, turning her, kissing her, kissing her with the desperation of a—

He had no idea how to classify his desperation—just knew it existed, for his hands were clamped around her body and his lips were pressed to hers, his tongue already exploring the taste of her, the shape of her lips, the hardness of those neat white teeth....

It could have been a minute or an hour later that she moved against him, pulling back, smiling weakly at him in the yellow outdoor light.

'Surely only a fool would kiss a woman with a hammer in her hand,' she said, but though her voice was steady, he could see the unevenness in her breathing, see the way she was drawing air deep into her lungs. To replenish what she'd lost during the kiss or to steady her heartbeats as he was trying to steady his?

She should have hit him with the hammer, Kate thought as she waved the tool aloft. Or hit herself! Her heart thudded in her chest and no amount of denial or sensible talk could convince her she *wasn't* attracted to this man.

'I don't do serious relationships.' The words were as blunt as hammer hits would be, his voice deep and husky as if he'd had to force it out past innumerable obstacles.

Keep it light! Kate warned herself.

'And you're telling me this, why?'

She even managed a smile as she asked.

'Because I'm about to kiss you again and I thought you should know,' he said, and before she had time to make sense of the statement, he'd turned the words to action. He reached out, removed the hammer from her hand and dropped it on the ground. One arm clamped around her, drawing her close against his body, tucking her into it as if to fit a missing piece of a jigsaw puzzle, then the fingers of his free hand grazed her chin, tipping her head, fingers running into her hair.

By the time his lips met hers, Kate was breathless with the delay, her body throbbing with a desire she'd never felt before. Had he felt it, tasted it with the brush of lips on lips, so that his mouth became demanding, insistent, forcing her lips open as if he needed to claim all he could of her in a kiss?

She was melting, floating, boneless in his arms, held upright by his strong hand against her back, the other tangled in her hair. And he murmured as he kissed—muttered, really—little words and sounds she really couldn't make out, although they sounded more like reprimands than endearments.

But the noise did nothing to diminish the potency of the kiss. If anything, it intensified the excitement, so when Kate realised she was making little moaning noises, she didn't try to stop them. She surrendered to sensation, enjoying the searing heat of desire along her nerves, the burning need settling at the base of her abdomen.

Crazy as a loon! Angus didn't think he'd ever used the expression he'd heard often in the U.S., but it was the only one that seemed to fit. Yet even as it echoed in his head, and he chided himself for his behaviour, he couldn't take his lips from hers, couldn't release her body from his clasp. He wanted her—dear heaven but he wanted her—and kissing her like this, feeling her response, there was only one place they'd end up and that was in bed.

Hers, obviously. He'd never paraded any of the women he'd occasionally enjoyed relationships with in front of Hamish.

She was so slight and delicate, like quicksilver in his arms, yet the breasts he could feel against his chest were real and soft and full and, as his hand slid to her butt, he felt its curves. But it was her mouth that still demanded most of his attention. Syrup sweet, that mouth! Maple syrup! Years in the States had given him a taste for it and now he tasted it in Kate—addictive.

Then she was gone, warm night air where her body had been, a distance of perhaps a foot between them.

'*Not* a good idea, Dr McDowell,' she said, although the flush on her cheeks and the glitter in her eyes suggested otherwise.

'You're going to deny there's an attraction between us?' He was still trying to work out how she'd slipped away from him, while thwarted lust was making him tetchy.

'Of course not.' She shook her head to emphasise the words, the wild red curls flying every which way.

'It'd be easier to deny the sun rising, but that's all it is, Angus, attraction, and at my age I really don't want a go-nowhere affair. If I'm putting time and energy into a relationship, then I'd like to think there might be some future in it.'

'So every relationship should lead to marriage? Is that what you're saying?' Maybe he was a tad more than tetchy!

'Of course not,' she snapped. 'I'm not entirely stupid. But I don't see the point of going into a relationship that has nowhere to go and you've made it clear anything between us *would* have nowhere to go. What was it you said? "I don't do serious relationships"? Well, that's fine, and I like the fact you set out the guidelines from the beginning, but I'm entitled to do the same, and I don't want to go into something just for the sex.'

'It wouldn't just be sex,' Angus muttered—not good that he was down to muttering already. Muttering was usually part of losing an argument. But he persevered anyway. 'We enjoy each other's company. We can have dinner, go to the theatre—'

Kate couldn't help but laugh, shaking her head at her behaviour at the same time, but unable to control the gurgles of mirth that were bubbling up from deep within her.

'Oh, Angus, if you could only hear yourself. We could go to dinner—yep, and then back to my place to bed. We could go to the theatre and—'

'Okay, I get your point,' he growled. 'I can even see it from your side and understand, but don't think for a moment this discussion is over because whatever it is between us is so strong I doubt either of us can resist it.'

The growl became a husky whisper as he added, 'Or can you?' before he took her in his arms and his mouth claimed hers once again.

Enjoy it while you can. That was Kate's last rational thought before sensation took over and she floated on the blissful cloud of desire he seemed to generate so easily.

It couldn't just be the way he kissed.

The thought eased into her head as she turned her lips away from his to catch her breath. There had to be more to the way he made her feel than just kissing. Perhaps the way her body fitted his had something to do with it. She pressed experimentally closer and went back to kissing. But not mindlessly this time, for her sensible brain was chiding her the whole time

Idiocy! Plain and simple. Stop before it becomes impossible to stop.

But she couldn't—wouldn't—because kissing Angus was the most exciting, enthralling, stupendous thing she'd ever done…well, that she could think of right now! Perhaps if they kept to kissing, a kissing relationship…

'You're not behaving like someone who doesn't want to get involved with me.'

The accusation was delivered with a warm breath close to her left ear and she shivered as his tongue flicked, then his teeth nibbled gently on her earlobe.

'I never denied the attraction,' she whispered back, kissing him this time, pressing her lips to his as a punctuation mark at the end of the sentence. Then a sigh filtered out and she pushed away.

'I do mean it, Angus. I really don't want to go into a pointless relationship—'

He moved but not so far away that he couldn't still clasp her loosely, holding her within the circle of his arms so his strong features were in profile against the yellow light and she could see his lips—*those* lips—move as he spoke.

'A lot of relationships turn out to be pointless,' he reminded her. 'There are never guarantees that everything will work out. Surely it's not so much how you go into them as how you come out of them.'

A hopeless mess, that's how I'd come out of a relationship with you, Kate thought, but she didn't say it. I've done that before and really do not want to do it again.

He was making some kind of point here, and she should have an argument to counter it, but her brain was still fuddled from the kissing and her body was suddenly very, very tired.

'I am not going to argue semantics with you tonight,' she said, then regretted saying anything when he grinned at her and restarted all the fizzing sensations that had been happening along her nerves.

'Aha, so that means we'll have another night to argue them.'

He was teasing her and suddenly she hated him—well, not hated, but definitely didn't like him very much. He'd awoken responses from her she'd never thought to feel and to him it was nothing more than a game—kissing, flirtation, an affair—with no more point than the kissing games young teens played at parties, practicing for love.…

'Go home,' she told him, and though his arms tightened momentarily around her, she stiffened and he didn't pull her close.

'No goodnight kiss?'

'No kisses period,' she told him, but as he walked towards the gate she remembered it was Friday night and called him back. 'Wait, I'll give you the car keys and the sat nav so you can take the car to visit McTavish. I might not be here in the morning.'

Angus turned and followed her into the house, into the kitchen, the only room he'd seen so far. She rummaged through a drawer in search of keys while he studied her, wondering why this woman of all the women he met in his day-to-day life should fire something in him, something so strong he knew he should be strengthening his resistance against her, not wondering how soon he could kiss her again.

'Ah,' she said, turning to him with triumph in her eyes, her smile so open and delighted he felt as if a hand had tightened around his heart. 'Not only keys but the sat nav, as well. You've used one? Can program it?'

He took the little device and nodded, knowing it was the same brand as the one he'd used in the U.S., but the hand clutching his heart hadn't let go and he suspected he'd have to rethink his ambition to kiss Kate again as soon as possible. He was beginning to suspect that kissing Kate could be addictive, and addictions were hard to break....

'Thank you,' he said, aware he sounded formal and aloof once more, the way he sounded at the hospital when he was talking to the parents of his patients.

And Kate heard it, too, for her dark eyebrows rose and her pink lips, still swollen from his kisses, twisted into a wry smile.

'Okay,' she said, as if she understood exactly what his tone had meant. 'Enjoy yourselves tomorrow. There's plenty of fuel in the tank if you want to take Hamish to the beach after you've been to the quarantine station.'

He nodded and departed, pausing in the doorway to look back at her, the smile gone from her face and in its place an unmistakeable sadness.

'Goodnight,' he said, for what else was there to say. An affair between them could *not* have any point and he wasn't going to lie to her to get her into bed.

Although, as he shut the gate between their properties, the discomfort in his body suggested that this stance was all very well morally and ethically, but physically, given that he wouldn't be able to avoid seeing her every working day, it might be difficult.

Kate was actually pleased when the phone rang at one o'clock in the morning. She might have been in a light sleep but whatever sleep she'd managed had been deeply disturbed, her body tossing and turning, feeling the magic Angus had generated, the heat, and wanting to satisfy it.

It was a good thing she was mentally strong, she told herself as she pulled on slacks and a T-shirt. She had a stock of laundered white coats in her locker at work, so all she had to do was clean her teeth, wash her face, tie her hair up in a bundle and get moving up the road.

A five-day-old baby girl had been admitted to the hospital with cold, clammy skin, rapid breathing and alarming cyanosis, her lips very blue. The neonatologist on call was doing X-rays, an ECG and an echocardiogram, but had called in one of Kate's team—she rather thought Oliver was on call this weekend—thinking they'd need to do a cardiac catheterisation to see what was happening in the baby's heart.

Kate considered what lay ahead as she jogged up the street, thinking, too, of the parents, so happy with their new baby, then panicked by her distress. She made her way to the treatment room off the PICU where she found not Oliver but Angus.

'You're not on call,' she told him, so bothered by the unexpected encounter her heart was racing and her mind in a whirl—not a good way to be before sedating a tiny baby.

'Oliver had a family occasion of some kind so I offered to do tonight for him. He'll owe me.'

Well! Obviously Angus was in hospital mode, all thoughts of hot kisses in her backyard well and truly gone.

Which is how it should be, she reminded herself.

And if he could do it, so could she!

'How long will you need?' she asked as she read the baby's chart, checking her weight so the sedation could be accurately measured.

Angus didn't answer immediately, but she was used to that now. She could imagine him running through the operation in his mind—inserting the catheter into a blood vessel in the patient's groin, feeding the wire carefully up into the heart, perhaps introducing dye so he could better see the problem, perhaps also, depending on what he found, needing to use a special catheter with a balloon at the tip to open up a hole between the left and right atria.

'Forty minutes! I should be able to do it in half an hour but we'll take the extra ten minutes just in case. It's a suspected TAPVR.'

Kate mentally translated the initials, thinking how frightening it must be for parents to hear that their child had total anomalous pulmonary venous return, when, in fact, it simply meant that the veins from the lungs, pulmonary veins, had somehow got themselves attached to the wrong part of the heart. Angus would find out exactly what was happening now, and later the baby would need an operation where the veins would be disconnected from where they were, and set into place where they should be, connecting to the left atrium. At the same time, the surgeon would close the little hole Angus was about to make, and the baby's heart should operate beautifully.

She checked the dosage of sedative and injected it into the intravenous line already attached to the baby girl, who lay, unresisting and lethargic, looking up at her until slowly the dark blue eyes closed and her breathing grew less laboured.

Kate took a blood sample from a second catheter in the baby's foot, wanting to check on the blood gases before the procedure, so they could compare it after Angus had completed the operation. A small oxygen monitor was attached to one of the tiny fingers, but Kate always checked the blood, as well, not wanting to rely on just one reading.

Angus nodded at her as if he agreed, then his eyes focused on the ultrasound screen as he slid the fine wire up the baby's vein towards the heart.

Kate watched her patient and the second monitor that told her exactly what was happening in the baby's body—blood pressure, oxygen saturation, heart rate and rhythm. She watched over the unconscious child while just a small part of her mind went back to the conversation she'd had with the nurse at baby Bob's monitor, the nurse who wanted to get out of the PICU before she had children because seeing the ones who had health issues made her nervous about having children of her own.

Yet Kate saw babies with congenital problems every day of her working life, so why didn't it bother her?

Because she knew they could be fixed?

Nonsense, not all of them could, although every day brought new procedures and treatments to improve the health not only of babies but of adults, as well.

But deep down she knew it didn't bother her because the longing for a child—or for the child she hadn't had—was far stronger than any fear of a congenital abnormality. It was gut deep, instinctually emotional—inexplicable really....

The straying thoughts made her glance at Angus, his lips—those lips—closed into a thin line as he concentrated on getting the tip of the balloon catheter through a tiny opening in the atrial wall. As she had suggested to him once before, maybe it was his work with children that made him so definite about not having any more.

She'd have liked to ask him again, liked to have had him as a friend, as well as a neighbour and a colleague, but after the kisses, that was impossible.

'Impossible!' she repeated, actually saying the word, although under her breath, so she could drum it into her head.

Angus glanced her way before returning his attention to the monitor, where she saw him pull the tiny, now-inflated balloon through the hole, enlarging it so the oxygenated blood could mix with the unoxygenated blood and ease the work the little heart had to do while they waited for the baby to grow strong enough to have an operation.

'Impossible? No such word!' he told her, and she heard the satisfaction in his voice as he withdrew the catheter and dressed the wound in the baby's groin.

'You really love your job, don't you?' Kate said, and he gave her a quizzical look.

'Are you telling me you don't?'

She shrugged. Of course she loved her job, but it was far less demanding than a surgeon's, so the risk of burnout—of falling out of love with it—was far less likely.

'I doubt anyone could work with babies like this if they didn't love it,' the nurse who'd been assisting said. 'And as for Kate, well, I've seen her here at four in the morning, anxious about a patient she might have sedated days earlier, just drawn by some instinct to come back.'

Kate shook her head, although she did remember the incident—a baby newly off the ventilator having a reaction to some drug the surgeon had prescribed. To this day she couldn't say what had brought her racing to the hospital.

'I think they send out thought waves, our babies,' she said, smiling at the nurse. 'It wasn't only me that night—I found Phil here, as well. He'd woken up with a conviction that something was wrong so we were able to stabilise the baby and get him back onto a ventilator. He came off two days later without the slightest trouble.'

Angus nodded; he knew what she was saying, although he'd never realised other people had that inexplicable sense of trouble from time to time. He followed Kate from the treatment room, the nurse wheeling the baby back into the PICU. Kate stopped by Bob's crib, smiling down at Mrs Stamford, who slept beside her baby boy.

'He looks good,' she said quietly to Angus, and taking in the pink cheeks of the infant, Angus had to agree. But Kate looked good, as well, although why he found her so attractive he couldn't have explained. To another man she might just be a slim, average-looking woman with wild red hair, but just being in her vicinity stirred his senses in ways he didn't want to consider.

'I'll walk you home,' he said, but she shook her head.

'I'll stay awhile,' she said. 'You'd best be off. You have a big day ahead of you, navigating around Sydney for the first time, visiting McTavish.'

Angus would have liked to argue, but she was right. He hadn't been sleeping when the call came, still disturbed by the after-effects of kissing Kate. But now he could walk away from her—in colleague mode again.

No worries!

He said goodnight and went along the corridor to the elevator foyer, but the sense of her came with him—'kissing Kate,' not 'colleague Kate…'

CHAPTER SIX

KNOWING she could have other emergency calls so needed some sleep, Kate left the hospital an hour later, walking slowly past the house where Angus would be sleeping, trying hard to think about work, not her colleague. But the kisses had stirred something deep inside her, and she had to wonder if a relationship—forget that, an affair—with Angus would be so very bad.

Okay, so it had no future, but what else was she doing? Going through the motions of a life, her social life consisting of occasional visits to a movie, or having dinner at friends' places, where a likely man would have been invited, her friends all committed to 'finding a man for Kate'!

From time to time, one of these available men would follow up on their meeting, inviting her for drinks, maybe dinner, but after a few outings, too casual to be called dates, one or other of them would realise that there was no…zing—that was the only word—between them and the relationship would be over before it had really begun. Yet she'd always remained confident that somewhere out there was a man for her—*the* man—the one who'd be a father to her children, a grandfather to her grandchildren.

Or was she wasting her life? Letting it slip away from her because of the loss of an unborn baby years ago and an absurd dream she'd had as a child?

She'd found the zing—boy, had she found the zing!—and she was going to let it go because an affair with Angus had no future?

Was she out of her tiny mind?

She realised her steps had slowed sufficiently for it to be called a halt and she was standing on the footpath outside Angus's house, staring at it like some lovelorn fool.

She had to get her act together, sort out some priorities here. But even as she moved on, this idea firmly fixed in her mind, she imagined the weight of a tiny baby in her arms, and longed to feel it for herself—her own baby in her arms, the future in its tiny form....

She'd lied to Angus—perhaps not lied but shifted the emphasis of her dreams—when she'd talked of her ambition to be a grandmother. Yes, that had been the precipitating event, that long-ago family gathering, but later, after the miscarriage, it was a family of her own she longed for, a baby of her own, someone who belonged to her, had her blood, her genes—although probably not her red hair.

Of course, *belonged* was the wrong word—no one could belong to another person....

She unlocked her front door and walked into the house, hearing the ghosts of children who'd lived there in the past when it was the family home it was built to be. The smell of the chemical in the product she was using to strip wallpaper off the living room walls struck her immediately. Well, at least this weekend she'd have enough work to do finishing that job to keep her mind off Angus and relationships and babies of her own.

'We saw McTavish and he remembered me!'

Had she been kidding herself when she'd thought she'd see no more of the McDowells over the weekend? Had she forgotten that Hamish now viewed her as his new best friend? She was bundling the last strips of the wallpaper, slimy and stinking, into the rubbish bin near the back lane when he erupted from the tunnel in the hedge.

'I'm sure he remembered you,' Kate told the little boy, who was now holding his nose as he stared at her.

'Phew, you smell,' he told her, and she had to laugh. If anyone told it how it was, it was Hamish.

'I do indeed, but I'm about to have a shower. I've been peeling the old wallpaper off a wall and it's a very smelly job.'

'Can I look, can I?' he demanded, excited as he always seemed to be by some new concept.

'Only if you tell your father or Juanita first. Did you tell them you were coming over?'

'We were both coming over,' a deeper voice said as Angus appeared through the gate. 'Hamish just took the shortcut.'

This time it wasn't just a cheek blush! Kate could feel her entire body heating, reddening, as she imagined just how she must look—scraps of wallpaper and stripping chemicals in her hair, bits sticking to her arms and legs. Her working attire, an ancient pair of cut-off jeans—cut off far too short—and an old T-shirt advertising a rock band long defunct.

'You found the place all right, then?'

It was a feeble response but she saw that Angus had her car keys and sat nav in his hand, and it was all she could manage.

'No problems,' he replied, although, possibly for the first time since she'd met him, she could see a gleam of what could only be humour in his dark eyes.

'Kate's pulled all the wallpaper off her walls and I'm going to look,' Hamish announced, breaking what could easily have become a strained silence, because her conversational spring had definitely dried up and he seemed content to stand there and study her dishevelled state—with that gleam in his eyes—for ever.

'We might be interrupting Kate,' Angus argued, but Hamish waved aside the objection.

'No, she was just going to have a shower, but we don't mind if she smells a bit, do we?'

Angus had to smile. Better to be smiling at his son's faux pas than be thinking of Kate stripped down in a shower. Why was stripping such a recurring theme in her backyard?

'Kate?' he said, and as he watched he saw her weigh her discomfort at having him in her house—and probably the smell—against the appeal in a pair of blue eyes. He saw her waver, then nod at Hamish.

"Okay,' she said, reluctance dragging out the word, 'you can come in but I warn you, there's nothing very exciting about a living room with bare damp walls. I thought I'd paint it once I had the wallpaper off, but it's kind of rough so maybe I'll have to repaper.'

She was leading the way into her house as she spoke, through the kitchen, up a hall, past a dining room and into the large room at the front of the house. Angus peered around, realising this house must have been similar to the one he was renting, before his place was converted into flats.

Hamish had climbed onto the window seat in one of two bay windows in the graciously designed room.

'If that hedge wasn't there, I could see my bedroom,' he said, excitedly working out the geography of the two places.

'In my house, I use that room as my study,' Kate told him. 'Do you want to see it?'

Hamish was off the window seat in a second, heading out of the room and across the hall. Angus followed more slowly, wondering at the very definite reluctance he was feeling. Was it something to do with seeing more of Kate's house and the possibility it might make him feel closer to her?

Or was it seeing how Hamish had connected with her that made him uneasy. She treated his son as she would an adult friend, accepting his enthusiasm for anything new and never speaking down to him. Once again Angus was conscious of a gap in his relationship with Hamish, and found himself frowning over the thought. He did things with his son—read him stories, listened to his prattle about his daily life—loved him dearly, but…

He turned his thoughts back to Kate but there was no less confusion there. The moment he saw the room he knew he'd have been better off not following, for this was obviously the room she'd chosen to furnish first, and though he didn't know her well, he knew the room spoke volumes about her. Two walls lined with bookshelves and books from childhood days with faded covers, through medical tomes and reference books to the latest thrillers, were crammed into the shelves. She had a desk, an old roll-top set against the third wall, but her laptop was on the cushioned window seat of yet another bay window and he could picture her there, checking something out, keeping up with friends through emails, perhaps doing something on the research she'd mentioned once.

The cushions on the window seat looked soft and comfortable, blue and green tones, muted but easy colours with which to live.

'You've made this space special,' he said, and saw the colour rise in her cheeks again.

'I did it first—I needed a space in which I'd feel comfortable. You should see my bedroom!'

It was a natural enough statement but the moment it was out—hanging there in the air between them— she coloured even more deeply and moved towards the bookshelves, pulling out a book which she showed to Hamish.

'This is an old book of mine about possums,' she told him, resolutely ignoring Angus. 'Would you like to borrow it?'

Of course Hamish would, which meant there'd be yet another thing to return. But Hamish and Juanita could return the book; he, Angus, was out of here. Since the bedroom remark all the sensations kissing Kate had generated were returning and he was becoming more and more aware that his libido was completely out of control. Keeping out of her life was the only answer. He had to get it into his thick skull that she was a work colleague, nothing more!

'See, Dad, see,' Hamish was saying, showing him the possum on the cover of the book.

'That's great,' Angus managed, then he glanced at Kate. 'But we really must be going. Kate wants to have a shower.'

Work colleague, work colleague!

'Thanks for returning the keys,' she said, not refuting her need to have a shower or urging them to stay. 'I'll see you back at work on Monday. Here, you can go out through the front door.'

She brushed past him, out of the study and down the passage to the door, which she opened, then stepped back. He'd have liked to think it was because she didn't want to stand too close to him—that her hormones were as active as his libido—but she could also have been saving them from the weird chemical smell of stripped wallpaper and, either way, all she was, was a work colleague after all.

By Monday the baby girl, Bethany Walker, who had been admitted on Friday night, was judged strong enough to have the necessary operation. Alex had decided he would do it, but had asked Kate to act as anaesthetist. She didn't know whether to be delighted because it saved her the uneasiness of working closely with Angus that day or to be disappointed because she *wouldn't* be working closely with Angus that day! Talk about confused!

'Howdy, neighbour.'

She was in Theatre, setting out all the things she'd need, checking and rechecking drugs and equipment, when Angus walked in.

'Are you looking for Alex?' she asked, dismayed to find the zing was right here in Theatre, in the area of their workplace where it was least expected—and most inappropriate.

'No, I like to check things out before an op,' he replied, showing no evidence of zing at all.

'But Alex is doing the op,' she protested—one-way zing was the pits.

Angus smiled at her which certainly didn't help.

'And I'm assisting,' he told her cheerfully. 'I might be okay with TGAs but the man's a genius when it comes to TAPVR, so I'd welcome any opportunity to see him at work or work with him as I will today. Is Clare our perfusionist?'

Angus wasn't sure why he'd asked the question, except that, although he was usually totally focused on his job when he was in Theatre, today he was feeling all the manifestations of the attraction his body had developed towards Kate's. He'd already decided after their strained conversation the previous day that he'd have to find a diversion. His next decision had been that he would ask Clare to have a drink with him one night or maybe dinner—go to a movie. He'd discovered back when they'd lunched together, that she was as new to Sydney as he was, and as friendless.

Kate hadn't answered his question, although she had shrugged her shoulders, so maybe she didn't know, or was she so intent in fiddling with syringes and cannulae and drugs that she hadn't heard him? He doubted that, although she may have been as determined to ignore him as he was to avoid her. He finished checking the instrument tray and left the theatre, switching his mind firmly to the operation ahead.

It went smoothly, Angus opening the little chest, spreading the ribs apart so Alex could get best access to the heart. The switch to the bypass machine went without a hitch and Alex's skill at separating out the wayward veins and reattaching them was, as far as Angus was concerned, a marvel to behold.

'Off pump!'

Alex gave the order and the whole team watched the tiny pale heart, willing it to beat, but it lay there, flat and flaccid while tension spread like noxious gas through the room.

'We'll have to shock her,' Alex said quietly, while Angus was already giving orders to Kate for the drugs the baby needed. Tension tightened but neither drugs nor electric current could restart the little heart. Angus had his hand in the baby's chest, his fingers oh-so-gently massaging it to keep blood circulating to the vital organs. Alex fired more quiet orders for different drugs, shocked again, to no avail, and Angus slid his hand back into place and continued massaging.

It was third time lucky. The third time the electric current hit the little heart it jolted; it heaved, then, rapidly at first, began to beat.

'Not arrhythmia, not now,' Alex muttered under his breath, because arrhythmia would mean more shocks, but while the whole team waited and watched, the beating steadied and a muted cheer went up. Little Bethany had made it—this far at least.

'Do you want to close or leave it open?' Angus asked Alex, and Kate held her breath. Leaving the chest open, covered only by a dressing, would mean Alex was anticipating more trouble.

'Close,' Alex said, and Kate imagined everyone let out a sigh.

'She's a little fighter,' Grace murmured, but the rest of the team grew silent, too shocked by the near loss to be chattering. Alex left the theatre; a resident, under Angus's watchful eyes, would close the chest, leaving in place drains and a pacemaker to keep the heartbeat steady. Like Bob, Bethany would be on a ventilator for a few days at least, watched over night and day in the special PICU.

Kate waited while the baby was transferred to a crib, then followed as it was wheeled to the PICU. But as Alex was there talking to the parents, she didn't stay, thinking she'd change and return in a short while to check on her charge. But once in the changing room she slumped onto a bench, feeling as if all her energy had been drained away by the tension they'd endured in Theatre.

Angus came and sat beside her, not speaking, just sitting, yet the bulk and warmth of his body, close to hers, was infinitely comforting.

'Why do we never expect those things to happen?' she asked him. 'Why is it always such a gut-wrenching shock?'

She didn't really expect him to answer, so was surprised when, after his usual thoughtful pause, he said, 'It's the optimism thing again. If you consider it seriously, how often do we have dramas during an op? Perhaps not as dramatic as today's, but small dramas?'

Kate thought about it, then had to agree.

'Nearly every operation,' she admitted. 'A bleed, a blood vessel that kinks, unexpected difficulty getting the patient on bypass—I guess there's always something to keep us on our toes.'

She sighed and shook her head, not comforted at all.

'So why was today different?' he asked.

She turned towards him.

'Because that baby died,' she told him bluntly. 'And for a little while it looked as if she might have stayed dead! That's not why we operate, for babies to die.'

Had her voice quavered? Had her eyes filled with tears? She knew she was emotional but didn't realise she'd let it show until Angus put his arm around her and hugged her to him.

'Did they all die, your family, that you need a new one? Was it more than your sister that you lost?'

His voice was so gentle, so full of understanding, that she let out the sob she'd been holding in her chest, then, realising where she was—and who was holding her—she pushed away, swiping tears from her face.

'Oh, for Pete's sake, Angus, don't encourage me to be maudlin. I can do that well enough on my own.'

'And here I was thinking you were an optimist,' he teased, and once again she saw a glimmer of a smile in his eyes.

I could fall in love with a smiling Angus.

The thought hit her like a hammer blow.

'Well, I am.' She spoke firmly and just as firmly moved away from him, stripping off her outer layer of theatre clothes and pulling on a white coat so she'd look professional even if she was feeling like a teenager on the threshold of love.

It couldn't possibly be love. It was attraction and tension, two powerful forces combining to throw her normal commonsensical self into turmoil.

'See you later,' she said to the man causing all the trouble. He was still sitting on the bench, not smiling now, but no less attractive.

'When later?' he asked as she was about to flit through the door, hurrying away from him.

She turned back, frowning now.

'Sometime, any time—it was just a phrase, like "goodbye,"' she grumbled at him.

'Only it wasn't goodbye,' he reminded her, watching her closely, something in that regard making her stomach uneasy again.

'It's an Australian goodbye. We say it all the time— "see you later"—it doesn't mean anything.' And in case he didn't get the message, she slipped a touch of sarcasm into her voice as she added, 'And much as I'd like to stay and discuss the vagaries and variations of the English language with you, I really have to go and check on Bethany.'

He nodded, then as she shot through the door she heard him say, 'I'll see you later,' and the shiver that slithered down her spine suggested he wasn't using the words as a farewell but as a promise.

Angus knew he should stir himself from the bench. He had a cardiac catheterisation on a teenager to do and patients to check before that, but he couldn't bring himself to move, his mind turning over the totally inane conversation he'd had with Kate.

Although the earlier conversation hadn't been inane. She hadn't answered his question about her family, but the great gulp of grief she'd given had spoken for her.

'Ah, Angus, just the man I want to see.' He turned to find Clare had joined him in the changing room. 'Have you heard about this hospital social they're having on Friday night? Apparently it's to welcome all the new staff, and as I hate walking into something like that on my own, I wondered if you'd mind if we went together.

We could grab an early bite to eat at that little restaurant down the road, then walk up to the hospital from there.'

Angus stared at the woman he'd been thinking he should ask out to divert his mind, not to mention his body, from thoughts of Kate, but now that she was here, asking *him* out, he didn't have a clue how to reply.

Except—

'*This* Friday?' he asked.

Clare nodded.

'Becky's put up a notice in our staff lounge.'

'I'm on call,' Angus told her, although he knew that was no excuse to not go to the shindig. After all, from the way Clare spoke, it must be being held at the hospital.

She raised her eyebrows, letting him know she knew he was prevaricating.

Feeling remarkably stupid, he rushed in to the breech. 'Of course I can go with you,' he said, then he shrugged. 'It's just that in the past I've tried to avoid hospital social activities. We spend so much time on the job as it is, it's always seemed unnecessary to return to the place when I don't have to.'

'But it *is* a way for the team to get to know one another better and for us to meet some of the hospital staff from other disciplines,' Clare pointed out. 'With Christmas only a month away, surely it's a good idea to get to know a few people.'

'Christmas!' Angus muttered. 'I keep forgetting about Christmas—I suppose because it's so darned hot it doesn't feel like November. I'd thought I might get home to Scotland this year for Christmas, until Alex pointed out that he likes to take on new staff in November, so everyone is settled in and able to cover for one another over the holiday period.'

'Believe me,' Clare said, 'this is easier than it used to be when staff were transferred from hospital to hospital at the start of a new year. You'd arrive in some country town you'd never heard of, and be thrown into New Year's Day hangovers, and fights and family break-ups all brought on by too much heat and too much alcohol. And that's not to mention the holiday road toll and all the car accidents we'd get.'

Angus studied Clare while she explained all this, seeing her lips move, her eyes sparkle, aware of how very beautiful she was, and wondering why that beauty failed to spark even a murmur of attraction in his body.

'So, Friday? Early dinner at Scoozi's? That suit you?'

Why on earth was he so reluctant? This was exactly what he needed—a woman and a beautiful one at that— to take his mind off Kate Armstrong.

'Providing I've not been called out,' he said, then it struck him that this was still far from organised. 'I haven't a car as yet so I can't offer to collect you,' he said, and she laughed.

'I just live down the road,' she said. 'I'm renting a small flat from Annie Attwood's father—Alex's father-in-law. He's in a wheelchair so he has the ground floor and he's turned the upstairs part of the house where Annie lived into two flats. Oliver's in the other one.'

Oliver's in the other one and you're asking me to walk into the social affair with you? It didn't make sense to Angus and he found himself asking her.

'Is Oliver not going?'

To Angus's surprise a faint blush coloured Clare's cheeks. Not a patch on Kate's blushes but a blush none-theless.

'I'm not sure,' she said, and that was that.

Clare went through to the showers and Angus pulled off his theatre gear and dressed, moving quickly because he'd already wasted too much time mooning about in the changing room.

Mooning?

Definitely mooning! He could hear his mother's voice, not scolding but chiding him. You're mooning about again, she used to say, back when he was a teen-ager. Is it a girl?

This time it is, Mum, and I don't know what to do about it

He sent the silent message to her, not that she could help, but admitting there was some mooning to be done over the Kate situation made him feel a little better.

And having a date with Clare for Friday night—well, surely that was a good thing.

CHAPTER SEVEN

IT TURNED into one of the busiest weeks Kate could remember, and although the two babies she saw as special, Bob and Bethany, continued to do well, it seemed everything else that could go wrong did. A child showed an allergic reaction to a drug he'd had before; a young teenage girl went into arrhythmia as they were feeding a wire through her veins to take photos in her heart. Problems they overcame but which left all those involved in the procedures with tightened tension.

Or was her higher-than-usual sense of anxiety caused by the fact that she was working so closely with Angus?

Not that he showed the slightest interest in her outside professional courtesy. It was as if, as far as he was concerned, the kisses had never happened. So why were they imprinted on Kate's lips? Imbedded deep in her mind?

She hoped she was showing as cool an exterior as he was, but she doubted that was possible, knowing how her body warmed whenever he was near her.

Maybe an affair would be okay....

But even as the insidious thought slid into her mind, she felt the heaviness of loss within her body—the loss of the baby she'd never carry, never hold in her arms, because if she fell in love with Angus, how could she ever marry someone else?

If she fell in love with Angus?

She was thinking about this as she mooched home on Friday afternoon. She'd left work a little earlier than usual, wanting to wash her hair—no easy task with its curls and length—before the social do that evening.

'You're early—it's not ready yet.'

Hamish's voice, ripe with accusation, greeted her. It seemed to be coming from behind the yellow sofa which she really had to move before the summer storms began and the old wreck of a thing became saturated and smelly with mould and who knew what else.

She peered behind it to find her small neighbour busy digging a hole.

'What's not ready yet?'

'My wombat hole.'

Kate smiled to herself. Hamish always managed to make the most ridiculous things sound rational.

'And why do you need a wombat hole?'

He looked up at her now, blue eyes gleaming with excitement in a dirt-streaked face.

'So a wombat can come and live in it, of course.'

'Of course,' Kate responded weakly, sinking onto the sofa and wondering if having children was as good an idea as she'd thought it would be. Imagine having three who all wanted to dig wombat holes?

'And why are you in my front yard when it's off limits to you?' she asked.

He kept digging, although he did turn partially towards her as he said, 'Juanita knows I'm here. I couldn't be digging it in the backyard because the wombat wouldn't see it there.'

Kate had to chuckle, picturing a large wombat strolling down the road in search of a hole, checking out front yards as it went.

'Did you have a story about wombats at kindy today?' she asked the small digger.

He shook his head, then sat back on his heels.

'Juanita bought me a book about one,' he explained. 'It's like the possum book only about a wombat so she knew I'd like it. She gave it to me because Dad's going out tonight. He won't be able to read my bedtime story, so she read it to me this afternoon when I had my rest.'

There was a lot of information in Hamish's words but the ones that stuck with Kate were 'Dad's going out tonight.'

To the hospital social?

That's where she was going, but mainly because her friend Marcie, a paediatric physician, would be there and it was some time since they'd connected.

But Angus hadn't mentioned he was going....

Why should he?

'You could help me dig if you wanted to.'

The digger had straightened up and was peering hopefully at her over the back of the sofa.

'I don't think so,' she said, switching her mind from the father to the child. 'In fact, come and sit beside me and I'll tell you some stuff about wombats.'

He came obediently enough and snuggled onto the sofa beside her.

'Do you know some wombats?' he asked.

She had to smile.

'Not personally,' she told him, 'but that's because they're not like possums. They don't live in the city, but out in the country. Wombats move very slowly, which means that if they lived in the city they'd be run over by cars or buses, so they stay way out in the country, although there are wombats in our wonderful zoo. Maybe one day your father will take you to the zoo. You can go on a ferry across the harbour, and that's fun, to see all the animals there.'

'Will you come, too?' he asked, snuggling closer, and she couldn't resist putting her arm around him and cuddling him against her, smelling dirt and sweat and little-boy smell.

'Come where, too?'

Kate closed her eyes and shook her head. One soppy cuddle with a little boy and she was caught. Hamish scrambled away from her.

'To the zoo to see a wombat. See, Dad, I made a hole for one, but Kate says he won't come because wombats don't like living in the city so I'll have to go to the zoo to see one.'

'Wombats?'

Angus had vaguely heard of such creatures, picturing in his mind something large and cumbersome, but his mind wasn't working as well as it should be, having taken off at a tangent when he'd walked down the road to see his son cuddled in Kate's arms.

His first reaction had been anxiety—Hamish had been hurt—but his son's bright voice dispelled that; the pair had been sharing nothing more than a hug.

While they talked about wombats?

He knew he was frowning but he couldn't pin down the cause for his inner uneasiness. Surely it couldn't be jealousy that Kate had achieved such closeness with Hamish so quickly? Fortunately Hamish's piping voice broke into his confusion.

'Can she, Dad, can she?'

Can she, what?

Before Angus had his mind straightened out again, Kate had answered for him.

'I've already seen them, Hamish, many times, and now I have to get inside. Stuff to do.'

She stood so hurriedly Angus knew she was escaping, not from Hamish but from him.

So she, too, was feeling confusion over the kisses they had shared. He wasn't sure if that made things better or worse as far as he was concerned, so he lifted his son off the sofa and set him on his shoulders, carrying him back to the house, letting Hamish's flow of conversation about wombats, Kate and zoos flow over and around him, anchoring him back in his real life—the father of this lad.

Father!

Again the knowledge of the wall between them raised its head, although now he considered it, it seemed, since coming to Australia, he'd been able to grow closer to his son. He'd certainly been able to look at his face—so like his mother's—without the oppressive guilt he'd once felt.

Make no mistake, the guilt still lingered—it would never go away—but it had lessened in its intensity and for that he was sincerely grateful, so much so as he set Hamish down on the floor, he hugged the little boy and whispered that he loved him.

* * *

Kate slipped her high-heeled sandals into a soft silk bag and slid her feet into flatties. She might not mind the walk to and from the hospital but in killer heels? No way! Although looking at herself, she hoped she wouldn't meet Angus on the way. The sexy black dress she'd bought for another hospital function, then been too cowardly to wear, was just fine, but with the flat shoes? No, it didn't work; it needed the high heels to set it off.

And just why was she thinking of sexy dresses and Angus in the same breath? Wasn't she avoiding Angus? Wasn't she determined *not* to have an affair with him? Isn't that what she'd decided as she'd washed her hair and spent a good hour straightening it, taming it into a shining auburn curtain that fell to her shoulders in long, obedient strands.

Even in the flat shoes she looked pretty good, but—

She shook her head, making the curtain of hair fly around her face. There was no way she could go to a hospital function dressed like this. Oh, she usually made some effort to look good, but a sexy black dress, killer heels *and* straightened hair? Her colleagues would be abuzz with speculation over which new member of the team she was trying to attract.

Sighing deeply, she pulled off the dress, but she was damned if she'd mess with her hair. She hauled her faithful black slacks out of the wardrobe and found a slinky black singlet top to go with them. It was hot enough to go with just that, but it was a trifle bare for a casual social at the hospital, so she dug around until she found a short-sleeved cardigan, black with silver threads through it, and used it to finish her outfit. No need for high-heeled sandals, the flatties would do.

As flat as her mood, she realised as she trudged up the road towards the hospital, no longer fearing she'd run into Angus. She felt thoroughly dispirited, in fact; although dispirited didn't begin to describe how she felt when, in the foyer of the staff elevators, she ran into Angus and Clare, obviously together.

It's a good thing, she told herself, but the pain in her chest gave lie to the assertion.

Was he staring at her? Angus hoped not, but he knew his eyes continued to be drawn in Kate's direction, for all that he was responding to Clare's conversation and listening as the two women exchanged greetings.

'Your hair looks great,' Clare was saying, and Angus found himself echoing the compliment, barely refraining from adding, All of you looks great.

'Thanks.' Kate's response took in both of them, although she was looking towards Clare. 'It takes such an age to straighten it, I don't do it often.'

Was it just the hair, or was it the slim but shapely body snugly encased in black that had him all but panting like a dog?

The elevator doors opened and he stood back as Kate and Clare entered, the pair of them engrossed in what he took to be a hair conversation, as Clare was tossing her dark locks while Kate smoothed hers down against her shoulders.

'Are you with us?'

Clare asked the question and if he'd been honest he'd have had to answer no, for his thoughts were bounding all over the place, which made it very difficult for his brain to control his wayward body. But he stepped into the elevator, being careful to stand closer to Clare than

Kate, but even in a large-size hospital elevator he was still too close to the woman who was disrupting his life.

It probably wasn't her fault, he'd just decided, when she brushed against him as she exited the elevator and his body went into a spasm of such hot desire he wondered if he could plead a sudden terrible headache and go home.

'Come on!' Clare was sounding impatient and he realised Kate had already entered the big room on an upper level of the hospital, while Clare was waiting patiently at the door.

Because she wants someone to see her coming in with me.

In one way the realisation was a relief, signalling as it did that Clare had no interest in him as a man, merely as a partner for this occasion. So he needn't feel guilty about the way he'd stared at Kate.

He joined Clare and together they entered the room, her hand slipping into the crook of his arm as they came towards a small cluster of their colleagues, both of them ducking to avoid some dangling Christmas decorations.

'Bloody tinsel! This close to Christmas I might have known they'd have tinsel everywhere,' Clare muttered, then she was smiling and greeting the team members, leaving Angus at a loss about the tinsel conversation.

Not that it preoccupied him for long, for there, just beyond this particular cluster of people, was Kate, the light shining on her fine white skin, and picking up the deep auburn colours in her hair. Somehow he made conversation with Alex and Oliver, smiled at a joke Becky made about doctors, then, with Clare fully occupied, he slid away, taking a drink from a tray a waiter held out, hoping his colleagues would think thirst had made him leave the group.

Deciding it would look bad if he made a beeline for Kate, he took a complete circuit of the room to get around to where she had been standing, but by the time he got there, she was gone.

'Hi, I'm Marcie, I'm a paediatric physician. You're one of the new cardiac surgeons, I believe.'

He introduced himself to Marcie, then left the conversational ball in her hands as he looked around for Kate.

'I know you worked in the U.S., but you're obviously Scottish. I did my paediatric training in Edinburgh. Did you train there at any time?'

Angus rattled off the salient points of his educational CV, and managed to hold a reasonable conversation with the woman, but apparently it wasn't reasonable enough, for finally Marcie said, 'If you're looking for Kate, she's over at the buffet. A tip for you for the future—any do like this, that's where you'll find her. She says it's because she doesn't like food that's been lying around too long so she gets in early. But, in fact, it's probably because she doesn't look after herself properly, always too busy doing something else—minding other people's children, working on her renovations or helping someone out somewhere. So she forgets to shop and forgets to eat until she's starving, then there's nothing in the fridge or pantry.'

Marcie's explanation finally ran down, but it left Angus not only with a fuller picture of his neighbour but also with a strong urge to be the one who *did* look after Kate. After all, if she didn't look after herself, someone would have to!

He was about to head towards the buffet, which he could see set up in a side room, when Clare reclaimed him.

'Let's go get something to eat,' she said, and although Angus had seen her demolish a dish of pasta that would set a footballer back on his heels, he was happy enough to go along with her—very happy, in fact.

Ha! So maybe Oliver was the focus of Clare's interest, Angus decided, checking out the crowd around the buffet and seeing only Kate and Oliver from their team. Kate and Oliver very close together, heads bent as they discussed something, Kate smiling at the man—

'Well, hi, you two—fancy meeting you here.'

Clare breezed up to them, tugging Angus by the hand until he came alongside. He knew Kate had taken in the linked hands but her expression told him nothing, which in itself was weird as Kate's face usually showed every emotion, if only in the variation of colour in her cheeks. But then, he was keeping his own reaction in check— the reaction he'd felt deep in his gut when he'd seen her with Oliver. Ridiculous, that's what it was. Apart from a couple of kisses, there was nothing between him and Kate, so why shouldn't she be standing close to Oliver?

And standing close didn't mean interest—wasn't he, Angus, standing close to Clare?

Not comfortably close, he had to admit that, although the crush now gathering around the buffet made it hard to move apart.

'Well, I'm taking my supper up on the roof,' Kate announced.

'Up on the roof? Isn't it off limits? Isn't that where the helicopter landing pad is?'

Kate smiled at him—more gut reaction.

'You haven't had the guided tour of the hospital, have you?' she said. 'There are two towers, linked on the odd-numbered floors with walkways. The helipad is on the top of the other tower. At the top of this tower, there's a wonderful roof garden, thanks to a television gardening show that did makeovers. Someone suggested that as the new buildings had taken up most of the grounds which once surrounded Jimmie's, we should have a garden on a roof. It's wonderful.'

She included all of them in her smile this time. 'Why don't we all go up?'

Was she mad, going up onto the roof with Angus? Even with the others present wasn't there a danger inherent in being out in the moonlight with him? Wandering a shadowy garden with Angus?

Although Clare seemed to have Angus firmly in hand, Kate reminded herself, to stop the mental questioning of her sanity.

'Won't it be windy up there?' Clare objected. 'It'll blow your hair.'

Kate shrugged. Clare had just offered her the perfect excuse to avoid the combination of moonlight, shadows and Angus, but she was too twitchy to stay here, making polite conversations with colleagues while the most beautiful woman in the hospital flirted with Angus. At least on the roof she might not notice Clare flirting!

'I'd like to see the roof garden.' Angus, who'd been putting two small appetisers on his plate, turned back to them to make this statement.

'Well, I'll keep an eye on Clare while you're gone,' Oliver said, far too heartily, some false note ringing in the words. But Kate had no time to be thinking about Oliver and heartiness or false notes, for it seemed as if she and Angus were headed for the roof garden, his hand clasped on her elbow as if to ensure she didn't escape.

There'd be other people up there, she reminded herself, *and you've got a plate full of food to eat, so it isn't as if you'll have time for kisses, not that he'd be wanting to kiss you if he'd come with Clare.*

Muddled thoughts popped in and out of her mind as they walked to the elevators, but once on the roof Kate realised her assumption that other people would be about was wrong. It was obviously too early for people to be slipping away from the party.

She chose a stone seat out of the wind—Clare had been right—and began to eat while Angus deposited his plate beside her, then prowled away, obviously intent on exploring this secret wonder.

'It's wonderful,' he declared, returning as she finished the last of the food she'd chosen and was eyeing off his meagre selection.

'It is,' she agreed, but looking at Angus, hearing the enthusiasm in his voice, she felt a pain so deep she could barely breathe.

He stood there in the moonlight, tall and strong, his accent making magic of his words—prosaic words like soil and ferns and watering systems—and she knew that it was love. Oh, people would argue that love didn't happen like this—in such a short time—but attraction, no matter how strong, couldn't cause pain as intense as she was feeling.

Her mind was battling this new revelation, but she knew sitting like a statue while it assimilated it was going to look odd, so she moved, picking up Angus's plate and helping herself to his appetisers.

'Do help yourself,' he said as she popped the second one in her mouth. 'I ate earlier.'

She looked up at him, stricken by her behaviour.

'Oh, I'm sorry, I wasn't thinking. I'll go down and get you some more.'

She stood so hurriedly she almost stumbled into him, and though she was sure he'd only put his hand on her shoulder to steady her, somehow she found herself in his arms, the plate she was still holding squashed between them.

'And waste this moonlight?'

He bent his head towards her and she could feel his lips—feel the kiss—before his mouth met hers.

'Angus, we can't!' she wailed, and heard the anguish in her voice.

He must have heard it, too, for he straightened.

'No, you're right. It's a work function and it's far too early for people to be returning to it looking rumpled and well-kissed.'

That hadn't been what she'd meant but it had stopped the kiss, which was a good thing.

Yeah?

Of course it was a good thing!

The two parts of her brain were arguing again, but as Angus had taken the plate from her hands, put it with the other one and was striding towards the elevators, she had little alternative but to follow.

Striding?

He was angry?

With her, for stopping the kiss?

Well, he's the one that actually stopped it *and* rationalised it!

Angus pressed the button, then felt a surge of fury that the doors didn't immediately open.

Fury!

What was wrong with him, striding off like that?

Feeling anger?

And with whom, himself or Kate?

Not Kate—it wasn't her fault he felt this almost uncontrollable urge to kiss her whenever she was within a yard of him.

Nor was she to blame that she had enough sense to pull back from the kiss!

She'd joined him by the elevator, not speaking, just standing there—within the dangerous one-yard zone but not by much.

The anger dissolved as quickly as it had surfaced, leaving him feeling confused and—

No, it couldn't be vulnerable.

He didn't do vulnerable.

'How did Hamish's mother die?'

Darn the woman! Had she sensed something? Slid inside him and ferreted out doors he'd slammed shut years ago? Somehow eased one open?

Yet might it not be time?

Around them a cool breeze rustled the leaves of the ferns and palms on the rooftop, and the scent of some sweet-smelling flower perfumed the air.

'Could we go and sit awhile?' he suggested, just as the elevator arrived and the doors opened.

Kate turned towards him, concern causing a small frown on her smooth forehead.

'You don't have to answer that question,' she said. 'In fact, it was rude and intrusive of me to have asked it, but as Hamish regards me as a friend, I thought—well, I wouldn't want to say the wrong thing to him.'

The inner tension that had eased when Kate asked the question tightened again. She was asking for Hamish, not out of concern for the boy's father.

The elevator doors had closed so he turned away, back towards the stone seat on which she'd been sitting earlier. He set down the plates on the end so she could sit beside him.

If she followed.

She did, although caution or regret was making her drag her steps.

'It's best you know,' he agreed when she slid onto the seat, close enough to touch, but not close enough for him to feel her body's warmth.

Angus looked straight ahead to where, between the branches and leaves, he caught glimpses of light in high-rise towers in the city. He'd told the story often enough, not regularly but from time to time, to explain to a colleague usually.

Kate was a colleague. Think that way!

'Jenna's pregnancy was unremarkable—she was well throughout, and her labour was hard but not overly prolonged. She was a doctor, like myself, so one would think if she'd had any preliminary signs of deep vein thrombosis—pains in her calves, tenderness on touching—she would have said, but she was blissfully happy, keeping Hamish close, showing him off to relatives and friends.'

His voice was flat, all emotion ironed out of it by the strength of his will, but Kate knew he must be reliving that pain, and slid closer, reaching out to take his hand in hers and hold it tightly.

He didn't resist but nor did his fingers respond to hers, simply lying limp in her hand as he continued.

'You'd know that DVT is often a forerunner to a pulmonary embolism, and Jenna knew that, as well, but if she was feeling breathless or had any other symptoms she didn't say. I wasn't there when she collapsed. I'd taken Hamish out to show some of my colleagues. They started anticoagulation therapy but she was dead within thirty minutes. Ridiculous that it can take such a short time for a young, healthy woman to die.'

Kate clung tightly to his hand. What could she say? What was there so say?

I'm sorry? A useless platitude, no matter how sincere the words!

She let the moment pass in silence, offering nothing more than whatever comfort he might derive from her clasp on his hand, then knew she had to probe again, because the pain this man was carrying was like an abscess that needed to be lanced.

'You can't possibly blame yourself,' she said, guessing this was how his thinking went. 'She must have wanted a child as much as you did, and what are the chances of a post-partum death by pulmonary embolism—very small, I would guess. Less than ten per cent?'

He stood, retrieving his hand in the action, and walked away, not towards the elevator this time, but towards the railing on the side of the roof garden that looked out over the suburbs towards the sea.

Unwilling to let him get away with silence, Kate followed him, coming to stand beside him, not touching him, but close enough for him to feel her presence.

'The mind is a strange thing, Kate,' he finally said, his voice deep and harsh. 'You'd think the scientist in me could rationalise what happened, using the figures I know by heart. Once she collapsed, there was nothing anyone could have done to save Jenna. It was just one of those occurrences that pop up to remind medical people they are not gods. But the emotional part of me cannot accept that.'

He turned towards her and put his hands on her shoulders.

'So, you see, sweet Kate, that although logically I know it wasn't my fault, emotionally I feel I was to blame. If it wasn't for me, she wouldn't have been pregnant. And yes, I know it was something we both wanted—a child—but I could never go through that again, never put a woman at risk that way, never have another child.'

He wasn't saying he could never love again....

It was a strange thought to bob into Kate's head, especially as Angus was drawing her close and she knew full well there'd be no stopping this kiss. But bob into her head it did, to lie there like a tiny seed, while her body responded to the touch of Angus's mouth, to the taste of Angus on her tongue. She slid her arms around him, holding him tight, kissing him with a passion she'd never felt before, knowing in a hazy kind of way that there was no pity in it, but sympathy at least, until the kiss became so fervid her mind went blank and she gave in to the longings of her body.

CHAPTER EIGHT

VOICES broke them apart—voices that told them others had come up to enjoy the cool breeze and beautiful views of the roof garden, or maybe to steal a kiss in shadows.

Angus looked at Kate, but her head was bent, so he smoothed the ruffled hair as best he could, thinking at the time how much better he liked her wayward curls, although the beauty of this shining curtain had taken his breath away earlier.

Who was he kidding? It was Kate herself who stole his breath.

She looked up at him now and he could see she'd been quietly renewing her lipstick, although the pale pink colour did little to hide the fullness of well-kissed lips.

'I think I'll go straight home,' she said. 'No-one will think anything of it—I rarely stay long at these occasions, and I've seen the person I came to see.'

Which obviously wasn't me, Angus realised, then chided himself for feeling put out. She saw him all the time at work; she didn't need to make a special effort. And she'd been kissing him, not some other man. She was here with him—

She was here with him!

The realisation released a lot of the tension that had built up again after the kiss.

'I'll walk you home,' he said, his body already stirring in response to this brilliant idea.

Green witch eyes studied him intently.

'Aren't you forgetting something?'

'Forgetting something?' He raised his eyebrows.

'Or someone?' Kate clarified, but obviously Angus still didn't get it.

'You came with Clare,' Kate reminded him. 'Surely you should see her home.'

'Oh, but it wasn't that kind of coming with,' Angus stuttered, and Kate almost laughed, almost but not quite. It wasn't really a night to be amused by seeing the usually oh-so-together Angus all confused.

'Whatever kind of coming with it was,' she told him, 'you should at least see that she's okay to get home. Besides, as I've told you before, I'm quite capable of seeing myself home.'

She was, but as she plodded up the street, a heaviness she rarely felt descended on her spirit. Angus had been honest with her from the start—no more children in his life—but the attraction between them, the attraction she knew he felt, had swayed her into thinking maybe something could come of a relationship between them.

Swayed her into thinking maybe he'd change his mind.

But now she knew how he felt, she had to cross that, admittedly remote, possibility right out of contention.

And why was she thinking of relationships of any kind with Angus when all they'd done so far was kiss?

Honesty propelled the answer: because she wanted there to be more than kisses—she wanted a relationship. And now that she knew she loved him, the need was not just for an affair kind of relationship but one that might possibly have a future.

With no babies?

Get real, Armstrong, you're so far ahead of the play here you're out of the field. There is no relationship! Get that into your thick head and get on with your life.

He caught up with her as she turned into her gate.

'Oliver is taking Clare home,' he panted, 'which I think is what she wanted all along.'

'So?' Kate demanded, angry with her body for responding to his arrival and angry with him for disrupting her when she'd only just got things sorted in her head, and had her wayward impulses back under control.

'So, I can see you home,' he said, less puffed now so he could smile as he spoke and it was the smile that was Kate's undoing.

Not that she could let him see it.

'I am home,' she pointed out.

'But I can see you to the door,' he whispered, the words zapping along her nerves like electric currents.

He hooked his arm around her shoulders and drew her close, kicking the gate open and walking her up the short path to the shadowed porch.

If he kisses me, I'm gone.

It was Kate's last rational thought. They'd no sooner reached the porch than Angus's lips captured hers and she was swept into the maelstrom of delight just kissing Angus caused. Swept into eddying currents of desire so deep and swift she knew there was no escape.

She eased one hand out of his grasp and dug in her pocket for a key, wordlessly unlocking the door and walking in, still in his embrace, his lips now seeking other places to kiss—her temple, just below her ear and the little hollow at the base of her neck.

Every kiss provided its own erotic thrill, each different, yet building and building the desire that was already flooding through her body.

'Bedroom, I think?' he whispered, the huskiness of his voice sending shivers down her spine, weakening the muscles in her legs.

He lifted her then, carrying her as easily as he carried Hamish, up the stairs and turning as if by instinct towards her bedroom at the front of the house.

She closed her eyes and tried not to think of the clothes scattered around on every surface, the skirt she'd worn to work probably on the floor, the sexy black dress cast aside on a chair. As long as they didn't turn on a light—

And *why* was she thinking about the disarray in her bedroom at a time like this?

She knew full well—it was to save her thinking about the consequences of what was about to happen. She was about to make love with Angus, and though the aftermath of that action might break her heart, she wanted it more than she'd ever wanted anything in her life.

Especially now Angus was kissing her again, only this time his hand was underneath her singlet, underneath her bra, touching her breast, feeling for her nipple. And pressed against her was the evidence of his desire, hard and strong, moving only slightly against her body but exciting her with the subtle movement.

She eased his shirt out of his trousers and slid her hands onto the skin on his back, feeling the silky smoothness of it, pressing her fingers into flat muscle mass and hard ribs, learning Angus through touch.

But her fingers couldn't possibly be exciting him as much as his were exciting her, for now he was cupping her breast and she could feel it grow heavy, her nipple peaking with desire, his tweaking on it sending fiery messages directly down to the sensitive nub between her thighs.

'Can we dispense with clothes?' she murmured against his chin, hoping she sounded less desperate than she felt.

'No sooner said than done,' he responded, and somehow, with hands flailing and feet moving, they stripped each other off, then came together again, skin to skin, less frantic now, savouring this moment of meeting properly, revelling in the togetherness of naked bodies.

'I grabbed some protection before I left the hospital,' Angus muttered, bending to retrieve his trousers and digging into a pocket before dropping a handful of foil-wrapped condoms on the bedside table.

'That many? What are you, the Scottish stud?' Kate teased, although the teasing was hiding her silly disappointment. Was she mad? She might want a baby but not an accidental pregnancy, especially with Angus, so why disappointment?

'You'll see,' Angus was saying as he lifted her again and tossed her lightly onto the bed, following her down so his body lay full-length beside her, on his side so he could lean towards her, touch her, kiss her, tease her with his tongue and fingers, and with words too, soft words that questioned and suggested. Their exploration of each other became a voyage of discovery until the teasing brought Kate to the very edge of orgasm and she cried out to have him deep inside her so satisfaction could be shared.

They'd used two condoms, Kate remembered that much as movement on the bed disturbed her exhausted sleep. She reached out for Angus but he was already up, dressing in the darkness.

'You're going?'

She hoped she'd sounded less desperate, less disappointed, than she felt! He sat down on the bed, and leaned over her, kissing her gently on the lips.

'I must, sweet Kate, for all I'd love to stay. But Hamish, knowing it's Saturday, will be bouncing into my bed at the crack of dawn which, in this upside-down country seems to be about 5:00 a.m.'

'Later now we're on summer time,' Kate corrected, although this totally unnecessary piece of information was nothing more than an attempt to mask the hurt she felt. Rationally she knew Angus had to get home to his son—of course he couldn't spend the night with her.

He pulled on his shoes, then bent to kiss her again, offering, as he stood, yet another piece of explanation.

'He'll be on a high because I'm taking him to the zoo to see the wombats.'

Kate waited, but the invitation she longed to hear didn't come, so she slid out of bed, pulled on a robe, fortunately slung over the bedpost nearby, and caught up with him at the door.

'There's a deadlock,' she explained, trying to sound as practical and matter-of-fact as he had. 'I'll lock the door behind you.'

She followed him down the steps, willing the idea of inviting her to the zoo with them to occur to him, but as he dropped a second goodbye kiss on her lips at the door she realised just how compartmentalised Angus's life must be. Okay, so she'd caught a glimpse inside one compartment tonight—the one labelled Jenna—but the Angus and Hamish boxes were still locked against her.

And probably always would be!

The realisation saddened her, but at least she knew where she stood and now it was up to her to decide where she wanted to fit into his life. Would she be happy to be in her own box? One marked Kate for Sex? Well, maybe he wasn't *that* crass! Maybe it was just marked Kate!

But, loving him as she did, could she handle it? She had no idea, and standing in the dark hallway wasn't going to supply one, so she went back to bed and curled up on the side where the scent of his body still lingered, memories of their lovemaking carrying her back to sleep.

She'd been right about the compartmentalisation of Angus's life, she realised when, after escaping to a friend's place in the Blue Mountains for the weekend to avoid him—and to think—she was back in the company of the professional Angus.

Was it easy for him, or did he want to lean into her when they were close, as she did to him? Did he want to touch her lightly as they passed, brush his fingers against her arm or back, as her fingers ached to do to him?

There was no sign that he did, but then, life at work had been hectic and there'd been little time for social interaction of any kind. Early in the week it was fairly standard chaos, except that two theatre nurses were off with summer colds and the team was working with theatre staff they didn't know, which always made things go a little less smoothly.

And even when she had no patients to check, Kate stayed at work later than she needed to, still uncertain in her mind—though not her heart—just where she wanted to fit in Angus's ordered life. She was determined to avoid accidental contact with him until she'd worked it out.

If she worked it out!

If she was right that he compartmentalised his life, could she accept that?

Or was she wrong about his attitude?

Although he'd have had to shut off part of himself after his wife died....

Her heart hoped she was wrong, but on top of the lack of an invitation to join him and Hamish at the zoo, Angus's behaviour at work, professional to the nth degree, told her she was right. Okay, so she didn't want a cuddle in the linen closet or a quick kiss in the procedures' room, but some acknowledgement of what had happened between them—a touch, a wink, an offer of a shared coffee break—would have made her feel less insecure.

The week went from bad to worse on Thursday, when they had a baby transferred into Jimmie's with hypoplastic left heart syndrome, a bad congenital defect where the left ventricle which pumped blood into the aorta, thence all through the body, was virtually missing. Kate first met the baby, Karl Sutcliffe, when she was called in to do the anaesthesia for the investigative procedures. He was such a chubby wee infant it was hard to believe he had a severe abnormality in his heart.

'Have you been involved in many cases of HLHS?' Angus asked, and knowing he liked to have people talking as he worked, she responded.

'Only one Norwood,' she said, naming the first operation that was usually performed on newborns with the problem, 'but I've been involved with a few who've had the bidirectional shunt inserted at six months and one little girl who had a Fontan at eighteen months.'

'That's the trickiest of the three,' Angus said, carrying on the conversation, although Kate knew ninety-nine point nine per cent of his attention was on this patient. 'Connecting the superior and inferior vena cava veins to the pulmonary artery can be very tricky, especially as the lungs have to be strong enough to adapt to the change.'

'Well, Phil did that one, and it went beautifully. I saw the little girl a couple of weeks ago when she was in for a check-up and she looked great.'

'Are we talking about Lucy Welsh?' Angus asked, glancing up at Kate, the dark eyes causing tremors she shouldn't feel at work.

'That's her,' Kate responded, trying to focus solely on work. 'Is she seeing you now?'

Angus nodded. 'That's right and she's doing really well.' There was a pause before he added, 'Okay, we're all done here.'

Something in his voice made Kate look more closely at him.

'And?' she probed.

He nodded to the technician who'd been handling the equipment, asked for a number of specific prints, then, as Kate checked the baby's blood gases, he sighed and answered.

'It's worse than the X-rays, ECG and echo showed. There's no ventricle at all, and the aorta is compromised, as well.'

'You can't operate?'

Kate hoped she sounded more professional than she felt, but hearing news like this always shocked her. Without an operation this baby would die.

'I'll talk to Alex, show him what I've found, but I doubt it.'

He sounded tired and more than ever Kate longed to touch him, even a light touch on his shoulder, but Angus was in work mode and every movement he made, every glance he gave her, told her this.

Angus saw Kate flinch and longed to reach out and touch her—nothing more than a reassuring brush of his fingers—but this was work and he knew from experience he had to keep his work life separated from his personal life.

Yet he owed Kate something.

'Cup of coffee?' he suggested. 'Once you've got him hooked up back in the PICU?'

'Where?' she asked.

He glanced at his watch. It was after five, the day had got away from him.

'If you're knocking off, let's make it Scoozi's. Hamish has a playdate with a kindy friend so won't be home until late. Besides, he and Juanita are used to expecting me when they see me.'

She nodded but he sensed she wasn't overjoyed by the idea. She'd been avoiding him—he'd figured that out quickly enough—but why? Embarrassment over what had happened Friday night? Or avoidance so there'd be no chance of it ever happening again?

His body didn't like that idea, not one little bit. Kate Armstrong had excited it in ways he'd never felt before and he'd hoped she'd enjoyed the experience enough to want to continue it.

He reached the restaurant first and chose a table in the outdoor garden section. A pergola overhead shaded the area from the worst of the day's sun so it was pleasantly cool, and he sipped his coffee and found his body not only relaxing, but stirring at the thought of seeing Kate in private—or more or less private, at least not at the hospital.

'Is there nothing we can do for that baby?'

So much for his body stirring! But he didn't have to answer straightaway, did he? He stood and moved to pull out her chair.

'Sit down, relax. Do you want a coffee or a drink—a glass of wine, maybe? I know they have that white you liked.'

She stared at him as if he'd gone demented, then her lovely lips clamped together in a thin line.

'You know that because you and Clare ate here last Friday night, I assume, and no, I didn't come for a drink, but for you to talk about that baby. Isn't that why you asked me?'

Kate heard the words come flying out before she could prevent them. What was wrong with her? Here she was, meeting Angus at *his* invitation, and she was carrying on like a shrew.

'Sit,' Angus said, but gently this time, his hand offering just the slightest downward pressure to her shoulder.

Damn him! Just one touch and she was jelly! Angry jelly, although she knew full well the anger was irrational. She slumped down into the chair.

'Coffee or wine?'

His repetition of the offer made her shake her head, but maybe a glass of wine would help her through whatever lay ahead.

'Wine, please.'

He gave her order to a waiter and settled back in his chair, reaching out across the table to grasp her hands.

'Yes,' he said, 'I sensed you needed to talk about the baby, but we need to talk about other things, as well, Kate. I came over to see you on Sunday afternoon when Hamish was asleep but you weren't there, and at work, well, I—'

'Like to keep things professional,' she finished for him. 'I did guess that.'

'But do you understand it?'

Did she? Kate thought about it, pleased her wine had arrived so she could take a sip and put off replying for a moment.

'To a certain extent, but as most doctors and nurses end up in relationships with other doctors and nurses, it's usually obvious what's going on around the place. In our unit alone there've been seven relationships that I know of, and it's only been set up a couple of years.'

He shrugged, the movement of his shoulders reminding her how the skin on those shoulders had felt, reminding her of too many things.

'It happens, but for me it's easier to keep things more—'

'Compartmentalised?' Kate offered the guess she'd already made about this man.

'I suppose so,' he admitted, then he stared off into space and she knew he was either thinking of some excuse for this behaviour, or wondering if he'd tell her the real reason.

'Back when Jenna died,' he finally began, and she knew he'd come down on the side of the latter. She also felt a tiny surge of happiness that he was opening the crack in that particular box just a little wider. 'We'd both been working at the hospital, so everyone knew us—knew us as a pair.'

He paused, his eyes once again on the greenery on the far side of the garden area.

'I had to keep working there—I had a fellowship, studying under one of the best paediatric cardiac surgeons in the business.' He turned back to Kate, dark eyes pleading for something—understanding?

'It was terrible, Kate. I could cope, just, with Jenna's death. I knew I had to come to terms with it and that in time I would, but the sympathy, the commiserations, of the staff around me—everyone knowing and wanting to help—it made it so much harder.'

'So from then on you shut yourself into a box called Work and thought that would shield you from emotion? Did you never think that maybe having people around you who knew you both might be a good thing? That their empathy and understanding and friendship and even love might have helped you through that time, even if it was only in giving you something to kick against?'

He stared at her, frowning slightly.

'I didn't see it that way,' he finally replied. 'And I still don't see it as shutting myself away in a box. I'm trying to explain that, at the time, it grated on me and I decided that I wouldn't mix my professional and private lives ever again.'

'Until you went to bed with me last Friday night!' Kate reminded him, making him frown even harder.

'But can't we keep that separate? Does everyone have to know?'

Kate shook her head, a sadness she didn't understand riffling through her senses.

'"Everyone" being hospital staff, or "everyone" being them plus Hamish and Juanita? Just how private a box do you want this relationship to be in?'

He threw up his hands.

'How do I know? You started the box thing—I don't see it like that at all!'

If he'd argued that he just wanted to keep things quiet at work, Kate knew she might have had a hope of a reasonable relationship with the man she loved, but he'd not answered the Hamish question, which hurt her more than she could say.

'Don't you?' she said. 'Okay, enough of boxes. I don't like them anyway. I like my world to be in circles, over-lapping rings that encompass all I do and all the people I love. So tell me about the baby. You feel there's no hope?'

Angus stared at her, seeing the pale oval of her face against the richness of her hair—curling wildly again.

'Angus?'

Had he been silent too long? What had she asked while he'd tried to analyse a very nasty constriction in his gut? The baby!

'I'll discuss it with Alex—in fact, I'm seeing him this evening before he flies to Melbourne for a conference. But I think the best we can do is list the baby for a heart transplant and hope that one becomes available while he's still well enough to survive an operation.'

'Poor kid—poor parents. Did you speak to them?'

Angus shook his head.

'Not until I've spoken with Alex so we can present them with all the information and options—however limited those might be. I've not been here long enough to know the ins and outs of the transplant listing system, how long a donor waiting list might be, how cases are prioritised.'

He might have been talking work but as he watched Kate lift her wineglass and drain the last mouthful, he couldn't help looking at her lips, thinking of the magic they'd wrought on his body such a short time ago.

Would he ever taste them again?

He wanted to ask, to find out how she felt about continuing a relationship with him, but what could he say? Can we have sex again?

Of course he couldn't.

'This is ridiculous,' he finally blurted out. 'I'm nearly forty years of age, sitting with a woman to whom I am incredibly attracted, and I don't know how to ask her if we've got anything going between us.'

Kate stared at him, then smiled and shook her head.

'Perhaps you should have got out a bit more and learnt a little about the way of the world.' She paused and the smile slid off her face. 'Yes, we've got something going between us, Angus. It's called attraction—a very strong attraction—strong enough for us to end up in bed together last Friday night. I've had a few days to think about it and, believe me, I did a lot of thinking. But I've always known that relationships that are simply for sex are not for me. I know they work for some people, but as far as I'm concerned, apart from the purely physical release, there's no fulfilment in them.'

Anger filtered into his head but he squashed it down. He wanted this woman in ways he didn't fully understand, and although so far in this conversation he'd done nothing more than turn her off him, he was determined to make a reasonable argument.

'You're making a judgement call on our relationship before we've even got to know each other properly. I won't accept it's just for sex. I like you, and I'd like to see more of you out of hospital hours. Are you afraid of what might happen? Are you afraid it might turn into a deeper relationship than you can handle? Is that why you're dodging it?'

'*I'm* dodging it? That's a laugh!

But although she'd snapped the argument at him, Kate knew he was right. Of course that was why she was dodging it. Because at the end, whatever happened, it wasn't going to lead to the family she had craved for so long.

So instead, she'd forgo any pleasure the relationship could provide? What if a grandfather for her grandchildren *never* came along?

'I don't know,' she finally admitted, her head and heart so at war with each other she felt exhausted.

'"I don't know" will do me for the moment,' Angus said, his tone exultant. 'Now, I'm meeting Alex at his house so I'll walk you home through the park. You are going home?'

She nodded, though walking home through the park was the last thing she wanted to do. The park was special to her, a favourite place, and she didn't want it tainted by the uneasiness she was feeling with Angus.

'You said the house where you live had been your family home, so you grew up with the park as a play-ground?'

Had he read her thoughts? They were on the path that led directly across it towards the street where they lived. It ran under spreading poinciana trees, already in bud, some showing the beginnings of the red-and-gold flowers that would shortly make a vibrant canopy overhead.

'We moved there after Susie died,' she said, not exactly answering his question.

She thought about it some more, then honesty propelled further explanation.

'Yes, I loved the park. I escaped to it as often as I could.'

'Escaped?'

She stopped by a sundial in the centre of a small piazza where several paths converged.

'You of all people would know that grief doesn't go away just because you move house,' she said. 'It came with us, and it haunted my parents' lives, so yes, I escaped to it. The park was light and sunny and even in the shadows it was warm.'

Angus felt a tension in his chest as he imagined the child Kate had been, alone with grieving parents, using the park as an escape from the darkness grief brought in its train.

Was *his* grief haunting Hamish?

He took Kate in his arms and kissed her gently on the lips, then simply held her, trying to work out the upheaval going on in his mind. He'd always put down the gap between himself and Hamish to Hamish's resemblance to his mother, but had he deliberately shut himself off from his child, as well as his colleagues?

Was Kate right about his behaviour, about his shutting himself away?

He'd have to think about it later, because right now the woman in his arms, held lightly but still held, was more important.

'Are your parents both dead now?' he asked, and she looked up at him and nodded.

'My mother died when I was eighteen. She'd been ill for a long time, or so it seemed. My father died three years ago. That's when I moved out of the house.'

'And you had no-one?'

She moved out of his embrace.

'Not really. I had someone after my mother died,' she said. 'Although probably no-one would have been better.'

The words weren't bitter but they had a hint of tartness in them, then suddenly she smiled, a proper smile, a 'Kate smile.'

'Didn't I tell you once not to make me maudlin! I had, and still have, a group of wonderful friends. I've had a great life and intend to continue enjoying it. Okay, so it had its share of bumps but all lives have their bumps. You have to live with that so you can enjoy the smooth bits all the more because of them.'

She marched off down the path so he had to hurry to catch up with her. There was more—he sensed that— more about the 'no-one' she'd probably have been better without. Not her father. A man, no doubt! No wonder she was wary about a relationship with him.

But wasn't he just as wary?

Wanting to keep it quiet?

Wasn't that unfair?

Belittling her some way?

He rubbed his hands through his hair, aware his mind was more confused than it had ever been. *His* mind, the mind he prided himself could work through any problem.

They walked in silence, crossing the road together, then parting without farewells, he to see Alex in the house further down the street, she to disappear into her house.

'So *that* has done a lot of good!' he muttered to himself as he walked through Alex's front gate.

'Talking to yourself, Angus?'

He looked up to see Alex's wife, Annie, heavily pregnant with their second child and positively radiant, cutting roses in the front garden.

And in his mind's eye he saw not Jenna but a pregnant Kate, and the image shocked him so much he stopped as if he'd hit a telegraph pole.

'Incipient madness!' he said to Annie.

'Comes with the job, I think,' she said sympathetically. 'Go on in, I think Alex is doing something about cold drinks.'

In a corner of the big living room a toddler played with coloured blocks, knocking over the towers Alex was building for him, then gnawing at random blocks.

'He's teething,' Alex explained, standing up to greet Angus. 'But then they always are, it seems. You'd know about it.'

Another stab of guilt. *Had* he known much about Hamish's developmental milestones? He supposed his mother had told him when teeth came through, and he'd dutifully admired them, but as a father?

This was doing his head in. Thank heavens Juanita had picked up their car today. He'd talk to Alex, then head for the beach, take a walk to clear his head. He'd heard you could walk for miles along a headland path from Coogee. He'd do that—

He caught up with Alex's conversation, saying yes to a cold drink, but thinking now, as Alex disappeared to get drinks, not of a solitary walk but perhaps a trip to the beach with Hamish. They could swim and play in the sand.

Ask Kate?

Not this time, there was a lot of catching up to do, but soon he'd ask Kate—

Ask Kate what?

CHAPTER NINE

'I HATE transplants.'

They were in Theatre. Oliver was preparing baby Karl. Angus was to do the operation as Alex was still in Melbourne, but it was Clare who voiced the emotion Kate also felt.

'Why?' Oliver asked as he cut open the tiny chest of the patient.

'For me it's because some other baby has to die.' It was Kate who answered. 'I know it means this baby will live, and one lot of parents will have the joy, but I always think of the other parents, the ones going home with empty, aching arms, and bruises on their hearts that will last for ever.'

'Just slightly melodramatic, Kate?' Angus had returned from speaking to the patient's parents in time to hear her words.

'I don't think so,' she said, barely glancing at Angus, who'd been avoiding her assiduously since their coffee and walk through the park a week earlier. Although, to be fair, with Alex away, Angus was busier than usual....

She'd been avoiding him, as well, although she'd seen plenty of Hamish, who, having been reunited with McTavish, was spending a lot of time adventuring in her backyard.

But when Angus spoke again, she was startled and just a little put out, for he was opening the box that was Jenna, not just to her but to his colleagues.

'My wife died suddenly,' he was saying, while Kate tried to concentrate on her job and ignore the emotion bumbling around in her chest. 'As a physician, she'd always been an advocate of organ donation, yet at the time of her death, when a woman from the organ donor program approached me, all I felt was revulsion. I was about to refuse when I remembered how vocal Jenna had been about it, and although it ripped me apart at the time, I agreed that they should take whatever they could use.'

He paused, and the normal sounds of the operating theatre seemed louder in his silence, then he added, 'But it does bring comfort later, when you can think more clearly, and to parents of a child that died to know their child didn't die in vain, I think that must, in time, be helpful.'

Kate stared at him, and though his dark eyes, all but hidden behind the magnifying loupe, turned her way, she could read nothing in them. Yet she sensed that this was probably the first time Angus had spoken openly to colleagues about his wife's death, and wondered if perhaps this, too, would be helpful to him.

Her love for him made her want to go to him, to put her arms around him and hold him tightly, but this was work, and here in this place, they were colleagues and nothing more.

Perhaps that's all they were anywhere; nothing had been resolved....

The talk around the operating table was purely profes-sional now, with the circulating nurse offering the latest information on the expected arrival time of the donor heart, the operating team counting down the minutes, preparing precisely, so little Karl's time on the machine would be as short as possible. And as the operation proceeded, Kate lost her reservations about transplants. Angus did the switch so swiftly it seemed impossible to think dozens of tiny stitches had been inserted as the new heart was set in place and connected to Karl's blood vessels, but now, as the heart beat on its own for the first time in Karl's chest, Kate felt the joy that *this* baby had survived.

Angus was in the PICU with Karl's parents when she and Clare wheeled the baby through. Clare was really in charge now he was on the ventilator, but Kate wanted to see him settled before she left the hospital.

And not only was Angus with the parents, but he had his arm around Karl's mother, who had tears welling in her eyes as she thanked him and his team.

'You've humanised me again, Kate Armstrong,' he told her later, catching up with her as she walked through the early-evening light along their street. 'And for that I thank you.'

He slung an arm around her shoulder and drew her close.

'I'm not saying you were right about the boxes, mind,' he added, 'but I'd lost my way and now I see a faint hint of a path ahead of me.'

Which meant what? Kate wondered but didn't ask, simply enjoying the feel of his arm around her, the solidity of his body against hers.

'So, dinner tonight at Scoozi's? Or somewhere else if you'd prefer? I don't know the places to go so you choose.'

Kate shook her head, remembering another conversation—dinner and sex, a movie and sex...

'Why?' she asked, perhaps a little bluntly, as they reached his front gate.

'Because,' he said, and kissed her, right there and then for all the world—or any of it that happened to be around at the time—to see. 'We're starting again. I'm courting you. We're not going to get tangled up in where we're going or what might happen in the future—we're going to take it one day at a time and see what happens.'

He kissed her again.

'That suit you?'

All Kate could do was nod, too overwhelmed by the sudden change in this man to take it in. Perhaps...

'Then why don't you come to my place for dinner,' she suggested. 'That way we can get to know each other a little better than we would in a restaurant.'

A sexy smile greeted this pronouncement, and before she could protest that that wasn't what she'd meant, he was kissing her again.

'I'll read Hamish his bedtime story and be in at eight,' he promised as they drew apart, and though Kate was reasonably sure her feet were touching the ground as she made her way next door, it felt as if she was dancing at least a yard above the ground, flying like a fairy in a bright bubble of happiness.

He came, they talked, and ate, and talked some more. They wandered through the park, hand in hand, kissing in the shadows, prolonging the agony of desire for as long as they could. Then suddenly both needing more than kisses, hurrying back to her house, to her bedroom, stripping off their clothes and lying together once more, not talking now, but letting their hands renew the exploration of each other's bodies.

It was a dream yet not a dream, Kate decided as the escalation of her desire blasted thoughts of the future from her mind. For the moment there was only now, and right now, here with Angus, was where she wanted to be.

His teasing fingers brought her to a whimpering, tremulous climax, and as he slid inside her, she shivered again, knowing that she would surely splinter into a million pieces the next time. But it was Angus who cried out loud when the moment came, his body shuddering with his release, his arms clamping her to his body as if she was a lifeline in a very turbulent sea.

They lay together, Kate holding him close, knowing so much had changed in his life recently he might feel totally adrift, and as she held him, he drifted off to sleep, and she watched over him in the moonlight that streamed through her window.

Would it go anywhere, this relationship?

Did it matter if it didn't?

Couldn't she simply take what she could out of it, and if a time came to move on, then she'd have memories to treasure in the future?

But even as she assured herself this was possible, she knew that she was wrong. The more time she spent with Angus, the more she learned of his convoluted personality, the more she loved him, and the harder any parting would eventually be.

So she held him as he slept and tried not to think, simply reliving the pleasure of the evening they'd spent together—the walk in the park, the kisses under the trees, the magic of his lovemaking.

'You should have woken me!'

It was two in the morning and she was sitting up in bed, still watching over him, having decided that was far more satisfying than sleeping beside him, when he came awake so suddenly she was startled.

But the accusation in his words startled her even more, and as she watched him pull on his clothes, she felt her happiness seep away, leaving only emptiness. How had she fooled herself that Angus had changed? Why had she thought that two kisses outside his gate meant he was willing for people to know they were in a relationship?

'I would have woken you soon,' she muttered, angry now at his reaction. 'I know you like to be home before Hamish wakes.'

'I've got to go—I'll see you later. You're on call this weekend? You'll be here?'

He was out the door, doing up his shirt with one hand, his shoes and socks in his other.

Kate stared at the empty doorway, then heard him call from the bottom of the steps.

'Don't forget to come down and lock the door before you go back to sleep.'

Go back to sleep? Ha! She was so confused she might never sleep again.

Maybe he hadn't meant to be so offhand?

Who was she kidding?

Dinner and sex, movies and sex—that was Angus's idea of a relationship and she'd known that from the start. Just because he was becoming more human in other areas of his life didn't mean he was going to fall madly in love with his next-door neighbour.

She must have slept for she was woken by a strange noise at her back door, and she pulled on a robe and made her way downstairs to find McTavish sitting on the doorstep, whimpering piteously.

'What's wrong, where's Hamish?' she asked the dog, then realised how pathetic that was.

She called the boy, thinking he must be hiding somewhere and McTavish couldn't find him, but there was no reply, and in spite of her sudden rush of anxiety a quick search of her backyard revealed no unconscious little boy.

Picking McTavish up, she was walking towards the gate when she realised she was hardly dressed for visiting.

'Come inside with me,' she told him, carrying him into the kitchen and putting some water for him into a bowl. 'I'll get some clothes on and we'll investigate.'

He sat beside the water bowl, the dark brown eyes in the pale Highland terrier face looking so sorrowful she had to hug him again before she went upstairs to change.

But going next door provided no answers. The little car Angus had bought was on the concrete pad in the backyard, but no-one was at home.

'Well, do you want to stay here or come home with me?' she asked McTavish, who put his nose against her leg by way of answer and followed her back into her yard.

'I don't have a dog door but I'll leave the back door open,' she told him, but apparently, having found one of the few humans he knew in Australia, McTavish wasn't going to budge from her side.

By late afternoon Kate was seriously worried, and although she'd phoned her neighbours frequently there was no reply, and no answering machine picked up. She'd never had reason to know Angus's mobile number and wondered about phoning the hospital and asking them to contact Angus on his pager. But she knew how much he'd hate that, so she sat and worried, cleaned her living-room walls down and worried, took McTavish for a walk in the park using a belt for a lead, and worried.

At midnight, when McTavish's scratching at her bed-clothes told her he needed to go outside, she let him out into the backyard and saw lights on next door, but they were upstairs in Juanita's flat and Kate didn't feel she knew Juanita well enough to visit her at midnight.

Instead, she tried to shoo McTavish back home, but although he went through the gate and wandered around for a while, he came back and followed Kate inside.

'Stuck with each other, aren't we?' she said, although by morning she knew she had to find out what had happened. Clutching McTavish's solid body under one arm, she went next door, to the front door this time, and pressed her finger on the bell. So what if it was barely seven; the dog was lost, well, kind of lost....

And so was she, but that was different.

Juanita came eventually. Not the cheerful, competent Juanita Kate was used to seeing, but a sleep-rumpled Juanita with dark shadows under her eyes.

'The dog! I'd forgotten all about him. He hasn't been here long enough for me to remember he's part of the family. Have you been looking after him?'

She reached out to take McTavish but Kate held on to her prize.

'What's happened?' she asked. 'He's been at my place since yesterday morning and I've tried to contact Angus any number of times.'

'You don't know?'

Juanita sounded shocked, but the look of her, and now the tone of her voice, was filling Kate with a strong foreboding.

She shook her head.

'It's Hamish!' Juanita said, her voice catching on his name, and tears welling in her eyes. 'Just suddenly on Friday night—he was sleeping in my flat because Angus was out, and he started crying, then he stopped, suddenly. One minute crying, then no crying. I went to check—he was asleep. He felt a little hot but he gets ear infections and a temperature sometimes and he was sleeping so I didn't wake him. Then in the morning— very early, it was still dark—he was going down the stairs to his own flat and he fell. Angus thought he'd knocked himself out and took him up to the hospital for X-rays but it wasn't the fall. He's got enceph—'

'Encephalitis?' Kate whispered, finishing the word that Juanita was trying to get out.

Juanita nodded.

'The doctors there say he must have had some kind of virus and this followed it, but until last night he's been well as far as we could see.'

'And Angus?'

'He is by his son's bed where he should be,' Juanita said, somehow implying it's where he should have been when Hamish was first ill. Not that Kate needed Juanita's words to make her feel guilty; she'd been feeling guilt since she'd first heard of the little boy's illness.

And if she was feeling guilt, how would Angus be feeling—Angus who was a world champion in the guilt stakes.

She handed McTavish over and headed straight for the hospital, then had second thoughts and turned back, returning home to get her hospital ID just in case she was stopped from entering the intensive-care unit where Hamish would be.

He was in a small room, hooked up to monitors, a haggard-looking Angus by his side.

'I'll sit with him while you take a break,' she said, coming close but not touching either the man or the comatose child.

Angus looked up at her, his dark eyes almost black with worry.

And regret!

Although maybe she was imagining the regret.

'I should have been there for him earlier in the evening,' he muttered, confirming her fears that Angus would be taking on entire responsibility for his son's illness.

'He could have sickened during the day, while you were operating, while he was at kindy—any time, Angus, and you know it.'

The dark eyes turned away from her, and though she longed to touch him, hold him, help to bear his pain, he'd erected a wall between them, so obvious she could almost see it.

'Take a break,' she said. 'I'm speaking as a doctor now, not a friend. You'll be worse than useless if you don't look after yourself and you know it.'

'He hasn't roused at all,' Angus muttered. 'They're giving him corticosteroids but there's little else they can do.'

'He knows me well enough now, Angus, for me to be with him if he does rouse, so go, if only to have a shower and get fresh clothes. Something to eat and drink.'

To her surprise Angus stood, ceding his place to her, and as she slipped into the chair he touched his hand to her shoulder.

'I'm sorry,' he said, his voice gruff with exhaustion, and although he was gone before Kate could question the remark, it filled her with a coldness she didn't want to consider.

She took Hamish's hand in hers, and talked to him, about possums and wombats and McTavish coming to visit her and staying the night, chattering on, hoping something in the stream of words might penetrate enough to rouse him. It was only when a different nurse came in to do his obs that she realised she'd been there over a change of shift, and checking her watch saw Angus had been gone two hours.

Maybe he'd had a sleep!

She was pleased for him but, stupidly perhaps, even more pleased for herself that he'd trusted her to sit with his son.

But his return, another hour later, was no cause for pleasure, his thanks spoken so brusquely Kate flinched.

'I'll stay a little longer,' she suggested, for in spite of his attitude she knew he needed support.

'There's no need,' he said, and now she did depart, stopping by the monitors to speak to the nurse in charge, a young man she knew quite well because he'd done a stint in the cardiac PICU.

'It's not good that he's not rousing,' he said. 'The swelling in his brain is down, and he's responding to physical stimuli but not to verbal ones.'

Kate walked home, worrying about this, knowing Angus must be frantic with concern. She found McTavish sitting forlornly on the yellow sofa and it gave her an idea.

A radical idea!

Could she do it?

Should she do it?

Perhaps it would be okay; after all, Hamish wasn't in the main ICU but in a room of his own outside the really sterile area.

She thought of the consequences, the insanitary aspects of it, then thought of a little boy that talk alone had failed to rouse from his semiconscious state.

Damn it all, it was worth a go!

'How do you feel about backpacks?' she asked the dog, remembering a friend who took her King Charles spaniel to the beach in a backpack.

She hurried inside, McTavish at her heels, and dug out a backpack that had seen better days but was still serviceable enough.

'I'll give you a run outside to do whatever you have to do,' she told him, leading him through to the backyard and chasing him around until he sniffed a bush or two and left his mark on one of them.

'Now,' she said, 'here we go.'

She lifted his chunky body, pleased he was still little more than a pup and hadn't filled out to true Highland terrier proportions.

Apparently used to being carted around by Hamish in unusual conveyances, the dog showed no objection to being treated this way.

'Okay, we're off,' she said to him, lifting him and slinging the backpack on her shoulders. With the friendly nurse on duty at the monitors she should be able to get the backpack in without question. It was Angus she was more worried about.

Would he object?

Of course he would; he'd think she was mad. But Hamish was his child, so obviously she'd have to discuss it with him first.

She stopped next door, knocked, then explained to Juanita what she was doing.

'Angus'll have his mobile in his pocket on vibrate,' she said. 'Could you give me twenty minutes to get up there and on to the right floor, then phone him. He can't use his mobile in there, so he'll have to leave the room to check the call and I'll grab him in the foyer and explain what I want to do.'

Juanita stared at her as if she was mad, then she smiled, a broad warm smile.

'It might work,' she said. 'I can tell him I've been speaking to his mother, which is true.'

They checked their watches and Kate took off, hurrying now, as the weight of the dog on her back seemed to be increasing all the time.

From an alcove outside the PICU she saw Angus leave the unit, hurrying to the elevator foyer to answer his phone. Kate caught him as he closed the phone, drawing him into the alcove so she could explain her idea.

'That is crazy. You can't take a dog into his room—he's in a hospital bed.'

Kate looked into his eyes, aware of the plea he must be able to read in hers.

'He's not responding to anything else, Angus,' she reminded him. 'Isn't it worth a try?'

Angus's fingers had found a way into the top of the backpack and he was scratching at McTavish and murmuring to him.

'He does love the dog,' he said, his voice so rough Kate realised he was feeling pain. Pain that maybe Hamish loved his dog more than he loved his father?

'Of course he does, but a lot of that is because McTavish relies on him. Maybe thinking McTavish needs him will be the incentive to push him to the surface, back to consciousness.'

The anguish on Angus's face was so obvious Kate touched his arm, then reached up and kissed his cheek.

'Worth a try?' she said as lightly as she could, for her heart was aching for this tormented man.

'Worth a try,' he finally admitted, then he found a smile that eased, just a little, her heartache. 'But you're the one who takes the rap if the hospital gets wind of it!' he warned, but he took the backpack off her and carried it into the room.

Once there, he grabbed a towel and put it on the side of Hamish's bed, then set the backpack on the towel. Kate held her breath as Angus opened it enough for

McTavish to poke his nose and paws outside. The little dog whimpered at the sight of his master and Kate lifted Hamish's hand to rest on McTavish's head.

'It's McTavish, Hamish darling. He's come to visit you. He's been missing you so much. Won't you say hello to him?'

Kate didn't know if it was her words or the dog's rough tongue licking Hamish's hand, but the blue eyes opened and the little hand grasped one of his dog's paws as he whispered, 'McTavish.'

To Kate it was the most beautiful word she'd ever heard and she knew tears were rolling down her cheeks, down Angus's, too, she realised as he bent to take his son in his arms.

Kate tucked McTavish back into her backpack, promised Hamish she'd visit soon, and left the room, dodging the nurse who'd entered in response to the change in Hamish's condition shown on the monitor screen.

Hamish's eyes had closed again, but through the window Kate could see that his fingers, rather than lying listlessly on the bed, were now curled around his father's hand, while Angus's free hand stroked his son's face and hair, his fingers trembling slightly.

As she left the hospital, she let McTavish out of the backpack, once again using the old belt as a lead. They walked home together, Kate pouring out her troubles to him.

'So you see, McTavish,' she finished, dropping down onto the yellow sofa and helping him jump up on it to sit beside her, 'just when the man was ready to accept that being human, which means vulnerable, was okay, this happens, and I know for sure he'll be shutting himself off from the world again—or from the world of human emotions.'

McTavish responded by putting his front paws on her lap and giving her chin a consolatory lick.

'*And* I'm going to be in trouble for taking a dog into a hospital—the one place in the world that's supposed to be a germ-free environment and who knows what germs you might have.'

McTavish was obviously bored with the conversation, as he'd now put his head on his paws, still in Kate's lap, and had closed his eyes, confirming his lack of interest with little snuffling snores. Juanita came along the footpath.

'Angus has called me. It worked, your idea?'

She was smiling with delight but Kate couldn't summon up more than a tepid grin.

'Yes, it worked,' she said, 'but I'm not sure Angus was too impressed—reckons if anyone gets into trouble it will have to be me.'

'Angus, phooey!' Juanita declared. 'He needs to be jolted out of himself that man, and though I wouldn't for the world have had this happen to Hamish, maybe it will be for the best in the long run.'

Not for me, Kate knew but didn't say.

'I hope so,' she said.

'I'm going to the hospital now,' Juanita said. 'Maybe I can nag him to come home for proper sleep.'

Then she shrugged her shoulders.

'And maybe not, but I try. You'll mind McTavish?'

Kate nodded, and watched Juanita bustle away.

'She's wrong, McTavish,' Kate told the still-sleeping dog. 'I think I managed to jolt him out of himself, just a little. But this, it's just jolted him right back to where he was.'

Alex flew home from Melbourne so Angus could take time off without leaving the teams two surgeons short, and McTavish returned to his home when Hamish came out of hospital, under strict bed-rest instructions.

Which left Kate all alone again. She went to work, and came home, phoning every evening to ask after Hamish, more often getting Juanita for the latest report but occasionally a totally formal Angus would tell her the little boy was progressing well. She longed to call in to see her young friend, but no invitation was forthcoming, so she stayed away, throwing a ball for McTavish in the evenings when he came to visit, talking to him— almost sorry the possums had left so she'd have had more company....

Baby Bob was out of the PICU and due to be medivaced back to a unit at the Port Macquarie hospital, so instead of going straight home on the Thursday afternoon, Kate made her way to the nursery to say goodbye to the Stamfords.

Bob was out of his crib, lying in his father's arms, and Kate felt such a surge of longing her knees felt weak.

'May I hold him?' she asked, and Pete Stamford handed him over. She tucked the little fellow up against her, talking quietly to him, amazed that the dark blue eyes seemed to be taking in every word she said.

'He'll be clever,' she told his beaming parents.

'Healthy is what we're after,' Mrs Stamford said. 'I was just telling Dr McDowell that a few minutes ago.'

'Dr McDowell? Here?' Kate asked, finding she now had a churning stomach, as well as weak knees.

'Apparently his little boy's been ill and he brought up some chocolates for the staff where he'd been treated, then he heard we were going home so called in to say goodbye.'

And I missed him! Kate wailed, but she kept the words inside, then told herself it was for the best. What did they have to say to each other?

'He might be back,' Pete Stamford added. 'He said something about a present for Bob because he was the doctor's first Australian patient.'

Which means I should give this baby back to his parents and get out of here, Kate's inner messenger declared, but it was already too late, for Angus was there, a small toy wombat in his hands.

'I thought I'd seen these in the shop downstairs,' he said, speaking to the Stamfords, though his eyes had glanced towards Kate as he drew near. 'My son just adores them.'

He handed the little toy to Mrs Stamford as Kate settled the baby in his crib. He'd be travelling north by ambulance, his mother riding with him, Pete Stamford, no doubt, driving right behind the medical vehicle.

'I'd better go. Good luck,' she said, then was surprised when Mrs Stamford reached out and pulled her into a hug.

'Thank you for everything,' the woman whispered, and Kate felt the tears that had started welling when she held baby Bob, now threatening to spill down her cheeks.

'It was nothing,' she managed to mutter, then added a general goodbye to everyone within hearing and fled the room.

Angus caught up with her in the elevator foyer where she'd been surreptitiously wiping tears from her cheeks. He came and stood beside her, not touching, or speaking, just being there. They entered the elevator together and rode it down, still silent, then, because she knew she couldn't stand the tension in this silence any longer, she broke it, asking, as they exited on the ground floor, 'How is Hamish?'

'He's fine, well enough now to be a handful as far as keeping him quiet is concerned. We've read every book ever written about possums and wombats and have moved on to platypuses and kangaroos.'

They'd moved towards the front entrance as she'd asked the question and he'd answered, but now Kate stopped, unwilling to walk home with him while her body ached to hold him, her hands to touch him, yet his whole demeanour yelled, Keep off.

'I'll drop some of my books in for him,' Kate said.

He'd stopped beside her, looking down at her, but it wasn't books he mentioned when he spoke again.

'You told me you weren't quite alone when your mother died,' he said, the words so startlingly out of context Kate frowned as she made sense of them. But making sense and saying something were two entirely different things. She could only stare at him.

'And you held that baby like he was something precious. Did you lose a child, as well? Is that what makes you long for one? Was the grandmother story just a cover?'

How had he done this?

How had Angus, of all people, swooped from swimming eyes while she held a baby, to her grandmother story being a cover in such a short time?

Confused didn't begin to cover how Kate felt, and that stirred anger.

'The grandmother story is true,' she said, and turned away, but he caught her shoulder and steered her into the café.

'Come, sit awhile with me. Talk to me, Kate. Help me here.'

She looked at him, still angry, but read a confusion to equal her own in his eyes.

Allowing him to steer her to a corner table, Kate slumped down in a chair, waited while he went to order coffee, then looked at him across the table.

'I don't think my life is any concern of yours, not any longer,' she said.

He spread his hands and shook his head.

'How else could I feel but guilty—not being home that night when Hamish first was sick? I'm not blaming you, Kate, but it brought home to me how dependent Hamish is on me, and how—'

'How you can't afford to have a life of your own because of that?' Kate demanded. Then before he could reply, she continued, the weird anger that had come from nowhere suddenly exploding. 'That's nonsense, Angus, and someone as intelligent as you should know it. It's just another excuse to hide yourself away from hurt, and don't tell me I don't know about hurt. I've felt it all, including, yes, a baby that I lost. When my mother died I was seeing a fellow student, Brian, and seeking comfort in his arms I became pregnant. He was horrified, wanted me to have a termination, but it was my baby and no way was I going to give it up, so we parted. Then two months later I miscarried. So, yes, there's more to my wanting children than my grandmother dream, but—'

'You *did* lose a child? It was a stab in the dark, when I said that, not something meant to upset you,' he said, but the stab had found its mark and suddenly Kate was too upset to stay in the café, no matter how good the coffee was. As the waitress approached with the order, Kate stood and hurried out, muttering something that might have been goodbye but was more a garbled curse.

The tears were too close again, and she was damned if she was going to cry in front of half the hospital staff....

CHAPTER TEN

'Two COFFEES?' the waitress said, and Angus waved to her to put them down. He probably wouldn't drink either of them, but he needed to sit awhile and try to sort out some of the emotional mess curdling inside him.

Of course Kate, who'd suffered so much loss in her life, would want children of her own—a family. Not only that, she deserved a family, deserved all the happiness in the world, in fact.

The thing about Kate, he'd discovered, was that she refused to be beaten by what life threw at her. She kept going, kept smiling, always positive, always up-beat, seeing the best in situations, the best in people. She'd even tried to dig out something worthwhile in him and, to a certain extent, succeeded because he was recovering his humanity, and for that he was really grateful.

He drained his cup of coffee and started on hers, not sure where all this rational thinking was getting him, although he now had a much fuller picture of the woman he loved.

Loved?

He set the cup back carefully in its saucer, certain it had been about to slip from his grasp.

Loved?

How could he love her? He barely knew her. But even as this excuse sprang from his brain, another part of his mind was denying it. Of course he knew her, knew her from that first day at work when she'd broken through Mrs Stamford's denial, and started his own process of rehumanisation, if such a word existed.

He pictured her on the yellow sofa, an arm around his son, and remembered the stab of jealousy he'd felt, but what he should have felt was pleasure, that finally he'd found a woman who would make the ideal mother for his son.

His son!

His only child!

Kate wanted babies, wanted a family, and knowing Kate as he now did he knew darned well one child didn't constitute a family in her terms.

And she deserved babies and a family, but was he the man to provide this? Fear grasped his heart as he considered losing Kate as he'd lost Jenna.

No, that couldn't happen!

It probably wouldn't, the scientist reminded him, but there was always that chance.

He left the coffee shop, half a cup undrunk. Alex had given him more time off, but he had patients he wanted to see—outpatients whose parents had often travelled hundreds of miles so their children could keep appointments. He wasn't going to push them on to one of the other specialists. Tomorrow he'd go to work, but taking appointments, not operating, so he'd be able to avoid Kate while he sorted things out in his head.

Avoidance was not so easy when he returned home to find her as he'd pictured her in his mind, sitting on the yellow sofa, Hamish by her side, McTavish as close as he could get to Hamish, Kate reading from a rather tattered storybook.

'This was my favourite as a child,' she said, holding it up so he could see the cover. It was a Dr Seuss book, and although he was reasonably sure Hamish had a newer and cleaner version, he could hardly complain. His son was sitting quietly, which was the main thing, and if the picture conjured up images of family in Angus's eyes, then that was his problem.

As was the distance in Kate's voice as she spoke, though when she returned to the story, she was animated once again, giving all the characters a different intonation.

The urge to join them on the yellow sofa was almost irresistible but he knew, until he'd sorted out how he felt about Kate—how could it possibly be love? He'd known Jenna for years before he'd fallen in love with her!—he had to steer clear.

On top of that was the fact that he had no idea how Kate felt about him. He had no doubt about the attraction, but love was a whole different matter. He tried to remember if she'd used words of love at any time, but knew it was a pointless exercise. If Kate had at any time mentioned love, he'd have backed off so quickly even kisses would have been off limits.

Waving a rather ineffectual goodbye, he made his way inside, but though he settled in the corner of his bedroom he'd made his study, determined to do some work, images of Kate blocked his mind. So he gave up, got the car, told Juanita he was going out for a while and headed for the beach.

He walked the coastal path, north towards another beach called Bondi, striding along until he came to a massive cemetery, perched on the edge of the cliff, gravestones looking out to sea. It was a place of such quiet beauty he found a bench and sat there, thinking of the past, reliving Jenna's death, then moving on to consider—really seriously—the future.

Needing to do something to stop herself thinking about Angus, Kate had spread drop sheets on the living-room floor, and was, rather inexpertly, rolling paint onto the uneven surface of the walls. It was a paint called white-on-white, which the man at the hardware shop had assured was perfect anywhere. What it seemed to be doing was highlight all the unevenness of the walls, and she was wondering if it was time to call in an expert when the front doorbell rang.

She looked down at the paint spatters on the old dungarees she was wearing, and frowned at the smattering of paint dots on her arms and legs, then as the doorbell pealed again, she sighed and headed for it, praying it wasn't someone important from the hospital.

'Angus?' The first word was generated by surprise, then fear took over. 'It's not Hamish, is it? He hasn't had a relapse?'

Angus shook his head, presumably answering her questions, not denying who he was.

She stared at him. He'd come to her so he must want something, but did she want him in her house?

Did she want him within a hundred yards of her, looking as she did?

Of course not, but he was there.

'Do you want to come in? It's just that I'm painting, as you can see, so it's not the best time, though what it's not the best time for, I don't know.'

The rapid heartbeats Angus's presence always caused had obviously turned her brain to mush that she was prattling on like this. And now he was smiling—more mush, although in her stomach this time.

'Not the best time for proposing, I guess,' he said softly, but she heard the words, just couldn't grasp the meaning.

'Proposing what?' she demanded, thoroughly disconcerted now.

'Marriage, of course.'

He was sounding a little tetchy now but how did 'marriage' and 'of course' get to go together?

'Marriage?' she echoed, just to make sure she'd got it right.

'Yes, marriage,' he grumbled—hardly loverlike.

'To me?'

'Of course to you.' He was snapping now.

'But I want children,' she reminded him, then suddenly realised they were still standing on her front doorstep, she completely paint-spattered, and he in shorts and a T-shirt that looked slightly damp.

'Has it been raining?' she asked, though she was sure she'd have known if it had been, but weather talk was good to get through awkward conversations.

He stepped towards her, smiling now, and put his arms around her.

'Kate, I'm proposing to you, not discussing the weather, but no, it's not raining. I just went for a walk, then needed a swim to clear my head, and it was hot so I went in fully clad—except for my shoes, of course.

Now could you please put me out of my misery and tell me if you're at least interested enough in me to consider a proposal.'

He kissed her, which was a big mistake as Angus's kisses always had the effect of starting such powerful surges of desire that her mind, even when it wasn't mush, found it hard to work.

'Could you at least say something?' he asked, raising his head several minutes later. 'I'm dying here!'

'You don't want more children,' she reminded him, and he kissed her again.

'It was nothing to do with not wanting more children,' he reminded her at the next kiss break. 'It was fear for the mother of the children, and that's still there and very real and if you marry me and we have more children I shall probably drive you insane checking you for DVT after each and every birth.'

Even with a mushy brain this was beginning to sound quite hopeful, but it had all been very matter-of-fact. Was it just the attraction?

Which, given the way she was kissing him back, she'd find very hard to deny!

'Is there more?' she asked when she'd pulled away and replenished enough breath to form words.

'Of course there's more,' he told her, but he must have thought she meant more kissing because that's what happened. Eventually he broke away, this time holding her at arm's length and looking down at her with such tenderness she thought her heart might split in two and all her blood seep out.

'When you walked out of the coffee shop, I realised how much I loved you,' he said, his voice so deep and husky it ran across Kate's skin like the brush of butterfly wings. 'Then I thought of all I knew about you, and how you, of all people, deserve the family you crave. I knew then that even with my fear of losing another person I loved, if I married you I'd have to give you the children you deserved, because otherwise I'd lose you anyway. Does that make sense?'

Kate melted into his arms.

'Not a lot,' she whispered against his damp shirt, hoping these weren't his best casual clothes because by now they probably had quite a lot of paint on them. 'But it sounded really beautiful.'

'So, will you marry me?'

Would she?

Why the uncertainty?

Because it was so sudden?

'Oh, Angus!' She held him tight and hoped her words didn't come out as a wail. 'Do you really want this? Are you sure it's not just a reaction to Hamish's illness?'

He pushed her away again, looking deep into her eyes, studying her as if to read what she was thinking; but if *she* couldn't figure out what was going on in her head, how could he?

'I really want it,' Angus said, wondering how a decision he'd made in the cliff-top cemetery had somehow become so difficult. 'I know it won't be easy for you, taking on someone else's child, but you and Hamish seem to get on well.'

At least the smile *that* brought to her face chased away the look of worry it had held earlier, but doubts were now springing in *his* mind, bursting out like sprouting plants. She didn't love him. Couldn't think of a way to tell him, to let him down lightly! She could think of nothing worse than being Hamish's mother— Oh, hell! Perhaps he should kiss her again.

But as he tried to draw her close she held him back.

'Tell me again why you want this,' she asked.

'Because I love you,' he said, slightly puzzled as he was sure he'd told her that before.

'Really love me?' she asked, and now he *had* to kiss her. But this time he punctuated the kisses with words, telling her things he couldn't ever remembering saying before, about how wonderful she was—her empathy with patients' parents, her calm control in all situations in the operating theatre, the instinctive way she'd known that McTavish could rouse Hamish. Then the way she made him feel, ten foot tall and invincible, the way just looking at her roused his blood to fever pitch, the way thinking of her made his body hard at inappropriate times—a catalogue of love-reasons tumbling from his lips, lips that still stayed close to hers, kissing in between...

'Now it's your turn,' he finished, breathless from words *and* kisses.

She looked at him, pale green eyes alight with mischief.

'My turn to kiss you?' she teased.

'Your turn to tell me things, little witch!' he growled, his arms still loosely imprisoning her.

There was silence for what seemed forever to his overburdened heart, then she smiled a funny kind of smile that made her teeth gleam and her eyes light up.

'I love you, Angus,' she said, and that was it, but it was all he needed to hear. He drew her close again, her head resting above his heart, and held her so she could feel its excited beat, and feel the flush of heat in his body.

'That's all I need to know,' he managed, his voice so gruff with emotion he didn't recognise it as his own.

'All we need to know, as well,' another voice said, and Angus turned to see Juanita, Hamish and McTavish sitting on the yellow sofa, smug smiles on all their faces, although it wasn't really easy to read *smug* in the expression of a Highland terrier.

He frowned at all three of them but it had little effect.

'If you will propose to someone on their doorstep, you have to expect to have onlookers,' Juanita continued. 'We were actually coming over to invite Kate to Hamish's getting-better party on Saturday afternoon, and got here just in time for the show.'

Angus knew he should be angry but Kate was laughing helplessly, just standing there in paint-spattered dungarees, laughing and laughing. So instead of being angry he put his arm around her and drew her outside, stopping in front of the threesome on the sofa.

'Hamish, do you understand what's going on here?'

'You've been kissing Kate,' he said, with all the aplomb of a four-year-old who knows about kissing. 'I kissed Chloe at kindergarten—it's kind of fun.'

'I've been more than kissing Kate,' Angus said, squatting down in front of his son, praying this would go better than his proposal had—at first!

'I've been asking Kate to marry me, so that means she'll be your new mother.'

Hamish nodded, apparently shrugging off this momentous news.

'Juanita told me that ages ago,' he announced, causing his carer to shift uncomfortably on the sofa. 'She said that Kate was just what our family needed. We just had to wait for you to figure it out for yourself. I did say I'd ask Kate for you, but Juanita said you had to ask or it wouldn't be right.'

Angus gave up squatting and collapsed onto the ground. Kate was laughing again and hugging Hamish, while Angus considered ways a doctor could get away with murder. But Juanita must have read his mind, for she reached out and touched his shoulder.

'It was in your eyes from the first time you saw her,' she said gently. 'Love like that doesn't happen often, so you have to seize it while you can. I just hoped you'd have the courage to do that, and you did. Congratulations!'

She leaned forward and kissed him on the cheek, then hugged Kate.

'Come on, Hamish, let's go back inside. We've a party to plan, then a wedding to arrange—we're going to be really busy for a while.'

They disappeared back into their house, Hamish asking if you could have balloons at weddings and would there be cake. Kate collapsed onto the yellow sofa and smiled at the man who was pulling himself off the ground. He sat beside her and took her hand.

'It's real, then?' he asked in a bemused voice.

'I think so,' she replied, just as bemused. 'Actually, now Juanita and Hamish are in on the act, not to mention planning our wedding, I don't think we can get out of it.'

She clasped his fingers tightly as she spoke, the happiness welling so deeply inside her she needed him to anchor her to earth.

'Not to mention McTavish,' Angus reminded her, then he kissed her and she knew he was all the anchor she would ever need. In spite of all the storms she had weathered in her life, she was now safely in port....

With Angus by her side!

EPILOGUE

BABY Hannah arrived nine months after the wedding, her father in attendance at her birth, her brother, Hamish, her first visitor. Kate held the tiny mortal in her arms, her heart so full of love for all her family she was afraid she might burst.

'Can I take her to school for show-and-tell?' Hamish asked, poking a cautious finger into his sister's rosebud mouth.

'Not this week,' Kate told him, 'but soon. She and I can both go but you'll have to have a lot of practice in holding her before we take her there.'

'Are you mad?' Angus demanded when Hamish and Juanita had departed. 'He can't take a baby to school for show-and-tell—think of the germs?'

Kate grinned at him and used their linked hands to tug him closer.

'No more fears, remember,' she said, kissing him on the lips. 'We're a glass-half-full family. In fact, in my opinion, our glass is full and running over, so stop worrying about every little thing. Now take your daughter for a walk—I need a shower before she demands another feed.'

It was a test, and Kate knew it. She also knew how hard it would be for Angus to walk out of the room, so she swung her legs out of the bed and held them up for his inspection.

'No swollen calves, no aches and pains, no redness or tenderness. I am fine, Angus, and you know it, so go.'

He kissed her again, then lifted Hannah out of her arms and left the room, walking the corridor with her, talking quietly, telling her how much he loved her, how much he loved her brother, but most of all how much he loved her mother. Telling her about family, about her grandparents who were due out from Scotland any day and how, one day, she, too, would have children and her mother would have her dreams come true—she would be a grandmother....

FREE BOOKS OFFER

To get you started, we'll send you
2 FREE books and a FREE gift

There's no catch, everything is **FREE**

Accepting your 2 **FREE** books and **FREE** mystery gift
places you under no obligation to buy anything.

Be part of the Mills & Boon® Book Club™ and receive your favourite
Series books up to 2 months before they are in the shops and delivered
straight to your door. Plus, enjoy a wide range of **EXCLUSIVE** benefits!

 Best new women's fiction – delivered right to
your door with FREE P&P

Avoid disappointment – get your books up to
2 months before they are in the shops

No contract – no obligation to buy

We hope that after receiving your free books you'll
want to remain a member. But the choice is yours.
So why not give us a go? You'll be glad you did!

Visit **millsandboon.co.uk** to stay up to date
with offers and to sign-up for our newsletter

2 **FREE** books
and a
FREE gift

M0JIA

Mrs/Miss/Ms/Mr   Initials

BLOCK CAPITALS PLEASE

Surname

Address

Postcode

Email

🌹 MILLS & BOON®

NO STAMP
NEEDED!

@ MILLS & BOON®
Book Club

FREE BOOK OFFER
FREEPOST NAT 10298
RICHMOND
TW9 1BR

NO STAMP
NECESSARY
IF POSTED IN
THE U.K. OR N.I.

FAIRYTALE
ON THE
CHILDREN'S WARD

BY
MEREDITH WEBBER

First published in Great Britain 2010
Harlequin Mills & Boon Limited,
Eton House, 18-24 Paradise Road, Richmond, Surrey TW9 1SR

© Meredith Webber 2010

ISBN: 978 0 263 87920 9

Harlequin Mills & Boon policy is to use papers that are natural, renewable and recyclable products and made from wood grown in sustainable forests. The logging and manufacturing process conform to the legal environmental regulations of the country of origin.

Printed and bound in Spain
by Litografia Rosés, S.A., Barcelona

Emily dropped a kiss on her mother's cheek. 'Isn't it fun having Dad around?' she whispered, and suddenly Clare's spring of happiness wasn't bubbling quite as high.

She knew it wasn't jealousy she was feeling, but disappointment of some kind—disappointment that the life she'd been providing for her daughter hadn't measured up...

'You need my pearls—the ones Gran gave me,' Emily declared as she inspected her mother for the last time. 'Wait here.'

She ran off to her bedroom and returned with the pearls that had been her great-grandmother's, making her mother sit on the bed so she, Emily, could fasten them.

'There,' she said, 'you're beautiful. Dad will surely want to marry you now.'

Clare knew the words were nothing more than childish enthusiasm, but once again the joy of the morning dimmed, and despair wormed its way into her heart.

How could she resist if it became a matter of two against one?

CHAPTER ONE

OLIVER RANKIN hated being late. He was a man who believed there were no acceptable excuses for it, and condemned the rudeness of it. But he was undoubtedly running late, due mainly to car trouble on his drive from Melbourne to Sydney—trouble that had delayed him twenty-four hours while a part was sent, apparently by camel train, from Melbourne to the Victorian border.

Then there was Sydney peak-hour traffic—unbelievable!

Eventually, however, the latest fellow appointed to Alex Attwood's paediatric cardiac surgical team pulled into the parking lot at St James Hospital for Children, abandoned his car in a board-members-only parking spot and raced into the building.

Fortunately he'd spent a month with the team earlier in the year so he knew where to go, but he still only made the meeting with a couple of seconds to spare.

Relief swamped him!

Until—

The world whirled before his eyes. Low blood pressure—all the rushing...

He dropped into a chair as Alex introduced him to Angus, the new surgeon on the team, and reminded him he'd already met Kate. Then he closed his eyes, and opened them again.

Carefully.

The apparition had come right into the room, later than he was.

A totally beautiful, totally mind-blowing apparition…

'And this is Clare Jackson, our new perfusionist,' Oliver heard Alex say. 'I'm more delighted than I can tell you to welcome Clare to our team as she trained in the US at the same hospital as Theo, and the oldies on the team will know how good he was.'

Oliver battled to sort out the disbelief in his head, to actually accept that the woman who still, from time to time, haunted his dreams was right here in this room.

Impossible!

Except it wasn't! There she was, head tilted towards Alex, so he saw her in profile, and caught the long line of her neck—the neck he'd loved to—

Clare Jackson?

He'd had the list of team members' names for a couple of weeks, but as she'd shown up on that as C. Jackson and most perfusionists he'd worked with had been males, he hadn't given a thought to the coincidence of surnames.

Alex was talking, but the words didn't penetrate Oliver's brain. Not only was Clare right here in this room, but apparently she was a team member. He'd be working with her.

She was a *perfusionist*?

From actress to lifesaving medical equipment expert in ten short years?

'Clare!' he'd managed to blurt out when they'd been introduced.

She'd nodded, lustrous dark hair swirling around her head, brown eyes half hooded, long eyelashes hiding any emotion those eyes might reveal at this unexpected reunion.

'Oliver,' she'd said, her voice still so familiar a tremor of excitement had shaken his body.

He tried to concentrate on Alex's introductions to the rest of the team, but how could he? He snuck a glance at Clare, and was annoyed to see that *she* seemed totally unfazed by this incredible coincidence.

Clare held her body very still, glad she'd learned how to do this years ago—back when she was a drama student at university, back when she'd first met Oliver.

Besides, if she held her body very still it might not fall apart, which was what it was threatening to do any moment.

Her body *and* her mind!

That he should be here—on the same team—was so unbelievable she had to wonder if it was some giant conspiracy of the Fates. Of course, even ten years ago, Oliver had been headed for a paediatric specialty, but he'd never mentioned surgery.

Whatever, it was indisputably Oliver sitting on the other side of the room, ignoring her in the politest possible way. Although what could he have said?

Long time, no see?

Not for Oliver the trite phrase, nor even idle conversation. The problem was that eventually the meeting would end and they would have to leave the room and *some* kind of conversation would obviously have to take place!

He'd come to claim Emily!

Nausea roiled in her stomach as the thought struck like the flick of a whip, but common sense prevailed. He'd obviously been as shocked to see her as she was to see him, and if he'd wanted his child surely he'd have got in touch back when she'd told him about the pregnancy.

Or in the intervening years?

And the fact that he hadn't—that he obviously *didn't* want to know his daughter—hardened her heart against him once again.

She could handle this! She could handle *anything*!

Easy to think, harder to do. Fear for her daughter fluttered in her heart, fear for Em's emotional stability.

Her mind ran wild.

Now he *was* here, wouldn't he *want* to see his daughter—to get to know her?

And if he still refused to acknowledge her, how would that affect Em?

Thinking about her daughter opened up a void so deep and black Clare felt as if she was teetering on a precipice, about to be plunged into a bottomless abyss.

Yet how could she *not* think of Emily, *not* put her first?

She'd have to talk to Oliver, find out what he wanted and whether Emily was part of it. Then she—perhaps they—could work out how to get father and daughter together—or not—with the least possible upheaval in Emily's life.

She sneaked another glance at the man causing such havoc in her mind, and this time felt her heart turn over. Silver threads had infiltrated his sandy hair at both temples, lending him an air of distinction, but Oliver had always been a distinguished-looking man—tall, lean, tanned, with dark brows above those startling pale green eyes. In profile slightly hawkish, the long thin nose tipped down just slightly at the end.

Pointing to his lips?

That had been a stupid fantasy of hers in her youth, for Oliver Rankin had the most beautiful mouth she'd ever seen, on a man or woman.

Oliver!

Huge inward sigh!

She tried to concentrate on Alex's words, but her mind was way back in the past.

With Oliver…

How had things gone so disastrously wrong between them? How had she been stupid enough to walk out on him?

Because he didn't want the child you yearned for, she reminded herself. Didn't want a child at all and definitely not right then for all it would have been an ideal time as far as you were concerned. But part of the stupidity had been thinking he'd come after you, and that somehow the two of you could have patched things up.

That hadn't happened!

She'd spent a miserable Christmas at home on the farm with her family, then the realisation had dawned that, wanted or not, she was going to have a baby.

Tentative delight…

Quickly quelled at the thought of Oliver's reaction.

Which hadn't come!

Unable to contact him by phone or email, she'd finally written, but when he hadn't answered her letters—had ignored her unexpected news—she'd decided she'd have to forget all about him, which, she'd admitted to herself even then, was easier said than done. Until the diagnosis of her father's illness had turned her family's life upside down and concern and grief for him had swamped the pain of losing Oliver. Then, within weeks of Em's birth, life had changed so irrevocably Oliver had been the last person she'd been thinking of.

No, that was wrong. She'd longed for him—for his presence, his support, to have him there to share her dread and fear....

And not having him, she'd turned to the man who *was* there—

She shuddered as she shook the memory away, and concentrated on what Alex Attwood, the team leader, was saying.

'Oliver, Kate and Clare, you'll all be working with Angus tomorrow. Clare, I know you've settled into your flat, so maybe you could show Oliver where his is. Did I tell you he's taking the other flat in Rod's house?'

Of course Alex hadn't told her! Excited as she'd been at coming back to Australia and getting a job in such an elite unit, she'd still have remembered if someone had said, Oh, and a chap called Oliver Rankin will be living next door! Not only remembered, but packed up and left.

No, she didn't run from men any more, but she'd have had time to at least think about this situation, to prepare herself.

To prepare Emily?

Oh, sweet reason, *what* was she going to do about Emily? For one crazy moment she thought of phoning the school and asking if they could take her as a full boarder rather than a weekly one, but it was hard enough on both of them to be separated five days a week.

Alex had turned to Oliver, and was explaining. 'The flat I arranged for you is in my father-in-law's house just down the road from the hospital. Rod Talbot, my father-in-law, is in a wheelchair so he has the ground-floor apartment and has turned upstairs into two small but comfortable flats. Of course, you don't have to stay there. Once you get to know the area, you might find somewhere that suits you better. Because of the proximity to the hospital, the flats are easy to let—not that Rod needs the money.'

'Rod Talbot?' Oliver repeated, his voice stirring so many memories in Clare's body she found herself shivering. 'Is he the writer?'

Alex nodded, and while Oliver talked about how much he enjoyed Rod Talbot's books—Oliver having time to read?—Clare muddled over the other information she'd received. The bit about Oliver being in the other flat in Rod Talbot's house—the flat with the door right opposite her door. Oliver living so close, sleeping so close…

A tremor of memory ran through her body before she brought her mind firmly back to the major problem.

Oliver spending his weekends next door to her and Emily!

Once again her reaction was flight. They'd go back to the States; she'd always find work there. But she steeled herself against such weakness—flight *wasn't* an option. She wasn't an emotional young woman any longer; she was a grown-up, mature—a qualified and respected career woman with an important position in a team that saved children's lives.

Even if she *did* feel like a teenager right now, with all the confusion and angst and dreadful insecurity that came with the transition from child to adult.

The meeting was breaking up, the anaesthetist from the second team taking the new surgeon off to the child-care centre. Dear heaven, had Oliver married again? Would he have children?

No, he'd been adamant about that, about never having children. That was why they'd split up. To a certain extent Clare had understood, because it had been soon after he'd found out a little about his own past, found out his life had been built upon a lie.

Thinking about that time—how hurt Oliver had been—diverted her thoughts from Oliver's marital arrangements, although if there *was* a wife, what would *she* think about Em?

It was all Clare could do not to wail out loud. How could this be happening to her? And now, when both she and Em were so excited to be back in Australia?

She pulled herself together with an effort.

Best not to think about Em! Not here, not now…

And it was useless to be speculating about Oliver's marital state, let alone whether he had children or not, although Rod had told Clare hers was the larger of the two flats, so a wife and children could hardly fit into the other one.

This realisation made her feel a little easier for all of five seconds, until it occurred to her he could have left his wife and kids—if he'd weakened on the children stand—in Melbourne while he settled in.

'Clare.'

Her name in his voice, a sound she'd never thought to hear again. *No-one* said her name as Oliver did! And no-one else, with just that one word, could send those stupid shivers down her spine.

After ten years?

It was unbelievable.

She'd heard of muscle memory—sportspeople talked about it. Was there such a thing as nerve memory, that every nerve in her body remembered…?

He was close now, waiting for her. The composure he wore like a well-cut suit to hide the emotional Italian inside him was so familiar she wanted to reach out and touch him, to feel the warmth of the man beneath that cool facade.

Was she mad?

Touching Oliver would be disastrous—had always been disastrous!—because one touch had never been enough.

She dug through her memory for an image of that last morning, not long before Christmas, when, all composure gone, fury and resentment had flared from his body and burnt in his eyes. That was the Oliver she needed to keep in mind.

Which was okay as far as resisting his appeal went, but what about the rest? What about Emily?

Clare felt physically sick, nausea spreading through her body. How could this have happened? She pulled herself together with a mammoth effort, hoping outwardly at least she might look composed.

'So we're to be neighbours,' she said, offering a polite smile, while her bewildered heart beat a wild tattoo inside her chest, and her thoughts ran this way and that like mice in a maze.

'It seems that way.'

Were his words strained? Was Oliver feeling the same mix of disbelief, and confusion—and surely not excitement?—as she was?

Of course he wouldn't be. For one thing, Oliver didn't do confusion.

Her heart skittered again but this time it was nothing to do with excitement—more like dread and fear and trepidation. She *had* to say something.

'I did write to you, you know.'

It sounded pathetic but at least it caught his attention.

'When?' he demanded, his voice hard and tight.

So hard and tight the tiny bit of courage that had prompted Clare to tell him faded, which meant the next words came out all breathless and confused.

'End of January, and again later in the year.

'You wrote to me at the end of January? Wasn't that a bit late, considering it was before Christmas you walked out? I'd definitely moved on by then, physically and emotionally.'

Pain stabbed through Clare's body at the last words, but what was he saying?

'You didn't get *any* letters from me—then or later?'

Glacial green—that's how Oliver's eyes could look… and *were* looking now.

'No.'

He shook his head to emphasise the word and, knowing he would never lie to her, Clare felt a stab of deep resentment—not to mention pain—as she realised he didn't know about her pregnancy. He didn't know he had a daughter, a daughter who would be right there in the flat next door to his come Friday!

She had to tell him!

Easy enough to have the thought but how to do it?

And when, and where?

This was hardly an appropriate time or place and, what's more, he was talking to her again, saying something, although with the wild furore going her mind it was a struggle to make out the words.

Forcing herself to focus, she realised his conversation was nothing more than the polite inquiries of old acquaintances catching up.

'But a perfusionist? What made you change course? What happened to life on the stage?'

Clare cast an anxious glance behind him, but there was no-one nearby to overhear an almost honest answer.

'Long story short, I moved to Queensland and studied science. I met a perfusionist who used to work with Alex when he was in Melbourne. I learnt more about it and decided it was the dream job as far as I was concerned. I began my studies in Brisbane, then went to Chicago to get more qualifications and experience, and here I am.'

Oliver knew he was staring at her, replacing his mental image of a twenty-five-year-old soap-star Clare with this more mature adult version—more mature, and even more beautiful. And the reaction in his chest was an ectopic heartbeat, nothing more. Ectopic heartbeats happened to some people all the time, and most people some time in their life....

But if he read the signs correctly, she was feeling even more strain at this unexpected meeting than he was.

'Alex was saying we're going to be neighbours.'

Could he really be having this stilted conversation with Clare? Clare who had laughed and loved and thrown herself into life with enormous energy and enthusiasm? Thrown herself into their relationship, making every moment they were together special and intense.

Until the day he'd told her he didn't want a baby and, unable to believe he'd never mentioned this before, unable to even discuss it with him, she'd walked out....

And he'd let her go, furious at her lack of understanding of his situation—*his* feelings in all of it! How could he have contemplated fatherhood when he didn't know who his own father was, didn't know himself? And how could he have considered marriage when his closest experience of it—his mother's three attempts—had been so disastrous?

He was reminding himself of this justification when Clare spoke again.

'You were saying you've read our landlord's books?'

'There's no need to sound so surprised,' he grumbled, memories of the past bothering him more than he'd thought possible. 'I've time to read these days.'

She smiled at him and he felt his heart miss another beat. Frequent ectopic heartbeats might be indicative of a problem of some kind, his medical brain told him.

'You didn't have time for any relaxation back then,' she said.

Except with you, he thought but didn't say, for there was a barrier between them, like a glass wall through which he could see and hear but not touch. Not that he would touch her, of course. No matter how much his fingers tingled at the thought.

Of course there'd be a barrier between them. It had been ten years; they'd split up. There were issues— wasn't that the word people used these days? So many unresolved issues it was more like a brick rampart than a glass wall between them.

Back to the present!

'My car's illegally parked downstairs. Can I follow you to the flat?'

'You can give me a lift.'

The moment the words were out of her mouth Clare regretted them. She needed to get away from Oliver, not spend more time with him, especially not more time in the privacy a car offered.

She needed time to think things through, to work out how on earth she was going to tell him about Emily.

Not that he deserved to know! He hadn't wanted a child.

The tiny whisper from one corner of her brain was tempting, but she slapped it down. Of course he'd have to know, and now they'd come together, didn't Em deserve to know her father? Hadn't Clare always told Em that one day they'd find him so she could meet him?

But 'one day' in Clare's mind had been when Em was eighteen or so—an adult who would understand the traumatic period of time that had been Clare's pregnancy, not to mention the aftermath of Emily's birth!

She should have directed him to the flat; it was just down the road. But here he was, saying he'd be delighted—ever polite, Oliver Rankin—and putting out a hand to usher her towards the door.

She moved, just in time to avoid contact with him, but knew that as well as the Emily problem, she had to sort *herself* out, to strengthen her body against the insidious physical weakness just seeing him again had caused. There was too much at stake for her to be distracted by attraction.

'I need to speak to Alex about something, so I'll meet you downstairs. The easiest way is to take the blue exit from the car park. I'll be down there near the gate in five minutes.'

Alex was still at the front of the meeting room, stacking some papers he'd spread out earlier. What excuse could she give? What question could she ask?

Had he noticed her hesitation that he looked up?

'Everything all right, Clare?' he asked. 'Emily settled in at school?'

'Just fine and dandy, and yes, she loves it,' she replied, hovering by her chair while Oliver left the room. But Alex's question had reminded Clare that Alex and Annie knew Emily, and Rod knew Emily—it wasn't as if you could keep a nine-year-old a secret.

Clare dropped her briefcase, which gave her an excuse to sit down. Knowing she couldn't just sit, she leant down to retrieve the leather case, fiddling with the catches on it while she tried valiantly to regain the poise on which she prided herself, the composure she'd fought so hard to achieve!

'I only know of Angus from his colleagues, but Oliver worked with us earlier this year,' Alex was saying. 'He's a fine surgeon, and if Angus is even half as good as people say he is, we've got a team that you'll discover is every bit as good as the ones you've already worked with. At least, I hope you find it that way.'

Clare smiled at him. He was so *nice*! He and Annie, his wife, had invited her and Emily for dinner the previous Saturday, and seeing their relationship—the obvious love they felt for each other—had left Clare wondering why relationships worked for some people and not for others.

Her body tightened at the memory…

Ached…

Oliver eased his car out of the parking space, thankful he hadn't been clamped. The signs to the blue exit were clear and easy to follow, but it took some manoeuvring to reach it. Clare came hurrying towards him, the movement blurring her image so he saw the beautiful girl who'd first caught his attention—the girl he'd thought was his for ever—running eagerly to meet him.

He couldn't fool himself about ectopic heartbeats any longer; his body was reacting to this bizarre reunion, to her presence, although that could be explained away as well. It was a while since he'd had a relationship with a woman, put off women by the words of his most recent lover who'd informed him he was nothing but an empty shell of a man, with no understanding of love whatsoever.

The woman Clare, not the girl he'd known, climbed into the car and pointed ahead.

'We go through the lights and straight down that road across from the park. I think most of the team seem to live along here, though maybe not the nurses, who'd be local Sydney people. It's such a pleasant walk to work I haven't considered buying a car yet.'

I, not *we*, Oliver thought, then he had to ask.

'You're on the team list as C. Jackson? You never married?'

He sensed her withdrawal and knew the glass wall was very definitely back in place.

'Once, for a very brief time. It was a mistake,' she said lightly, turning to look out the window at the houses they were passing. 'We're four more down, the house with the red door. There's a common foyer on the ground floor, and stairs up to a landing. The two flats open off that. They're fully furnished and very comfortable but I guess Alex already told you that.'

She might as well have said, Mind your own business, changing the subject from marriage to accommodation so swiftly, yet the thought of Clare with someone else had sent a shaft of pain through his belly.

Ridiculous, of course; he'd been with other women.

He pulled up outside the house she'd indicated, double-parking as all the marked spaces were already occupied.

'There's a garage around the back. Rod has a vehicle that's been adapted for a wheelchair but there'd be room for another car. Drive on and I'll show you how to get into the lane. Sorry, I didn't think of it earlier.'

Clare knew she was babbling as he followed her directions, but sitting in the close confines of the car with Oliver was even worse than she'd imagined. Somehow she'd been transported back to when they'd met and she'd fallen so helplessly in love—to when *any* time with Oliver was special. Her stupid body was responding to his presence, her physical delight totally uncontrollable no matter how much she tried to overcome it with strong mental warnings.

Even the panic and worry she was feeling over Em did little to dampen her reactions.

'Park here—I'll get the gate. You can ease the car into the yard while I go in and check with Rod if it's okay to use the garage.'

Finding the gate shut had been a relief. She all but leapt from the vehicle, opening the two sides of the gate, then hurrying to the rear door of Rod's flat.

He was in the small conservatory at the back, his gnarled arthritic fingers pecking furiously at the keyboard of his laptop. She knocked on the glass.

'I hope I haven't ruined your train of thought,' she apologised, 'but Oliver, Dr Rankin, has arrived and has a car. Can he park it beside yours in the garage?'

Rod waved away her apology and wheeled towards her, coming out to meet his new tenant.

'Can't help you with your cases, mate,' he said to Oliver a little later when the car was snug inside the garage and Oliver was heaving two cases from the trunk.

'I can,' Clare found herself offering, but Oliver, being Oliver, refused her offer, carrying them both himself.

'Come through my place,' Rod suggested, and led the way into his flat, always neat and tidy, the minimum of furniture allowing his chair to move freely through the apartment. He opened his front door, showed them into the foyer and handed Oliver a set of keys.

'Clare will take you up,' he said.

'No papers to sign? No lease agreements?' Oliver asked.

'If you're working for Alex, you're okay,' Rod replied. Then he smiled. 'Actually all the financial details will be in a folder on your kitchen bench. Annie, my daughter, organises all of that for me. Her phone number is there as well as mine, so phone if you need anything or have any questions.'

He then looked from Oliver to Clare before he added, 'Or ask Clare—she's been here a week now, settling in, so she knows her way around.'

He turned from Oliver to Clare and added, 'Have you heard from Emily this week? Does she still think the school's the best in the world?'

Emily! Emily! Emily!

The name hammered in Clare's head, but she *had* to reply.

'She still loves it,' she managed to say, although her vocal cords were so tight it was a wonder the words came out.

'Emily?' Oliver repeated as he followed her up the stairs.

Could she faint? Clare wondered. Faint and topple backwards down the stairs, possibly breaking her neck which right now, extreme though it might be, seemed preferable to answering Oliver's question.

'My daughter,' she managed, forcing the words through even tighter vocal cords, so she sounded shrill, if not hysterical.

'Fancy that! So you got the child you wanted,' Oliver said as they reached the landing. The ice in his voice was visible in his eyes as he looked down at her and added, 'Got the child and dumped the husband once his usefulness was over? Was that how it worked?'

Clare could only stare at him, her mind a chaotic battlefield, one voice yelling at her to tell him right now, another suggesting physical assault, while a third was advocating flight. She steeled herself against them all, looked him in the eyes and, hoping she sounded far more cool and in control than she felt, said, 'You never used to be spiteful, Oliver.'

After which she turned away to unlock her door, and dive into the sanctuary of her flat. Oliver's voice saying her name was the last thing she heard before she shut him out.

She leaned against the door, shaking with the hurt he'd inflicted, trying to breathe deeply, desperate to stem the waves of panic that washed through her mind and body.

Ten deep breaths, wasn't that the rule—no, maybe that was counting to ten before you murdered someone. Well, there was an idea!

Three deep breaths…

Now think rationally!

Monday was as good as done, which meant she had four more days—four days to find a way to tell Oliver Emily was *his* daughter before Em came home and almost inevitably met him in person.

Clare's mind went back into panic mode and breathing deeply didn't seem to help.

Of course she had to tell him. Forget that his reaction just now had been so hateful. He *had* to know!

But the hub of it all was Emily. As far as Clare was concerned, Emily's welfare, her happiness and emotional stability, had to be protected at all costs. Forget how Oliver might feel about Em's mother, forget how Em's parents might feel about each other—or whatever kinds of messes they'd made of their respective lives—at the heart of whatever lay ahead was Emily's well-being.

CHAPTER TWO

OF ALL the impossible things to have happened! Oliver set his cases down in the small foyer and took a look around. Small sitting area, the open plan revealing a dining nook in a bay window and a kitchen behind a high bench at the back.

She had a child.

Stop thinking about Clare; look around your new home.

He could move; Alex had said it would be okay.

No, look around.

Neat, tastefully furnished, all he needed in the way of space. He turned aside, into a reasonably sized bedroom, again a bay window, this one overlooking the front yard and the street and park across the road, while down a small hall he discovered a bathroom and a second bedroom, small, but furnished with a good-size desk as well as a bed, so it was obvious any single tenant would use it as a study.

Or a tenant with a child could use it for the child.

How could he live next door to Clare's child—the child he'd denied her?

A child who wasn't a toddler, if she was at school. Why hadn't he realised just how desperate Clare had been?

Because he'd assumed getting pregnant had been a whim, that's why. Possibly something to make his commitment to her more—

More what?

Binding?

No, she'd known all along he had no intention of marrying and he'd assumed she'd understood that meant no children.

He closed his eyes but her image was once again imprinted in his mind. Not the image from the past, but the image of the new Clare, more heart-stoppingly beautiful than ever.

He swore quietly to himself. Why was he letting her affect him this way? On top of which, the fact that she had a child was none of his business. Where was his self-discipline? Surely he was professional enough that he could treat her as a colleague.

But even as that thought formed in his head another part of his brain was echoing with mocking laughter. As if that's possible, it was saying, when your libido jolts to attention any time she's around. Ectopic heartbeats indeed—be honest, it's lust, mate!

Had it been more than lust the first time? Maybe not love—he wasn't sure what love entailed—but definitely he'd felt a deep affection for her. How could he not when she'd been so beautiful and open and honest?

So loving!

Did she still see their relationship as five wasted years?

No! It was in the past. This was now. And if the child—Emily, Rod had said—was at school, Clare hadn't exactly hung around mourning their break-up.

He gripped his head hard in his hands and squeezed to stop the mental arguments and to shut out the memories.

He would *not* think about Clare! He would *not* think about the past. He would move on, continue moving on, and if a tiny part of his mind kept questioning whether he'd ever really moved on from Clare emotionally— well, it was such a quiet voice he could ignore it.

She'd moved on, that was for sure. Changed careers, had a child—he doubted she'd ever given him a passing thought.

Until today, of course…

So?

Forget the past!

He took a deep breath, retrieved his cases, carried them through into the bedroom and began unpacking. He had chests with household items awaiting despatch in Melbourne, wanting to settle in and make sure he liked the flat before having them forwarded on, but for now all he needed to unpack were clothes, the one set of sheets he'd brought with him, a couple of towels and books— lots of books, although many more were in the chests. Reading had become his escape, but from what?

It was the first time he'd asked himself that question and now he had to probe further. Was it an escape from thinking too deeply about the sterility of his life? Or an escape from the inner emptiness his old girlfriend had pointed out to him? Or even an escape from feeling anything at all—for anyone…?

He gave a scoffing laugh, and shook off the stupid introspection. Reading was an escape from the intensity of his work, nothing more! And this unfamiliar delving into his psyche was the result of tiredness, having driven through the night to make the meeting this morning, stopping only for a couple of short breaks for safety's sake.

And considering work, rather than the escape from it, he should read up on tomorrow's op. With specialists all over the world, someone was always trying something new—discovering a tidier, or more effective, solution for the myriad problems they encountered.

He found his laptop, opened it on the desk in the second bedroom and settled down to search the internet. Hours later, stiff and tired, he closed the laptop and went in search of food—or information about food.

He found the folder in the kitchen and leafed through it. There was a selection of takeaway menus at the back of the notes—ha, food! He selected one and made a phone call. He'd eat, then shower, and get a good night's sleep—practical, sensible decision making, that's what was needed here.

A tap at the front door, his flat's front door, made him wonder how people got in—how his pizza would get in. Did the outer door have a bell of some kind, an arrangement whereby it could be opened from upstairs? Had Annie's notes explained? He'd read them again, but first see who was at the door.

Clare!

A very twitchy, uptight-looking Clare for all she smiled politely at him before explaining, 'I thought I should tell you about the doors. On your keys you'll have a bigger shiny silver key, it's for the deadlock on the outside door, but if someone comes to visit you there are bells outside the front door. I've just labelled your bell with your name. You'll hear the ring inside, and the button on that phone thing in the hall—this… Pressing it releases the door lock.'

She'd come in to show him the door-opening mechanism and was so close he could have taken her in his arms right there and then. He could feel her in his arms, feel her curves snug against his body, smell the perfume of her hair in his nostrils. He'd bend his head, just a little, to capture her lips—

He was losing it! Seriously insane! He had to pull himself together, get sorted, all that stuff.

'Thanks,' he managed when she turned to look at him, perhaps puzzled by his wooden stance and lack of response.

'No worries,' she said, then she frowned and looked more closely at him. 'Are you okay? I know it's hardly flattering to tell someone they look terrible, but you look exhausted.'

'Car trouble on the way from Melbourne meant I had to drive through the night. One good night's sleep and I'll be fine.'

Clare turned to leave, uncertain whether to be glad or sorry. She'd buoyed herself up to tell Oliver about Emily, using the key explanations as an excuse to knock on his door. The plan was she'd casually offer dinner, and they could sit down in a civilised fashion and discuss the situation, though the problem of quite how she'd bring it up still loomed large in her mind.

But seeing how tired Oliver looked and finding out why, it was immediately obvious this wasn't the time to be telling him he had a daughter, especially as he was operating the next morning. What he needed was a good night's sleep, not a bombshell that was likely to rock his world and quite possibly prevent any sleep at all.

Part of her was relieved, but the other part aggravated that the telling would continue to hang over her head.

Then there was dinner—he had to eat… Should she still ask?

'Thanks for explaining about the locks and keys,' he said as she dithered in the doorway, so conscious of his body she wondered if he could feel the tension building in hers. In her mind his hand reached out for her, touched her shoulder, drew her close. She'd sink against him, feeling her body fit itself to his and—

The jangling buzz of the outside bell sounded in his flat, shocking her out of the stupid dream. He smiled as she looked at him, ashamed of her thoughts and puzzled by the intrusion.

'Good thing you labelled my bell,' he added. 'I ordered a pizza for dinner.'

As Oliver pressed the button to release the front door lock, using the phone to tell the delivery person to come on up, Clare scuttled back across the landing, all but diving into the safety of her own flat.

Although as a refuge it was now severely lacking in serenity and peace, given who her neighbour was, and the wayward turns her mind was taking.

Back when he hadn't replied to her letters, she'd put him out of her life, swearing never to think of him again.

But not thinking about him had proven difficult when their child had inherited his green eyes and curving, inviting lips.

* * *

Clare knew she needed a good night's sleep, but how could sleep come when the huge, insurmountable problem of how to tell Oliver was cluttering up her mind and sitting like an elephant on her chest?

Earlier, when she'd gone in with the key excuse, she'd decided just coming out with it would be the best. Oh, by the way, my daughter, Emily, is your child.

But now that seemed impossibly, horribly flippant. She *had* to find some better way to say it.

Oliver, there's something you should know?

No, that wouldn't work. She'd lose courage after the Oliver part and ask about his mother or something equally inane.

Could she begin with self-justification? I did try to contact you; I phoned and wrote, then—

No, she couldn't do that because it would mean explaining about Dad dying and even now thinking of that time still hurt too much for her to talk about it.

Finally, with herculean determination, she lulled herself to sleep, only to wake before dawn, tired, cranky and so uptight she thought her limbs might snap apart as she moved.

But move she did. Although she'd spent many hours at the hospital the previous week, getting to know the machine she would be operating, now she was anxious to get up to the theatre for one last check.

She showered and dressed, blotting everything from her mind except work, excited yet slightly apprehensive about her first day as part of the team.

Slightly apprehensive?

Understatement of the year, and although she was focusing on work, the other problem set aside, it had to be the thought of working with Oliver that had her twitching like a snake on drugs.

An image of him flashed across her mind—the now-Oliver with silver streaks in the tawny hair, and fine lines at the corners of his green eyes. More lines forming parentheses in his cheeks when he smiled, his lips still as mesmerising as ever, a pale line delineating their shape.

Em's lips!

But it was better to think of Oliver's lips than the problem of Emily right now. Thinking about Emily would put her mother into a panic again and a panicking perfusionist was of no use to anyone.

Unfortunately thinking of Oliver didn't do her much good either. Look at it this way, she told herself. Yes, it was an unbelievable quirk of fate that had brought them together again, but they'd met as colleagues now, nothing more. Two professionals, working in the same team, working to save the lives of tiny babies.

Forget the fact you still feel an attraction to the man!

Forget Emily—well, not Em herself, but the problem she presented right now. Concentrate on work.

In the kitchen, she turned on the simple pod coffee machine that had been her treat to herself when she'd moved to Sydney, and dropped two slices of frozen fruit loaf into the toaster. Had Oliver found the shops? Did he have food to eat? Coffee?

The temptation to tap on his door and ask him was almost overwhelming, but it was barely six and their official working hours began at eight so it was likely he was still asleep. Besides, the more times she saw him outside of work hours, the more opportunities she would have had to tell him about Emily, and the angrier he'd be when she *did* tell him, that she hadn't told him earlier.

Did that make sense or was her lack of sleep making her stupid?

She sipped her coffee, returning to the mental excuse of not knocking on the door in case he was still sleeping.

An image of a sleeping Oliver popped obligingly into her head—Oliver in boxer shorts, his back bare, lightly tanned, the bones of his spine visible as he curled around his pillow in sleep. An ache started deep inside her, and she left her toast half eaten, the coffee cup still half full, hurrying to the bathroom to clean her teeth, then fleeing her flat which was, she realised, just far too close to Oliver's for her peace of mind. It was the proximity dogging her, reminding her, teasing at her body. If she moved—

But how could she when Alex had been kind enough to arrange the accommodation and she already felt settled here?

Or had done!

Although if she shifted…? *No!* her mind shrieked at her. Of course you have to tell him.

Oliver pushed his bedroom window to open it wider, sure there must be a breeze somewhere in the stillness of the summer morning. Below him the front door clicked shut and Clare strode into view, marching with great speed and determination up the path, then along the street, striding now—exercising or escaping?

But escaping from what? Not him, surely.

He laughed at the thought, a mocking laugh, but didn't leave the window, watching until a slight bend in the road took her out of sight.

Clare!

He showered and dressed, reminding himself that both of them had changed in the ten years since the split. Now they were mature adults and could meet and treat each other as professional colleagues, nothing more, though the thought of her with a child niggled at him.

For one thing, where was the child now? She hadn't had a child with her and there was no noise coming from next door.

Clare with a child.

Why did that hurt him?

The physical attraction he still felt towards her was probably nothing more than an emotional hangover from the past, some glitch in programming, possibly to do with the Italian revelations. And feeling this strong attraction, it was only natural that he'd been on the brink of taking her in his arms yesterday evening, when the front doorbell had sounded.

Saved by a pizza!

Think of food, not Clare.

Rod's daughter had left some basic groceries in the flat—milk and butter in the fridge, coffee, tea, bread and spreads in the pantry. He'd have to find the supermarket and do some shopping, and until then he could eat at the hospital. In fact, if he left now he could have breakfast there; maybe that's why Clare had left so early.

She wasn't in the little coffee shop in the foyer, nor in the canteen, so he ate a solitary breakfast, then made his way not to the teams' rooms but to the theatre, wanting to refamiliarise himself with the way Alex had it set up.

'Oh!'

Clare was there ahead of him and she must have sensed his presence, for the startled expression burst from her lips before he was fully through the door.

Not that she was unsettled for long, greeting him with a smile—a very professional smile—and a cheery, 'Good morning, Oliver,' for all the world as if they hadn't shared an extremely passionate relationship, albeit ten years ago.

'Do you always begin this early?' he asked, because two could play the calm and controlled game. She smiled again.

'First-night nerves,' she told him. 'I've spent a lot of time here in the past week, but I'm still anxious about the machine, which is stupid as it's exactly the same make of machine as I operated in the States. It's just that—'

She stopped abruptly and he saw a faint colour appear in her cheeks.

'Just that…?' he prompted, hoping professional conversation would halt the disturbances in his body.

'You'll think I'm barmy, but to me the machines have personalities, maybe idiosyncrasies would be a better word, and until I get to know each one personally I won't know what to expect.'

Clare watched him carefully as she explained her unease, and to her surprise, she caught no hint of a smile. In fact, Oliver was nodding as if he understood what she was saying.

'You have so much to think about, with the responsibility for the respiratory and circulatory functions of the lungs and heart. I can understand you wondering if the machine has quirks you need to watch for. You've got the oxygenator, the pumps, the filters, the reservoirs and tubing, so many component parts that can go wrong.'

And now he smiled, sending tremors of remembered delight through Clare's body, in spite of her determination to remain on strictly professional terms with him.

'But have things ever gone badly wrong for you? Has there ever been a disaster you couldn't overcome?'

She found herself smiling back at him, professionally, of course.

'Tubes kinking, the membrane oxygenator failing, the machine turning off automatically when a clot or bubble gets into the tubes? I've seen most of the calamities that can happen, and had to cope with a few, but generally the machines, providing they are serviced regularly and checked before every operation, work brilliantly.'

Oliver heard the pride in her voice and recognised the dedication she had to her profession—speaking of which...

'It still seems a strange choice for someone who had stars in her eyes and an established career as an actor.'

He saw her shoulders lift in a slight shrug.

'Things happened, Oliver, that changed my goals. I'd done well in science at school, so a switch to that seemed logical.'

Which would have made sense, only her voice had tightened as she spoke, and he sensed a tension in her

body. Or was he fooling himself that he was still so at-
tuned to her he could feel her emotion, sense that she'd
told maybe not a lie but certainly not the whole truth?

'Then perfusion.'

He shook his head, as much at his own imaginings
as at her choice of career. But at least her smile was
back—a bright smile now.

'If I'd known how much I would love this job I'd
never have bothered with anything else. What amazes
me is that there are so many jobs out there that no-one
even knows about. I mean, the career adviser at my
school didn't mention perfusionist as a career option. In
fact, he'd probably never heard of it either. By chance, I
met a perfusionist and that was it.'

'So here you are.' Nice, normal conversation; he'd
be able to handle this. Always assuming the attraction
he still felt towards her wasn't obvious to everyone who
came in contact with him when she was around.

She bent her head as she answered, presumably
checking some component of the machine, and Oliver
found himself studying her, once again imagining he
could sense tension in her voice.

'It can't have been easy, handling training and a
child.'

It was a throwaway remark, the kind anyone might
make, yet he saw her tense. No sensing it this time; he
actually saw her stiffen.

Why?

'Mum helped out.'

Obviously that was the only answer he was going to
get, so should he keep the conversation going?

Might as well; it was awkward enough as it was without silence extending between them.

'How old is she?'

More silence, then Clare looked up at him.

'She's nine,' she said, before returning to whatever she was doing, fiddling with the machine.

'Nine? As in nine years old?' he muttered as a rage he'd never felt before, not even when his real father had denied him, burnt through his body. 'You're telling me you were so desperate for a child you went from me to him, whoever he was? Or were you already seeing him? Cheating on me? Did he offer marriage? Is that what swayed you? And did he offer before or after you announced you were pregnant, eh?'

Clare had never heard such anger in his voice, yet this was hardly the time to refute his hateful accusations. He was about to operate on a vulnerable infant. He needed to be calm and composed, totally focused on the job, not struggling to comprehend the fact that he had a daughter.

What's more, *she* had to be calm and composed as well! Later she'd get angry. Later she'd tell him....

Right now, she had to defuse the situation somehow.

'It is none of your business what I did or didn't do, Oliver, and right now I really need to get on with this.' She looked up at him again, saw the harsh anger in his face and hated the contempt she read in his eyes. And though her own anger burned at the injustice of his words, she pushed it aside, adding calmly, 'And you probably want to check out the theatre, although didn't Alex say you'd worked with them before?'

For a moment she thought he'd reject the conversational shift, but when he nodded she knew she'd succeeded in tempering the tense emotional atmosphere in the room.

At least for the duration of the operation!

'I *have* worked here before.' Clipped, crisp words, but Clare knew he was turning his focus to work.

'Do we know yet if we have a patient?' she asked, pursuing professional conversation, although he was still unsettling her, prowling around the perimeter of the theatre, distracting her with his presence when she didn't need distraction.

'Last I heard about the TGA Alex listed yesterday was that he hadn't arrived,' he said, and this time his voice sounded more relaxed—*his* professional self taking over.

'So we wait,' Clare responded, determined to match his tone. 'If Angus is as good at doing a switch of the great arteries as Alex seems to think, it will be exciting to watch him at work. Do you know any more about the patient?'

Oliver shook his head.

'But you still have more contact with them than I do,' she added. 'I usually only get to meet patients when they come into Theatre, although with older children I sometimes do blood collection for autologous blood transfusions should one be necessary. My main contact with newborns is after the op if they go onto ECMO.'

Could she really be having this conversation with Oliver, when the echo of his accusations and the spectre of Emily hung in the room like twin thunder clouds?

'Extracorporeal membrane oxygenation—of course, you're in charge of those machines as well.'

'Terrible necessities,' Clare said. 'Some babies need them post-op but they can do so much damage to the organs if we're not really careful.'

She continued on about the problems the machine could cause, but Oliver had stopped listening to the actual words, hearing instead the confidence and professionalism in her voice, noticing the tension had lessened.

Maybe it had never been there. Maybe he'd imagined it!

Or maybe she was as good as he was at compartmentalising her life. It had taken him a mammoth effort, a few minutes ago, to block out the implications of the age of Clare's child, but he'd done it, because the baby they were about to treat had to be his sole focus for the next few hours.

His pager buzzed against his belt and he glanced at the message.

'Looks like it's all systems go,' he said, and heard Clare's pager buzz at the same time.

'Good luck,' she said, smiling now, no hiding the excitement in her eyes. She was rising to the challenge that lay ahead, totally professional, the adrenaline rush in her veins lighting her up from within.

So why was he seeing black shadows hovering over her—the shadow of another man, another man's child? Why was totally inappropriate anger festering inside him?

'Good luck yourself,' he said, blotting the dark clouds from his mind, repelling the anger from his body. In eighteen years of professional life he'd never allowed his work self to be distracted by outside issues and he wasn't about to start now.

And the tension he was feeling at the base of his spine was because he was working with a new team, nothing else.

Other members of the team breezed in, inconsequential chat filling the air as people went about their allotted tasks while the atmosphere in the theatre seemed to tighten in expectation of the operation that lay ahead.

'You're opening?' the circulating nurse asked Oliver.

In work mode now, totally focused, he nodded, then examined the instruments she'd laid out on a trolley. It would be his job to open the tiny chest, cutting through skin and the rib cage, using retractors to hold the ribs open and allow a clear field for operating.

'Do you need a small suture?' the nurse asked, and Oliver thought about what lay ahead. As he separated out the pericardium—the fine sheath of protective tissue that surrounded the heart—he would often take a tiny piece of it, and secure it to a spot in the baby's chest, in case the surgeon needed it later to repair a hole in one of the interior walls of the heart.

The baby!

It seemed impersonal to think of him or her that way, but every one of them was very real to Oliver and every one he was involved in saving was special, even though his contact with them, at this stage, was minimal.

The baby!

His mind wavered for a moment—Clare's baby, the one he hadn't wanted, intruding—but only for a millisecond.

'Leave a suture there—I'll ask Angus when he comes in. I know from working with Alex that he always likes to have a piece of tissue in reserve.'

The nurse slipped the threaded needle onto the tray, while Oliver checked he had all he needed, shifting a couple of instruments into an order he was used to, in spite of the fact he would rarely pick up an instrument himself.

'Okay, folks, we have a baby to save.'

Kate Armstrong, the anaesthetist, erupted into the room, nodding and smiling at everyone, then stopping beside Clare to discuss drugs and dosages. Oliver studied the two women—Clare, tall and straight, Kate smaller, but with so much animation in her face she seemed more of a presence. Her vibrant red hair was wrapped in a scarf, but its energy seemed to escape so she had an aura of liveliness about her.

Yet it was Clare who drew his eyes, although he didn't know this Clare at all....

He likes her. The thought came to Clare as she watched Oliver looking at Kate, and it niggled in her chest in a way it had no right to niggle, especially after the angry, hateful accusations he'd thrown at her earlier.

No, apart from whatever relationship he developed with Em, Oliver was no longer her concern. He could like whomever he cared to like, though for a moment Clare wished she had the same kind of lively personality Kate had—a personality that attracted men. Instead, she had a face and figure—outward things—that drew their attention.

The arrival of their patient put an end to any extraneous thoughts. As the nurses set the patient up for surgery, and Oliver, as the first assistant, began the simple part of the operation, Clare checked and rechecked her machine, watching the monitors, talking quietly to Kate from time to time, discussing the blood values they were getting.

But she watched Oliver as well, noticing how gently his hands touched the infant, how carefully he cut and opened up the little chest. She smiled to herself, remembering how much he'd loved his paediatric patients, back when they were together, how special he had thought each and every one of them.

Was that why she'd been so stunned when he'd said he didn't want children? Although they'd never discussed the subject until she brought it up that fateful time, she'd always assumed, somewhere down the track, Oliver, loving children as he did, would want children of his own.

CHAPTER THREE

ANGUS arrived and the operation proceeded smoothly, Clare relieved for the baby's sake when it was successfully completed. But her job wasn't done, not with the baby still on a support system. She and Kate accompanied him to the small recovery room off the main cardiac PICU, Clare concerned about her first patient as part of this elite team, while Kate explained that she always wanted to see her patients come out of the anaesthetic. When Kate left for a moment to check something on the ward, Clare looked down at the little boy with tubes and monitor leads practically obliterating his small body.

'They're so vulnerable,' she whispered to herself. 'But so valiant.'

'They are indeed! We do terrible things to their bodies and they come out of it so well.'

She looked up at his voice, still startled by it, still unnerved by the coincidence of Oliver being in the same team.

Unnerved, unsettled and, remembering his remarks in Theatre earlier, angry.

Definitely angry.

Very angry.

But when Angus came in to check on the patient, Oliver left.

'Look, there's no point in all three of us being here,' Kate said, soon after. She waved her hand towards Clare and Angus. 'Why don't you two grab a coffee break— in fact, it's past lunchtime. The canteen is good, and cheaper than the coffee shop on the ground floor. You know where to go?'

Why was Kate so keen to send them away?

Not that it mattered. Kate was right that they did not all need to be there. It was a very small room. Angus was apparently open to the suggestion, for he was already holding the door for Clare.

But it was Oliver she *should* be talking to. As hateful as his words had been earlier, she *had* to tell him! Not that she could tell him in a hospital canteen…

Although where *could* she tell him?

Was there an optimal place for telling a man he had a nine-year-old daughter?

'Yes, I'm glad that first one's over,' she said to Angus in reply to his polite conversation about the op. But as they reached the canteen she knew she had to stop asking herself impossible questions about the Oliver situation and toss the conversational ball back to Angus.

'I'm using the same machine, but did you find the set-up much different to the way you worked in the States?'

After that it was easy, normal conversation about work, but although Angus was a very good-looking man with dark hair and eyes and a soft Scottish accent that should be sending ripples up her spine, neither looking at nor listening to him did anything to her.

He was a nice man, she decided, a little reserved and without the magnetism that drew her to Oliver, but very nice all the same.

Magnetism?

Oliver?

Wasn't her reaction to him—the physical attraction thing—just a hangover from the past?

And how could she even think of being attracted to a man who thought so little of her?

There were no ripples up her spine from Angus because she was totally spineless!

'I really should go back,' she said as, coffee finished, the conversation dried up. She needed to escape, preferably to a dark cave where she could hide out while she sorted out her life.

Or at least until she worked out how to tell Oliver her child was also his.

A week ago, life had seemed so simple, been such an adventure. She and Em coming back to Australia, setting up house, just the two of them, for the first time. Now everything had erupted into chaos.

'Are you all right?' Angus asked, and Clare realised she'd been twisting her table napkin so tightly it had curled into something that looked very like a miniature noose.

'Nervous about the baby,' she said, hoping her voice wouldn't reveal her lie.

'So, let's check on him together,' Angus said.

Together was good. She wouldn't be on her own if they ran into Oliver.

Which they didn't, although the baby—now named Bob—had his parents with him at the moment, so Clare contented herself with sitting by the nurse on duty at his monitor, watching the information feeding out from all the paraphernalia attached to him.

Oliver didn't reappear, which was both a relief and a cause of anxiety. She *had* to talk to him!

But just imagining that conversation filled her with such apprehension she found herself literally shaking. Bob was doing well and she had no excuse to hang around so she made her way to the team tea room, thinking another strong coffee might settle her nerves and, once they were settled, surely her brain would start working again.

No, that was the coward's way out. Oliver wasn't in the PICU, but he'd have an office somewhere in the unit rooms. On his first full day of work, he wouldn't be seeing patients but he was likely to be in his office, reviewing files of children he would be seeing later in the week, patients he'd be taking over from the specialist who'd left the team.

Bypassing the tea room, and the meeting room next to it, Clare made her way down the corridor to where Becky, the unit secretary, had her office.

Was fate telling Clare not to do this now because Becky was absent from her desk?

Nonsense, the names are on the doors. You've passed Alex's and Angus's offices; Oliver's is probably next. It wasn't but it *was* further down the corridor. Dr Oliver Rankin!

Before she could lose her nerve as she had last night, Clare knocked and heard Oliver's voice bid her enter.

He was sitting at a wide desk, files stacked in neat piles all over it. The light from the window behind him threw his face into shadow, making any expression impossible to read, but just seeing him brought back the angry accusations he'd made earlier and the injustice of them made her own anger rise.

She was about to let fly—to just come out with the fact that Emily was *his* daughter—when he disarmed her with a smile.

And an apology!

'I had no right to speak to you as I did earlier,' he said, standing and coming around the desk to where three easychairs were set up with a small coffee table in the middle.

Now she could see his face, but although she studied it closely, she couldn't read the motive behind the words.

Should she accept them at face value?

When he had her so churned up she felt she might be physically sick at any moment?

No way!

'No, you had no right at all, Oliver,' she said, quelling the nausea that clutched at her stomach. 'But I haven't come to talk about that—well, not about what you said. But yes, about Emily, my daughter—our daughter.'

The words were out before she realised it, and now hung in the air between them like graffiti letters on a big balloon.

'*Our* daughter?'

Such steely contempt in his words and his eyes that Clare shivered, but Oliver had put her down once today; he wasn't going to do it again!

'Yes, *our* daughter,' she snapped. 'What with Christmas and being distraught over our break-up I didn't realise I was pregnant until late January, and then I tried to contact you but you'd left the apartment and your mobile number and email address had changed, and when I called the hospital they said you'd left but wouldn't tell me where you'd gone. I phoned your mother but she wouldn't speak to me, so I wrote to you at your mother's address and, now I've met up with you again, I realise you must never have got the letters, although at the time I did wonder if you hated me so much you didn't care about your child.'

The words came tumbling out so quickly Clare realised she must have practised them more often than she'd thought. Maybe in the dream state before she went to sleep some nights, when memories of Oliver had crept like whispers into her heart.

But now they *were* out she slumped into a chair, as if getting rid of them had stolen her strength.

Oliver looked at her, elbows on her knees, bent head held in her hands, an image that could be called despair.

Obviously he was thinking of how Clare looked because he couldn't take in the enormity of what she'd told him, and thinking about something else was far preferable to trying to make sense of the blurted-out confession.

He had a child?

Her child was his?

A girl called Emily?

It was a nice name.

He groaned and took a turn around the room, unable to believe he'd had such an irrelevant thought at a moment of such magnitude in his life.

'You wrote to me? Where?'

This wasn't quite the issue either, but anger had begun to burn deep inside him and he had to get it out.

'At the apartment and your mother's house. I even wrote care of the hospital but it was returned. I wrote when I couldn't contact you by phone or email, and I wrote again when Emily was born.'

Now some of his anger found a new target—oh, there was still plenty for Clare but right now it focused on his mother.

'She must have destroyed the letters,' he said, speaking to himself, hearing the tightness of his fury in his voice. 'But you could have phoned her again, told her about the baby—'

'Would she have passed on the information if she wasn't passing on the letters? Maybe she already knew, maybe she'd read them before destroying them. She never considered me good enough for her son, so would she want a grandchild if I was the mother?'

Clare looked at him and shook her head, adding in an exhausted voice, 'Anyway, it's all irrelevant now. You didn't know. I thought you did and I hated that you didn't care. The point is that Em's missed nine years of knowing her father, although I've talked to her about you, and now you—well, we, I suppose—have to decide where to go from here. Given that she's just started at a new school and is boarding for the first time, I don't want her upset.'

'Boarding? You've sent a nine-year-old to boarding school? Didn't I tell you what I thought of parents who dumped their kids in boarding schools? Don't you remember me telling you how much I hated it?'

Once again Oliver was aware this was a side issue, but it was all he could manage as his mind was still

struggling to accept he was a father. Clare was standing up again now, and she touched his arm as she
explained.

'She's a weekly boarder, so she comes home every
Friday and leaves again on Sunday evening. Up until
this year, Mum lived with us and looked after her when
I was studying or at work, but I knew it was time Mum
had a break—she's got other grandchildren to fuss over.
And Em's mad for horses so this school is ideal as they
can take riding lessons, and have horse camps during
the holidays. My cousin Caitlin is a senior at the school
and she's keeping an eye on Em as well.'

'Em!'

The name came out as a roar of pain or rage. Oliver
wasn't sure which it might have been; he only knew he
had to move, to get away from Clare before he exploded
and did or said something he might regret. He went
back behind his desk, staring at the neat stacks of files
he'd made on it, wishing his mind was as well ordered,
instead of the churning, swirling mess boiling around
inside his head.

He had a child, a daughter—Emily…Em!

Clare moved towards the desk, though warily, he
thought, stopping out of touching distance, her arms
wrapped around her chest as though she was cold, or
maybe fearful.

'I hated my name being shortened when I was at
school,' he snapped, and she stared at him as if she
couldn't fathom what he'd said, although more likely
she was puzzled as to why he'd said it.

Join the club!

'Oliver,' she said quietly, 'I know I've dumped a bombshell on you and you'll need time to think about it, but we don't have to talk about it any more right now.'

She reached out her hand as if to touch him across the table, to bridge the gulf that had widened between them, but anger still held sway within him and he turned away from the proffered hand, staring blindly out the window.

She *could* have found him!

She'd *chosen* not to!

And there was more to this than she was telling—the timing was just *too* suspicious.

He swung to face her.

'*You knew you were pregnant*—that's why you left! All that talk of it being a good time for you to take a break from your career, about how easy it would be to write you out of the show by sending you on an overseas holiday, then you could come back in later. You had it all worked out! When did you stop taking the pill? How far back had you planned this? Before Owen told me he wasn't my father, or did you do it after that, knowing how I felt?'

The words were like a fist to Clare's stomach and she flinched away from him.

But not for long!

'It was not planned,' she said, standing very upright and speaking with cold deliberation. 'Nor did I know when we parted. There is just no way I would have kept something like that from you. I thought you knew me well enough to realise that.'

No response, while his face, with the setting sun behind it, might have been carved in granite so little did it reveal.

'Anyway,' she continued valiantly, though her heart was pumping wildly and her body shaking with the tension, 'this is not about the past, and what did or didn't happen, but about Emily and whether or not you want to be part of her life as her father.'

'And you expect me to decide that now?'

The growled words seemed to Clare to contain a hint of menace, and once again her body flinched, but she stood her ground.

'No, Oliver. I know you need time to assimilate this, and to consider things, but you must realise I had to tell you.'

Oliver stared at her for a moment longer, then turned away again.

Had she been pregnant?

Surely it was too big a coincidence that she'd left him because he didn't want children, *then* discovered she was pregnant! Far too big a coincidence!

And as for not being able to contact him. She *could* have found him.

His anger built again, then faltered as a cool voice whispered through the random thoughts cartwheeling through his head.

She thought she had.

Maybe.

He wasn't ready to concede that yet.

'Oliver!'

He turned to face her again, taking in her upright posture, her head held high, challenge in every line of her body.

'This is not the time for recrimination,' she said, voice cool, although he thought he caught a slight waver in it. 'You can think what you like about me but what you have to decide is how much involvement you want to have with Emily, then we have to work out how and when to tell her. She has to come first in all of this. We're adults and we're supposed to be able to handle flak in our lives—she's a child and it's our duty to protect her.'

Oliver bit back the 'you're her mother, you tell her' response that leapt to his lips. Emotional reactions were *not* appropriate right now. Clare was right. They had to put the child first. But for possibly the first time in his life, his usually clear and analytical brain had gone AWOL. He couldn't string two thoughts together, let alone form a plan for introducing a nine-year-old to her father.

And did he want to be a father? It was all very well deciding in principle that he didn't want a child, but now he knew one existed, how was he going to handle it?

By rejecting her as first Owen and then his birth father had done to him?

Totally unacceptable.

Unthinkable.

Anger burned, directed once again, possibly unfairly, at Clare for putting him in this position, but before he could find words to release it, she was speaking again.

'Perhaps if you could get to know her as a person first, then we do the father thing later,' she suggested.

'You mean do things with the two of you at weekends, then in a few weeks, if she doesn't take against me for some reason, announce that I'm her father?'

Boy, was that ever a legitimate reason for anger release!

Clare felt her shoulders slump again as this new wave of Oliver's attack washed over her. She sat down again, the better to absorb it.

Of course they couldn't do that to Em.

'I'll have to tell her straightaway—explain you never got my letters, and so you didn't know about her. She knows your name anyway. I've talked about you—'

'And told her what?' Oliver demanded, fury still reverberating in his voice. 'That her father didn't care enough to want her? That I didn't want a child at all?'

His accusations were so unjust Clare couldn't help herself. She glared at him across the desk, although she knew anger only bred more anger and that arguing was futile.

'Well, did you? At least be honest, Oliver. We split up because a child was the last thing you wanted—then or ever. And you had logical reasons to back up your stance—your own childhood, not knowing who your father was, not wanting to pass on an uncertain heritage to a child. You were definite enough!'

But even through her anger she could still feel the manifestations of attraction, all the physical magnetism that Oliver had always exerted over her. And feeling them, looking at him, seeing his pale, tight face, she wanted nothing more than to go to him and put her arms around him, to comfort him as he grappled with this momentous, life-altering news.

She was pathetic.

After the way he'd behaved, *she* wanted to comfort *him*.

'How much does she know about me?'

The physical reactions lessened at the abrupt question, but at least it was something Clare could answer honestly.

'Quite a lot. She knows you're a doctor, a paediatrician, and from when she was quite young she decided off her own bat that the reason you weren't around like some other kids' fathers was because you were too busy looking after sick babies.'

Oliver felt a growl beginning deep down in his throat, but he held it there, breathing deeply, knowing getting angry again wouldn't help anything. Clare's words had somehow made his daughter come to life, and though his anger at Clare still simmered deep inside him, a different churning had begun. He'd been cheated out of nine years of his daughter's life and was now expected to step into a fatherhood he hadn't wanted.

With an effort of iron will, he forced himself to calm down, to think rationally.

He mentally repeated what Clare had told him, and realised it might help them sort the 'telling Emily' problem out.

'I've been overseas—so have you—so obviously we couldn't have been looking after the same sick babies up until now. But surely if she knows about me, can't you just tell her we've met up again? Exciting news—her father's working in the same place as you are!'

He got that far before apprehension swamped him, and he stood from behind the desk to pace again.

'*Would* it be exciting news for her?'

'It would be the ultimate in exciting news for her,' Clare said, so softly he had difficulty making out the words.

'The problem is,' she continued, 'where do we go after the excitement. I can't give her a father who really doesn't want to be a father, one who's not willing to go the whole way. That doesn't just mean going to parent-teacher meetings and taking her to the zoo, but guiding her path through life, teaching her right and wrong, disciplining her when necessary and helping her cope with things like bullying, and jealousy, and teachers she thinks are mean to her at school.'

She paused, then while Oliver was still trying to take in all she'd said, she added, 'You'd have to be a dad.'

How could he be a dad?

He, who'd never really known his father—well, the father he'd thought was his?

Owen had been cold, reserved and distant. Because Oliver wasn't his blood son? Perhaps, but even as a step-father he hadn't been much of a model for Oliver to follow, and the men who'd come into his mother's life after Owen hadn't bothered to pretend to be interested in their stepson.

'I'll leave you to think about it,' Clare said, standing again, but Oliver was so lost in his own thoughts he barely heard her, simply nodding, although he realised the conversation was far from over.

Escaping from Oliver's office had been relatively easy, but escaping her thoughts and turbulent emotions were an entirely different matter.

Except that she still had work, and turning her mind to work would at least block out any thoughts of Oliver and where they stood in regard to Emily.

She made her way to the PICU where Bob was now installed. At least she didn't have to worry about how he looked. He lay in his crib, all pink and contented, totally beautiful if you ignored the dressings and tubes and monitor leads. Not wanting to intrude as both his parents were by his side, Clare checked the machine was working smoothly, that all the settings were correct, then slipped away, stopping by the outside monitors, where she watched the screens which were confirming he was doing well.

'I'm leaving the hospital now,' she told the nurse who was watching Bob's screens, 'but I'll have my pager, so if there's any change don't hesitate to contact me.'

'You and all the rest of the team,' the woman said, smiling at Clare and pointing to the list of numbers by the monitors. 'This little guy has captured a lot of hearts in a short space of time.'

'They all capture mine,' Clare admitted. 'So small and so resolute, the way they come through the terrible stresses we put on their little bodies. Every one of them is a miracle.'

'Aren't all babies miracles, especially for their parents?' the nurse asked, and Clare nodded her agreement.

Think of Bob, she told herself as she left the hospital. Think of the part you play in saving the lives of babies like him. Think positive, woman! You can handle this situation. Em will handle it as well. Okay, so it might be a bit awkward at first, but eventually the three of them should be able to find a way to fit Oliver into Em's life, and Em into his, without too much disruption.

* * *

When Clare left his office, Oliver replayed in his mind the list of things she'd said he'd have to do—a very small part of dadhood, he imagined—but though theoretically they all seemed doable, the idea of someone bullying his daughter at school filled him with a white-hot rage.

Clare would have to handle things like that, but what about all the other stuff he heard parents discussing, like how much television their children should watch, and the perils of the internet.

He slumped down into his chair, banged his head against the desk and groaned.

Being a father in name only wasn't an option—Clare had made that abundantly clear—but could he take on the task that was becoming more mountainous every time he thought about it, new worries like adolescence and dating sneaking into his head?

Damn the woman! Surely it would have been easier if they'd been together all the time, and he'd have had the opportunity to grow into the job.

Feeling justifiably aggrieved now, he stacked the files into one pile. He'd have to read them some other time, some time when he might manage to take in what was in them. For now he had to think, had to talk some more to Clare, had to work out just where in his life he could fit a daughter.

Or where his daughter might fit him in!

Clare would have to help him. Had she gone home? He glanced at his watch and realised it was late enough for her to have left the hospital, but with baby Bob Stamford on ECMO would she be on duty?

She wasn't in the PICU, although according to the Stamfords, she'd just left. He set off for his flat, striding down the road, feeling hard done by again. How could he possibly be a dad? He found the source of his aggravation sitting on the front fence.

'Most fathers learn on the job,' he told her without any lead-in conversation at all, 'so it's easier than having it dumped on them like this.'

She studied him for a moment, then half smiled.

'At least be honest with yourself, Oliver,' she said. 'How much learning time would you have had? Had we still been together, how often would you have been home to bathe Emily, or change a nappy, or play with her, or read her a bedtime story? You're thinking of you now, all qualified, but back then?'

She was right but no way would he admit it, although a change of subject might be in order.

'What are you doing sitting out here?'

It was a full smile this time, though her flushed face suggested it was hiding embarrassment.

'Changing the subject? I forgot my keys. I kind of rushed away and must have left them in my locker at the hospital. Rod's not home, so I was hoping you'd eventually return and open the front door.'

'And your flat? How do you propose to get into that?'

The smile became more natural.

'I keep a key above the door. I've always had a key hidden somewhere outside in case I lost mine, or Em lost hers and something happened and she needed to get in. Rod's usually home downstairs, but she knows if he's not home Annie's got a key for the outside door, so all bases are covered.'

A horror he'd never felt before crept into Oliver's bones, turning the marrow to ice.

'She's nine years old,' he said, restraining the yell to a muted roar. 'Why on earth would she ever be out on her own and need a key to get back in? What kind of a mother are you, to be letting a nine-year-old roam the city on her own?'

Feeling incredibly weary, and sorry she'd ever started the Emily conversation, Clare stood.

'For your information she doesn't roam the city on her own, but things happen. I just believe she must always know how to get into her own home, in case something *were* to happen when she *might* find herself alone and need the refuge of her home. She also, if you want to know, has a mobile phone and a cab charge card. I realise it's so unlikely it's stupid to even talk about, but what if she ran away from school? You did several times, I remember you telling me. What if she has your running-away-from-school gene?'

She walked towards the door, then realised the man with the key was still standing where she'd left him by the fence.

'Do you have to think ahead that much?' he demanded. 'All the time? Do you have to imagine every possible eventuality and plan for them? Is that what parenting is all about?'

Clare walked back and stood beside him.

'You can never imagine every eventuality, believe me, but you can plan for the ones you do imagine—that way you sleep better at night. Not well, mind you, because there are always bits of child worry buzzing about in your brain, but better.'

She touched his arm to draw him towards the door, feeling exhausted by the tension and emotion of the day, and wanting nothing more than to have a hot shower and collapse into her bed.

He walked with her towards the porch, obviously thinking over what she'd said. Finally he unlocked the front door, opened it and stood back for her to enter first. The sensor light came on and she climbed the steps, every one an effort, but when she reached above her lintel for her key and opened the door, he stopped her with a hand on her shoulder.

'You do realise we'll have to get married,' he said.

CHAPTER FOUR

CLARE stalled in the doorway.

Surely Oliver couldn't have said what she thought he'd said!

Dismissing it as some kind of hallucinatory madness, she took another step into the sanctuary of her flat, but that didn't stop her hearing his next words.

'It's the only sensible thing to do—and the best thing for Emily, you must admit.'

Now she had to acknowledge the words were real. She spun towards him.

'Are you mad? Get married? What on earth put such an absurd idea into your head?'

He'd followed her into her flat, for now he was there, right in front of her, his body sending out those weakening subliminal messages, her own body, lacking any steel at all, responding.

'Everything you read tells you that children brought up by two parents are better adjusted than those from single-parent families.'

'That's rubbish and you know it. For as many articles you find saying that, there are just as many to refute it. As if a child isn't better off with one happy, well-adjusted parent than with two who are at war all the time.'

'But would we be at war?' he asked, so softly she wondered if she'd imagined the words. But when he leant towards her and added, '*All* the time?' she knew exactly where the argument was going. The physical attraction she'd been trying to deny since he'd come back into her life hadn't been all one way, and now Oliver was going to use it against her.

She could have moved, should have moved, but her legs refused to obey the instructions from her brain. Perhaps because they'd been very weak instructions, while the one from her brain to her lips—don't kiss him back—was positively pathetic.

His mouth claimed hers, capturing her lips and defeating any feeble resolve she might have had, for kissing Oliver was so mind-blowing she could only feel, and touch, and kiss him back.

Feel.

Surely there was a better word to describe the wave of languorous warmth the kiss brought with it, to describe the way her body grew heavy with excitement, the way her nipples peaked and tingled as they brushed against his chest. This wasn't feeling; this was bliss. It was wonderment and ecstasy and a hunger so deep and haunting she began to ache with it.

She wanted more; she wanted all of him, her body splayed across his now, he her sole support. The kiss had left her lips, his mouth moving to her temple, then her ear, her skin shivering beneath his attentions. Then those questing lips found her neck, the hollow where the heavy thunder of her pulse would be a dead giveaway of her arousal.

Clare knew she should break away, or at the very least stop responding to his kisses, but it was as if ten years had never been—no, that was wrong. It was the gap of ten years, that huge, insurmountable gap, that made the kisses so mind-blowingly intense. Heat raced through her body, not languid warmth now but something fierce and searing, burning away memories and scars she'd thought would stay for ever.

Oliver's body hummed with excitement, stirring, hardening, seriously hungering for the woman in his arms, his erection hard against her belly. His hand skimmed her breasts, felt the peaked nipples that told of her excitement, then he caught one lightly in his fingers and—

She was gone, pushing away from him, shuddering, shivering, pale as milk. He reached out for her but she spun away.

'Please go, Oliver!'

The words were shaky, strangled, but he heard pain and terror in them, so crystal clear he backed away without a second thought, shutting her door behind him.

But after unlocking his own door, he didn't go inside. He remained on the landing, listening, worried now that there was something seriously wrong. His mind was totally occupied by Clare, Emily pushed into the background, although he knew he'd have to give *that* matter more thought.

And soon!

For now, he stood in his hallway, the door still open, wondering about Clare, puzzling over her extreme reaction.

Puzzling wouldn't help, especially as the reasons that leapt to mind were very discomforting.

He'd think about Emily instead, but his mind wouldn't move past the whiteness of Clare's face and the horror in her dark eyes as she'd backed away from him.

Was she okay?

Of course she was. She was probably in bed by now.

Bed.

As he'd kissed her, ideas of bed had inevitably filtered into his mind, certain that the kisses would lead—if not tonight, but one night soon—to them resuming their physical relationship.

Until she'd flinched away...

It wasn't frustration gnawing at him now, preventing him from even considering his major problem—he had a daughter. It was that flinch—Clare's reaction.

He'd hurt her, he knew that, back when they'd parted. Then, not hearing from him and assuming he'd ignored her letters about her pregnancy would have hurt her even more.

But that had been emotional hurt. Could it extend to the physical, to the extent that she'd all but fainted when he'd touched her breast?

He shook his head.

There was no way he could guess the answers to his questions and he suspected he was thinking of Clare to stop himself thinking of his daughter—of Emily. But how could he think about a child he didn't know? Where did he start?

Feeling anger rise again, he moved, striding into the living room and slumping down into one of the surprisingly comfortable armchairs. Rod Talbot knew his furniture. And why was he thinking about Rod Talbot and furniture? Again the answer was Emily.

Perhaps if he didn't think at all, simply went about his business as if nothing had happened, his subconscious could chivvy away at the problem and maybe come up with some answers for him. Answers to questions like how do you get to know a nine-year-old? How do you even talk to a nine-year-old?

No, he knew how to do that—he'd had patients who'd been nine. He *could* talk to children, even if all the practice he'd had had been with patients, not daughters.

A daughter!

What did she look like?

Why hadn't he asked Clare?

He glanced towards his still-open front door, but there was no light visible beneath her door, and no sounds coming from her flat.

He could wake her up and ask her, ask to see a photo—surely he deserved that much!

Pride restrained him.

Pride and the memory of her milk-white face...

He took himself to bed, only to find images of small girls flocking through his head—small girls with dark eyes and hair, pigtails maybe, toothy smiles. Did she need braces, was she tall or short? He gave an anguished moan and sat up. If he wasn't going to sleep he could do some work. Alex had mentioned a new case coming in, an infant with Down syndrome and the added complication of an atrioventricular septal defect.

Because AVSDs were more common in children with Down syndrome, most of them had an echocardiogram soon after birth, even if no heart murmur was audible. Oliver opened his computer, doing a search through restricted medical sites for the latest information on the operation and its success rate. He was pleased to see it was now listed at ninety-seven percent success rate, though some patients, less than ten percent, had to return to Theatre later in their life for further surgery due to a leaky mitral valve.

Reminding himself of the procedure was a good idea, for now he could go to bed and run through it in his head—every intricate step—until sleep claimed him.

Slumped on the side of the bath, Clare held her head in her hands and tried to think, but her brain was exhausted by all the emotional upheaval of the evening and her body was drained of all energy.

How could she have reacted like that? What must Oliver have thought? Why hadn't she *known* that this might happen?

Tears streamed down her face—she, who thought she'd emptied out all the tears provided for her lifetime years ago!

She wrapped her arms around her body, shivering and shaking, ashamed that the nightmare of the past should have come back to haunt her at that moment, and in that way. And what must Oliver have thought of her behaviour, one moment responding to his kisses with all the fervour of a lover and the next shrinking, fleeing from him.

Mentally unbalanced—that's what he'd think, and from there it was only a small step to wondering if she was a fit mother for his daughter.

No! Don't make things worse. You can handle this.

She nodded her response to the voice in her head. She'd have a shower and go to bed and not think about anything but sleep.

Well, sleep and Emily. Forget the past and think of the future. Go forward, that's what they both had to do. They had three days to work things out. Em had phoned at daybreak this morning to tell her there was a party of some kind at the boarding school—year-twelve students leaving?—so she wouldn't be coming home until Saturday morning and could Mum please collect her at nine.

Of course Mum could, Clare had assured her, and although normally she'd have felt a quick stab of depression at missing out on another night of her daughter's company, with the advent of Oliver into her life again, the extra night had seemed like a blessing.

Oliver!

How could he think getting married would solve anything?

Although maybe he'd changed his mind about that idea after she'd pushed away from him.

Not that she could think of marrying Oliver, not now she knew how she'd react to his touch. He'd expect them to have a sexual relationship—why wouldn't he expect it when he knew the attraction was still so strong between them?—but it would be impossible.

Memories, images, flashed across her mind, things she thought shut away forever tumbling through her head, making her feel so dizzy she had to sit again, breathing deeply to calm herself as she shoved the memories back where they belonged—back into the past.

She stripped off her clothes, then did something she rarely did—looked at her naked body in the mirror. The scars on her breasts were faint now, probably more in her mind than on her skin, but as she looked at them shame flooded through her.

No, she couldn't marry Oliver!

Turning away from the tormenting image, she stepped under the shower, hoping having the water run hot and hard would wash away the ache of regret that grew inside her.

Of *course* she couldn't marry Oliver.

But wouldn't it be the best solution for Emily?

A platonic marriage?

A likely idea! Maybe if she hadn't kissed him, hadn't responded to his kisses like some sex-starved maniac, she could sell the platonic idea, but now it was too late.

Too late to even dream of such a thing, although later, as she lay in bed, she did dream of it, even feeling his hands on her body, exciting it as only Oliver could, then the dream turned to a nightmare, Oliver looking at her and backing away, repulsed by scars that had grown all over her body—scars that even in the dream she knew she didn't have.

Damaged goods!

Did he say the words in the dream, or had she heard them as an echo in her head? Either way she woke in the early hours of the morning to find her pillow wet with tears.

She had to sleep. It was nothing but a bad dream. They'd work things out, she and Oliver, without having to get married. Getting married was just another dream, a different kind of dream—a foolish daydream that he'd awoken with his words.

Years of practice had taught her how to turn off her churning thoughts before she went to sleep, but tonight none of her strategies worked, until she thought of Emily, and remembered the excitement in her daughter's voice this morning, the delight that she, a newcomer, had been included in the party.

Em's joy was proof that being the child of a single-parent household hadn't done her any irrevocable harm thus far. And thinking of Emily, happy and secure, helped Clare block out all the horrors the night had stirred up, and she was able to drift back to sleep.

Waking up, however, was a different matter. Happy and secure Emily might be, but when told she was about to meet her father...? How was she going to react to that? Clare had been so uptight about telling Oliver, she'd given little thought to the problem of how to introduce Emily to her father.

Unrefreshed from the restless night's sleep and still feeling the effects of the stress-ridden previous twenty-four hours, Clare made her way to work. She was in Theatre with Alex today and hopefully Oliver would still be working with Angus, but she'd no sooner arrived in Theatre to have a chat to her machine, than Oliver appeared.

'I'd like a photo if you've got one.'

Great opening! Although she should be thankful he was speaking to her at all, after her behaviour the previous evening. She faced him without flinching, outwardly at least. Inside she was flinched so tightly it was a wonder she hadn't shrunk, and it seemed to her haunted mind as if the air in the theatre had become dense and heavy.

'Of course I've got one,' she replied, hoping the flinch wasn't obvious in her voice and that the dense air would allow the passage of words. 'I've probably got a hundred, and yes, I'll find one, but Emily has been keep-ing a scrapbook for you, and she'll want to give you that herself.'

'Keeping a scrapbook for me?' Oliver echoed. 'What on earth do you mean?'

'Just that,' Clare told him, relaxing a little now and allowing herself a small smile at his bewilderment. 'It was her idea so we'll wait and let her explain, but I did tell you I've always answered any questions she's had about you, so it's not as if you'll be a complete stranger to her.'

'She'll be a complete stranger to me,' Oliver re-torted, and now, feeling his pain, Clare released a little of hers.

'Let's not go there, Oliver,' she said, guilt over her abrupt reaction last night ensuring she spoke gently. 'What's done is done. Let's look ahead and work out what we can do to make the outcome best for both you and Emily.'

Oliver glared at her, but as other staff members were drifting into Theatre, the conversation had to cease.

He sorted through what he knew about the patient, a four-month-old baby girl with a complete atrioven-tricular septal defect, meaning the walls between the heart's right and left atria and right and left ventricles were incompletely formed so oxygenated blood from the lungs to the left atrium crossed to the right and went out again to the lungs, at far too great a pressure.

'Has she been suffering congestive heart failure?' one of the nurses asked as Oliver studied the notes while waiting for the patient.

'Apparently not,' he said, 'which augurs well for us. That might be why Alex has decided to operate early rather than wait a couple of months for her to be stronger.'

The doors eased open and the gurney holding their patient was wheeled in, the infant looking so small, Clare felt a pang of concern, although she knew this operation was more or less routine for surgeons of the calibre of Alex and Oliver.

The team went smoothly into action, Clare more apprehensive than she'd been with baby Bob, probably because she was working with Alex for the first time.

'The tricky part is sorting out the valves—dividing the common valve we see in the defect into working mitral and tricuspid valves.'

Clare watched as Alex stood back to let Oliver do this delicate procedure—a sign that the team leader had the utmost confidence in his fellow. Alex must have known Oliver could be trusted to complete the intricate task successfully, and so it proved, his gloved hands handling the instruments swiftly and surely.

'Off pump.'

This time it was Oliver giving the order, the work on the little heart completed. Clare watched with the others, waiting nervously for the heart to beat, waiting, waiting. Alex massaged it, giving orders for drugs, then finally the heart moved of its own accord and a quiet cheer went up.

'We'll leave a pacemaker in her chest,' Alex said. 'The stitches we put in for the ventricular patch are very close to the tissue that supplies the electrical stimulus that makes the heart beat.'

The pacemaker fitted, Oliver closed the chest, and once again Clare couldn't help but notice the care he took to get the closure neat, and the gentle way he touched the infant's body.

He cares about his patients, she realised, although she'd known that back when they had lived together. He'd always spoken of them with genuine affection and part of the reason he had worked such long hours was because he went the extra mile for them—stayed at the hospital if there was any problem, or if the parents were overly concerned.

Would those qualities make him a good father?

Would professional care translate to personal care?

But was it caring she wanted for Emily from Oliver, or love?

Both, of course, but it was the love she wondered about. Could Oliver learn to love?

'I think she'll do well enough without ECMO, but be prepared for a call, Clare,' Alex was saying.

'I always am,' Clare told him. 'Now, what about baby Bob, am I taking him off the machine today?'

'You'll have to see what Angus thinks, but he was hopeful about it,' Alex told her. 'Oliver, maybe when you've changed, you and Clare could go and check it out.'

It was natural Alex would suggest they went, as both of them had been involved in Bob's operation, but the way Alex had paired their names made a shiver run down Clare's spine.

Oh, that it could be!

Dreamtime, Clare, get on with reality.

Oliver made his way into the locker room, wanting to change and be out of there before Clare came in. Bad

enough that every time he saw her his body responded—
something that had never happened to him before in
professional situations, although he'd had relationships
with colleagues—but to see her stripping off was asking
too much of restraint.

Not that seeing him half naked appeared to affect
her, for she'd come in, gone to her locker, picked up her
mobile and appeared to be frowning at the message on
it.

'Bad news?' he asked, a new anxiety banishing any
thought of attraction. Bad news could involve Emily.

But Clare's rueful smile assured him it wasn't all that
bad.

'In a way,' she said, coming across to him so she
could speak quietly, yet pausing at arms length, tension
coming in waves from her body for all she'd been smiling. 'I thought we had until Saturday to figure out a plan
but here's a text from Em.' She handed him the phone.
'I assume you can understand nine-year-old texting.'

Oliver looked at the message which made no sense
at all.

Nx wk not ths, cu 5 F

'"Next week not this, see you at five on Friday,"'
Clare translated, making the original immediately
obvious. 'Em had phoned earlier in the week about a
party this Friday night but apparently she'd got the date
wrong.'

'She's only nine and you're letting her go to parties?'

Oliver had to keep the demand to a whisper as other people were now in the room, but it was all he could do not to explode when Clare reacted with a smile.

How could she smile about a nine-year-old and parties?

'It's at the school,' she explained, 'in the boarding house, in fact—a party to farewell the senior students. She'll be quite safe and I doubt it will go on later than nine—well, not for the junior school boarders anyway.'

'How was I supposed to know that?' he muttered but he was talking to himself, Clare having disappeared into one of the shower cubicles, returning only minutes later, fully clad in civvies once again.

'You ready?' she asked, and he was about to ask, Ready for what? when he remembered they were going to find Angus to check if baby Bob should come off ECMO.

Was he rattled by her presence, by the stuff that had happened between them last night, or was the knowledge that he had a daughter distracting him from his usual cool professionalism? It had to be the latter, Clare decided. Finding out something like that would distract the Sphinx. He was pulling a white coat over his striped business shirt and the sleeve caught.

Without thinking, she reached out to straighten it, but touching him was a mistake. Once again her body was responding to Oliver's, heating and swelling with a longing that she wondered if she could ever conquer.

Of course she could—she had only to remember how she'd reacted to his fingers on her breast and shame would be better than a cold shower.

Yet the longing remained, stirring up anger. The voice in the dream had been right—she *was* damaged goods....

She headed out the door, away from any temptation to touch him again.

'So, we've got until Friday to come up with a plan?'

Oliver fell into step beside her as she headed for the PICU.

So much for attraction! He was obviously feeling nothing, and now she came to think of it, that kiss last night hadn't been about attraction on his part; it had simply been to prove a point—to prove marriage could work between them.

Unfortunately it had failed in the worst possible manner, but refusing to dwell on that again, she turned her full attention to Emily.

'I don't suppose we need a plan,' she admitted. 'I think I'll just tell her you're working here. It must be fate, I'll say. She'll like that bit. She'll think the gods were doing it just for her—for all I know she's been praying for this to happen, so maybe that's how it *did* come about.'

'And what about you? Do you believe it's fate?'

Clare turned to face him.

'I think it's just the most bizarre coincidence of all time, and I find the thought that there *might* be Fates who play around with the lives of humans to this extent scary.'

Extremely scary, she could have added, but she didn't want to sound paranoid, especially as Oliver was studying her with a strange expression on his face. Not exactly amused, but questioning somehow, and suddenly she was swamped, not with the attraction that had been confusing her so much—the bodily reactions—but with remembered love for this man.

At least, she hoped it was remembered love, not a new infection of the insidious disease, because love between them would be impossible.

'I don't know about the Fates playing with our lives,' he was saying, while Clare assured herself it had to be remembered love. She couldn't possibly *still* love him and there hadn't been time to fall in love with him again, especially as they'd been arguing for much of the time. 'But I could believe that this was meant to be. Why else would we have been brought together if not for Emily and me to get to know each other?'

'I can't answer that,' Clare said, aware she'd spoken shortly, but so thrown out of kilter by the feeling she'd had—the love idea—it was surprising she could speak at all. 'Let's forget all about it for the moment and see how Bob's doing.'

Oliver followed her into the PICU, but for once his mind wasn't totally on work. Something was upsetting Clare, something quite apart from introducing Emily to her father. Something from her past? He knew without a doubt that the attraction between them was as strong as ever, yet she'd ended the kiss in a panic, fear in her eyes....

Suspicion sneaked into his mind... She'd been married—not for long, a mistake...

Did he remember her saying that?

The hot rage that grew inside him was so unexpected and so strong he had to close his eyes lest they reveal his emotion.

You're only surmising, the few working neurones in his head reminded him. Now stop leaping to conclusions and think of your own problems. Think of Emily, of Clare in the context of a mother, not a lover.

'Are you concerned your relationship with Emily will change?' he asked, not realising where they were, by the monitors, and that Angus and a couple of nurses had probably heard the question.

'Who's Emily?' one of the nurses asked, and although Clare threw a scathing glance at Oliver, she ignored the question, asking one of Angus instead.

'Are we taking Bob off ECMO?'

'I think so,' Angus said. 'Originally I thought maybe he'd need another day but he's doing so well I think we should give him a go on his own. Let's take him into the procedure room and disconnect him, although I'll keep the cannulae in place just in case. You want to do it, Oliver?'

Oliver felt a swell of pride, enough to get his mind one hundred percent back on work. In some fellowship situations the fellow was a dogsbody, rarely given the opportunity to do much operating, but Alex had been definite that he worked differently—he actually wanted his fellows doing major surgery. And although disconnecting Bob from the ECMO machine wasn't major, it was still a responsibility that Angus, too, was giving to Oliver.

After the procedure was completed, Oliver spoke to the nurse who would monitor Bob, 'We'll need full blood values now, and continuous readings. Any sign that he's slipping back, just page me.'

He glanced at Angus, who nodded approval that Oliver had taken responsibility for the task right through to completion—sorting out the next stage of Bob's care.

Angus walked away, and a nurse wheeled Bob back out into the PICU, but Oliver waited, watching Clare fiddle with her machine, securing lines and turning off the monitors.

'What do you do now?' he asked her. 'Hand it over to one of the techies to clean and sterilise?'

'Theoretically yes,' she said. 'I did that up in Theatre with the heart-lung machine, because they have the gear there to do it more efficiently than I could and they know the routine. But the ECMO machines, I like to do them myself. It's such a dicey thing, having a baby on one of them, that I want to know every one is working perfectly.'

He waited until she wheeled the machine out through a rear door, and would have liked to follow, just to see how it was made ready for the next patient.

Or was the real reason he wanted to follow because he wanted to spend longer with Clare, with the very professional Clare he felt he didn't know at all?

He'd told her he thought it was meant to be, them coming together so he could meet his daughter, but although the thought of that meeting generated equal amounts of excitement and sheer terror, his finding Clare again was a whole different ball game. Something deep inside him told him that this, too, was meant to be, but the emotional upheaval of the things he'd learned in Italy might have made him susceptible to such fancies.

And she obviously didn't share his sense of rightness about their meeting up again, mocking him when he suggested marriage, making it sound like an indecent proposal. Yet her response when they'd kissed was undeniable—the physical attraction that had flared between them from their first meeting had, if anything, become stronger.

Until…

He shook his head, admitting he had little knowledge of what went on inside Clare's head—any woman's head, for that matter—and here he was, about to get another female in his life.

Emily.

He checked on Bob before leaving the PICU, went into the recovery room to find Alex with the baby girl they'd operated on earlier and, having assured himself he wasn't needed with either patient, wondered how he'd find Clare again. Suddenly the need to see a picture of his daughter had become urgent. He'd missed nine years and didn't want to miss another minute, but, of course, fate wasn't *that* co-operative, for Clare had disappeared.

CHAPTER FIVE

CLARE should have been relieved that Bob was off ECMO, and that the morning operation had gone well. She'd even managed a brief conversation about Emily with Oliver without falling to pieces, but none of these reassuring things lessened the agitation she was feeling. Inner agitation—twitchy; she felt twitchy.

Unwilling to go home lest she run into Oliver, she paced the tea room, pleased there was no-one to observe her agitation. Not much to attract the attention in a tea room, although there was a corkboard on one wall, covered in small notices, photos and postcards.

To divert herself from thoughts of twitches, attraction and Oliver in general—even from thoughts of Emily—she studied it.

The postcards must be from people who had worked with the team at some time, and she smiled to think where some of them had ended up—Italy, South Africa, even one from someone who'd moved on to her old hospital in Chicago. The photos were obviously of children who had been through the cardiac paediatric unit. All the photos were evidence of the success of cardiac surgery with the kids smiling and happy.

But it was a small notice decorated with balloons and streamers that caught Clare's interest.

Wanted—Bodies, it was headed, the words compelling attention.

Jimmie's Entertainment Unit is looking for people willing to give up some time between now and Christmas Day to ensure that all the children in hospital over the festive season are visited and treated to a little silliness.

Clare had to smile. These days professional clown 'doctors' were involved in most children's hospitals, but she knew from experience that volunteers were usually needed to augment the clowns' appearances, especially at Christmas when most entertainment units made a special effort.

Now here she was, back where she'd started. She'd taken out a pen to make a note of the contact number when she realised that the first meeting of the expanded entertainment group was tonight. A map at the bottom of the notice showed her how to get to the canteen in the other tower where the meeting would be held.

She had her pager, and another perfusionist was on duty, so there was no reason why she shouldn't join the troupe.

Although the performances would be close to Christmas when Emily would be home…so could she spare time away from her daughter? Or would Em be happy to join in?

Clare knew she would. Emily had often come to work with her, usually on weekends when Clare wasn't on duty but had wanted to call in to check on a particular patient, and Emily had enjoyed visiting the children's ward and chatting to the small patients. Best of all, she loved the babies and would stand outside the nurseries, peering through the glass, giving all the infants names as if they were her dolls.

Clare smiled at the thought, and for the first time since Oliver's stupid comment about marriage and the subsequent kiss had sent her spinning back into turmoil, she felt the dark cloud of unhappy memories lifting. In fact, the thought of performing again, even if it was only a bit part in a Christmas pantomime, was so therapeutic she made her way to the second tower with brisk, excited steps.

But no sooner had her spirits lifted than the cloud was back, and all because the first person she saw as she walked into the canteen was Oliver—large as life and twice as handsome—although she doubted it was his looks that made her heart race. Oliver could have looked like an ogre and he would still have the same effect.

'Did you come because you knew I'd be here? That's pretty close to stalking.'

She spat the words at him as soon as she drew near, so was disconcerted when he looked more puzzled than guilty.

'I'm sorry. I should have realised you'd be interested but I didn't give it a thought. Becky, the unit secretary, was printing out the notice as I went past her desk and she more or less bullied me into coming. She made out it would be a good way for me, and other new members of the team, to meet some staff from other sections of the hospital, but what she was really doing, I think, was making sure someone from the unit would turn up.'

Idiot that I am, of course she'd be interested, Oliver was thinking to himself. And here he'd allowed Becky to talk him into it, because he hadn't been able to find Clare but had guessed she was still at the hospital, not at home.

'Okay, listen up, everyone.' Someone had stepped onto a table to open the meeting. 'I've put out a plea for extra people as I thought we might do a pantomime this year. We can have the Starlight Room for the main performance, but I wondered—if we have enough people— if we could run two or three similar shows, the second and third ones with smaller casts so they can perform in the wards for the children who can't be moved.'

Having worked with hospital entertainers from the time she was doing her drama course at university it was easy for Clare to imagine this proposal, the smaller units doing little more than appearing in costume in the wards. Oliver, however, looked confused.

'I'll explain later,' she whispered to him as the speaker introduced himself as Dr Droopy, then waved a hand to four other people who were the regular hospital clowns, introducing them in turn.

'I thought we'd do *Cinderella* which is a fairly easy pantomime, and so for the smaller performances we'd need only seven characters—Cinders herself, the prince, two ugly stepsisters and their mum, and a fairy godmother, plus an announcer-cum-voice-over-person. For the Starlight Room performance we need mice and jokers and extras for the ballroom scene—say, twenty if we can get them. So that's thirty-four in all—let's make it thirty-five minimum.'

He looked around.

'Now, there definitely aren't thirty-five people here, so I'd like you all to do some active recruiting, preferably within your own wards or units. That way, if you miss a rehearsal because you're on duty—and that's the only excuse I accept—there's someone handy to let you know what you missed.'

One of the other clowns was working his way through the gathering collecting names, contact numbers and places of work.

'Good,' he said when he reached Clare and Oliver. 'You two can be the nucleus of the cardiac department's show. Got anything against being an ugly stepsister?' he added to Oliver, who shrugged his shoulders as if it didn't matter, although he did wonder what he was getting himself into.

'You, of course,' the clown said to Clare, 'will be Cinders.'

'Cinderella is fair,' Clare pointed out. 'I can do ugly—I can be an ugly sister or even the stepmother.'

'No way,' the clown told her. 'We need *some* beauty in the show.'

He was flirting with her, Oliver realised, and against all logic his blood began to heat with something he hesitated to call jealousy but could be little else.

'Or fairy godmother—that's what you can be. We'll have a beautiful—' the fellow was saying now, but Clare cut him short.

'No way, the fairy godmother should be a bloke and a big bloke at that. I've done enough panto to know that. Anyway, you've got other names to gather and it seems to me that Dr Droopy is the boss and he'll decide who plays what.'

The clown gave her a disappointed look and moved on. Dr Droopy was asking everyone to try to recruit more bodies and announcing the next meeting the following week.

'Same time, same place,' he finished, and the crowd began to disperse.

'Actually, I don't think I'd be very good at pantomime,' Oliver said to Clare as they walked towards the door. 'I only came because Becky seemed to think someone from the unit should attend, but as you're here—'

Clare spun to face him.

'Don't you even *think* of backing out, Oliver Rankin,' she said. 'In fact, given what Droopy said, you should be thinking of who you can con into joining us, not deserting a ship before it's even begun to sink!'

He had to smile at her vehemence.

'Hey, all I said was that I didn't think I'd be very good.'

Now she was smiling too.

'No one can be bad at pantomime,' she said. 'Making mistakes just makes it funnier—people will think you did it deliberately. Besides, everyone has to get involved in something over the festive season and anything is better than putting up balloons and tinsel.'

The enthusiasm in her voice died away at the end of the sentence, the change in her tone so obvious he had to ask.

'You don't like balloons and tinsel?'

She studied him, the smile gone now.

'Balloons I don't mind, even plastic evergreen I can handle—after all, I have to have a tree for Emily—but tinsel? It's like love, isn't it? Pretty and shiny when you first come across it, then before you know it, it's fallen down and people have walked over it and it's dirty and tawdry and done with.'

Oliver stared at her in dumb astonishment. Yes, ten years had passed since he'd last seen Clare, but bitterness had never been part of the eager, laughing, loving woman he had known. Without thinking, he reached out and touched his hand to her cheek, looking down into her dark eyes and seeing a stormy unhappiness he couldn't understand.

Although the memory of her face last night, white and fearful...

She blinked and moved away.

'Don't mind me,' she said, without looking back at him. 'Not a good time for me, Christmas, and with all the unrelenting jollity and goodwill it's hard to always put on an act.'

'Yet you're joining the panto,' he pointed out.

She spun back towards him.

'That's for the kids,' she said. 'Besides, being in the panto gives me a great excuse for not going to a lot of the parties that are usually on at the same time. With the panto you can plead rehearsals, costume fittings, costume sewing, a multitude of excuses that no-one ever questions.'

'Is it because we broke up when we did that you're so vehemently anti-Christmas?'

He *had* to ask.

She scanned his face, studying him for a moment, then shook her head.

'Maybe, though I'm not actually anti-Christmas— you can't be when you have a child—just anti-tinsel. You wait and see, two days after Christmas and the floors will be awash with it. It will be sticking to your shoe when you least expect it, and curled in corners of the elevators every time you go up and down. It's all-pervasive, everywhere—tired and dirty and worn.'

Like love?

Oliver wanted to pursue it, but sensed she was already regretting saying as much as she had. Was it their relationship that had made her feel this way, or her marriage? Although it wasn't relationships or marriage she was talking about; it was love.

And what did he know about love?

Not a single, solitary thing.

He shook his head as he followed her into the elevator and sneaked a glance into the corners for any rabid tinsel.

Clare believed in love. Love for her family, love for her friends, love for him at one time. Back when he'd known her, love had guided her life. So why had she taken this stand? How had love gone so bad for her?

A relationship that ended badly, a marriage that didn't work out—of course she'd be put off love. Yet could a woman as full of love as Clare had been set it aside like dirty tinsel?

He sighed inwardly, realising he didn't have a clue how this new Clare felt or thought.

But they'd be sharing a child. He *should* know her better.

'Will you have dinner with me?'

The question was out before he could give it proper consideration, and apparently it had surprised her almost as much as it had surprised him, for she was staring at him as if he'd suddenly spoken in tongues.

'Have dinner with you?'

Incredulity rattled the words.

Fortunately he had a perfect excuse.

'You could tell me more about Emily, and you have to remember it's been ten years since we saw each other. A lot has happened to both of us in ten years. Won't it make it easier for us, considering we're linked by Emily, if we fill in some of the blanks?'

'I guess.'

The response was so reluctant Oliver had to smile.

'Don't overwhelm me with enthusiasm now,' he said. 'We could go to the beach—down to Coogee. There are plenty of restaurants there to choose from, and if we sit on the pavement there'll be a sea breeze.'

They'd reached the ground floor so she didn't answer immediately, but once they were clear of the crowd exiting the elevator, she turned towards him.

'Do you know Sydney well, that you know about restaurants at Coogee?'

As questions went it was a fairly average one, but it lit a minute spark of hope in Oliver's gut. At least she was going along with the idea.

'I stayed at a hotel in Coogee when I was here working with Alex earlier in the year. It was close and easier than looking for a furnished apartment.'

An ordinary conversation in the busy foyer of a children's hospital, yet Clare felt tension coil within her body. Oliver's excuse for dinner was to talk about Emily, but would he bring up the marriage idea again? Was he thinking he could discuss it over dinner in a public place where her reaction couldn't be too volatile?

Her heart quivered at the thought, although common sense decreed he was hardly likely to bring it up again after the way she'd pushed him off last night.

'Don't look so stressed—it's only dinner,' he was saying. 'We both have to eat.'

She nodded, agreeing they both had to eat, assuring herself she could get through a dinner with him without falling apart.

'This is really stupid,' she told him, pretending to a lightness she was far from feeling. 'Here we are, once in a relationship together, and behaving with the formality of two people discussing a blind date.'

'Well, it feels a bit that way to me,' Oliver said, so quietly Clare wondered if she'd really heard him.

Blind dates were awkward things, and Oliver, over-loaded with a magnetic attraction for women, could never have felt that awkwardness.

Could he?

'Do you have to check on Bob?' he asked, and when she nodded he continued, 'Then I'll go home to get the car and meet you back here—when? Half an hour?'

'Half an hour's good,' she said, although, contrarily, given that this was far from a date, she had an urge to make the time longer so she could rush home and change out of the neat and practical jeans and polo shirt she'd worn to work this morning.

Ridiculous reaction! Here she was, going out with the man to talk about their daughter, and she was worrying about how she looked?

It was because of the way her heart had reacted when he'd mentioned dinner. With that one casual invitation she'd regressed to the twenty-year-old she'd been when she first met Oliver, when he'd come into her life and swept her off her feet. Her heart had raced, her blood heated, and hope had lightened her entire body.

She made her way to the PICU, wishing she hadn't thought about teenage-type reactions because now her heart was aching with the remembered love she'd had for Oliver—love that she'd thought would last for ever....

There was a restaurant set on a cliff top just along the ocean-side walk north of Coogee, Oliver remembered. It would be quieter there than a sidewalk café. He tried to remember the name of it, but drew a blank. However, it was unlikely it would be busy on a Wednesday night so they could take a chance on getting in.

And why did he want to take Clare somewhere quieter than a sidewalk café?

The question was an obvious one, but no easy answer came to mind.

'We're going where?' she asked when, once she was settled in the car, he tried to explain about this particular place.

'Just along the cliffs from Coogee,' he told her, 'but the problem is, I walked there when I went before and, while I assume you can drive, I don't know the name of the place, so I can't look up the address. Do you mind a walk?'

'What *kind* of a walk?' she demanded, and he turned to smile at her.

'Maybe a mile at the most—you know me, hardly the walking type. In fact, I remember you nearly killing me walking up and down the hills at your farm. My feet were made for pushing accelerators and brake pedals, not for tramping around sodden paddocks with grass a foot high.'

She laughed and it seemed to Oliver as if his chest had filled with helium, so light did he feel.

Clare's laughter, one of the first things he'd learned to—

To *love* about her?

Had he loved her? Loved her and not wanted to admit it because he was determined not to be undermined by some indefinable emotion?

Is that why losing her had been so painful?

'What's wrong? Are we lost?'

He slid the car into a parking spot close to where the ocean-front walk began, and turned to look at her.

'Nothing's wrong,' he said, but he wasn't so sure because his mind was still stuttering around over the possibility that maybe what he'd felt for Clare all those years ago *had* been love, and that he'd just not known it because love wasn't something that had featured in his life up to that point.

'Come on, we walk from here,' he told her, hurrying to open her car door, but she was already out, still frowning slightly at him, as if she'd read something in his face earlier and wasn't at all convinced by his answer to her questions.

Why had laughing at the memory of a happy time they'd had together made him frown?

Clare joined him on the path that led up a grassy slope towards the cliff top at the northern end of the lovely curved beach.

And was he still annoyed at whatever made him frown that he was striding out now as if they needed to reach the top in record time?

Not that she couldn't match his strides. She'd kept her fitness up in Chicago, loving the walks she and Emily would take around the lake. The freedom of movement and fresh air had relaxed and invigorated her after long, and often tense, sessions in Theatre, but as well as that, the walks had been a special bonding time with her daughter.

But in the present, in the fraught and nervous now, as Clare fell into step beside Oliver, she regretted agreeing to this outing. *She* might know it wasn't a date but her body wasn't convinced, reacting when their arms brushed, heating when he touched her shoulder and pointed out to sea.

'Are those dolphins out there?'

She stopped and stood beside him, her eyes following the direction of his finger, and after a few seconds three sleek forms broke the surface of the water, way out beyond the breakers—three dolphins frolicking in the sea.

'They're beautiful, aren't they?' she breathed, speaking quietly because she'd always loved these lissom creatures, feeling some kind of kinship with them, although why she didn't know.

'You told me once you thought you'd been a dolphin in a previous life,' Oliver said. He'd spoken just as quietly as she had, yet a strange excitement ripped through her body.

No, no, no, no, no! You can't go all gooey just because he remembered a chance remark. We were together five years—more if you took in the courting time before she moved in with him. He *had* to remember some bits of it.

But the excitement refused to be dampened, so as they moved on Clare made sure she walked just slightly behind him, so they couldn't brush arms, or accidentally touch in any way.

The view from the top of the path was brilliant, the sea at dusk an inky blue, contrasting with the white of the plumes of water that flew into the air where the waves battered endlessly against the cliff.

'I do love the smell of the sea,' Clare murmured, stopping to take the salty air deep into her lungs, but as Oliver stopped beside her, her nerves grew taut and a deep yearning to be held—and hold—hollowed out her body.

Or maybe it was hunger.

It had better be hunger. Holding and being held had ended in disaster, she reminded herself.

She moved, heading along the path, berating herself for her stupidity in agreeing to have dinner with Oliver, because being with him was just too confusing.

They followed the path to where the sea had gained purchase in the land, hollowing out a deep inlet, and perched above it the restaurant, blending in with the rocky landscape, only visible because it was well lit.

'Inside, or on the verandah?' the waiter asked when they entered the building.

'Verandah!'

They answered together and Clare had to smile at their reaction, remembering they'd always preferred outdoor dining when there was an option. The waiter led them to a table on a deck cantilevered out over the water below, water that surged and retreated, moving restlessly but without the fury of the waves that broke against the cliffs.

Restless? Was that how she felt? Did that explain the hollow feeling?

Of course it didn't...

Then what did?

'A glass of wine or something soft?'

Oliver looked at her over the wine list he was studying, but his eyes seemed to be asking a different question, a thousand questions—how was she, where had she been, what had been happening in her life...?

As if eyes could convey that much.

'Lime and soda, thanks,' she said, adding, 'I'm starving,' as she opened the menu and started to read the choices.

'Balmain bugs with chilli sauce.'

The waiter had returned for their drinks order but Clare felt he might as well take the food one at the same time; that way they'd be served more quickly. They could eat and leave and she could sort out all the confusion inside her once she got home.

She was wondering where the conversation should go when Oliver spoke.

'I've spent the past few years in the UK, then I went to Italy before I came back to Australia.' Oliver wasn't sure why he'd come out with this in the pause following the waiter's departure with their orders. There'd certainly been no conversational lead into it, but suddenly the words were out there.

Because they'd come to talk about their daughter?

Because subconsciously it was disturbing him that Emily shared his unhappy heritage?

Clare appeared startled by the conversation, then she frowned.

'Holiday or more than that?'

'I went to the village where my mother grew up. Ever since Owen told me I wasn't his son—and you'd remember *that* fun time in my life—I've been torn between wanting to know more about my father and denying him completely.'

'Denial was winning when I knew you,' Clare reminded him, but gently because she remembered how shattered Oliver had been at the time.

Oliver shrugged.

'I probably should have stuck to it,' he said, sorry now that he'd brought it up. Surely he could have made conversation about their patients, or the weather, or the ocean—anything!

'Bad stuff?'

The dark eyes still studied him, assessing—familiar.

'Not that bad. Pretty average really, although not as bad as Owen had made out when he told me. His version was that my father could have been any one of a dozen young local men. He claimed it was because of my mother's reputation in the village that her family sent her to the relatives in Australia.'

He paused; then, with his eyes fixed firmly on Clare's lovely face, he added, 'Do you wonder I didn't want children? Didn't want to pass on that kind of legacy?'

She shook her head, her eyes almost black in the shadowy light, dark with sympathy.

'So, did you find your father?'

He heard her empathy in the words and remembered how supportive she'd been when he'd found out about Owen. She'd wrapped him in her love and then, within months, he'd rejected her.

Damn it all, the conversation was bringing back too many memories.

Still, he could hardly stop now—hardly not answer her question.

'I found out who he was—meeting him was something else altogether. Neither he, nor anyone in the village, not even my grandparents who are still alive, wanted anything to do with me.'

'I'm sorry it was a bad experience,' Clare said, pain for him so acute she was having trouble breathing. Oliver had suffered one rejection when he'd learned Owen wasn't his father; for this to happen…

'You hear so many good stories about people finding their birth parents that you forget it doesn't work out for everyone,' she added. 'Can you put it behind you now? Go forward rather than looking back?'

He didn't reply, studying her instead, surely not trying to read anything behind the words.

'I mean it, Oliver,' she added. 'That wasn't a trite remark but genuine sympathy because I know how much that part of your past worried you.'

Still no response, so she ploughed on. 'But the past *is* past. Now, let's not spoil a good meal by dwelling on it. Look forward, go forward.'

He smiled at her, and for the first time in her life she understood the phrase *the world stood still*, for it happened to her right then and there. It was a smile, no more, but although she tried her best not to respond to it, her body ignored her, sending waves of heat simmering along her nerves, twitching at her muscles and tightening her lungs.

No!

It won't work.

You learned that last night.

Get over it.

'You're right,' he said, 'and I'm sorry for burdening you with that business, but you were there when I first found out that I wasn't Owen's son, so it seemed natural to tell you.'

Natural?

Forget heat and twitching muscles, woman, and get with the situation here.

Fortunately the waiter arrived, giving her an excuse to stop considering anything but food. She turned her attention to the plate in front of her.

'It looks and smells delicious.'

She glanced up at Oliver as she spoke and, because he was so familiar, even ten years on, she began to relax.

'Thank you,' she said, 'for suggesting this, for bringing me here. It's a magical place. I lived near the lake in Chicago and Em and I walked there often, but it's not like being near the sea.'

Oliver watched as she used the silver tweezers to pull the flesh out of the bug's case. She was concentrating on the task, the corner of her bottom lip caught between her teeth. 'Look forward, go forward,' she'd said, but could anyone completely wipe away the past?

Could she, whatever it was?

Successfully removing the meat, she cut a chunk off and popped it in her mouth, sighing blissfully when she chewed and swallowed.

'Aren't you going to eat?' she demanded when she caught him watching her. She waved her cutlery towards his plate where a thick slice of rare Wagyu beef shared a plate with chargrilled vegetables. 'It looks good.'

'I'll eat,' he assured her, cutting into the beef. 'But tell me about you. Where is "forward" for Clare Jackson? Where are you looking to go?'

Dark eyes flicked towards him, unreadable, then she concentrated on sorting another mouthful of food.

'Strange question, when I've just begun a new job, but since you ask, I aim to be the top paediatric perfusionist in Australia. That's where I'm going. I'm going to be on the board of the Australasian Society of Cardio-Vascular Perfusionists, and I'm going to train and examine and be involved with the development of the career path for future perfusionists.'

He had to laugh, shaking his head at the same time, because she sounded so totally convinced that this would all happen.

'Sounds like a plan,' he teased and watched a faint colour rise in her cheeks.

'It's been my plan for some time now,' she said quietly, and he wondered just what had happened in her life that she'd needed to define herself again—to find a new career path, however unusual, and to aim for the top in it.

The marriage that was a mistake?

Whatever had generated her reaction last night?

He cut some more steak and chewed on it, wondering at the same time, thinking...

The past is past, she'd said, and while Oliver was willing to let their shared past lie where it was, he couldn't help but wonder about the past he hadn't shared with her.

'And you?'

Because he was still thinking of Clare's past, the words made little sense until she added, 'Where are you going? You've this fellowship with Alex—that's, what, a year? And after that?'

After that?

He hadn't thought that far.

Well, he had. Originally he'd hoped to work with Alex, then, as the dutiful only child of a mother who was getting older, move back to Melbourne, taking up a senior position in one of the paediatric cardiac surgical units there—

'Hey, you're supposed to be telling me, not just thinking about it,' Clare reminded him. 'This is regular dinner conversation—you ask a question, I reply, then I ask one and you reply, remember?'

'Who knows?' he replied, dodging the issue, because his feelings towards his mother, a woman who had lied so often to him, were far too complex to go into over dinner. Too complex for him to think about most of the time, which is why he considered duty rather than love when he thought about her. 'Things happen, plans change. We've the perfect example of that with Emily. Obviously now I've got to factor her in, factor you in.'

Had his voice sounded strained that Clare reached out her hand and caught at his fingers, squeezing them lightly?

'We'll work it out,' she said quietly.

And suddenly he realised just how good it was to sit with Clare like this, doing nothing more exciting than eating dinner in a special place. He even found himself relaxing.

'Your family?' he asked. 'They're well?'

'They're all in Queensland now,' Clare told him, but he sensed the question had been ill-timed, for suddenly her voice sounded strained and tight. But as he watched he saw her rally, her spine straightening and colour returning to her cheeks. 'My dad died and we sold the farm. My brothers bought a property on the Darling Downs in Queensland—they do some cropping and raise Black Angus. They're lovely beasts, the Black Angus, docile and really good doers, and best of all, as far as my brothers are concerned, there's no twice-daily milking.'

'I'm sorry to hear about your father. I know how close you were.'

It was his turn to offer comfort, turning her hand in his to gently press her fingers.

She took back her hand and shrugged.

'These things happen,' she said, but her voice told him she wasn't over her father's death, that it still hurt her more than she would admit. He looked around, seeking distraction, wanting to regain the mood of pleasant companionship he'd felt earlier.

'During the day you can sometimes see big kingfish in this inlet,' he said, apropos of nothing.

'You'll have to show me some time. We could bring Em,' she replied, and though that, too, was probably nothing more than a throwaway line, the thought of coming here again with Clare sent a surge of excitement through him.

Though the 'bringing Emily' part brought back all the fears and insecurities that had been nagging at him since he'd learnt he had a daughter.

He called for the bill, paid it and they left, Emily not discussed at all, and an uncomfortable silence stretching between them.

Was Clare, too, feeling discomfort in the silence that she chatted on about their patients and the operations, sticking solely to work talk the whole way home? Then, as he drove into the garage and stopped the car, she was out in a flash, thanking him and taking off through the shadowed garden as if chased by demons.

By the time he reached their shared landing, she was gone, her door shut and the muted sound of a radio or television coming from behind it.

CHAPTER SIX

No OPERATIONS, just patients to see—regular check-ups, query patients referred from GPs, patients in for various tests. Oliver found the change refreshing, enjoying again the interaction between the children and their parents.

His final patient of the day was, by chance—there it was again—a nine-year-old girl, a little charmer who'd been born with a partial AVSD which had been repaired when she was twelve months old.

'I really don't need to be still seeing a specialist,' she told him with the utmost confidence, 'but it makes Mum feel better so I do it.'

She talked on, seeming to know a great deal about her operation, explaining, when he mentioned this, 'Oh, I'm in a chat room with some other kids who've had heart surgery. We talk about all kinds of things, compare scars and stories of how nearly we were to dying, although I think most of us exaggerate that part.'

Did all nine-year-olds use the word *exaggerate* with such confidence? Oliver wondered, upgrading his image of his daughter from a just-past-starting-school stage to an almost teen.

I'll never cope. The panic-stricken thought rendered him momentarily speechless, but fortunately his new young friend was now telling him about a boy on the chat list that she thought fancied her, though meeting him might be difficult as he lived in England.

'Dr Rankin worked in England—he might know him.' Was the nine-year-old's mother trying to stem the flow of conversation?

And how likely was that in a country of more than forty million people? He was about to point out the impossibility when another panic struck him. This nine-year-old girl—a child—had a boy who fancied her.

Not *his* daughter! he decided savagely, but now the child was telling him the name of her boy friend—two separate words, Oliver told himself, not one—and the name was ringing a bell.

'Is he from Leeds?' he asked, getting back into the conversation with some difficulty.

'Yes, he is,' the delighted child replied. 'Do you know him?'

Oliver shook his head. This was taking coincidence too far. He refused to believe in Fates that pushed human lives around on some kind of cosmic chessboard, but—

'I actually operated on him a few years ago,' he admitted. 'Like you, he had an AVSD when he was an infant, but he had a full separation, not a partial like yours, and he needed another op a year or so ago to stop his mitral valve leaking.'

'What's he like?' the excited girl demanded. 'Is he as good-looking as his picture? Does he really have a tattoo?'

Oliver closed his eyes. Nine-year-old girls could not *possibly* be turned on by boys with tattoos. He refused to believe it.

'I don't remember a tattoo,' he managed to reply, then he turned the conversation off the boy in Leeds by reminding his patient he had to examine her, and keeping the talk to purely professional matters.

'I'll tell him you're my new doctor. He'll be so excited,' the girl told him as she left, while her mother, waiting until her daughter was out of earshot, smiled at Oliver in a harried kind of way.

'She's got two older brothers and, believe me, driving them around to sporting practice and games is a small price to pay for having boys. The elder one is thirteen now, and I swear he's not even aware girls exist, except for the ones who play soccer with him.'

Oliver went back into the office, sank down into his chair and rested his head on the desk. He thought of banging it against it, but he'd done that one other afternoon and knew it didn't help.

How could he possibly be a father to a nine-year-old girl? He didn't know the first thing about fatherhood and, never having had a sister, knew even less about young girls. Images he had of pretty little things playing quietly in a corner with their dolls or perhaps doing scales on a piano were obviously so out-of-date he needed a crash course of some kind.

He'd start with Clare. Forget marriage, forget attraction; they had to concentrate on Emily. Having kept his daughter from him all this time, Clare owed him, and she could begin repayment by bringing him up-to-date on what his daughter loved and hated, thought about, dreamed of and generally believed in as far as nine-year-old life was concerned.

He found Clare sitting on Becky's desk, chatting away about something—clothes probably. Hell, did the clothes thing begin in childhood with women? Would he have to learn about child fashion as well? He'd have to make a list.

No, Clare would have to make a list. Emily's likes and dislikes—that kind of thing.

'Are you heading home?' he asked her, then added in a very firm voice before she had a chance to refuse, 'We could walk together.'

'Very masterful,' Clare murmured to Becky, and the two women smiled, further raising the aggravation he was feeling towards the whole female sex. But Clare had slid off the desk and showed every sign of being willing to walk with him, for which he should be pleased.

Not so. Walking with her, even in a reasonably crowded hospital corridor, reminded him of the other aggravating aspect of the female species—the fact that they could give out some kind of emanations that made the coolest of men feel warmth building in their bodies, and carnal thoughts slipping into their minds.

He forced himself to think of the purpose of this walk.

'Does Emily think boys with tattoos are cool?' he asked, or maybe demanded, for Clare stopped walking and turned to him with so much astonishment on her face he felt totally stupid.

'I can explain,' he said as the elevator doors opened and they stepped into the crowd inside.

'I'm sure you can,' Clare told him quietly, 'but perhaps not here.'

So they rode down in silence, which wasn't good for the emanation thing, but at least battling it took his mind off Emily for a few minutes.

Should she apologise for her behaviour last night? But how could she apologise without some explanation? And how could she explain that telling Oliver of her father's death had brought back so many bad memories she'd barely been able to breathe?

Clare stood beside him, trying to convince herself that guilt over her abrupt departure last night was making her feel so fidgety. It couldn't possibly be desire—not when she knew anything between them would be impossible.

And Oliver only wanted to walk with her to talk about Emily.

She took the lead in case the conversation didn't go that way.

'What's this about boys with tattoos?' she asked as they left the hospital and headed through the grounds towards the traffic lights at the corner of their street.

'I've been talking to a nine-year-old girl,' he replied, his voice so laden with doom she had to hide a smile as she turned towards him, relaxed now that the conversation *was* about Em.

'Ah! A nine-year-old girl who fancies a boy with tattoos?'

The lights changed and they crossed, jostled to and fro by the mass of people, so it wasn't until they were alone on their street that Oliver answered her.

'She thinks *he* fancies her! Please tell me our daughter isn't into boys! I realise fancying boys or them fancying her will come into the picture sometime and I don't know how the hell a father handles things like that, but I thought I'd have a kind of breaking-in period.'

'I think you're safe with Em,' Clare told him, her heart filled with joy at this evidence that Oliver was actually considering himself a father, before he'd even met his daughter. 'At the moment she's horse obsessed and I've encouraged that because to me it's better than being clothes obsessed, and believe me, some nine-year-olds are. They know the cool brands, all of which are expensive, and won't be seen dead in anything else.'

'I think I need a list,' he announced.

He thinks he needs a list? Clare muddled over it for a while, then had to ask.

'What kind of list?'

'An Emily list—what she likes and doesn't like. Food and games and stuff, then perhaps another list of things she does, and hopes and dreams…'

'And pop stars and TV stars and boy bands and clothes,' Clare added, smiling now at the thought of the endless lists she could make out. 'It won't work,' she added, although the warm feeling inside her grew stronger, because Oliver cared enough to ask for lists. 'Nine-year-old girls don't have strong allegiances. What or who she likes this week could be completely different next week. It makes buying presents very tricky because you might think she's still reading school stories and she's decided they're old hat—that is *not* a nine-year-old's expression but one of mine—and she's wanting some other book altogether.'

'I'll never be able to do it,' Oliver said, so much despair in his voice Clare had to touch him. She reached out to pat his arm, feeling the muscle beneath his shirt, feeling all the things she still felt when she touched Oliver, no matter how unbelievable that might be.

'Of course you will—you're good with children.'

'Other people's children,' he reminded her as they turned in through their gate. 'What if I cook dinner and you write lists. Or if you don't like the thought of lists you could just sit there and talk about what she thinks and does and talks about so I can get a sense of her.'

He was following her up the stairs as he made the dinner suggestion, and whether it was the idea of sitting in Oliver's kitchen while he cooked dinner, or his presence behind her on the stairs, she didn't know, but a shiver of apprehension had slithered up her spine and left the nerves in her back tingling.

To be honest, other nerves were tingling as well—deep-seated nerves—so relief flooded through her when he added, 'Oh, no, I can't do that. I haven't shopped, and although Alex's wife left the basics in the flat for me, they certainly don't run to cooking dinner.'

Clare had reached the landing at the top of the steps and was unlocking her door when he joined her.

'Is there somewhere close by that we can eat?' he asked. 'Actually, that's a better idea. You can talk and I can make the lists—or take notes—about whatever I might need to think about later.'

He took her arm and turned her back towards the stairs.

'Come on.'

'Right now? Forget it. I am going inside. I'm going to kick off my shoes and have a long cold drink and then a long cool shower. Besides, you bought dinner for me last night.'

'Well, tonight we can go Dutch—and you're right, if we shower and change we'll be fresher. I noticed in the notes Annie—that's her name, isn't it?—left for me that there are a couple of restaurants within walking distance, casual places with good food, she said. I'll pick the closest, is that all right?'

Oliver knew he was pushing Clare, but for all that he believed she'd tried to contact him about Emily, he still felt he was the injured party here. After all, *she'd* left *him*, and he deserved a little consideration.

'You have to eat,' he reminded her, 'and you can't deny me the opportunity to learn as much as I can about Emily before I meet her, now can you?'

She studied him for a moment, her hand still on the key in the door.

'As long as that's all it's about, Oliver,' she said sternly. 'No more kisses. Emily's future is far too important to me to risk disturbing it with muddled thinking.'

Oliver was about to smile but caught it just in time. Best not to look triumphant, but he couldn't help but comment on her words.

'You're saying our kisses muddle your thinking?'

'Of course they muddle my thinking,' she said crossly. 'They always have, and now you're back, it's even more disturbing. I mean, we hardly know each other, and there's other stuff—a *lot* of other stuff. It's impossible...'

With that she flung open her door and stepped inside, her back to him so he could afford to smile, for if her words weren't confirmation of the fact that she was still as much attracted to him as he was to her, what were they?

'How long do you need to get ready?' he called after her. 'Shall I knock in half an hour?'

'Okay' came the reply as the door closed between them, and although it had all the enthusiasm of someone agreeing to an enema, Oliver felt a lurch of excitement.

He'd rushed Clare with the marriage suggestion, but it was the perfect solution. She'd obviously suffered some trauma in their years apart—either in her marriage or maybe in childbirth—but together they could sort it out, especially as the attraction between them was as strong as ever.

They'd put the past with all its hurts behind them, and begin again. Married! That way, he could be part of his daughter's life, taking up his rightful place as her father, and Clare could continue to handle the main parenting stuff, just as she'd been doing for nine years.

He ignored a slight qualm of conscience about this imagined arrangement, assuring himself that in time he'd grow into the parenting role and all would be well. In the meantime, he was going out to dinner with Clare, and if he remembered the map Annie had drawn, their route would take them through the park, and if walking through a park in the moonlight didn't soften Clare's attitude to kissing, he didn't know what would.

He's doing it again, Clare admitted to herself as she kicked off her shoes, then dropped into an armchair, leaning back against the headrest and letting the tensions of the day ease from her body. Rushing me headlong into something without giving me time to think. That's how we got together in the first place—attraction, bed, let's move in together.

Yes, he needed and deserved to learn more of Emily, but she knew him well enough to realise he hadn't given up on the marriage idea. Obviously there would have to be a relationship of some kind between them—they shared a daughter—but knowing Oliver he'd use that as an excuse to push or pull her somewhere she didn't want to go.

Couldn't go.

The thought caused an ache in her heart. She'd reached out and touched him earlier and, touching him, had known she loved him. It had been as simple as that. No need to question whether it had never gone away, her love for Oliver, or whether this was new love. It didn't matter because it was simply there, deep in her heart, and there it would stay no matter what.

She almost sighed, then realised she seemed to be spending a lot of time sighing these days, so shut it off and straightened in the chair. Loving Oliver might be a fact, but it was an irrelevant one—a secret she had to keep to herself.

It was also a secret she couldn't allow to have any bearing on the decisions she would make about Emily's future.

Right now she had to think clearly of the future, not the past, and of practical matters, not love. For Emily's sake she had to set aside her personal issues and concentrate on the best outcome for her daughter.

She nodded acknowledgement of this decision and rose out of the chair. Time to shower and dress for dinner, to arm herself against whatever seductive wiles Oliver might choose to use. Though to be fair, it probably wasn't his fault that his body held such a powerful attraction to hers.

Nor were her memories his fault.

Perhaps if she remembered those two things, she could have a normal, adult conversation with him.

* * *

'You look great!'

Three words, a conventional, probably meaningless compliment, and her resolution about the seductive wiles of his body dissolved like sugar in hot water. And so much for deciding not to put on any make-up. Given the limited time and the decision to ignore attraction, all she'd done was shower, pull on a long cool summer dress, then whip her hair up into a clasp on the top of her head, again for coolness.

'You clean up okay yourself.'

She returned the compliment, but made sure he *knew* it was nothing more than polite conversation by turning from him to lock her door.

In fact, he'd cleaned up so far ahead of okay that for a moment he'd stolen her breath—and her resolve. He was wearing a dark blue shirt that for some perverse reason made his eyes seem greener, and stone-washed jeans that hugged his hips like a lover, revealing the swell of his butt and thick muscled thighs.

'So…Emily, horses, you say. Does she have a horse?'

They were across the road and on the path leading through the park, the lights already on, although it was barely dusk.

Great, Emily conversation. Clare knew she could handle this, although she now realised that any time she was with Oliver, especially alone with Oliver, was like walking across a floor littered with broken glass— shards of broken dreams?—so she was always aware of having to tread especially carefully.

What was the question?

Horses.

'Does she have a horse? Are you kidding? Do you have any idea how much the care and feeding of a horse costs? Different in the country, where a horse can live out in a paddock and eat grass, but in a city? They have to be stabled and exercised and brushed and combed and fed, daily tasks beyond the ability of a nine-year-old who also has to go to school.'

Oliver listened to the words, but part of his brain was considering his companion—how beautiful she looked in the long, swishing dress with its fitted top cupping her full breasts, and the thin shoulder straps revealing the smooth golden skin of her shoulders and the pure, taut lines of her neck.

Emily. They were talking about Emily.

'How much?' he asked, and Clare stopped in mid-stride to turn and face him.

'How much what?' she asked, her dark eyes shadowed to almost black, and genuinely puzzled.

'How much does it cost to keep a horse in the city?'

She frowned at him, then shook her head.

'I've no idea—not in actual, up-to-date figures—but I know it's a lot. But the reality isn't the cost of keeping the horse, but a nine-year-old's forever changing goals and passions. Next year—forget that, next week—it might be swimming or hang gliding or who knows what. For the moment, the school provides an adequate outlet for the horse mania. Students who are interested ride one afternoon a week, and there's the horse camp in the holidays. If she keeps riding, and does well at it, proving she's committed to it, then later on I'll think about a horse.'

'*We'll* think about a horse,' Oliver corrected, but the conversation had puzzled him enough for him to ask, 'How do you know these things about changing goals and passions and nine-year-olds? Are there books?'

Clare smiled, such an open, delighted smile it made something stir inside Oliver's chest. He hoped he wasn't back to ectopic heartbeats.

'There are books—hundreds of books—but I was a girl myself, and though at nine a horse would have been an acceptable passion for someone who lived on a farm, I wanted to be a surfer like my brothers. I nagged and nagged for a surfboard for my birthday but Mum and Dad had enough sense to start me off on an old one of Steve's. I was still learning to stand on it when a friend got a pair of hamsters and surfing was forgotten in the bid to become a hamster tycoon. I've forgotten what came next, but Mum no doubt remembers every one of my enthusiasms—all the things I'd absolutely die if I didn't get, have, try.'

Had his face betrayed his reaction that she reached out and grasped his arm?

'Oh, Oliver, I'm sorry. I forgot what a miserable excuse for a childhood you had.'

He stepped towards her and slipped his free arm around her shoulders.

'Don't be sorry about your happiness—it's beautiful to see,' he told her, then he kissed her, very lightly, on the temple, where a blue vein pulsed beneath her golden skin. 'And that's a caress, not a kiss,' he added as he turned away, steering both of them along the path, but keeping his arm firmly around her shoulders.

It was obvious the physical attraction between them was as strong as ever, however much she might shy away from their kisses and make rules about not kissing again. So surely if he promoted the attraction, even with a casual hand holding their bodies close, it would be a good thing....

A good thing when she'd flinched and paled and drawn away from him in fear or pain?

He shook his head, determined this night would be different. This night would be about Emily.

It was wrong, walking with Oliver like this. It made Clare think all kinds of things she shouldn't think, like might not being married to him, being a family with him and Em, be a good idea.

She forced herself to think of how she'd shrunk away from him when he'd kissed her, her movement sheer instinctive fear. And how she'd fled from him last night, afraid it might happen again.

No, marrying Oliver—marrying anyone—was an impossible dream.

'There's the restaurant.' He pointed ahead, and Clare felt a sense of relief that the far-too-intimate walk was nearly at an end. Although they still had to walk back.

'I'll pay tonight,' she said. 'You got the bill last night and—don't argue—I'm a working woman and pay my own way.'

'When I've not contributed one penny to my daughter's upkeep for nine years? Forget it!'

She glanced at him, about to argue that he'd said they'd go Dutch when she saw the set expression on his face. The argument died on her lips as she imagined how emotionally overwhelming it must be to suddenly discover you have a nine-year-old child.

If they were married, she could be more supportive to him, help him in his dealings with Em.

And happily go to bed with him?

She was back on the field of broken glass again.

'Have you been here before?'

The nice, normal question pulled her out of useless speculation.

'No, but I believe it's very popular with hospital staff. Oh, damn, I hadn't thought about that, and here's me hoping to keep any relationship between us quiet until after we've got Em sorted out.'

Oliver stopped walking on the pavement outside Scoozi, and looked at her.

'You used not to worry about every little thing. In fact, you plunged into life as if welcoming the rocks as much as you welcomed the diamonds. Is it motherhood or something else that makes you so cautious now?'

Something else, maybe both—but neither was a reply she intended giving.

'Have you considered it might just be age?' she said as lightly as she could, given the memories he'd stirred up again.

He studied her for a moment longer, then shook his head.

'Age doesn't change a personality,' he said quietly, then he took her elbow and guided her into the restaurant, agreeing with the waiter who met them that, yes, the garden courtyard would be a lovely place to eat this evening.

Clare looked around her, accepting that some of the other patrons would inevitably be hospital staff but pleased that no-one from their team was dining there tonight. So Emily would be a safe topic of conversation; actually, Emily would be the only safe topic, given the physical tension that still stretched between herself and

Oliver. Some of her colleagues were already aware she had a daughter; in fact, Alex had already met Emily, but now that Oliver had come into the picture, explaining *that* relationship—well, that was too complex to consider right now.

'Tell me about the school,' Oliver suggested, as if he, too, had decided his daughter was to be the focus of their conversation.

'It's a great place—unbelievable. I'd heard about it over the years because Mum's youngest brother lives on a property out in western New South Wales and his daughter Caitlin has been a border there since she was about the same age Emily is now. Over the years, we've stayed with Uncle Ken in holidays so Em already knew Caitlin, and it was Em who decided, when we came back to Australia, that that's where she'd like to go.'

'Is it some distance from where we live? Is that why you opted for the boarding option?'

Clare shook her head, then paused as the waiter set down their drinks and took their food order.

'It's a ten-minute ride in a taxi, or if she was a day girl a school bus would collect her outside the door,' she explained. 'But as I think I told you, Mum lived with us up until now so she was always there for Em. However, it was time we let Mum go back to her own life, and although I work fairly regular hours there are times I'm called out at night or work late and I couldn't have Em being on her own. Weekly boarding gives us the best of two worlds as she has friends among the other boarders to do things with after school hours, and we have the weekends together.'

Together.

Although he'd felt he'd been handling this emotional bombshell quite well up to now, that one word caused such pain he actually winced.

Go forward, he repeated to himself. Think of the future, not the past.

'The text message—did it say what time you could collect her?' he asked. 'I was so impressed by your ability to translate it, I've forgotten what it said.'

'Soon after five,' Clare replied, then her dark eyes met his and she studied him for a moment before adding, 'I'd suggest you come with me, but that's too sudden. Give me time to get her home and tell her, then can we leave it up to her?'

'How, leave it up to her?'

Oliver was aware he was growling, but now a new gigantic worry had loomed up in his mind.

What if she wasn't excited about having a father?

What if she didn't want to meet him?

Keeping a scrapbook was one thing, but *meeting* her father…

CHAPTER SEVEN

EMILY's meeting with her father so far exceeded any expectations Clare might have had, that by the end of the weekend she was beginning to feel she was being excluded from a secret society.

Surely she couldn't be jealous of Em's delight in finding a father, nor feel put out that Oliver had slotted into the role with so much ease it seemed impossible the pair hadn't known each other forever.

Having delivered the news in the taxi ride home—incredible coincidence, maybe meant to be, et cetera—Clare shouldn't have been surprised to find that Em's first thought on arriving at the flat was to meet her dad.

'Can I call him Dad?' she'd asked, doubt in her eyes for the first time.

'You sort it out with him,' Clare had replied as she'd knocked on the door, behind which, she guessed, stood a very anxious and uptight Oliver.

By the time the three of them had finished dinner—Em's favourite lasagne always cooked by Clare on Friday nights—together in Clare's flat, Emily and Oliver were chatting away like old friends, and the name *Dad* was falling easily off Emily's lips, and was seemingly as easily being accepted by Oliver.

Saturday they'd gone to the beach, then Saturday night to a movie Em just *had* to see. 'Does it worry you she seems to take such weird stuff as vampires and werewolves for granted?' Oliver had asked. So it wasn't until Sunday afternoon, not long before Em was due back at school, that the scrapbook came out.

'My gran did scrapbooking so she helped me put it all together,' Emily said shyly as she handed the carefully decorated book to Oliver. 'Gran says it will tell you the story of my life in pictures mostly, although there are words as well.'

Oliver was sitting on the couch in Clare's flat. He seemed to have been there all weekend and his presence had been even more unsettling than the instant rapport the pair had achieved.

Now he patted the couch for Em to sit beside him, and with her by his side, pressed against him, he opened the book.

And frowned.

'That's when I was born,' Emily said, pointing to the first photo. It was a newborn-baby photo like a hundred others Oliver had seen, but it was the set of pictures on the other side of the page that had him frowning. These were pictures he'd seen before as well—a baby in a special-unit crib, tubes and monitor leads attached.

'Those are when I had my operation. I had a PDA. Mum said I needn't put those pictures in, but I think that's because looking at them makes her sad. But I don't remember and it was part of me, so me and Gran decided they should be there for you.'

'You had a PDA—you know what the words mean?'

'I used to know them,' his daughter answered cheerfully, 'but I forget. A little something went wrong with my heart and I had to have an operation—that's when Mum stopped being an actor and started being a perfusionist, because of my operation and learning all about babies with bad hearts.'

Oliver heard the words but his eyes were now on Clare. How could she have kept this from him?

How could she have not contacted him when *this* happened?

She must have read the anger and accusation in his eyes for she shook her head, just slightly, warning him to let it go for now, nodding to the new page open in the book which Emily was keen to show him.

He turned back to his daughter, banking down his anger, but determined to have this out with Clare later. She *could* have found him. He'd written enough papers that simply searching his name on the internet would have produced some hits.

'Are you looking?'

Emily's voice brought his attention back to the book, and looking at the pages, photos of his daughter as she grew older, the surrounds of each one decorated with small bears or balloons or pretty flowers, he felt such a surge of love for this child who'd done this for a father she didn't know that he forgot his anger and simply enjoyed the gift, not only of the scrapbook, but of a daughter.

The explosion came as they drove away from the school, leaving behind a little girl so full of excitement and delight Clare was worrying more about whether Emily would get sick with it, than any repercussions from the photos.

'She had a patent ductus arteriosus and you didn't think to tell me that before I met her?'

The accusation reverberated through the car, bouncing off the closed windows, unmuffled by the leather upholstery.

'We haven't had that much time to talk, and why tell you anyway? She had the op, video-assisted thoracoscopic surgery to tie it off. She's fine—I never think about it.'

Clare hoped she sounded calmer than she felt. Yes, she'd always discussed Emily's health with her mother, but she'd never had to answer to anyone for the decisions she'd made on Emily's behalf. Now, here was Oliver—who hadn't wanted a child in the first place—demanding full disclosure of his daughter's life.

'*Never?* She doesn't have ongoing specialist appointments? You didn't have her heart checked out before this riding business started? Are you sure she should be riding? Is it safe?'

Clare felt her own explosion building, and the tension of the past few days uncoiled in a flaming rush of words.

'Do you seriously think I'd put her life at risk allowing her to do something she's not fit to do? Where do you get off, walking into her life and criticising me, second-guessing my decisions? Of course she has regular check-ups, though only once a year now she's older. She's seeing Alex here, and yes, he did agree there was no problem with her riding. I'm not entirely stupid, you know!'

She paused for breath but her fury wasn't spent.

'Nor did I keep a daily health diary just in case you might one day turn up in her life. She had whooping cough when she was two in spite of having had the immunisations. Do you want to know that as well? A greenstick fracture of her wrist at four, caused by falling off her bike when she persuaded Mum to take the training wheels off? What else?'

'You're being ridiculous now,' he growled, but Clare didn't care. The togetherness of the weekend had been bad enough, but now to have Oliver carrying on as if all that had happened in the past was somehow her fault was just too much. On top of that, she hated thinking back, especially to that period of time after Emily's birth, which was jammed tight with so many bad memories she tried never to think about it.

'*You* brought it up!' she snapped, the tension between them as palpable as the electricity in the air before a storm.

Oliver didn't reply, his silence intensifying the pressure in the atmosphere as they finished the short journey home.

He dropped her off in front of the flats and drove off, Clare so relieved to be out of the car, she didn't care where he went. But just in case he was simply putting the car away, she fled up the path, unlocked the door and bolted up the stairs to the refuge of her flat.

Refuge? When she was listening all the time for the sound of a vehicle in the back lane, or the growl of the garage doors opening?

She had a shower, hoping hot water might ease the aching tightness their conversation had caused in her muscles. It was okay they'd parted as they had. Seeing how good he was with Emily had intensified the love Clare felt for him—but only by about a thousandfold. And after a weekend of such togetherness some traitorous part of her brain had been thinking maybe marriage wasn't such a bad idea.

A platonic marriage, of course.

Which would go down *really* well with Oliver!

But now she was sure he was sufficiently annoyed with her to have forgotten he'd ever suggested it, which should make her feel relieved, not uptight and disappointed.

And angry.

She turned off the water, wrapped a towel around her body, found a copy of Emily's health file and left it on Oliver's doormat, then made herself toast and jam for supper, and went to bed. She might not sleep, but at least with all the lights out Oliver might think she slept.

Or had gone out.

That thought made her think some more, her mind tracking along a completely new path.

His assumption that they should marry indicated he was assuming she had no social life at all.

Which she didn't, but that didn't mean he should assume it.

Could she conjure one up?

Pretend?

He had a daughter!

Oliver stood on the top of the cliff above Coogee Beach and looked out to sea, trying to assimilate the information, the reality of it.

Emily had been real enough when she was there— chatting so unselfconsciously, showing so little reserve to a virtual stranger, so childishly confident in the love of the adults she knew that she hadn't seemed to doubt for a moment he would love her.

He had doubted—oh, how he had doubted. Yet when he'd looked into those green eyes, familiar from the face he saw in the mirror every morning, something had swelled inside his chest, filling it to capacity, making him feel light-headed and woozy.

Stress, that's what he tried to put it down to, but her lack of awkwardness should have dispelled stress within seconds and that strange wooziness had remained with him all weekend, less all-encompassing but still there, swelling to maximum power again when she'd given him the scrapbook.

Was it love?

Could you feel love so instantaneously?

So intensely?

How could he know so little about love that he had to ask himself these questions?

Not wanting to think about the answer to that conundrum, he turned his attention to the future, except that thinking about the future meant thinking about Clare and, right now, thinking about Clare fanned the doused embers of his anger.

Logically he could accept that she had done her best to contact him when she discovered she was pregnant. Intellectually he could accept that not hearing from him, she would assume he didn't want to know his child, especially after the way they'd parted.

But the newly discovered emotional person inside him still blamed her and, blaming her, felt she was the one with the responsibility of sorting out where they went from here.

Because they *were* going somewhere.

All three of them.

The idea of being a part-time father was totally unacceptable. Emily deserved better than that. She deserved a family.

Oliver spun around and retraced his steps to the car. He needed to talk to Clare and he needed to talk to her now.

Clare was lying in bed, not even pretending to sleep because her mind refused to settle, when she heard footsteps on the stairs.

Oliver was returning.

The footsteps hesitated on the landing and she knew he'd have found the file—the photocopy she always kept as they moved the original file from one specialist to another.

She hadn't left a note, just the file, but surely it was self-explanatory. Yet she didn't hear a key turning in his lock, instead there was a tap at her own door, then a louder knock.

Depleted of all energy from the emotionally fraught weekend, she didn't answer the summons. Let him assume she was asleep.

Or out?

She wasn't sure where the idea had come from, but suddenly the idea of avoiding Oliver for the next few days was intensely appealing. If she could just have a few days to herself—to go to work, come home and pretend life was normal—then by next weekend she might be able to think clearly enough to work out where they went from here in Em's relationship with her father.

It wasn't hard. Monday's operation was a complicated one that Alex and Angus were doing so she wouldn't have to see Oliver, and she knew Oliver was working Tuesday and Wednesday evenings, having swapped his weekend duty with Angus so he, Oliver, could spend time with Emily. Clare could go to the pantomime meeting without fear of seeing him there.

Thursday—well, she wouldn't get too far ahead of herself just yet, but if Monday's op was a long one, and there was no surgery scheduled for Thursday, she could probably take the day off and start on her Christmas shopping. She'd like to get something special for those nieces and nephews up in Queensland, and something extra special for her mother, who'd been such a rock in her life since Em was born.

Plans are one thing but, in reality, avoiding Oliver was difficult when he catapulted down the stairs behind her as she was leaving for work the next morning.

'Wait up. I want to talk to you.'

'And asking so politely too!'

Okay, so snapping at him was petty, but after a week of unadulterated tension, she was desperate for a little Oliver-free time.

'It's about *our* daughter,' he growled, his voice telling her he probably wanted to see as little of her as she wanted to see of him.

She shrugged off the sniping comment.

'Was any explanation given for the PDA? According to the file she was slightly premature but four weeks is nothing these days. Did the paediatrician who saw her think it might have been genetic?'

Clare sighed.

'I really, really don't want to think about that time,' she muttered. 'You might not believe it, but it wasn't exactly a high point in my life. I've given you the file, what more do you want?'

She was striding up the road, trying not to get ahead of him but to escape the relentless awareness that stirred her senses whenever he was close.

'I want to know the nitty-gritty stuff. If we have another child, should we be prepared that this could happen again.'

'If we have another child?'

The words came out so loudly three pigeons nodding to one another on the roof of a nearby house took flight, the whirring flutter of their wings echoing in Clare's head.

Along with a lot of other confusion.

'Why on earth would you suppose we'd have another child? How's that likely to happen? Immaculate conception?'

He didn't touch her, but he was walking far too close to her, invading her space in a way she did and didn't like, her body and mind set on different paths.

'I told you I thought we should get married, and having met Emily I'm more convinced than ever that it would be the right thing for her.'

'For *her*?'

Forget pigeons, now she was causing the heads of the pedestrians waiting at the lights to swivel towards Oliver and herself.

'And what about me? Where do I come into it?'

Fortunately the lights changed so the pedestrians moved off the kerb while she and Oliver were still approaching, but she did mute her voice as there were people everywhere.

'We'd be doing it for Emily,' Oliver muttered at her, but it was too late—she'd taken off across the road, although the signal was already flashing. And with those words following her like a trailing streamer, she fled into the hospital.

She *had* to keep out of his way!

Oliver checked the patients in the cardiac PICU, then collected his outpatient list from Becky.

'I've got four more staff members from our unit willing to be in the pantomime,' she told him.

Pantomime? That's where his tumultuous week had really taken off.

'I'm only telling you because I know you're on duty Wednesday night and won't be able to make the meeting, but I'm sure someone will tell you all about it. And Friday night, there's a staff welcome party. I've put a notice on the board in the staff lounge. Alex likes everyone to be there because it's a chance to meet staff from other departments.'

'If I can't make it I'll explain to Alex,' Oliver told her, thinking that on Friday afternoon he'd be going with Clare to collect their daughter from school. Or was this Friday the party Emily had been chattering on about?

He'd have to ask Clare.

Given the rage she'd been in when they parted, this wasn't an appealing idea, but surely, eventually, she'd see the sense of his suggestion.

But asking Clare anything proved difficult when he couldn't track her down. From time to time, he did see her at the hospital, but never in a situation where he could discuss the very personal matter of their daughter.

'It will have to come out sometime,' he said when he did meet her in an elevator one day.

'What does that mean?' she demanded.

'Exactly what I said. Everyone will eventually know we have a daughter, so now she knows about me, would it be so bad if people overheard us discussing her here at the hospital?'

She threw him a glance that would have melted rock and exited the elevator, although he was sure she'd have no patients on the orthopaedic floor.

And catching her at home was impossible. He'd been on duty himself for two nights, and when he knocked on her door on Thursday evening there was no response. Unless she was living in the dark like a mole, she wasn't at home.

'Not that it's any of your business,' she told him coolly when he caught up with her on Friday and, rudely he supposed, asked her where she'd been. 'But there *are* on-duty rooms at the hospital, and there's been a very fragile baby on ECMO. Where else would I have been last night?'

Embarrassed, but still unreasonably angry, he was searching for a reply when her pager buzzed and she was whisked away. No doubt to the fragile baby on ECMO.

He could follow. He knew the baby in question and there was no reason why he shouldn't go into the cardiac PICU, but he also knew he'd be better off stepping back a bit, working out what was really upsetting Clare—apart from marrying him—before he blundered in again.

He all but growled. *He* didn't blunder. His relationships with women usually ran smoothly. They were well-planned campaigns, mutually satisfying, and ending in if not friendship, then definitely with accord.

Except, of course, his relationship with Clare.

Clare woke on Friday morning, aware her days of avoidance were over. This afternoon she would have to go home to the flat, to make sure things were ready for Emily for the weekend.

Thank heavens she'd had the forethought to ask Angus if he'd mind accompanying her to the staff party that evening, using the excuse that she hated walking into functions on her own. She'd sweetened the request by offering to buy him dinner at Scoozi first, and she hoped that Oliver might take the innocent outing as a date and so let go of the ridiculous idea that they should marry.

She shivered at the thought, aware after the kiss they'd shared that while her body might ache for the satisfaction only Oliver could give it, the dark memories in her mind would always make her draw away from him.

Now she sighed.

Her heart had been telling her she loved Oliver—whether still or again—since shortly after he'd walked back into her life, but the reality of it was now gaining ground in her mind. And loving him, as she was reasonably certain she did, she couldn't possibly marry him. She refuted the damaged-goods label her head kept throwing at her, but she *had* been damaged, physically and emotionally, in the past, which meant she definitely wasn't good marriage material.

Oliver was contemplating knocking on Clare's door to ask her if she'd like to have dinner with him before the staff get-together when voices from the footpath made him glance out the window.

Clare and Angus?

Had they met by accident? Oliver was vaguely aware that Angus also lived somewhere on this street, although closer to the hospital, he thought.

So why was he down here? Crossing the road with Clare? Walking into the park?

Oliver spun away from the window. What was *he* doing, spying on his neighbour like this?

The knot in his gut told him the answer. He was jealous. Jealous that Clare was walking and talking with another man.

And why?

He couldn't answer that one, but he knew it was unreasonable to be feeling like this. For all that he still thought they should marry for Emily's sake, Clare had walked out of his life a long time ago and was under no obligation to be faithful to him.

Not that he could assume she was being unfaithful with Angus—a man she barely knew!

And if that wasn't the epitome of confused thinking, he didn't know what was. He took himself off to the kitchen, fixed a toasted sandwich, ate it in front of the television news and told himself he wouldn't go to the party.

After which he told himself to grow up!

* * *

Poor Angus. Had their dinner conversation been as boring to him as it had seemed to her? Clare wondered about this as they entered the hospital, relieved when Kate joined them in the foyer.

'Your hair looks great,' Clare said, admiring the gloss and gleam of Kate's carefully straightened hair.

'Thanks,' Kate replied. 'It takes such an age to straighten, I don't do it often.'

And although not one cell of Clare's body had responded to Angus, good-looking though he was, she was suddenly intensely aware of him—of *his* tension.

Was he interested in Kate?

Had she, Clare, unintentionally bumbled her way into something she hadn't understood?

Confused and a bit embarrassed, she continued to chat with Kate about hair as they entered the elevator together.

Angus didn't follow!

'Are you with us?' she asked, and he moved in to stand beside her, although she was sure most of his attention was on Kate.

At the door of the function room, Clare realised she'd once again lost Angus. Kate had plunged into the crowd, but what was the point, Clare thought, of coming with Angus if they didn't walk in together?

She slipped her hand into the crook of his arm as they moved towards a cluster of their colleagues, ducking to avoid Christmas decorations, Clare muttering to herself about the tinsel but smiling at the team members.

Then not smiling as she realised Oliver was part of the cluster. But at least she had Angus as backup, for all he seemed to be very distracted.

They stood and chatted for a while, Oliver disappearing as Becky told a doctor joke, then Angus, too, drifted off. Clare took a drink from a tray and looked around the room, hoping it appeared that her gaze was wandering casually over the throng, rather than looking intently to see where Oliver had gone. She was considering another circuit when her heart gave an excited little blip and she realised it was the back of his head she could see, over by the buffet laid out for their supper.

But in spite of the urge to talk to him—so much for keeping her distance—wouldn't it look too obvious if she just wandered over there?

Angus was not far away, so she'd grab him first.

'Let's go get something to eat,' she suggested, and although Angus looked slightly startled—he'd seen the dinner she'd eaten—he fell in with the plan.

So he could see Kate, who was also by the buffet?

Clare shook off the confusing thoughts and took Angus's hand, all but dragging him along.

'Well, hi, you two—fancy meeting you here.'

Was she making a point? Oliver wondered. Why else was she holding hands with Angus?

Or was she using him as a shield? Protection?

'I knocked on your door,' he said as she drew close.

'I left early,' Clare replied, their conversation so stilted it hurt her to think they'd come to this.

Kate was talking about taking their supper up onto the roof, suggesting all four of them went.

'Won't it be windy up there?' Clare protested. 'It'll blow your hair.'

Kate shrugged off the comment, but before Clare could speak again, Oliver had made the decision for her.

'Well, I'll keep an eye on Clare for you while you're gone,' he said, probably to Angus, although Clare was sure the words were also meant for her.

She shouldn't have avoided him all week. Avoidance didn't solve anything, especially when there were things of major importance to sort out.

They were adults. They could discuss things rationally.

Well, almost rationally—just standing near him right now was sending all the wrong messages to her body.

'Can *we* go somewhere and talk?' he asked, speaking her thoughts and so confusing her a little more. Was he feeling what she was feeling? Would this talk be personal?

'About Emily?'

He shook his head, answering two of her questions, one asked and one unasked.

'About you,' he said, then he reached out and tucked a swatch of hair behind one ear. 'About you,' he repeated, but so softly it was little more than a breath of air puffing from his lips.

'We can't leave yet,' she managed, although now he'd asked she wanted nothing more than to talk to Oliver, to let out so much of the poison she had bottled up inside her. Once he knew about her past he'd stop pressing her about the marriage thing and they could have a good relationship with each other and their daughter.

'But soon,' he said, then he turned away as Alex tapped him on the shoulder, asking him to come and meet a surgeon from the general ward.

Clare watched him go. She was aware of feeling nervous yet relaxed—two diametrically opposite emotions existing side by side within her.

She chatted to various members of the team, met people from other wards and disciplines, but was aware all the time of Oliver's presence in the room, as if her sensory receptors were tracking every move he made.

'So, now can we leave politely?' He came up to stand behind her, and she turned towards him, smiling as she nodded her response.

Oliver doubted he'd ever been as aware of anyone in his life as he was of Clare through that seemingly endless evening. Was it her beauty that stirred him so deeply, the outward serenity of her even features, the tumbling mane of hair, swept up off her neck tonight, though tendrils had escaped to trail against the golden skin?

She slipped her hand inside his elbow, his arm crooking to tuck her fingers into place.

'Didn't you have a date?' he asked as they wove their way towards the door.

She raised dark eyebrows at him.

'Been spying on me?' Then she shrugged. 'I came with Angus. I asked him, not the other way around. It was stupid—infantile—thinking if I avoided you we wouldn't have to talk, but Em deserves we do the best we can for her, so maybe if we get all the talk out of the way we'll see a path ahead more clearly.'

'What kind of talk?' Oliver asked cautiously. They were alone in the foyer outside the reception room, most people still enjoying the hospitality provided.

She pulled a face, gave another little shrug.

'The other night—I can explain...'

But she was looking pale again so he put his arm around her and ushered her into the elevator, keeping his arm there so she was tight against his side.

'Let's wait until we get home,' he murmured, nodding to the people entering on the next floor down.

She didn't argue, but he could see the lines strain had drawn on her face, and feel the unhappiness tightening her body.

What could he do to ease her pain? At least alleviate it slightly so the walk down their road wouldn't be so agonising for her. They were back to ground level now, and the foyer was as busy as it always was.

But usually—

'Here,' he said, and drew her into one of the small rooms that were part non-denominational chapels and part simply quiet spaces where people could release emotions and regain their fortitude before facing again some of the horrors they had to deal with in a hospital situation.

And in that private space he kissed her, not passionately, but gently, carefully, trying to tell her without words that he was there for her. She nestled closer, not responding to the kiss intensely, but responding nonetheless.

Was it because this room had held such emotions that images of how Clare's life must have been seemed to flash across his mind? First discovering she was pregnant, not hearing from him, hurt beyond words that he should care so little for her news—alone with her misery at what should have been a time of excitement and delight. Then Emily's birth, alone again, and frightened, when she discovered her baby had a problem.

He folded his arms around her and held her close, not kissing now, but wanting to say so many things.

'You need never have to face things alone again,' he murmured against her hair which was tumbling down from its clasp and feathering against her shoulders.

She snuggled closer for a moment, then drew away, lifting her hand to touch his cheek.

'If only it was that easy,' she whispered, then she took his hand and led him out of the room. 'Let's go home. We'll talk there.'

CHAPTER EIGHT

For a flat that had much the same furnishing as his, Clare's place was so distinctly different. It had the feeling of a home, something he'd never achieved in any of the rented apartments he'd had over the years.

He didn't for a moment believe that only women could make a place homely, so…

'I guess I never really cared about where I lived, not in the sense of wanting it to offer anything more than shelter and a certain amount of comfort and security,' he said as Clare led him into the living room and continued on to throw open the bay windows.

She turned and looked at him, eyebrows raised in query.

'This place—I didn't take much notice at the weekend, with Emily here—but it looks homely,' he explained.

'You mean messy and untidy,' Clare said, coming forward and picking up a magazine from the arm of one chair and tossing it into a wicker basket on the floor by the couch. 'Call it rebellion, or perhaps it's just the natural outcome of having a child around the place. There is always stuff hanging around.'

Oliver nodded. He could see the evidence of Emily's existence, a handpainted card on a side table, a hair ribbon tied to the stem of the large-leafed plant in one corner of the room, a butterfly on a stick stuck into a smaller pot plant on the windowsill.

But though these snatches of his daughter's life caught his eye, his mind was back on the first thing Clare had said.

Rebellion.

'Rebellion?'

He repeated it out loud and saw her shoulders lift as she took in a deep breath.

'Do you want coffee or tea, a drink? I have some wine, but no spirits.'

He shook his head.

Another deep breath, then she gestured to the arm-chair.

'Then let's sit down. I have to tell it from the begin-ning or you won't understand.'

She threw him a half-smile before adding, 'Actually, you might not understand anyway. Most of the time I don't myself.'

Clare watched Oliver sink down into the comfortable armchair, then seated herself on the couch, drawing up her legs under her, almost unconsciously making herself as small as possible.

Less of her to hurt?

'When I left you, I went home to the farm. It was only a week before Christmas, you remember. Everything was fine. I mean, I was miserable, but the family were all kind and supportive and I pretended to be okay. Both my brothers were still living at home, and my sister, who'd shifted to Queensland, was down for the festive season, and life went on. Then one day Dad fell down.'

'Fell down?'

Clare paused, recalling so vividly that day in the dairy when her father had seemed to trip and fall, but then had failed to get up.

'Apparently he'd been feeling lousy for a while, but being Dad hadn't said anything. Mum had noticed he was dragging one foot but when she asked him about it he brushed her off. It was Christmas—everyone was busy, but cows still had to be milked. With Dad only half there we all dug in and got through, then in the New Year, Mum insisted he see the doctor.'

This was where the telling became difficult, Oliver realised, and knowing how much Clare had loved her father, he got out of the chair and came to sit beside her, not touching, just being there.

'Eventually,' she said, nodding as if accepting his move, 'he was diagnosed with motor neurone disease—right about the time I diagnosed myself as being pregnant.'

Clare had told him this bit looking down at her lap, toying with a button on her skirt. Now she looked directly at him.

'You'd know about MND. In most cases it progresses very rapidly. We all wanted Dad at home because we knew he'd be happiest there, so although Liz went back to Queensland, I stayed on at the farm to help out. Steve's mate Barry used to come three or four days a week to give a hand with the milking. He'd changed to beef cattle so was free. I contacted you and didn't hear, but there was so much emotion flowing around the place, Oliver, that not hearing from you was just one more thing to set at the door of unkind Fates.'

She offered him a smile, but he could hear the pain of those days in the huskiness of her voice and see it in her tortured dark eyes. He ached to touch her, to hold her, but something in her stillness warned him off. The glass wall was there, and though he suspected it was fragile, he didn't want to shatter it right now.

'We moved Dad into a hospice the week before I gave birth to Emily. Mum was staying there with him, and while by then I wasn't much use to the boys around the farm, I could still help out by shopping and cooking. When my waters broke, four weeks early, Barry was there, having called at the house to drop off a couple of casseroles his mother had made for us. He took me to the hospital and he stayed there with me. Mum couldn't leave Dad, and my brothers were busy at the farm, so Barry stuck around. He was wonderful. Just having someone there when I was told about Em's PDA, just having someone to lean on—I was so grateful to him.'

Oliver stood and strode across to the window, aware *he* should have been the one supporting Clare, so aware of it the awareness hurt.

Yet how could he have been there? How could he have known?

He stopped himself grinding his teeth just before he did damage to his tooth enamel, but the anger and frustration inside him was almost too much to bear— especially as Saint Barry was now front and centre in Clare's thoughts.

'So you married him?' Oliver found himself growling. Better that he ground his teeth but he couldn't stop the words from bursting forth.

Huge dark eyes studied him—unreadable in their intensity.

'Not then,' she finally whispered. 'First I tried to find you, then Dad died. Mum was devastated—lost. Em had her op, and the boys sold the farm. I had to stay in Victoria as Em was still seeing specialists and *then* I married Barry.'

Oliver assimilated the words. Really assimilated, for they seemed more to seep through his skin and into his blood than enter through his ears. And with them came the pain Clare must have suffered, the gut-wrenching loss of a beloved father, the fearful news that her newborn daughter had a heart problem, the isolation when her family moved away.

Damn the wall! He reached for her and drew her close, holding her as he would hold a hurt child, offering comfort, nothing more.

Clare melted against him, the tension of the telling of the story draining out, the warmth of Oliver's body so seductive that for a few seconds she imagined maybe everything would be all right.

Could she pretend that was the end of things?

Would Oliver accept that one failed marriage was enough to put her off the institution for life?

Probably not, but she was all talked out for one evening, and sitting like this, with Oliver's arms around her, was so close to heaven she didn't want to move, or think, or do anything much at all.

Just sit and let the bliss of it wash over her.

Just sit and not think at all.

But life didn't allow time for such luxuries. Oliver was turning her in his arms, slipping his fingers beneath her chin, turning her head, so she had to look at him.

Or so he could kiss her?

A deep shudder ran through her body, quickly relieved when his lips moved to speak, not to kiss.

'The marriage didn't work?'

She considered shaking her head, then knew she needed to say the words.

'The marriage didn't work,' she repeated, and this time knew he must have felt the shudder for his arms tightened around her and his head lowered so he could drop soft kisses on her hair.

So comforting. So very, very comforting.

But unacceptable! She was probably giving Oliver false hope about the marriage idea.

She eased herself away from him, pushed her hair back off her face, pulling it into a bundle and knotting it out of the way.

'I'm sorry, but getting rid of all that pent-up emotion has exhausted me,' she said, and watched his face, wanting to see some reaction, but reading nothing in it, or in his green eyes.

All he did was nod, then he stood up off the couch and walked towards the door, pausing there to ask, 'I take it we can go together to collect Emily in the morning. We can go in my car? What time?'

Clare frowned at him, unable to believe she'd been towed so far back into the past that the present—including her daughter—had gone completely from her mind.

'We can collect her at nine, which means leaving here about a quarter to.'

She knew she was still frowning, but that was because she realised she needed some time away from Oliver, the intimacy of telling him about the past now weighing heavily on her.

But she'd tried avoiding him last week and avoidance hadn't achieved a thing. They had to forge a way forward together, to find a life that would be stable and enriching for their daughter.

'Are you okay?' he asked, still hesitating in the doorway. 'Do you want me to stay?'

He smiled at her.

'Even to stay as a friend, not a lover?'

'I'm fine,' she lied as love for this man she was turning away swept through her, shaking her so badly she needed him to leave so she could sit down alone and put herself together again.

Emily was tired and cranky. A rainy afternoon during the week had meant she'd missed her riding lesson; the party had been gross.

'That's terrible,' Clare translated for Oliver's benefit.

'The music was really lame,' Emily's plaint continued. 'Dad, can I have a guitar?'

As Em was sitting in the front seat next to Oliver, Clare had no chance to send a silent signal to him that guitar ownership had already been discussed and knocked back.

'I'll have to talk to your mother about it,' Oliver replied, and Clare gave him a tick of approval.

Emily produced a theatrical groan.

'Mum'll say no, I know she will. She'll say I'm already having riding lessons and I'm playing soccer and when would I have time to practise and what's the point of having one if I don't practise?'

She mimicked Clare's voice so well Clare had to hide a smile. They were driving down the back lane, the garage door sliding up in response to the remote, so Oliver had an excuse not to reply, though he did say, 'Ah!' in a thoughtful voice.

'I've got an old guitar back home in Melbourne, hardly used,' he said to Clare while Emily had found Rod sitting in the garden and was telling him about her week—sounding far more excited about it than she had when telling her parents.

'Should I get it sent up for her?' Oliver finished.

Clare shook her head.

'Let's wait and see,' she suggested. 'She might want a flute next week.'

Then she smiled at him.

'Got a flute tucked away at home?'

Oliver looked at this woman who had been through so much, yet could still smile and joke and carry on as if life was the great adventure she'd always thought it. Something quivered inside his chest—not attraction for sure—something far more subtle than that.

Something he didn't want to think about.

Emily had joined them, bouncing up and down with excitement.

'I asked Rod if he'd come and talk to my class at school about being a writer and he said yes,' she announced.

Oliver looked across at Rod, who nodded and smiled.

'I love talking to kids about writing,' he admitted. 'They're so full of enthusiasm. Clare, can you organise a time with the school, perhaps check they really want an old man like me coming to visit?'

Clare moved towards their landlord and bent to kiss his cheek.

'Of course I will and thank you,' she said, then she straightened and looked at her daughter. 'Em, you've got your key? How about you take your things upstairs, then get a cup of tea going for Oliver. I'll be up shortly and we'll sit down and plan our weekend.'

Emily stood her ground.

'Are you going to tell Rod about Dad?' she asked, and Oliver wondered by what intuition a nine-year-old could fathom such a thing. He'd guessed that's why Clare was lingering in the garden, believing it was only right that Rod should know what was going on with his tenants.

'Come on,' he said to his daughter. 'What your mother wants to talk to Rod about is none of our business.'

The green eyes flashed towards him, rolling in a manner that said, Not you too, without the words, but Emily led the way around the side of the house, dug her key out of her overnight bag and opened the doors.

'The girls at school thought it was weird that I suddenly had a father,' she told him as she stomped up the stairs. 'They wondered if I'd change my name.'

She reached the landing and turned towards him, face-to-face as he was still a few steps behind her.

'Will you and Mum get married?' she added, the simple innocence of the question stealing Oliver's breath.

'Let's get that cup of tea going,' he told her eventually, 'and work out what we want to do over the weekend. Have you ever seen horse races? I thought we might go this afternoon, not so much to see who wins the races but so you can check out the thoroughbreds as they parade around the ring. Would you like that?'

'Could I have a bet?'

It was the last question Oliver had expected and he frowned at this apparently knowledgeable small person who'd come into his life.

'What do you know about betting?' he demanded, and was rewarded with a cheeky grin.

'Melbourne Cup of course. *Everyone* knows about the Melbourne Cup! The teachers even let us watch it on the television because they say it's part of the Australian culture.'

Put firmly in his place, Oliver repeated the question. Would going to the races interest her?

'I'd like to see the horses,' she told him, heading for the kitchen and lifting the electric kettle to fill it with water. 'Because they brush them somehow so they have patterns on their rumps, and I'd like to learn to do that for when I have my own horse.'

Oliver rather doubted she could get horse-grooming lessons at the races, but he liked the idea that he'd thought of something that might interest her—that he, not Clare, had come up with the outing.

Clare.

He took the kettle from his daughter and filled it for her, although she assured him she could manage.

Was he fiddling around in the kitchen so he didn't have to think about the trauma of Clare's life in that year after they'd parted, so that he didn't have to feel, well, guilt that he hadn't been there for her?

The story had spun around in his head as he tried to sleep the previous night, and snippets of it—things he wanted to ask about—kept coming back to him.

'I'm going to change. Mum has her tea black,' Emily announced, apparently happy to leave him in charge in the kitchen, though she'd no sooner left the room than she reappeared. 'Do I wear going-out clothes to the races?'

'Perhaps we'd better consult your mother before we decide definitely that's what we'll do,' he told her, and she frowned ferociously at him.

'I thought a man could decide things like that on his own,' she said. 'Anyway, Mum won't mind. She likes horses too. She used to live on a farm, you know.'

Before Oliver could work out a reply to this conversation, Clare appeared.

'I explained to Rod,' she said briefly, then she turned to Emily. 'You're not changed yet?'

Emily heaved a theatrical sigh.

'Dad says we can go to the races, but we have to ask you first, so I don't know if I should put on going-out clothes, or beach clothes or what.'

'Go to the races?'' Clare echoed faintly. Bad enough that she had to give their landlord a brief explanation of their convoluted relationship, but now, apparently, she had to make a decision about going to the races.

'It'll be fun,' Oliver said. 'Here, I've made the tea, and I've told Emily we won't be betting, just going to look at the horses and we needn't stay long.'

Unable to think of a valid reason for *not* going to the races when it was put like that, Clare nodded at her daughter.

'Going-out clothes, something cool, and the hat Gran gave you for your birthday.'

Emily skipped off into her bedroom and Clare sank down onto the stool in front of the kitchen bench.

'The races?' she said, looking at Oliver across the tea things.

'She likes horses,' he said, though he looked so embarrassed Clare had to smile.

'Have you been thinking all week of outings you could offer her?' she asked. 'We don't have to go out, you know. She can just as easily spend the weekend at home, with a high treat being a walk across the park for a pizza at Scoozi for dinner.'

Oliver nodded, but still looked put out.

'I suppose it's because I've missed so much of her,' he said, 'that I feel I should be making up to her all the time.'

He paused, then he reached across the bench and touched Clare lightly on the cheek.

'Making up to you as well,' he added softly.

Clare felt the touch. It felt like love, although she knew it was sympathy and understanding. She wanted to grasp his fingers and hold them to her cheek, but his hand had moved away already, and besides, it would have been unwise.

'I'll go and put on some going-out clothes,' he said. 'I imagine we can get lunch out there. Shall we say leaving here at eleven-thirty?'

Clare nodded, her mind already scooting off touches and love and delving feverishly into her wardrobe.

Going-out clothes?

She didn't go out.

She had one kind of all-purpose black dress she'd worn the previous evening, suitable for everything from dinner parties, to hospital functions, to funerals. But going-to-the-races clothes?

She dashed across the landing, banging on Oliver's door.

'I haven't got any going-out clothes.' She all but wailed the words, catching herself in time and trying to sound like a reasonable adult. 'I don't want to disappoint Emily, so how about you take her?'

Oliver looked at Clare for a moment, then shook his head. He left her on his doorstep while he walked across into her flat, knocking on Emily's door.

'You decent?' he asked, and the door opened to reveal Emily already dressed in a pretty but simple sun frock that had been part of her birthday present from Gran.

'Your mother hasn't anything to wear,' Oliver told the child. 'Where's the nearest place we can buy going-out clothes for her?'

'Ooh, can I come too? Can I help you choose? The shopping centre just up the road has a boutique with some super grown-up women's clothes. I've been telling Mum for ages she needs to buy some decent gear. She came to the school my first week in jeans and a jacket she bought in Chicago—can you imagine?'

Clare slumped against the doorjamb and shook her head in bemusement. Between them, her daughter and her daughter's father were disrupting her life so much she wondered if she'd ever get it back on track.

But within minutes she'd been swept off between the two of them, and hustled into a boutique, where Emily darted around pointing to clothes she thought her mother should buy, while Oliver sat down in an armchair obviously provided for male companions, and gave every indication that he was ready for a show of some kind.

Not that Clare intended parading in front of him, although once she had a pretty patterned skirt and top on, she was so unsure of how she looked—so unused to seeing herself in going-out clothes—she did actually go out of the changing room to ask him what he thought.

She looked so nervous and uncertain Oliver's first instinct was to take her in his arms, but knowing that would be disastrous in a shop, *and* in front of Emily, he studied the outfit.

'You look fantastic in anything,' he told her, 'and those colours look great on you. Are you happy with the two pieces or would a dress be easier?'

By now Clare was looking distinctly embarrassed, and when she muttered something about a skirt and top being more practical because she could get more wear out of them, it made him wonder if maybe she had no going-out clothes because of financial restraints. He had no idea how much she earned, certainly less than him, and with school fees and uniforms and riding lessons and rent...

'Try on the other things and show me, then we'll decide.'

'Try on the brown spotty dress first,' Emily put in, then she came and sat beside Oliver on the arm of the chair. 'She never buys anything for herself,' she confided to him. 'She says it's because she doesn't need to, that she has enough clothes for work and weekends and that's all she needs. Mum's idea of dressing up is putting a jacket over her jeans and polo shirts.'

It was an artless conversation but Oliver was struck by the enormity of what had happened because his mother, out of pure spite, didn't forward on a letter. For ten years Clare had struggled on her own, or with whatever help her mother could give her, while he'd never hesitated to buy the latest laptop, or a new Italian suit, or take a skiing trip in the Alps.

He wanted to buy her everything in the shop, to fill her life with the things she'd been denying herself. He wanted to marry her and take care of her for ever so she never had to scrimp and save again.

She came out in the brown dress with the white spots, and he stopped thinking altogether, his mind numbed by the vision in front of him. The dress was probably fairly ordinary as dresses went. It was made of some silkily soft material so the skirt swirled softly around her long legs, while the V-neck of the top showed the shadow of her breasts, the whole effect breathtaking.

'Told you it would be super,' Emily said, leaping up from the arm of the chair to dance around her mother. 'It *is* super, isn't it, Dad?'

Oliver found it hard to respond. It was indeed super, but the beauty of this woman had taken his breath away and his mouth was too dry for words.

'Well, that's okay, but I can't buy it anyway. I can't wear black sandals with it and that's all I have, so I'll get the skirt and top which are more sensible anyway. I can wear the two pieces separately, mix and match.'

'With your jeans!' Emily groaned in a long-suffering voice, rolling her eyes in mock disgust at the same time.

'Well, the top would look good with jeans,' Clare said crossly, and she disappeared back into the changing room.

There she sat down on the little stool and tried hard not to cry. The brown dress was so classically cut and elegant, she'd felt a million dollars in it, but it was the look in Oliver's eyes when he'd seen her in it that had really struck deep into her heart. He had looked at her as if she was beautiful and for a moment she had felt beautiful—something she hadn't felt for a long time.

And wanting that feeling to last, she really wanted the dress, wanted to walk beside him in it....

Being maudlin will get you nowhere, she told herself sharply, standing and carefully removing the dress, returning it reluctantly to its hanger. She put on her own clothes, then carried the skirt and top out of the changing room to find her daughter and Oliver had disappeared.

'They said to wait,' the store attendant said. 'I'll just get the dress from the changing room.'

'I'm not taking it—just these two things,' Clare told her, but the woman bustled away, returning with the dress and putting it down on the counter.

Emily's excited voice told Clare the others were returning, her daughter bursting through the door with three pairs of sandals in her hands.

'Try these on, Mum,' she insisted. 'Dad said the least he can do is buy you a pair of sandals when he hasn't been con—'

She stumbled on the word and Oliver put in 'contributing' for her, so Emily could finish her explanation.

'—contributing to my clothes or school or anything. If you get a pair of sandals you can buy the brown dress which looked super on you.'

Emily hustled her to the chair Oliver had used earlier and knelt to slip off her mother's sneakers, replacing them with delicate, strappy sandals.

'Perfect,' she said, and Clare had to laugh—her daughter a saleswoman at nine.

'Try on the others as well,' Oliver advised. 'You might like one of the other pairs better, or you could have all three.'

'No-one needs three pairs of white sandals,' Clare objected, and now the saleswoman got involved.

'Hush your mouth!' she said sternly. 'You'll be struck out of the fraternity of women if someone heard you say that.'

Clare smiled as a happiness she couldn't remember feeling for a very long time welled up inside her, bubbling like a spring freed from some obstruction.

'I'll take this pair,' she said, choosing the sandals she'd first tried on, then she looked up at Oliver. 'You don't have to do this, you know,' she told him, but all she got in reply was a short shake of his head before his attention turned to Emily.

'Come on, kid,' he said. 'We'd better get these back to the shoe shop and pay for the ones we're taking.'

He turned aside to speak to the saleswoman, while Emily gathered up the shoes, keeping the discards in one hand and the pair they were to buy in the other.

'Back soon, Mum,' she said, then she dropped a kiss on her mother's cheek. 'Isn't it fun having Dad around?' she whispered, and suddenly the spring of happiness wasn't bubbling quite as high.

Clare knew Oliver's reasoning behind the gift of the sandals and—it appeared when she went to pay—of the clothes, and though she felt awkward about accepting such things, she would do it graciously. But Emily's whispered comment had hurt her in a way she didn't fully understand.

She knew it wasn't jealousy she was feeling, but disappointment of some kind—disappointment that the life she'd been providing for her daughter hadn't measured up....

'Hey!'

Oliver had returned and was standing beside her, and his hand rested lightly on her waist as he murmured the word.

'We're going forward, remember. Just enjoy Emily's delight.'

Clare nodded, wanting so much to be a full participant in this new family of three, but knowing it could never be, not the way Oliver wanted it.

They returned to the flats where Clare changed into her new finery, eliciting cries of delight from her daughter.

'You need my pearls, the ones Gran gave me,' Emily declared as she inspected her mother for the last time. 'Wait here.'

She ran off to her bedroom and returned with the pearls that had been her great-grandmother's, making her mother sit on the bed so she, Emily, could fasten them.

'There,' she said, 'you're beautiful. Dad will surely want to marry you now.'

Clare knew the words were nothing more than childish enthusiasm, but once again the joy of the morning dimmed, and despair wormed its way into her heart.

How could she resist if it became a matter of two against one?

How could she deny her daughter life in a family situation—two parents living together, not in separate flats?

She shook her head, knowing she couldn't resist or deny, yet knowing she couldn't marry Oliver either.

CHAPTER NINE

THE afternoon at the races was an unqualified success. Emily was fascinated by the patterns on the horses' rumps and totally infatuated by the beautiful thoroughbreds.

Clare felt like Cinderella, decked out in fancy clothes, knowing all the time the ball would end and she'd be going back to the reality of her life with only minor changes.

'I don't intend to talk to you about things tonight, with Emily around,' Oliver said to her when they returned home after eating dinner at a Chinese restaurant near the racecourse. 'But tomorrow night—we'll sort it all out then.'

He paused, possibly listening for sounds from Em's bedroom, for the little girl had been tired enough to head straight to bed.

Then he continued, 'She asked me if we'd get married, did you know that?'

Clare stared at him, unable to believe Em had spoken that way to a man who, for all he was her father, was still virtually a stranger to her.

'She's only nine. It probably seems to her the kind of thing adults do. She's no idea what marriage really means, or what being married might entail for the two people involved. All she wants is a mum and dad at home like other girls at school, although statistically speaking there are probably as many different home situations as there are girls in her class.'

Oliver studied the woman he'd decided he would marry, the woman he'd been so proud to have by his side this afternoon, the woman who appeared, on short acquaintance, to have done an excellent job of bringing up his daughter.

'We'll see you in the morning,' she said, telling him the conversation was over for this evening, but his thoughts stayed with him as he made his way into his own flat.

He knew Clare still had feelings for him. He'd seen it in her eyes from time to time, when she thought he wasn't watching her, yet she held to this stubborn resistance against their marriage.

It wasn't lack of attraction—that still ran strong between them, so strong that even standing close to her he could feel it thrumming in both their bodies.

So why?

Because she felt the failure of her first marriage was her fault?

Because she was afraid she'd fail again?

The Clare he'd known had been afraid of nothing. Well, maybe snakes, but a lot of people had an atavistic fear of snakes. But she'd had no emotional fear, throwing herself into love as wholeheartedly as she'd plunge into the ocean on a hot day.

Ah! Was it *his* fault? Had their split made her cautious about loving again? Had he hurt her so badly she feared to love again?

Useless speculation! They'd talk tomorrow evening, after they'd dropped Emily back at school, and in the meantime he'd read about a great restaurant on the rocks beside the beach at Bondi, not far from where they lived. They could all three go for breakfast there, then wander through the Sunday markets, have a swim and be home in time to do whatever Clare had to do to get Emily ready for her return to school.

He pulled out his mobile and dialled Clare's number, telling himself he was phoning her to make these suggestions to her, not because he wanted to hear her voice just one more time before he went to bed....

Togetherness crept up on you, Clare decided when once again they were in Oliver's car, heading for Emily's school. Em was chatting on to Oliver about all the things she'd have to tell her friends when she arrived, turning to ask Clare if she could invite one of the country girls home next weekend and to remind her to phone the school about Rod coming to talk.

The wonderful breakfast at the beach, the walk, the swim, had all left Clare so pleasantly tired she agreed with everything, although she knew when she got back to the flat she'd have to write herself a note about phoning the school—about Rod and about the boarder coming to visit.

When she got back to the flat.

Would they *have* to talk?

Could she plead exhaustion?

She thought not, although it would be real enough. She was usually tired after a weekend with Em because they always tried to pack as much as possible into it, but tonight it was emotional exhaustion.

It weighed her down and dogged her footsteps as she walked from the car to the front door of the house, then up the stairs, making every step an effort.

'Too tired to talk?' Oliver said when they were both on the landing.

She nodded, then shook her head.

'No, let's not put it off any longer,' she mumbled, tension twining through her body as she said the words, tightening as she led him into the flat where she dropped onto the couch, but in the middle so he couldn't sit beside her.

Not that it stopped him. He sat and edged her along, then put his arm around her.

'Of course we can put it off,' he said, so gently she felt like weeping. 'There are better things for lips to do than talking anyway.'

And with that he kissed her, so softly at first it was barely the brush of skin on skin, the touch of a rose petal.

But it was never going to be enough, his mouth moving against hers, testing and tasting her lips, his tongue exploring, not delving yet, but teasing her so she responded with her own tests and tastes, melting against Oliver's body, revelling in the feeling of being held not tightly but securely in his arms.

The heat she'd been trying to hold at bay crept through her body once again, and desire so strong she wondered if it would overcome all else sang in her blood. His lips devoured hers now, hungrily seeking deeper and deeper responses, responses she was happy to give.

Mindlessly she floated on a sea of sensation—being in Oliver's arms, kissing Oliver and being kissed by him—time and troubles fading into oblivion while remembered bliss tweaked her nerves and coursed through her body.

Oliver had gripped her hair, tugging gently so her head fell back and his lips could find her neck.

Did every woman have erogenous zones along the line of the blood vessels in the neck, or was it only she who shivered with delight when his lips pressed against her skin, and his tongue delved into the hollows where neck and torso joined?

His mouth was moving lower, buttons sliding open on her shirt, her hand against the back of his head, feeling the roughness of his hair.

Oliver!

She was twenty-five again—no, twenty, when all of this was new and exciting, when kissing Oliver was an exploration of a whole new world of sensation. His tongue slid into the deep cleavage between her breasts, increasing the longing in her body, so she pressed against him, nibbling at his ear, sucking on the lobe, sliding her tongue into the hidden whorls, feeling his reaction in his hardening erection.

It would be all right, she told herself. This was Oliver. She was safe. It would be fine. She needed love; she wanted it, wanted him.

Wanted him?

The words began to echo in her head and were blotting out the wonderment kissing Oliver had provided.

'Oliver!'

She breathed his name, and although she knew it must have taken a superhuman effort, he pulled away from her, still holding her, but not tightly, to him—not kissing her.

'I can't do it,' she whispered, her voice hoarse and her body shaking. 'I'm not teasing you—I thought I could, but I can't.'

He sat there, looking at her, no expression at all on his face.

So many explanations, none good, were racing through Oliver's mind he couldn't speak. He couldn't react at all. Something was very badly wrong here and until he knew what it was he couldn't begin to think about it, let alone do anything to make it right.

His immediate reaction to this second rejection had been anger, but that had been his libido talking. One look at Clare's face told him every word she said was true. She *couldn't* do it!

And there was no need to be coy about it and pretend he didn't know what 'it' was. They'd both been so worked up sex had been all but inevitable.

All but.

He took her hand in both of his and looked into her beautiful and unutterably sad and weary face.

'Can you talk about it?'

She shook her head, then bent it so her hair hid any expression from him.

'I thought I could do that as well, but now…'

So what to do?

She needed him—or someone. He knew that as surely as he knew he loved her, though why that revelation struck him right now he didn't know. He could hardly say it at the moment; she'd think he was using it as a weapon—something to force the issue of whatever it was she was hiding.

So he sat and held her hand in his, waiting, barely thinking, but willing to sit there all night if that's what was required.

So her movement startled him. She snatched her hand away, straightened up and looked directly at him. Then, holding his eyes, she ripped open her shirt and wrenched her bra aside, revealing her full and beautiful breasts, as proud and upright as they'd been when she was ten years younger, but—

Scarred?

He stared, unable not to, at small white lines like snail tracks, and bruised knotted tissue.

'Oh, my darling,' he whispered and took her in his arms again, holding her, not knowing what to say or do, except to hold her, murmuring now of love, telling her— talking, talking, talking, while her silent tears soaked his shirt.

Had she really stripped off her shirt and bra? Shown Oliver her scars? How *could* she have done that? How utterly embarrassing? How on earth was she going to face him in the morning?

Worse, how had she ended up in bed? Her last memory was of sitting on the couch, saturating Oliver's shirt with stupid, senseless tears, while the poor man talked of love, no doubt to try to stop her crying.

Clare clambered out of bed, pleased to see she was wearing her knickers, though nothing else, and headed for the shower, hoping to wash away the disjointed memories and get her mind into work mode once again.

But as she stared at the toast she'd made, and tipped her coffee, untasted, down the sink, her stomach squirmed at the thought of seeing Oliver again, working with Oliver today, pretending that nothing untoward at all had happened between them.

She left the flat, escaping. As far as she remembered Oliver was doing a PDA today, the same operation Emily had had, tying off the little duct that before birth carried blood between the arteries but after birth was supposed to close. No heart-lung machine required, but she wouldn't be at Jimmie's anyway; she'd been asked to assist at a hospital across town where a complicated adult operation was taking place.

Following the instructions the perfusionist at the other hospital had given her, she caught a train to town, changed there to another line, then felt a surge of delight as the second train took her on the famous bridge across Sydney Harbour, the wondrous sight of the Opera House down below. She'd been promising Emily a trip to the centre of the city to take in these sights, but they'd finally decided to leave it until Em had Christmas holidays so they could possibly stay a night in town.

'He's been on a ventricular assist device,' the perfusionist explained when Clare had been shown to the theatre and introduced to the man she'd only known as a voice on the phone. 'But as no heart has become available—rare blood group so it's going to be hard to find one—we're going to take out the old device and put in a more modern version of it, one we think will make him more comfortable.'

Having worked with teams putting these devices that helped the heart beat into adult patients in Chicago, Clare was only too happy to assist, but things went horribly wrong when the old pump was disconnected and it was discovered that the man's blood vessels were so damaged attaching a new device would be difficult.

'Heart surgeons can do anything!' the lead surgeon announced with more bravado in his voice than he must have been feeling.

Clare watched the monitors on the heart-lung machine, in sole charge now as the other perfusionist worked with the surgeons to find viable blood vessels in the man's chest.

'Maybe an external pump,' one of the surgeons suggested, but the lead man shook his head.

'The whole idea of doing the op was to give the man better quality of life. Is tying him to a hospital bed for however long it takes to find a heart a better quality of life? No, we'll do this. We might have to put in stents from good tissue in the blood vessels, and connect the stents to the LVAD.'

Clare checked the clotting factor of the man's blood, and the oxygenation, checked all the pumps were working, worrying about air bubbles now the man's chest had been open for so long. Then, eight hours after they'd begun, the job was done. She'd been spelled from time to time, forcing herself to eat and drinking coffee by the gallon, but now that the man was in the hands of the regular perfusionist and the anaesthetist, the weariness of the long hours in Theatre all but overwhelmed her.

'We've plenty of duty rooms you can crash in,' one of the nurses, perhaps sensing her exhaustion, offered.

'I think I might do that,' Clare told her. 'I don't think I could face the trains at this time of night.'

The nurse summoned an aide who led Clare along strange corridors, eventually opening the door of a typical on-duty room.

'There are toiletries in a sealed package in the cupboard—not much choice, male or female—and some theatre pyjamas if you want something to sleep in. Help yourself to tea or coffee or anything you might find in the refrigerator, but check the use-by date on any sandwiches. Who knows when the fridge was last stocked up.'

Food was the last thing on Clare's mind. She collapsed into bed, only to be called at four. They were taking the patient back to Theatre and, as the first perfusionist had been with him all night, could Clare assist?

'I've let Jimmie's know you're still here,' the head theatre sister told her when she joined the team in the theatre once again. 'Thank heavens you opted to stay the night.'

The team worked swiftly, knowing the man's life was already at risk. This second operation in twenty-four hours put strain on his entire body, not just his failing heart.

The surgeons spoke quietly, suggesting options, discussing and dismissing them while they removed the device they'd inserted the previous day.

'Maybe an external pump is the only answer,' one said.

'We still have to connect it to his heart, and to do that we have to connect it to blood vessels, and that's our problem—finding a couple that can take the pressure.'

But eventually they did it, although Clare stayed around until midafternoon, afraid if a blood vessel began to leak they'd have to open the man's chest again.

'All good!' the lead surgeon finally declared. He turned to Clare. 'You can go back to your babies now,' he said, 'but thanks for the hand and thank Alex for lending you to us. I know how tight your team is, so lending someone out is a strain on everyone.'

Clare was feeling too weary to do more than nod acceptance of the man's kind words. She changed into her civvies, pleased she'd washed out her undies and they'd dried while she slept, and caught the train back to the city, dozing as they crossed the bridge, changing trains, then finally arriving at the station just across the road from the rear of Jimmie's grounds.

It was only as she stared at the place that was fast becoming so familiar to her that she remembered it was Tuesday—rehearsal day for the pantomime.

Feeling certain that Oliver intended dropping out and not sure if anyone else from the cardiac team would turn up, she muttered the age-old words—*the show must go on*—and made her way to the canteen in the second tower.

Fate was apparently still in its capricious mood for the first person she saw was Oliver. In fact, she probably saw a lot of people before him but he was certainly the first to stand out in the crowd.

Tables had been pushed back and an area representing a stage marked out on the floor. Dr Droopy was clutching a bundle of paper, and Clare realised with some surprise that they had moved as far as scripts.

Oliver had seen her come in and now he made his way, unobtrusively he hoped, towards her. He didn't know why, given how angry he'd been to find she'd disappeared on him again. Not having seen her all day at the hospital, he'd knocked on her door last evening. No reply.

His immediate reaction had been fury. Damn the woman! He understood why she'd avoided him the previous week, but once she'd decided to tell him things, surely she shouldn't have been hiding herself away again? His anger had burned through the night, so he'd felt foolish—even ashamed of himself—when Alex had explained Clare was on loan to another hospital.

He didn't doubt that the tension he'd been feeling since he'd seen her scarred breasts had fired the anger, which, in retrospect, was more against whoever had hurt Clare than against Clare herself.

So with all this turmoil messing his head, he finally came to stand beside her in the small throng of people Dr Droopy was already calling to order.

'I've decided against the separate performances but still want people from all of the wards to do guest appearances there. Even if it's just a wander through the wards in costume a couple of times, it will make all the children feel included. The main performance now will be much bigger and grander and I've some preliminary scripts here for you to take.'

There was general muttering among the cast, but Oliver's attention was on Clare, who looked pale and tired.

'Rough op?' he asked, resolutely refraining from putting his arm around her and giving her a hug.

She offered him a weak smile.

'Two of them, both rough, and there's no telling if the poor patient is out of the woods yet.'

'We can only do so much,' Oliver was telling her when Dr Droopy stopped in front of them.

'You're the cardiac lot, aren't you?' he said.

'That's us,' Oliver responded, wondering what had happened to the other four Becky had mentioned.

'Good,' Dr Droopy told them, then he consulted his list. 'Clare Jackson, right?' he said to Clare, who nodded.

'I want you for Snow White.'

'Snow White isn't in *Cinderella*,' Clare objected.

'It's panto,' Dr Droopy reminded her. 'I thought as we were only doing the one performance—though probably two or three times—I'd put a lot of other nursery characters into it. With the ball scene we can have whoever we want there.'

'Makes sense,' Clare told him. 'The little kids these days seem to know the name of every princess ever written. My daughter certainly did.'

'How old is she?' Dr Droopy demanded.

'Snow White?' Clare was frowning at him now.

'No, your daughter! I'm after mice. Could she be a mouse?'

Clare hesitated but Oliver stepped in.

'I'm sure she'd love it,' he said, then he turned to Clare. 'She'll be on holidays soon, so will be able to come to rehearsals.'

Clare gave him a look that suggested there'd be further discussion on the subject later, but she didn't object. In fact, she offered Emily's name to the pantomime director.

'And you,' Dr Droopy continued, turning to Oliver, 'will be the fairy godmother. I thought I might get someone really ugly to begin with but we can do wonders with make-up.'

Oliver began to protest but as Clare was laughing and it seemed so long since he'd heard that delightful sound, he shut up.

The other clowns passed scripts around, and a rough read-through began, but Oliver's attention was more on Clare than the familiar words being read out in different voices—on Clare and the hurt she had suffered, presumably at the hands of her ex-husband.

He knew enough to understand the physical scars were probably the least of her worries, that the emotional scars would be the ones that took longer to heal—might never, in some cases, heal.

But what could he do?

How far into her space would she let him intrude?

'You look exhausted. I'll get a cab to take us home?' he said as the rehearsal broke up.

'A cab home? It's just down the road, Oliver. I'm not made of glass!'

True enough but Clare *did* feel fragile. That was the natural outcome of a combination of little sleep and the emotional outpourings of Sunday evening. But the feelings of acute embarrassment she was now conscious of in Oliver's company were worse than any tiredness.

Shouldn't she have simply told him she'd never marry again? Couldn't she at least have kept him at arms length? But to show him the scars, to reveal herself that way, not so much physically—although, oh, boy, did she ever do that—but emotionally as well? Had she been crazy?

They left the building together, Clare careful to walk far enough away from him they didn't accidentally brush against each other.

'Come and eat with me,' Oliver suggested as they went up the stairs to their flats. 'I'd actually intended asking you yesterday and bought some chicken pieces. I do a mean Moroccan chicken.'

Clare tried to smile. The idea of Oliver cooking—not just a grilled steak and chips but from a recipe—was enough to make anyone who'd known him smile. But she'd lost her smiles somewhere and the best she could manage was a shake of her head.

'You *will* come,' he told her. 'You will sit down, have a glass of wine, leaf through a newspaper or watch something mindless on the television while I cook, then eat and go home. No talk, no pressure, Clare—I promise you.'

She heard the sincerity in his voice and, when she looked up, saw it mirrored in his eyes.

'I don't deserve you should even speak to me,' she whispered, and the softness in his eyes vanished as anger blazed in its place.

'You will never say that again!' he said, icy words slicing through the sultry summer air. 'You are deserving of so much more than me, deserving of the best of everything. You are beautiful and kind and good. You're an excellent technician with a top-class reputation. You are a woman our daughter will always be proud to call her mother, and one she can aspire to be like.'

Clare stared at him, then felt her throat thicken, but she refused to cry again. Swallowing the lump that threatened to choke her, she said a simple, 'Thank you,' then sank down into Oliver's armchair and stared into space.

Oliver's words replayed themselves in her head and she knew they were a gift she could never repay.

Knew also that they might spell the beginning of an ending for the past. Oh, she'd got beyond her marriage break-up, forged a career and made a life for herself and her daughter, but deep inside she knew she'd never grown emotionally, never healed the scars that weren't visible.

Could she heal with Oliver's help?

Not when he'd promised not to pressure her.

When he'd promised not to touch her…

Tired as she was, she stood and walked towards where he was chopping things in the kitchen.

'Can you put it all away and order pizza later?' she asked him.

He looked up, so obviously puzzled that now she had to smile.

'Why?'

She came around the bench to stand beside him, and reached up to kiss him on the lips.

'I want you to take me to bed.'

He put down the knife but otherwise didn't react, silence stretching tautly between them.

'You're exhausted. You haven't thought this through,' he told her, brushing his fingers against her cheek. 'Sex is the last thing you need.'

'Yes to the first, but no to the second and third. I've done nothing but think about it ever since we met again. I've thought about whether I could go through with it, whether I'd let you down, whether you'd be so repulsed you wouldn't want me.' She hesitated, then continued, 'Please, Oliver, I really want to do this, but if you find my…my scars…off-putting, then just say no and I'll never pester you again.'

Oliver couldn't speak, so he wrapped his arms around her and held her close, smelling hair shampoo and garlic from the recipe, his mind churning at a million miles an hour.

What was she really asking?

Why now?

She was tired and vulnerable; could she handle it?

His body thought it was a great idea, but then his body was so obsessed with her it had thought cooking dinner for her was a reason to tighten.

His brain was still throwing up questions when she pushed away from him, far enough to look into his eyes.

'I'm not asking you to do this as a kind of medicine— you know, a cure of some kind. I'm asking because if we're to even contemplate a future together we have to know if I can do it. Do you understand that?'

That's when he saw the fear and knew the effort it was costing her to make this suggestion, to give herself to him.

'I understand you are offering me a gift beyond price,' he said, his voice rasping out of a thickened throat. 'You are offering me total trust, my darling woman, and that is so special I feel unworthy.'

He lifted her into his arms as easily as he might lift Emily, the gift she'd given him instilling power as well. In his bedroom he set her down gently on the bed, then knelt beside her, leaning down to kiss her lips, her eyelids, her brow and temples, then her lips again. His hand moved to her shirt, unbuttoning it, his fingers running across her chest, her belly—gently, softly, barely brushing her skin.

Still kissing her, he undid the snap on her jeans and slid the zip down, his hand delving further now, fingers tangling in the curls, seeking the moist lips beneath them.

They moved on the bed, adjusting to each other, he shedding his trousers and shirt, while Clare tugged off her jeans and top. He didn't touch her breasts, although later he would—later he would have to, to show her without words how beautiful she still was.

For now it was enough to feed their arousal with lips and fingers, exploring and remembering, Clare's hips lifting in encouragement as his fingers slid inside her. She stilled, and held him tightly, and he felt her muscles spasm once, again, and then relax. A sound that was little more than a whimper whispered from her lips, then she guided him into the slick depths and they moved together, remembered rhythms raising the excitement until Oliver could bear no more and spent himself inside her, her sigh of quiet delight suggesting she'd also enjoyed release.

They broke apart and she curled into him, but he knew they weren't finished. Holding her against his body, he undid the clasp on her bra. At first she stiffened, then, although he could feel reluctance in her muscles, she allowed him to remove it.

Now he knelt above her again, straddling her but keeping his weight off her body. He turned on the bedside light and dimmed it to its lowest setting. With his eyes on hers, he bent his head, and kissed first one breast, then the other.

She lay motionless beneath him but he could feel her...if not fear, then trepidation. With infinite tenderness he let his lips follow the lines of the scars; he kissed the tiny puckers, and lapped around her peaking nipples, forcing himself to relax, reminding himself that this was now and this was for Clare and she didn't need more anger in her life.

'Beautiful,' he murmured, taking one nipple gently into his mouth, teasing at it with his tongue.

She stiffened, then relaxed, beginning to move, to use her hands against his skin, exciting him again, as if to tell him she was now enjoying his attentions.

'Are you sure?' he asked as her fingers coaxed excitement from his body.

'Oh, yes,' she murmured, and this time as he plunged inside her the cry of release was loud and heartfelt, her muscles clasping and releasing, draining him completely.

CHAPTER TEN

THEY lay together, still joined, and haltingly the words came out.

'He was so good, so supportive, the whole time Em was in hospital, then he told me he'd bought a farm of his own. We'd have our own place—Em could grow up in the country as I had.'

She paused and Oliver rubbed his hands across her back, massaging the muscles he could feel tensing beneath her skin.

'I don't need to know,' he said.

'I need to tell,' she whispered.

'He said, let's sell your car and buy a newer dual-cab ute, safer for the baby than my old ute or your old car. Mum had bought a baby capsule and we used it in my car to take her home. It was close to Christmas and he'd decorated the house with tinsel. I cried to think he'd done that just for me. Later—maybe just a day or two, I can't remember now—he took my car to town to buy the new ute. Ordered it, he said, but coming up to Christmas it might take a while.'

She paused and snuggled closer, and Oliver found his arms tightening around her.

'The house on the farm was old, but I didn't care. I planned to do it up, bit by bit. He liked it tidy, liked things neat, so I was happy to have things to do. It was isolated, you see, but with Em to care for and the house, it didn't seem to matter.'

Her voice was growing quieter, as if whispering the memories might somehow make them less horrifying.

'Sometimes, when Em had been fretful and things around the house hadn't got done, he'd look around the messy room and sigh. Not saying anything but I'd feel that I'd disappointed him. Then one day, we were about to go to bed, and Em woke for a feed. It must have stirred his jealousy, and it triggered something in him I'd never have guessed was there.'

Anger so deep and hot he wondered he could keep it capped seemed to boil within Oliver, but he realised that, now she'd started, Clare needed to go on. He could only hold her, aching for her, fearing what he was about to hear, wondering if he could maintain his control.

'The new ute never came. I couldn't leave the house because we couldn't put the capsule in his old vehicle. He picked up groceries when he went to town. Sometimes he'd have a drink while he was there and after that would be rough with me—squeeze my breasts too hard. Mum had sent a box of Christmas decorations, some old ones I'd loved as a child and new ones, too, for Em's first Christmas, although we knew she was too small to know. I cut a little tree in the bush not far from the house and decorated it. It was Christmas—everything would be all right.'

She was shivering now, remembering, and Oliver could do nothing but hold her close and listen as the poison of that time was lanced from her soul.

'But Christmas meant parties, not that I'd go. I wouldn't enjoy them, he'd say, and besides, how could we take the baby? He'd meet some mates and have a drink and that was when he hurt me. He was always sorry afterwards, always promising it would never happen again, but one night, sometime in January, he grabbed my breasts and scratched them with his fingernails, scoring them and pinching me so hard I had to muffle my cries in the pillow in case I woke Em and he hurt her.'

Oliver felt her face pressed hard into the curve of his neck and knew his skin was wet with tears.

Was there more?

Could he listen to more?

Control his urge to find this man and murder him?

Then Clare's whispered words began again and he had to strain to listen.

'I realised just how jealous he was of my baby, of my feeding her, of my giving her any attention at all, and that's when I knew I had to leave. I waited until he slept, and knowing he'd been drunk so he'd sleep deeply, I took the capsule and Emily and left, walking not along the road but across the fields. The neighbours all around knew us both—knew Barry better and liked and respected him—so I had to get as far away as I could, carrying Em in the capsule because I knew I'd need it if I found someone to give us a lift.'

Oliver heard the words, so flat and emotionless, but in his mind he saw the woman he loved, trudging across the fields on the peninsula southwest of Melbourne, and he felt the fear she must have felt, the agony of desperation.

And understood her courage.

'I had a school friend in a small town near Apollo Bay. It was morning by the time I got there, so I went to her place. She didn't ask a single question, just put me and Emily in her car and drove us to the airport, paid for my ticket to Queensland on her credit card, bought some food and coffee for me, and once I was safely on the plane she phoned Mum to meet me at the other end.'

'Did he look for you?'

Oliver was surprised his voice had worked, so choked up did he feel.

Clare nodded against his chest.

'But not for long,' she whispered. 'Both my brothers flew south to see him. I don't know what happened but they came back and told me he wouldn't bother me again. Later Steve apologised, saying he had no idea Barry could behave that way. Apparently when they'd arrived, Barry had shown them the pile he'd made of my and Emily's clothes and all the gifts she'd been given. He'd put the Christmas tree and decorations on the top. He'd soaked them in petrol and had apparently been waiting for an audience for he set fire to it in front of them.'

'He was mad,' Oliver muttered. 'He must have been.'

Clare kissed his cheek.

'I thought so for a long time,' she said softly, 'but in the end I think perhaps he was just obsessed. For some reason I'd become the object of that obsession.'

She shivered and Oliver held her close again, murmuring not sweet nothings now, but talking of her courage and his love.

Thinking a pizza delivery after midnight might disturb Rod downstairs, Oliver made scrambled eggs and toast, coaxing Clare to eat until her body realised it needed fuel and she ate the lot.

Once she was fed, he took her into the shower, where he soaped her body, washed off the soap, dried her down and tucked her back into bed, his bed—Clare as docile as a child, allowing him to take care of her, although maybe she was so emotionally spent she could do nothing else.

He lay in bed beside her, knowing he should sleep, but wondering about how she might wake up in the morning, not wanting her to feel uneasy or embarrassed that she'd bared her soul to him.

'It was a gift without price,' he whispered to her when she did awake, sitting up uncertainly on the side of the bed.

'Making love?' she queried, a little frown puckering her forehead.

He shook his head and smiled at her.

'Telling me,' he said. He sat up, kissed her lips, then patted her lightly on the back. 'Now we've got to get to work. Tonight we'll need to catch up on our sleep, but by Thursday we should be rational enough to talk about where we go from here, okay?'

She was still frowning, so he kissed her again.

'No more today,' he told her. 'Don't think about the past or the future. Let's get to work—there are babies to be helped.'

Now she smiled, and Oliver's heart scrunched as if a giant fist had gripped it hard.

Was it love?

It had to be.

Clare wrapped his robe around her and dashed across to her flat to prepare for work, while Oliver moved into the bathroom, realising as he showered just how vulnerable love made a person.

It held you hostage, trapped you—yet the face in the mirror was smiling at him, so could it be all bad?

Obedience seemed the safest course. Clare kept her mind on the day ahead as she dressed for work. One of the things she loved about her work was the uncertainty of it, not knowing what case they might have to deal with next.

Oliver tapped on her door as she finished dressing. She called to him to come in, still feeling slightly anxious about the welter of emotion she'd dumped on him during the night. But when he kissed her, not with heat but with what felt like love, she put the past behind her, and delighted in his company even if all they were doing was walking to work together.

They went first to the PICU, where Oliver introduced her to the baby whose PDA he'd fixed on Monday. The baby's mother was in a chair beside his crib, dozing while her infant slept.

'You might have missed Em growing up but don't regret missing all the worry that went on when I discovered she had a problem,' Clare told him as they left the unit, knowing there was a team meeting in ten minutes. 'You feel so helpless, so useless, and although you know your child's in expert hands, not being able to do anything yourself is incredibly frustrating.'

Oliver squeezed her shoulder, just as Becky emerged from her office, heading for the meeting room.

'Aha,' she said. 'Cupid strikes again!'

'We're old friends,' Oliver told her, surprising Clare as they hadn't at any stage discussed how they'd handle their relationship at work.

'Oh, yes?' Becky said, eyebrows rising and a teasing smile lighting up her face. 'And don't think you're the only ones. Have you seen how Angus looks at Kate?'

Clare shook her head. She wasn't into hospital gossip, but usually if there was something going on within a team as small as theirs, there'd be some kind of buzz.

'Too absorbed in our own reunion,' Oliver whispered to her as Becky dashed away, 'but now Becky knows, the whole world will. Does it worry you?'

He turned to look at her, his green eyes showing his concern.

Clare pondered it for a moment, then shook her head.

'Not that we're going to stand in a team meeting and make an announcement,' she said, 'but no, if people begin to realise we're together, then that's okay.'

She stopped and studied him again, aware she must be frowning.

'Oh, dear, that's assumption on my part. Just because you were kind to me last night—it needn't mean more than that, Oliver, truly it needn't.'

She was looking so harried Oliver had to reassure her, dropping a light kiss on her lips in spite of their location in a hospital corridor.

'Except it does,' he told her firmly. 'I love you, Clare, and probably always have. I've wasted ten years of both our lives, and in doing that I put you into a position where you were alone and then abused. I can never make that up to you, but from this day forward I will do everything in my power to help you forget that time. I just hope my love for you will be strong enough to do that.'

'Am I interrupting something important?' Alex asked, edging past them in the corridor.

'Yes,' Oliver told him, putting his arm around Clare's shoulders to steer her up against the wall. 'We'll be with you in a minute.'

He'd intended kissing her, right there and then, but Kate was coming, and Angus, and the junior surgeon, so he made do with a brush of his fingers across her cheek, then led her into the meeting room where the entire team was awaiting their arrival, a smile on every face, and speculation in their colleagues' eyes.

Circumspection meant they kept to their own beds on the weekends when Emily was home, but every other night they spent together and, safe in the cocoon of bed and darkness and Oliver's love, Clare let out the pain and anguish of her brief marriage, then told of how she'd remade herself, determined for Emily's sake not to be a victim, and not to let the past drag her down.

Oliver would hold her and marvel at her strength and courage, unable to believe his love for her could still increase every day. With Emily, they shopped for Christmas decorations, Emily insisting they wait and buy a real tree, Oliver insisting they do without tinsel in their plans—so tacky, he said to his daughter, winning a warm smile from the woman he hoped to soon make his wife.

Two days before Christmas, the three of them turned up for the final performance of the pantomime. Oliver had only done one stint as the fairy godmother, having to do an emergency operation on the afternoon of the first one. But tonight he was back; in fact, both the fairy god-mothers were there, and their jealous behaviour towards each other had the audience laughing with delight.

Emily had made friends with the other mice and had spent the previous night with one of them, Mia, the daughter of a nurse in the orthopaedic ward. With the performance over, the small Emily mouse bounced up to Clare and Oliver, who were still in costume as they planned to do a visit to the wards.

'Mia and I decided we'd be bridesmaids when you two get married,' she announced. 'And Mia said the right way to propose, Dad, is to get down on your knees—or maybe one knee, I don't remember now—but if you're going to do that, can I watch?'

'Can we all watch?' a deep voice said, and Clare turned to see Dr Droopy standing right behind them, and behind him most of the cast.

And now she looked around it seemed the audience had stayed on as well, surely not expecting more of a performance. But before she could speculate further, the fairy godmother—grotesque make-up, wig, huge fairy wings and all—was down on one knee, reaching for her hand, asking her to marry him.

The cast and audience applauded and the mouse jumped up and down, then Oliver was on his feet, taking her in his arms, enfolding her and Emily, encompassing them both in his love.

'Did Snow White really marry the fairy godmother?' Clare heard a child's voice ask.

'In fairy stories anything can happen,' someone responded, but Clare was beyond caring what other people thought. She had her own happy ending right there.

SCOTTISH
BORDERS
LIBRARY
SERVICE

Medical Romance™

THE MOST MAGICAL GIFT OF ALL
by Fiona Lowe

Dr Jack Armitage's trip is delayed when an unexpected gift is left on his doorstep…a little girl! His replacement Dr Sophie Norman didn't expect to be a stand-in mummy—but whilst ensuring this little girl has a magical Christmas to remember they find the most magical gift of all: a family.

◆

CHRISTMAS MIRACLE: A FAMILY
by Dianne Drake

In the village of White Elk, Dr James Galbraith needs help from his ex, Nurse Fallon O'Gara. Fallon is only too happy to give it, but she's hiding a heartbreaking secret. As the snow flutters down Fallon finds safety in James's arms, and is finally ready to become mother and wife.

**On sale from 5th November 2010
Don't miss out!**

MILLS & BOON®

are proud to present our...

Book of the Month

Proud Rancher, Precious Bundle
by Donna Alward
from Mills & Boon® Cherish™

Wyatt and Elli have already had a run-in. But when a
baby is left on his doorstep, Wyatt needs help.
Will romance between them flare as they
care for baby Darcy?

Mills & Boon® Cherish™
Available 1st October

*Something to say about our
Book of the Month?
Tell us what you think!*

millsandboon.co.uk/community
facebook.com/romancehq
twitter.com/millsandboonuk

2 FREE BOOKS
AND A SURPRISE GIFT

We would like to take this opportunity to thank you for reading this Mills & Boon® book by offering you the chance to take TWO more specially selected books from the Medical™ series absolutely FREE! We're also making this offer to introduce you to the benefits of the Mills & Boon® Book Club™—

- **FREE home delivery**
- **FREE gifts and competitions**
- **FREE monthly Newsletter**
- **Exclusive Mills & Boon Book Club offers**
- **Books available before they're in the shops**

Accepting these FREE books and gift places you under no obligation to buy, you may cancel at any time, even after receiving your free books. Simply complete your details below and return the entire page to the address below. You don't even need a stamp!

YES Please send me 2 free Medical books and a surprise gift. I understand that unless you hear from me, I will receive 5 superb new stories every month including two 2-in-1 books priced at £5.30 each and a single book priced at £3.30, postage and packing free. I am under no obligation to purchase any books and may cancel my subscription at any time. The free books and gift will be mine to keep in any case.

Ms/Mrs/Miss/Mr _____ Initials _____

Surname _____

Address _____

_____

_____ Postcode _____

E-mail _____

Send this whole page to: Mills & Boon Book Club, Free Book Offer, FREEPOST NAT 10298, Richmond, TW9 1BR

Offer valid in UK only and is not available to current Mills & Boon Book Club subscribers to this series. Overseas and Eire please write for details.. We reserve the right to refuse an application and applicants must be aged 18 years or over. Only one application per household. Terms and prices subject to change without notice. Offer expires 31st December 2010. As a result of this application, you may receive offers from Harlequin Mills & Boon and other carefully selected companies. If you would prefer not to share in this opportunity please write to The Data Manager, PO Box 676, Richmond, TW9 1WU.

Mills & Boon® is a registered trademark owned by Harlequin Mills & Boon Limited. Medical™ is being used as a trademark. The Mills & Boon® Book Club™ is being used as a trademark.